I0691844

Endeavour Island

A North Queensland Cadet Adventure

C.R. Cummings

Also By
CHRISTOPHER CUMMINGS

Endeavour Island

A North Queensland Cadet Adventure

C.R. Cummings

DoctorZed
Publishing
www.doctorzed.com

This 1st Edition published 2024 by DoctorZed Publishing

DoctorZed Publishing books may be ordered through booksellers or by contacting:

DoctorZed Publishing
10 Vista Ave
Skye, south Australia 5072
www.doctorzed.com

ISBN: 978-1-7636975-8-4 (sc)
ISBN: 978-1-7636975-9-1 (ebk)

A Cataloguing-in-Publication entry can be found at the National Library of Australia
www.nla.gov.au

Cover design © Scott Zarcinas
Cover image: Island © Brainstormoff | Dreamstime.com

Printed in Australia, UK & USA

DoctorZed Publishing rev. date: 20/09/2024

Dedication

This book is dedicated to

Helen, Rosemary, Eve, and Anne

who
at various times in my youth

introduced me to
the wonder and delights of romance
on sunlit, sandy beaches
and moonlight kisses under the palms.

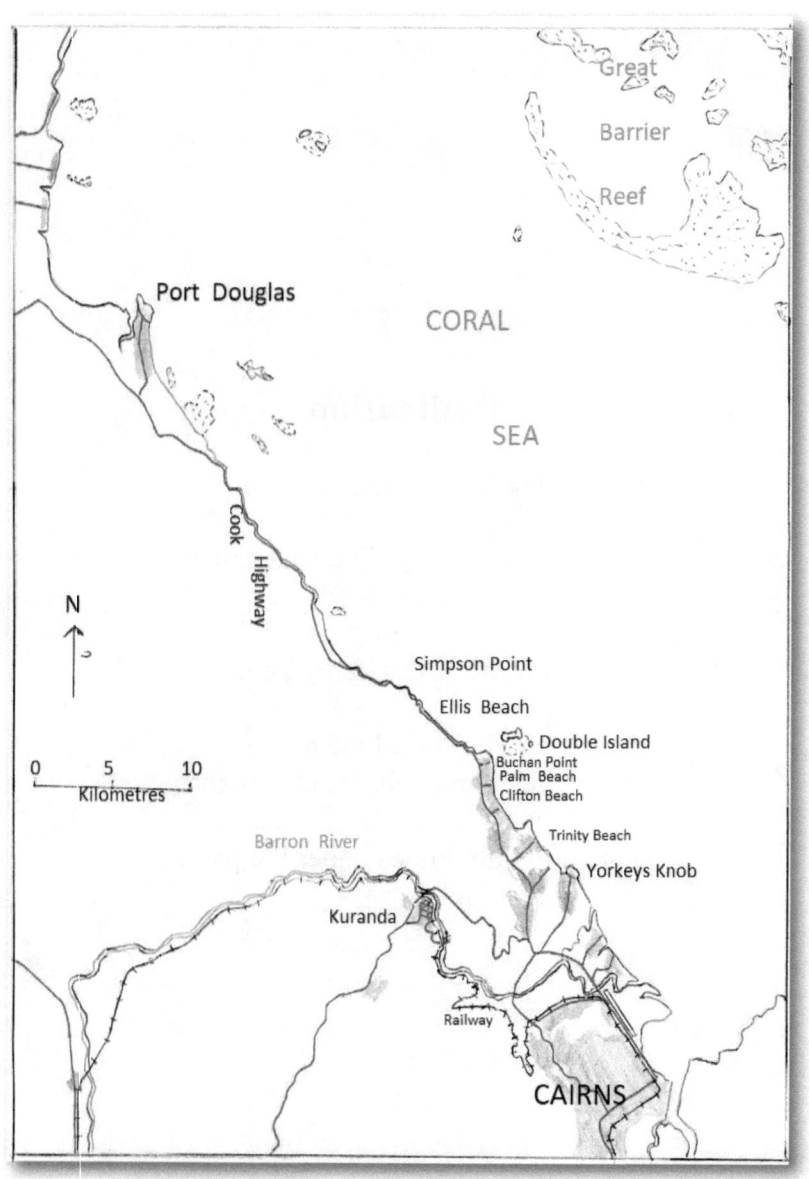

Great Barrier Reef

Port Douglas

CORAL

SEA

Cook Highway

N

Simpson Point

Ellis Beach

Double Island
Buchan Point
Palm Beach
Clifton Beach

0   5   10
Kilometres

Barron River

Trinity Beach

Yorkeys Knob

Kuranda

Railway

CAIRNS

Chapter 1

TREASURE HUNT

The Coral Sea, 20 kilometres north of Cairns, North Queensland
Saturday afternoon, 17th of March.

Eight sail boats strung out over 2 kilometres of sea.
The wind from the North East at 10 knots.

Cadet Able Seaman Carmen Collins, blonde and blue-eyed, 15 years old, leaned outboard to see better and then glanced at the compass she held in her hand.

We are winning, but only just, she thought.

Close behind on the port quarter raced the nearest rival, a 'Corsair' commanded by Cadet Petty Officer Crisp. Carmen chewed her lower lip and studied the set of her boat's sails.

Those lubbers from the Starboard Watch will catch us if we make a mistake, she thought.

She turned to her younger brother seated next to her. "Andrew, just ease that mainsheet a trifle," she ordered.

"You sure?" Andrew countered, his eyes flicking from her to the sail above him.

"Don't argue little brother. I'm the captain," Carmen replied. She knew that the air flow over the sail had to be just right to get the full 'Bernoulli effect' when tacking upwind. Sometimes that meant not hauling the sail as flat as possible.

The 'Corsair' drove its bow into a larger than usual wave and spray flew aboard. Carmen closed her eyes for a moment and then wiped her face. She smiled, loving every minute of the race. Being summer in the Coral Sea meant that the water was quite warm so getting soaked was no big deal. In the sail boat with her were her brother Andrew, who was a year younger and a rank lower in the Australian Navy Cadets, and his friend Blake.

Again Carmen studied the following boats. Apart from Crisp's boat it looked a no-contest. The next two boats were nearly a kilometre behind and were both 'Port Watch', one being Petty Officer George's and the other Leading Seaman Page's. Another few hundred metres back were two more: Armstrong's and, she thought, Austin's. The last two, both 'Starboard Watch', were so far back she could not make out who was in each but she knew they were commanded by Pocock and Kent. Both safety boats were back with them.

That's because that ham-fisted lubber Kent capsized, she thought.

Now she turned her attention to where they were heading. About a kilometre ahead on her port bow was a rocky headland. The chart, safe from spray in its plastic case, told her that was Simpson Point, the northern end of Ellis Beach. The beach itself, three kilometres of lovely golden sand, was now on the port beam. Behind the beach were the Cook Highway and then a range of steep mountains that rose for about 600 metres in a wall that extended north and south for many kilometres.

The next clue is in that little cove just north of Simpson Point, Carmen thought.

She ran back in her mind over the clues they had so far discovered, just to check that they were going to the right place. Satisfied, she held her course. The fact that Crisp's boat was sailing an identical course also reassured her.

They must believe that is the place as well, she told herself.

The cadets, who during the week were just normal school students, were spending the Sunday on a sailing and teamwork exercise. This was being run as a 'Treasure Hunt' and had been going on since early that morning when they had launched the boats at the Yorkeys Knob Marina. It was the first exercise of its kind that Carmen had taken part in and she was really enjoying it. The hunt was really a test of sailing ability, with the extra challenge of having to work out what the clues meant, and to navigate from one place to the next. The clues were just messages in plastic bags which had been placed in position by the adult Officers of Cadets of the Navy Cadet Unit.

To add spice and challenge, each clue was either in a code or was some sort of puzzle or cryptic clue. Several had been coloured drawings of naval flags, spelling out names or distances and magnetic bearings. Others had been in Morse Code and a couple had been merely mysterious words. So far they had found eight clues. First, they had sailed north

8

along the coast to Taylor Point, then in to Clifton Beach. Next, they had sailed along close to the shore to Palm Beach and then out to Double Island. The next leg had been in behind Buchans Point, then up to Ellis Beach, where they had stopped for lunch, being held to timings by the officers. The last leg had been out to sea to one of the motorboats, with Lieutenant (ANC) Ryan, the unit's XO, and the two senior cadets in it.

Now they were racing towards the shore and Carmen was sure there must only be one or two more legs, if only because it was getting late in the day.

We will have to get the boats back to Cairns and clean up, she thought.

That led to more anxious glances back at Crisp's Corsair. It was slowly but surely gaining, edging up a metre or so every minute. Carmen carefully studied the set of her boat's sails again, then considered the angle at which she was tacking into the wind.

Instead, of trying to tack up to windward as sharply as we can, should we try for greater speed over the ground by running more off the wind? she wondered.

Having considered all the options again, Carmen held to her course. *Not far to go now. If nothing goes wrong (touch wood!) we should just beat them to the beach.*

She again glanced a Crisp's boat, then turned to Andrew and Blake. "You two be ready to jump out as soon as we run aground," she said. "Leave the boat to me. Andrew, you search along to the left and Blake, you go the other way," she instructed.

Both boys nodded, their eyes continually flicking to the pursuing boat and then back to the shore ahead of them. Another glance around got Carmen worrying. Out to sea she could see masses of dark clouds with curtains of rain under them.

The weather is going to get worse soon, she told herself.

Already she was sure that the wind had become stronger, and she again checked the set of the sails. The boat was really flying along now, the cadets having to lean out on the windward side to help balance her. Carmen found the whole experience exhilarating. Normally they only sailed in the relatively sheltered waters of Trinity Bay, or on Lake Tinaroo, so being out on the more exposed open coast was thrilling.

The waves were bigger than she was used to, but not by much. Even now she estimated they were only about 1.5 metres. That was normal.

She knew that very large waves, say 10 or 15 metres, only blew up as the result of tropical cyclones. In that case the cadets would not be allowed on the water anyway. Normally the wave height was kept down by the damping effect of the Great Barrier Reef. Along this stretch of coast the mighty chain of reefs was about 30 kilometres offshore and the 'fetch' inside was too short to allow the building of large waves.

But the wave pattern had abruptly changed, and Carmen was made uncomfortably aware of this as the Corsair suddenly pitched and rolled alarmingly, her bow butting into the crests and sending spray flying.

The water must be shallower than it looks, she decided, noting that they were now sailing into the inshore zone where the waves began to break. That presented her with another set of problems. *Do we quarter the waves or run in square with them?* she wondered.

A moment's experimentation quickly decided her. She turned to run straight in and almost immediately regretted the decision. The boat lost speed as it sank down into the trough behind a passing wave and she felt it roll uneasily. The mainsail slatted and Andrew was only just quick enough to pull the sheet tight and prevent a gybe.

"That was close!" he cried.

Then the next wave overtook them and the boat rolled even more alarmingly as they picked up speed. Carmen saw that they would have no choice but to run straight in for the last 25 metres or so but decided to try to quarter the waves until then. She estimated that the shore was now only about 250 metres off. That meant first continuing on a beam run, then gybing to a do a run back to the small beach, which was now opening up among the large boulders on the point. She knew it was a risk as they would have to sail a greater distance but she did not feel confident of being to hold the boat upright with the wind directly astern.

She called orders to the two boys and then brought the wind onto the starboard beam again. Almost at once the sickening rolling motion eased and their speed increased so that they began to skim along at almost the same speed as the waves.

Andrew frowned and shook his head. "They will beat us now," he called, gesturing to the other Corsair, which was steering straight in.

"Too bad! I don't want to capsize in the surf," Carmen called back.

Andrew wasn't happy and didn't agree with her, but she pressed her lips together and stubbornly held her course. They now matched the speed of the waves and skimmed along at a really exciting speed. Carmen studied the shore they were now rapidly approaching. She saw that the northern end of Ellis Beach ended in a scatter of large rocks. The highway climbed up into a belt of dry savannah woodland as it went further inland across the end of a long spur. As always, she wondered why the bush on this coast was brown and dry, yet turned to dense tropical jungle on top of the range. The foot of the spur was a mass of black rocks, some quite jagged, others large smooth boulders. Beyond them, just around the curve of the point, was a short section of beach. This was their objective.

To reach the beach at a favourable angle, Carmen decided they needed to sail on till they were near its far end. She kept glancing ashore, checking angles and estimating the wind direction. Within a minute they were only a hundred metres out and level with the jagged rocks marking the northern end of the beach and the moment of decision was fast approaching! Carmen bit her lip and found her heart beating rapidly.

If I muck this up, we will get a soaking, she thought.

She called out, "Get ready! We are going to do a gybe to port. When I say 'Ready about' you hold that mainsheet tight Andrew."

She knew, from many duckings, that the main reason for capsizing during gybes was the boom of the mainsail swinging across too quickly, upsetting the balance before they could adjust or ease the sheet. She was also acutely aware that it was the control of the tiller that was the next most important element. Having several times in the past experienced that sickening feeling of skidding around out of control while trying to gybe she gripped the tiller extra hard this time.

To add to the stress Carmen could see Crisp's boat was already much closer to the beach. She pressed her lips together and carefully studied the waves and angles, making herself hold their course even though the temptation was very strong to start turning earlier.

Now! she decided. "Ready... About!" she called.

As carefully as she could she moved the tiller to bring the boat around, then firmly centred the rudder while Andrew hauled in the mainsheet. Blake slid down into the hull and gripped the boom to help control its swing. As soon as the boom was centred, Carmen nodded to Andrew and he pushed it across and began to very carefully ease it out. Carmen at once applied counter pressure with the rudder to hold the now swiftly skimming Corsair on the new course. Blake pulled the jib across and held it firmly. A wave slid under them but they were now around and racing along on the new run, the wind just on their port quarter.

Made it! Carmen thought, but she did not relax.

She aimed them at the small beach and then studied the angles. The other boat was now only about thirty or forty metres out from the beach and would obviously get there first, but it was not moving nearly as fast.

It's going to be close, Carmen thought.

Then she saw Crisp's Corsair slide down the back of a wave and roll alarmingly. As it wallowed in the trough the next wave caught it up and broke, white froth cascading into it.

Pooped! she thought, watching the foam swirl into the other boat.

There were cries and anxious faces over there and suddenly the other boat swung up over the next wave as it passed, and then broached and rolled. One second it was upright, the next it was over. Carmen saw the cadets spilling out into a welter of foam as the boat capsized.

By then her own boat was only 20 metres from the other boat but she did not try to stop. That would have been both pointless and dangerous that close to the beach. Besides, the waves were only breaking about a metre high. It was just the normal sized surf they swam in when they went to the beach. She thought that the people were safe but their boat might have a few things broken. So instead Carmen concentrated on keeping her own boat under control. They shot past the other boat, which now lay on its side in the breaking surf, heads bobbing among the foam.

The beach was only 50 metres away by this and all of Carmen's attention was taken up by conning her own boat. Staring anxiously ahead she noted small rocks awash in the surf to port but also an area of more sheltered water in their lee. She aimed for this and a moment later the boat surfed ashore on a breaking wave, grating to a stop in the relatively sheltered area.

As soon as the boat touched bottom, Andrew had the centre board up and eased the mainsheet. The boat at once slewed round and Blake leapt out, to grab the bow and push it further around. Carmen pulled up the rudder and also sprang over on the upwind side. She landed in waist deep water and was thankful she was wearing sandshoes as only then did she think about stingrays and stonefish. She splashed forward and heaved the bow around into the wind.

"Get going!" she shouted.

Andrew had now secured the centreboard and loosed the main halyard. The mainsail began to shiver and flap wildly but also started to slide down the mast. Carmen held the bow until she was sure the boys were searching for the next clue, then lay with all her weight on the bow. This lifted both rudder and stern and allowed her to use the next wave to slide the boat backwards up onto the beach. As soon as it was as far up as she could push it, she slid off and ran around to the stern, then started hauling the boat higher, dodging the flailing boom as she did.

Within a couple of minutes she had the boat safely on the beach and the mainsail lowered and lashed. Only then did she look around. First, she looked out to see if the cadets in Crisp's boat were safe. Counting three heads, and noting the arms holding the now upright Corsair as it drifted in stern first on the waves, she turned her attention to the search.

As ordered, one boy had gone each way and even as she looked Carmen saw Andrew point to a plastic bag containing a piece of paper which was taped to a tree trunk.

"Here it is!" he shouted.

Leaving the boat Carmen sprinted across the beach to meet him. "What does it say?" she called.

Andrew stopped running, glanced out at Crisp's boat, then read, "It says: 'Twenty paces north, big rock'."

"Pace it out then," Carmen called.

She could already see a large rock at the right distance and was starting to feel a tingle of excitement at the possibility of having won.

Andrew did so. The 20 paces did take him to the base of a large boulder. He bent and looked into a cleft underneath it. Almost at once he let out a cry and bent down.

"Here it is!" he called, straightening up with the next clue in his hand.

By then Carmen had hurried across to join him. "Well? Read it," she said.

Andrew frowned, then read, "Ten paces west. Spikes."

"Spikes?" Carmen queried.

She loooked around the beach and up among the rocks and bush behind it. The ground in from the beach was a jumble of big boulders and areas of exposed black rock, with clumps of grass and just enough trees on the steep slope to qualify as a forest.

"What about that Pandanus?" Blake suggested, pointing to a lone

Pandanus Palm which grew at the top of the beach a few metres further along.

"They have spiky leaves," Andrew agreed. "Let's try it."

He turned to face west, which was towards the pandanus, then paced out ten paces. This brought him to the tree. He bent and looked around it. Almost at once he let out a cry and bent down.

"Here!" he cried, pointing to another message taped to the back of the trunk. "Two paces north, dig, it says," he read.

"Oh bummer! We should have brought spades," Blake grumbled.

"Too bad, we will dig with our hands," Carmen said. "The treasure won't be deep."

So saying she dropped to her knees and began scooping sand away. The two boys joined her and they quickly dug out quite a reasonable hole. From time-to-time Carmen stopped and looked around, wiping perspiration from her face. It had become very hot and the afternoon sun blazed down on them. The clouds dropping rain were still out on the horizon, but the humidity had become truly tropical.

Must rain here soon, she decided.

She noted that Crisp now had his boat in on the beach thirty metres further along and he and one of his crew were walking over to join them. She noted that he had left the smallest boy in the whole unit, young Recruit Kit Walker, holding grimly to the bow of their boat. Further out were two more boats running in, their sails spread 'wing-and-wing'.

Petty Officer George's and Leading Seaman Page's, she noted.

The other four boats were still well out, at least a couple of kilometres away, and only one of the motorboats acting as safety boats was in sight. It was punching in through the waves towards them, throwing up bursts of white spray as it did.

Just as a wet and grumpy looking Petty Officer Crisp reached them, Andrew let out a cry and pointed into the hole. Carmen looked down and saw he had exposed the top of a metal container. Andrew and Blake at once redoubled their efforts, quickly uncovering a grey metal box. It looked brand new and was only the size of a shoebox. Andrew grabbed a small handle on top and lifted the box clear of the sand, then brushed it to clear more grains clinging to it.

"The treasure! We win!" he cried happily.

"Open it," called Seaman Toms.

Andrew tried to. After tugging at the handle and failing, he slid his fingers around the rim of the lid and tried to prize it up. A look of bafflement crossed his face.

"I can't. It's locked," he said.

"We will have to wait for the officers," Carmen said.

She looked up to check how far away the motorboats were and in doing so saw four civilians walking towards them along the beach: two men and two women. At first she took no notice, the sight of people having picnics and swims on the beaches being so common. However, something about the look on the first man's face made her look again.

The first man was tubby and middle aged, with a round, red face. He wore white shorts and a bright 'Hawaiian' shirt. On his head was a white 'Panama' hat and he had a bag and a beach towel over his shoulder. Behind him came a tall, thin man with a sun-tanned complexion. He wore jeans but had no shirt on. His longish brown hair was tied back in a pony tail and he had a large gold earring in his right ear. In one hand he carried a bag and in the other a spade. Both women wore straw hats and sunglasses and had beach towels over their shoulders and both had long, bare legs which looked very attractive. One woman was a blonde and wore a shirt, half undone and tied in a knot at the front to expose her middle. She wore tight white shorts. The other woman, with a harder, more angular face, had black hair and wore a long shirt, open at the front, over a red one-piece bathing costume.

Even so, Carmen was not interested in them. She turned her attention back to the problem of opening the 'treasure chest'. Thus she was surprised when the tubby man stopped near them and said, in quite a conversational voice, "I will take that box thanks."

Carmen looked up and frowned. "I beg your pardon?" she said.

"You heard me, give me the box," the man replied.

"We found it," Andrew answered. "It's the prize from our treasure hunt."

"I don't think so," the man insisted.

Andrew stood up. "It is so!" he replied.

The man shook his head and pulled out a key which hung on a chain around his neck. "This is the key to open it," he said. "It is ours. Give it to me and don't argue."

Andrew stood up and gripped the box, looking puzzled but stubborn.

"But we found it," he insisted.

The man became impatient. "Stop mucking us about kid! Give me the box."

"No!" Andrew replied.

The man shook his head with annoyance. "Get it off him, Dan."

"Yes Mr Barrett," replied Dan, the thin man with the pony tail. He stepped forward and held out his hands. "Give it to me kid!"

Andrew shook his head and pulled the box away, then turned to try to run. Before he could, Dan acted. To Carmen's dismay, the man sprang forward and struck at Andrew with the spade. The flat of the blade struck Andrew hard on the arm, causing him to cry out and drop the box.

At that, Carmen jumped forward. "How dare you! That's assault," she cried, blocking the man from picking up the box.

She was more puzzled than scared but now her anger made her act. Before she realised her danger the man named Dan swung the hand holding the bag and knocked her backwards. At that, Andrew, who had been rubbing his arm, stepped forward, raising his fists.

Dan raised the spade threateningly. "Back off kid or you will get hurt," he snarled. "Now get out of my way."

"No! Leave us alone!" Andrew cried angrily.

Dan swore and swung the spade in a vicious arc. Andrew jumped back just in time and most of the other cadets retreated a few paces to get well clear. Petty Officer Crisp called out in alarm but Dan ignored him.

Carmen was now so outraged and angry that she again stepped in and grabbed the spade by its handle, to prevent Dan hitting Andrew again.

"Leave us alone!" she called.

Thump!

Before she realised her peril, Dan let go of the spade and punched her hard in the face. Carmen reeled back, still gripping the handle of the spade. Dan followed, seizing the spade again. There were shocked gasps and Carmen tried to step back, her senses spinning from the blow.

As she did, Mr Barrett said to the black-haired woman, "Lana, pick up the box."

"Stop her!" Andrew yelled angrily.

Mr Barrett shook his head. "Leave it alone and back off you kids," he snarled.

Carmen was both puzzled and angry but now she was shocked to see that Mr Barrett was holding what looked like an automatic pistol and pointing it at Andrew.

What the hell is going on? she wondered in bewilderment.

Cadet PO Crisp looked shocked. "Is this some sort of a joke?" he asked.

"No joke at all," Mr Barrett snarled. "This is a real gun, so back off. You kids are just in the wrong place at the wrong time. Now pick up the box Lana."

At that moment, the blonde woman cried out and tugged at Mr Barrett's sleeve. "Mr Barrett! The cops!"

Carmen looked up the beach in the direction the blonde was pointing and was astonished to see half a dozen people, some wearing police uniform, clambering down over the rocks.

What on earth is going on? she wondered.

One of the policemen yelled out, "This is the police! Stop where you are! Put your hands up!"

Dan swore, then moved. Before Carmen realised what he intended he had dropped the spade and grabbed her arm. He twisted it up behind her back, then pulled a large black automatic pistol from his bag and shoved it up against the side of her skull.

Into her ear he snarled, "This gun is loaded little girl, so don't try anything foolish." Then he turned to yell at the police, "Back off coppers, or this kid gets blown away!"

Chapter 2

IN TROUBLE

Until the man named Dan had grabbed Carmen, Andrew had been more puzzled and angry than frightened. Now, as he saw the fear in Carmen's eyes, he suddenly realised that the situation was real.

I don't believe this! he thought. *Who are these people? What is going on?*

He stepped closer in a half-hearted attempt to block the black-haired woman named Lana from picking up the grey metal box. Her response was to whip out a small automatic pistol and point it at him.

"Back off boy!" she hissed.

Andrew looked at the small pistol, noting how shiny the silver metal of the barrel was, even as wave of cold shock coursed through him. He froze and put his hands half up, then watched helplessly as Lana picked up the box and stepped back next to Mr Barrett.

Mr Barrett took the box off her, then shouted to the watching police, "Keep back you coppers! Don't try to stop us or this girl gets a bullet in the head."

Andrew was stunned. He stared at his sister in dismay, then at last found his voice. "Let her go, you... you bully!"

Mr Barrett glanced at him, then looked around, muttering obscenities. Dan moved over next to him, dragging Carmen with him, holding her tightly so that he half hid behind her from the police.

"What are we going to do now, Mr Barrett?" he asked, anxiously scanning the watching police, who were now crouched behind the rocks along the top of the beach.

Andrew now noted that all of the police were armed and he went cold with dread. At that moment, one of the safety boats arrived. Andrew saw with relief that it was the larger boat with the CO, Lt Cdr Hazard, aboard. It surged into the small cove and rounded to, ending up facing out to sea, its engine matching the waves. An anchor was tossed over the bow and the boat began drifting in stern first.

Things will be alright now, Andrew thought, relief mixing with his mounting concern for Carmen. He was sure that it was all some sort of silly misunderstanding, and the CO would soon fix things up.

Instructor Petty Officer Evans, the unit's Boats Officer, tilted the outboard engine to get the propeller clear of the water. Then he and Lt Cdr Hazard jumped over the side and began wading ashore. They were joined by Lt Sheldon, the Training Officer. It was only five metres to the beach, and they covered it in less than a minute. But by the time the officers were sloshing up onto the beach Mr Barrett had acted.

"That's what we want!" He pointed to the motorboat. "Let's go!"

"What about our car?" Blondie queried.

Mr Barrett shook his head. "No, too risky. The cops can just follow us and might catch us. We will take the boat."

The four crooks, still holding Carmen as a shield, began making their way sideways down the beach. Andrew went to follow but was restrained by Cadet Petty Officer Crisp. He was scared now and shaking, but also appalled by the fact that the people were taking Carmen with them. He heard the police calling out to Lt Cdr Hazard to shove off, to go away, but the sound of the waves drowned out most of it and the three OOCs just looked puzzled and stood waiting as the group moved towards them. PO Ferguson, their female instructor, who had been at the wheel of the boat, remained aboard and began packing things away.

Andrew saw Mr Barrett shove his gun into Lt Cdr Hazard's face and then gesture toward where Andrew and the others waited. A look of shock and dismay crossed the faces of the OOCs as they realised what was going on. But it was too late. Faced with the threats of both the guns and of possible harm to Carmen they had no option but to step aside. They were then ordered to hold the motorboat while the crooks climbed aboard. Reluctantly, they did so, standing in waist deep water.

As they did, Andrew began to hope that the crooks might let Carmen go but was appalled to see her start to struggle. She grabbed at the side of the boat and refused to climb aboard. Dan put his arm around her neck and appeared to be choking her. Then he hit her hard on the side of the head with his pistol. By then Lana had climbed into the boat and Andrew was shocked to see her suddenly strike PO Ferguson, who was protesting at their treatment of Carmen, on the head with her pistol.

This led to a protest from Lt Cdr Hazard, who was in turn struck very hard in the face by Mr Barrett, also using his pistol. Lt Cdr Hazard slumped into the surf. Lt Sheldon and PO Evans both let go of the boat and grabbed him, then backed off, despite the threatening guns. Mr Barrett then ordered the blonde to help Dan get Carmen aboard. With some difficulty Carmen was roughly dragged up into the motorboat and held by Lana. Mr Barrett then passed the grey box up to Lana.

Next Mr Barrett organised Dan and the blonde to push the boat back into the surf. For a moment Andrew hoped they would be unable to achieve this but was further dismayed by seeing that the crooks apparently knew how to handle a boat. Having pushed it into deeper water the blonde clambered nimbly aboard. Then Dan hoisted himself in, Mr Barrett holding it steady and bows on to the waves as it bobbed in the surf. Dan climbed into the bows and grabbed the anchor chain, then turned and called to Mr Barrett, who then heaved himself aboard.

"Oh why don't the police do something?" Blake wailed.

Andrew shook his head in near despair, but he knew why: it was just too risky. All the while the blonde and Lana had guns pointed at Carmen and PO Ferguson. By this time the police had moved down to fire positions behind the rocks at the top of the beach. A glance showed that two were actually Customs Officers and that two more, in plain clothes, had appeared further up the slope. One of these was talking on a hand-held radio.

Dan quickly hauled the boat out into deeper water. By then Mr Barrett had lowered the outboard motor and moved to the controls. As a puff of smoke and a swirl of water appeared at the stern of the motorboat, Andrew led out a sob and cried, "Oh no!"

It just didn't seem fair that these thugs could just climb into a strange boat and make it work!

Lt Cdr Hazard was now kneeling on the beach, and he yelled at the boat but the crooks took no notice and his words were drowned out by the roar of the motor as the throttle was opened. The boat surged forwards, punching into the waves. Dan stood in the bows, balancing despite the bucking motion, while he hauled the anchor aboard. He tossed it into the boat, then turned to make an obscene gesture.

By now Andrew was sick with apprehension. Poor Carmen! What would they do to her? He seethed with helpless rage and found he had tears streaming down his face. Grinding his teeth with anger and despair, he stood and watched as the motorboat punched out through the waves.

Suddenly there was a commotion in the boat. Heart in mouth with anxiety, Andrew saw a flurry of movement, then a person fell backwards over the side, a person in dark blue clothes and a yellow life jacket. Was it Carmen? Or PO Ferguson? He could not tell but he saw a head appear, bobbing in the wake of the motorboat.

Then another horrible thought came to Andrew as he saw Dan and Lana both lean over the stern and aim their pistols.

Oh no! They are going to shoot her!

However, Mr Barrett turned his head and said something and no shots were fired. Andrew could now see that it was PO Ferguson who was in the water. He bit his lip with anxiety lest the crooks circle back to capture her again. A couple of seconds showed this was not likely, then another couple indicated that the crooks were definitely leaving her behind. By now they were nearly a hundred metres offshore.

Because they still have Carmen as a hostage, Andrew reasoned.

Andrew now clung to faint hopes that the other boats might somehow save Carmen, but these hopes swiftly faded as he watched. The stolen motorboat turned slightly to port and headed north. This meant that it passed the next two sail boats at a distance of several hundred metres. This left PO Ferguson bobbing in the waves and Andrew began to worry. It was not any concern over the instructor drowning, as she wore a life jacket, but rather over the things he knew for a fact lurked in the tropical sea; sharks and jelly fish being the main ones. Having spent nearly fifteen hours drifting in the sea the previous year after a plane crash, he knew with vivid certainty what it felt like to be in that predicament.

"Oh I hope one of those boats sees her," he muttered, his eyes watching the approaching boats anxiously.

It was Cadet PO George's boat who finally took note of the wildly waving and pointing people on the beach and turned towards PO Ferguson. As she was hauled aboard the bobbing sailboat Andrew breathed out with relief, not realising he had been half holding his breath for some minutes.

I hope she isn't hurt, he thought.

Then his eyes went back to the rapidly retreating stolen motorboat. It had turned more to starboard and was angling out to sea but well away from the next two boats. The last two boats, and the second safety boat, were still a kilometre out to sea. Andrew had pinned faint hopes on that second boat, the one with Lieutenant Ryan on board, but now he shook his head sadly.

They won't even notice that the power boat punching out through the waves is our cadet boat.

The two boats passed nearly a kilometre apart and soon after that the stolen motorboat sped into the first of the rain squalls sweeping in from out to sea.

As the stolen motorboat vanished into the greyness, Andrew felt his heart tighten up and he let out a little sob. Although he rarely showed it, he actually loved his sister very deeply and now he could only stand helplessly. The ghastly thought that he might never see her again crossed his mind, to be replaced by the equally horrible one that added the word 'alive' to the sentence. Tears prickled in the corners of his eyes and he bit his lip.

"Oh please God!" he murmured. "Please keep her safe and return her to us!"

He stood there, trying to come to grips with the reality of it all. A few minutes earlier he had been happily daydreaming that they were in a real sailing ship, an 18th Century square-rigger, being pursued by pirates across the Caribbean (not 'Swallows and Amazons' on an English lake as Carmen had suggested). Now it was all just mind-numbing dread!

By this time Lt Cdr Hazard and the other OOCs had been briefed by the police and customs people on what had happened. They also stared out to sea, straining to catch sight of the stolen boat amid the drifting curtains of rain. Lt Cdr Hazard was furiously angry.

"How dare you people not warn the cadets!" he snapped angrily.

"How were we to know you lot were going to barge in to our operation!" retorted a grey-haired, middle-aged man in a grey suit, a Commonwealth Police Inspector Andrew learned when the man identified himself.

Lt Cdr Hazard stepped closer and glared at him. "As soon as our cadets came ashore you should have moved to warn them and keep them safe," he snapped. "I don't care what long-running surveillance operation that compromised. The safety of these kids is more important than any drug bust!"

"Shh!" cautioned the equally angry inspector. "Loose lips sink ships."

"I'll sink your bloody ship if you don't start taking action to rescue my cadet!" Lt Cdr Hazard grated angrily. "Now get some assets moving!"

"Don't you threaten me!" blustered the inspector, but even Andrew could see he was worried.

Lt Cdr Hazard gave a short, bitter laugh, then said, "If it takes wrecking your bloody career to save Carmen then I will do it gladly, now act!"

"I already have," replied the inspector. "We have two cars going north along the highway; and the state police have been notified and are also sending cars to help. Even as we speak my people are contacting the navy and air force, and we hope to have helicopters in the area within half an hour or so."

He pointed to where another plain clothes policeman was busy talking on a mobile phone.

"They will need to be quick," Lt Cdr Hazard replied. "It will be dark in a few hours. And any aircraft are going to need thermal imaging or infra-red surveillance equipment to work in this rain that is coming in."

That was what was really gnawing at Andrew as well. The rain didn't look heavy, and it certainly wasn't from any sort of storm, was just normal summer rain showers, but it was now spread across half the horizon and looked to be thickening up out to sea.

Feeling very stressed and angry, he strode over to stand beside Lt Cdr Hazard. "Carmen is my sister. You must save her, please."

"We are doing all we can," replied the inspector.

"So what was in the grey box?" Andrew asked. He had a shrewd idea but wanted to confirm it.

"I can't tell you," the inspector replied.

Andrew noted the senior customs man flash a warning glance at the inspector. That nettled him so he said, "It was drugs or something wasn't it?"

"I can't say," the inspector repeated woodenly.

"I can!" Andrew snapped angrily. He was nearly in tears by this time and kept casting glances out to sea. There was now no sign of the stolen motorboat. It had vanished in the spreading rain showers. He said, "How come those crooks came here? They were looking for that box, weren't they?"

"Yes," the inspector muttered.

Lt Cdr Hazard looked puzzled. "So where was this box they took?"

Andrew pointed to the hole in the sand beside the pandanus palm.

"There, sir. The note said: Two paces north, dig. So we did."

"North?" Lt Cdr Hazard queried. "My note said three paces south."

"Oh no! There couldn't be two notes on the same pandanus palm!" Andrew cried. He strode over to it and looked, then felt sick inside. There, placed under a stone at the base of the trunk, was another note. He picked it up, then fished the other note out of his pocket. At once the different handwriting was obvious.

Even a different type of pen, he noted.

The inspector and the customs officer both came to look at the notes and the policeman took them off Andrew, saying they were now evidence. The inspector was then distracted by another plain clothes policeman calling him over to talk on a mobile phone. Andrew felt sick inside and shook his head in disbelief. "But why this tree?" he muttered.

Lt Cdr Hazard made a wry face and gestured along the small beach. "Because it is so obvious," he suggested. "It is the only pandanus palm on the whole beach."

"But why would the crooks put their drugs here?" he asked.

The customs officer just shook his head. That annoyed Andrew, who was puzzling over the whole business. So, obviously, was Lt Cdr Hazard.

He said, "I suppose for the same reason I did. The beach is isolated, yet easy to find. The highway is just up there a hundred metres, so they could walk down from a car, get the box and then quickly drive on."

Andrew nodded, thinking it through. "That would explain why they were all dressed for a picnic on the beach. That way they wouldn't attract any attention at all."

"I think you are right," Lt Cdr Hazard said, glancing at the customs officer, who tried to keep a poker face.

"But why would they bury it here sir?" Andrew asked. "Why wouldn't smugglers just sail in and go ashore to hand it over? I mean, it's a bit risky just leaving something very valuable." He knew that smugglers had to be involved because of the customs involvement in the operation.

Lt Cdr Hazard looked at the customs officer and then at Andrew. "I'd guess that there are two gangs, and they are trying to arrange it so that the authorities cannot link them together."

"How sir?"

"If the people who smuggled the drugs in by boat put them here a few days ago they could now be a thousand kilometres away and have a good alibi ready. There would be no provable link between them and the people who collected the drugs."

Andrew could tell by the fractional nod of the customs officer's head that Lt Cdr Hazard's theory was probably right. He asked, "So you think some smugglers came in from the sea and left the drugs here, sir?"

Lt Cdr Hazard nodded, then said, "Yes. They might have come off a passing freighter, come ashore in a fast boat, hidden the goods, then returned to the ship; or maybe came off a passing yacht or fishing boat. Something like that."

That made sense to Andrew. He said, "But there must have been communication for the crooks to know where to pick the stuff up. And how did the police know about it?"

That got him a blank stare from the customs officer. *An undercover operation maybe?* Andrew speculated, having seen such things on TV.

At that moment, the next two sailboats ran ashore, and Lt Cdr Hazard went hurrying down the beach to PO Ferguson. The inspector came back and also went over to see how she was. Andrew followed slowly, noting that the last four sailboats, and the second safety boat, were now all only a few hundred metres offshore. They were being overtaken by drifting curtains of rain.

We will get wet in a minute, he noted with half his mind, not caring at all. Feeling sick at heart, Andrew stared out to sea. *I wonder where Carmen is?* he thought miserably.

Then, he sobbed and muttered, "Oh! How am I going to tell mum!"

PO Ferguson looked very upset and had to be helped up the beach. Lt Cdr Hazard took out his own mobile phone and despite a protest from the inspector, called for an ambulance and then contacted the local navy HQ. He then phoned two more OOCs who were waiting with trucks at Ellis Beach.

By then the last of the boats had run ashore. The cadets stood in a group discussing the incident. All of them kept turning to look out to sea in the direction that the stolen motorboat had vanished. Andrew stood with them, but felt quite isolated and lonely. His friends Luke and Blake stood beside him, but then moved off to show the others where the clues had been. They also dug up the actual 'treasure'. This was only a carton full of chocolates in gold-coloured wrappers but the sight of them barely registered on Andrew's consciousness.

The rain arrived. That also went almost unnoticed by Andrew and most of the others. It was warm, tropical rain and merely cooled things down nicely. Luckily it was just a steady downpour, and the wind speed did not increase to any extent. Lt Cdr Hazard explained the situation to Lt Ryan and the other OOCs who had arrived on the second motorboat, then had Cadet CPO Pike, the Chief Bosuns Mate, line the cadets up. Still stunned by the shock of what had happened Andrew moved to stand with the others.

The roll was checked and then Lt Cdr Hazard moved to speak to them. He told them that everything possible was being done to find Carmen and they were now to sail the boats the 2km back to Ellis Beach, where the trucks were waiting. Andrew stood shivering in the drizzle, barely comprehending this, his mind out at sea. He did note that Lt Cdr Hazard and the other adult staff looked deeply shocked and upset and that helped. It certainly increased his liking and affection for them.

They care, he told himself. Not that he had ever doubted it.

Lt Cdr Hazard came over. "Do you feel up to sailing Andrew? You can go back in one of the police cars if you like, or in the safety boat."

The thought of travelling with the police or customs officers had no appeal. Andrew glanced at them and wrinkled his nose in disgust.

"No thanks, sir. I'm alright. I'll sail."

CDTCPO Pike was detailed to take command of Carmen's boat and he called Andrew and Blake to get the boat ready. That at least got Andrew's mind off Carmen for a few minutes, but only until they were afloat and heading out of the small cove. As they beat out over the waves Andrew kept glancing northwards, hoping against hope for a glimpse of the stolen motorboat. All he could see were drifting rain squalls and grey clouds. There were a couple of yachts visible right out on the horizon, but no sign of any motorboat.

Shock and despair numbed Andrew, and he reacted to orders like a zombie as they tacked the boat around Simpson Point and southwards parallel to the beach. The rain eased off and sunlight sparkled on the water, although other showers could be seen out to sea and to the north. CDTCPO Pike was a good sailor and he steered a course well out to keep out of the zone where the waves were breaking. The trip to Ellis Beach only took about half an hour and by then Andrew was beginning to recover from the initial shock.

He helped beach the boat and unrig it, half his mind still on the sea to the north. His emotions were in turmoil and he found he was shaking with a mixture of anger and apprehension. "Bastards!" he muttered savagely, referring to the crooks.

"If they do anything to Carmen!" But he knew that was just empty release.

I will never see any of them again. And maybe not Carmen either.

Now that hurt!

It hurt even more when his mother and father arrived by car as the cadets were loading the boats onto a truck. Lt Cdr Hazard met them and explained the situation and Andrew was unable to hold back his tears as he hugged his mother.

"It'll be alright, Mum," he said. "They will find her."

But that didn't stop his tears and in his heart he felt a chill of dread. Even seeing a low flying helicopter hurrying north out to sea did little to help.

They will be too late! he thought gloomily. *Oh poor Car! What has happened to her?*

Chapter 3

PIRACY

Carmen lay in the boat and allowed the rain to run down her face. It felt refreshingly cool and that was a relief after the numbness of the previous half hour. Her senses were still reeling from the blows she had received, and she tried to gather her thoughts and get her emotions under control. The initial feelings of almost paralysing fear had worn off somewhat, to be replaced by a mixture of dread, outrage and apprehension.

When Petty Officer Ferguson had struggled free and fallen backwards overboard Carmen had also tried to escape. In response Lana, the black-haired woman, had struck her very hard in the face with the gun she was holding. The blow had stunned Carmen and knocked her down. For the next twenty minutes she had lain there, barely conscious.

Now she was fully alert again, and very aware that her whole head throbbed with pain. There was the nagging worry that a bone might be broken in her cheek, but this was overlain by the greater anxiety over her possible fate. Carmen lay still and studied the situation through half closed eyes for a while.

Where are we going? she wondered, *and what will they do to me?*

It was the answer to the second question that worried her the most. Now that the first shock of unreality had worn off, she was painfully convinced that the crooks were dangerous and desperate.

I suppose while they need me as a hostage I will be alright, she told herself.

Spray had been wetting her for some time and the pattern of the buffeting and pitching of the boat told Carmen that they were heading out to sea in a northerly direction. Then the rain turned cold and added to her misery and chilled her even more.

The woman named Lana leaned over and looked at her. "She's awake," she said.

"Is she then?" replied Mr Barrett, the chubby, red-faced man in the Hawaiian shirt. "Sit up girl and tell us what the bloody hell you people were up to, and don't try any funny tricks."

Carmen struggled to sit, easing her buoyancy vest to rest her back against the bulwark. A glance to port caused her to suck her breath in. She got a glimpse of distant mountains through a grey mist of rain.

Oh heavens! We are a long way from shore, she thought in dismay.

Mr Barrett must have read her thoughts for he gave a mirthless laugh and said, "It will be a long swim sweetie, and without a life jacket you might not make it. Take it off."

"She could take off more than her lifejacket," suggested the pony-tailed man, leering as he did.

"Shut up, Dan, and keep your filthy mind on your job!" snapped the hard-faced blonde woman who was steering the boat.

Seeing no option, Carmen undid the buoyancy vest and shrugged it off. She then wiped drops from her face and turned to face Mr Barrett, who was obviously The Boss.

"Let me go," she said, trying hard to keep the quaver out of her voice.

Mr Barrett shook his head. "Just tell us what you were doing on that beach," he insisted.

Carmen did. When she had finished, Dan swore and growled, "So it was just pure bloody chance!"

"Yeah, but it wasn't pure bloody chance that the coppers were waiting there," Mr Barrett said grimly.

Carmen now noted that he still gripped a large automatic pistol. The grey box was on the seat next to him.

"Whad'ya mean?" Dan asked.

Lana made a face. "He means that there is a traitor in our organisation," she replied in a tone with a vicious hiss.

Mr Barrett nodded. "That's right. Someone grassed, and when I find out who it was, they are a dead duck!"

"Well it wasn't me!" Dan replied, but he sounded anxious to Carmen.

"Better not be," Blondie hissed.

Lana, who had taken over the steering, turned. "Where are we going Mr Barrett? Do you want me to hold this course?"

They all turned to look. Carmen could just see over the foredeck. She was surprised to see through the rain a thin white object sticking up out the sea a few miles away, or at least out of a greyish blur. Then she realised it was a lighthouse on a flat island. A moment's thought gave her a name.

Low Isles, she told herself.

That meant people and boats and she felt a sudden surge of hope. Her hopes soared even higher when she noticed a yacht only a few hundred metres away on the port bow. It was just nosing out of a passing shower and appeared to be heading on an opposite course.

Mr Barrett pointed to the yacht. "That's what we want. Put us alongside Lana," he ordered.

For a few seconds Carmen's hopes went even higher. She twisted in her seat to look at the yacht. It was an ordinary cruising yacht, ten or twelve metres in length, white hull, single mast, jib and mainsail set. There were people visible on it.

Why do the smugglers want to go to the yacht? she wondered. *Are they going to put me aboard?*

That hope was almost instantly dashed when Mr Barrett said to her, "You keep down girlie, and no calling out, or else!" Then he said to Dan, "Dan, you get aboard and stick them up. Blondie, you make fast. Okay Lana, come around astern of her and come alongside on her lee side on the same course."

The language was so nautical Carmen almost expected Lana to answer 'Aye, aye sir!' Instead, she nodded and said, "Yes Mr Barrett."

Carmen bit her lip and tensed. *They are going to steal that yacht,* she thought. *But why?*

All she could then do was sit and watch, with reluctant admiration at Lana's boat handling, as the motorboat swung across the yacht's wake and surged up alongside. As they nosed in, Carmen could see faces staring at them, curiosity all over them.

Five people, she noted.

Three adults and two children. Only one of the adults was male, a chubby chap in his forties in a red shirt. The children looked quite young, a girl of about ten and a boy who looked younger.

As the motorboat turned in and slowed to match the yacht's speed, Carmen saw puzzled frowns turn to concern on the adult's faces. The man called out to them to watch where they were going, then cried out in alarm as the motorboat closed right in. Once again, Carmen had to admit grudging approval of Lana's skill as the two vessels touched gently.

Dan sprang across, pistol in hand. He gripped a stay to steady himself, then pointed the gun at the man.

"Heave to!" he snarled.

Blondie scrambled across at the bows, taking a mooring line with her. She wasn't nearly as skilful and almost fell between the two boats as they bucked on the waves. Mr Barrett stood beside Carmen, holding her down with one hand and pointing his gun with the other.

The man was dumbfounded, then angry. "What the? Who the devil do you think you are? Get off my boat!" he shouted.

The women watched, wide-eyed and anxious. The children stared open-mouthed, obviously with no idea what was really happening. Dan stepped across to the cabin roof and crouched to aim better.

He grinned and said, "We'um pirates mister. Desperate Dan at your service. Now do as you are told and heave to before I plug ya!"

The man looked baffled and angry. He shook his head and glanced from Dan to Mr Barrett, then at the women and children.

"Get off my boat!" he called, but not nearly as belligerently as before.

"Turn into the wind!" Dan snarled.

To emphasise that he meant business, he pulled the trigger. Carmen saw the puff of smoke, instantly whipped away by the wind. She gasped in fright, fearing the man had been shot. However, Dan had aimed over his shoulder. The women screamed. Carmen saw the blood drain out of the man's face and her heart went out to him as his facial expression changed to one of a sick looking helplessness.

Now he obeyed. The yacht rounded to and came to a pitching standstill, head to the wind. Dan kept him covered and called over his shoulder, "Ease the mainsheet, Blondie, and don't let that jib flog itself to bits!"

Lana had matched the movements of the yacht, and the motorboat came to bobbing rest beside the yacht. Mr Barrett thrust his gun into his waistband, scooped up the grey metal box and stuffed it into Dan's carry bag, slung this over his shoulder, then stood watching. Judging his moment to a nicety, he stepped across onto the yacht. His obvious skill annoyed Carmen even more.

Mr Barrett turned and called back, "Okay Lana, wreck the radio, and make sure the engine won't ever work again, then come across."

"We should sink it," Lana called back.

Mr Barrett shook his head. "No. These people can go in it."

"Why not bump them off?" Dan queried.

It took a moment before the full import of Dan's casual question sank in, but when it did Carmen was chilled to the soles of her feet. She experienced an intense wave of sheer terror.

How callous! How could they? she wondered, seeing the look of stark horror in the face of the woman who was now holding the small boy.

To Carmen's intense relief, Mr Barrett shook his head. "No, they go in the motorboat. Get on with it, Lana."

Dan curled his lip. "I still reckon they should walk the plank. Dead men tell not tales."

Blondie now spoke up, her voice shrill with anxiety. "Don't you dare, Dan! I don't want to go to jail for murder."

Mr Barrett nodded. "Blondie's right, Dan. Nor do I. Doing five years for smuggling will be bad enough without adding twenty for murder."

The man had found his voice now and one of the women began weeping hysterically as the full import of what was going on hit her. The little girl huddled with her mother, who looked absolutely terrified. The man kept saying that they couldn't take his boat and that they had no right, but Dan just grinned and held up his pistol. Meanwhile Lana had got to work. She tossed a walkie-talkie radio across to the yacht, then located the main radio in the power boat. She wrenched the microphone off, then tried to smash the set with her hands. Failing in that she pulled out the shiny little silver automatic and aimed it.

Bang! Bang!

Carmen flinched at each shot. She saw shards of smashed plastic fly off the radio. One of the women screamed. Lana then pulled open a locker under the dashboard and looked through it. She removed the EPIRB and some flares and tossed them across as well. Next, she turned and moved past Carmen to the stern. Here she pointed her pistol at the outboard. Again the gun cracked twice. Lana then bent to look at the engine and put another shot into it from the side.

"That should do it," she called as she turned.

Her eyes met Carmen's and she gave a cruel grin. For a second Carmen feared that the hand holding the silver pistol would aim it at her head, but Lana just gave her a sardonic smile and made her way forward again. She tossed over the crooks few possessions and then sprang across to the yacht.

As soon as she was gone, Carmen struggled to her feet and stood. Lana met her eyes again and gave a warning shake of the head. All Carmen could do was stand and watch, easing her cramped and stiff muscles as she did. The two boats were now bumping together, the rubbing strake on the slightly higher yacht hammering down hard on the gunwale of the motorboat. As this threatened to overturn the motorboat, Carmen reached across and tried to steady the boats by holding them apart.

The unfortunate people from the yacht were then forced to transfer. This wasn't all that easy, or safe, as the children had to be passed across. Carmen helped with this, holding them to stop them slipping down between the erratically bobbing boats. One of the women was so frightened she froze up and could not jump.

That got Lana angry and she pushed her, hard. "Jump, you silly cow! Or I'll toss you overboard."

Terrified, the woman tried to spring across but misjudged it and fell heavily into the motorboat, despite Carmen's efforts to grab her. She was helped to a seat on the other side and then the man jumped across. He looked utterly miserable. When all were across Mr Barrett told Blondie to cast off. The painter was untied and the motorboat shoved off.

The yacht then got under way. Once again, Carmen watched with frustrated jealousy as the smugglers demonstrated they were very competent sailors. Lana took the wheel and had the yacht under control at once. Dan and Blondie trimmed the sails, working the 'coffee grinder' winches and belaying as though they had done nothing else for years. Mr Barrett stood and gave an amused wave. Then he pulled a mobile phone from his belt. He pressed a number and held the phone to his head while the yacht curved away to port.

As the yacht gathered speed and sheered off, her owner gripped the rail beside Carmen and shook his fist. "Bastards!" he cried. "I'll get you!" Then he turned to Carmen. "Who are they? And who are you?"

Carmen sat down and almost wept with relief. *Still alive,* she mused.

For a minute she eyed the angry man, favouring him with a cold stare. Then she began to shiver. "I'm a navy cadet," she said. "Those people (she almost called them pirates) are smugglers and they took me hostage to escape from the police. This is a navy cadet boat."

As soon as it sank in that she was not one of the gang, the people became much more friendly. The woman holding the little boy said, "Looks like they whacked you a beauty."

33

Carmen nodded and gingerly touched her right cheek. Now that she was aware of it, it wasn't just numb. It ached and throbbed and was very tender. She found she was unable to speak as reaction set in. To hide her tears (an Able Seaman shouldn't cry, she told herself) she turned away.

She was surprised at how far away the yacht already was. *Heading northeast,* she noted. *They must be going out to sea.*

She could see that the yacht's course would take it well to seaward of Low Isles. But it was no good. The tears came out in great wracking sobs. The other woman moved to hold her. Carmen snuffled for a while, half her mind still noting what the yacht was doing. She saw it vanish into a rain squall, then reappear much further away.

By the time she had told her tale, she could only glimpse the yacht's mast in the distance, and even that was hidden half the time by rain. She focused her thoughts inside her own boat. The boat was drifting and rocking quite a lot but to Carmen's eyes there was no particular danger.

Not so the other woman. She wailed about them being drowned and about not being found. That annoyed Carmen, particularly as the man did nothing to calm her and because the children both looked frightened and cold. The other woman looked sick.

"We are quite safe," Carmen said irritably. "This boat won't sink, and even if it does there are life jackets."

She knelt to a locker and pulled some out, insisting that the women and children put them on. She found her own on the deck and put it on.

If nothing else it cuts down the wind chill on my body, she thought, aware that her wet clothes felt quite cold as more rain drenched them.

"But what if nobody finds us?" the woman wailed.

That did annoy Carmen. Trying to sound much more confident than she actually felt she replied, "Lady, that is the least of your worries. Look, there is the coast. We are drifting towards it. Besides, I'll bet my CO has the navy, the air force, the coast guard and the police all out looking for us right now. All we need to do is sit and wait. It might be a bit boring and wet but that is all."

So saying she sat down and stared towards the distant coastline, trying to identify features. More rain swept in and she shivered.

I hope they do find us soon, she thought. *I'm cold and those kids look like they are freezing.*

Chapter 4

PHONE CALLS

Andrew was not allowed to return to the depot with the other cadets. His parents drove him straight home. Once there he was hustled out of his wet clothes, through a hot shower, and into dry clothes. By then it was 5:30 pm.

All the while he had been in the shower Andrew kept an ear open for the sound of the telephone, hoping for news of Carmen. Now, as he combed his hair, he heard the phone ring. Dropping the comb he hurried out of the bathroom and along the passageway towards the phone. He was too late. By the time he arrived his mother had picked it up.

"Hello? Mrs Collins speaking," she said. Then she listened for a second and Andrew felt his heart wrenched by the changes to her expression: from anxious hope to concern, to puzzlement, then to annoyance. "Who? Oh yes, I remember you. Yes, you want Carmen? Oh!"

There was a moment's frozen silence and Andrew saw his mother's face crumple into despair and tears. She sobbed, then said, "Sh... sh... she's not here at the m... mo... mom... (sob)... moment... (sob). You... what's that?... No... You haven't heard?... I... Alright... He is here. Just a moment." She caught Andrew's eye. "For you," she sniffled and held the phone out

Andrew walked over, wondering who might be calling him. His mother said, "Letitia, that girl from Townsville. Please don't talk for long, just in case..." Then she burst into tears and hurried away.

Andrew was torn. He wanted to hurry after his mother to comfort her, but he also wanted to talk to Letitia. He had met her during the school holidays in January when he and Carmen had been staying with Aunty Bev and Uncle Mel in Townsville. Letitia! Andrew had never met anyone like her: a year older than him, golden haired, big breasted, (voluptuous was the word that most readily came to mind!), and very uninhibited. She had given him several glimpses of delights he had previously only dreamed about. The mere mention of her name got his heart beating faster.

Andrew put the phone to his head and swallowed. He found that his mouth had gone dry and his throat had constricted. "He... hello?" he said. He realised his palms had gone sweaty and he wiped them one at a time on his shorts.

"Hi Andrew! How are you?" trilled Letitia.

The sound of her voice bored into Andrew's deepest consciousness, and he felt his heart leap. *She is so desirable!* he thought.

"Hello Letitia. I'm okay, look, I'm sorry, but... but Carmen isn't here. This... this isn't a good moment," he said, wondering how to explain.

"Oh I'm sorry. I will call again later if that's alright. When do you expect her back?" Letitia asked.

That really twisted Andrew's heart. Suddenly he burst into tears. *When?* he wondered. Words like 'never' flitted across his mind. Then he realised Letitia must be wondering as she said, "Andrew? Is everything alright?"

With an effort he calmed his sobbing and said, "No. Sorry I got a bit weepy, but Carmen's been kidnapped."

"Kidnapped!"

"Well, taken hostage really," Andrew replied. His mind flooded with vivid images of the drama on the beach, and he shook with emotion.

Letitia obviously didn't know how to handle that as she stammered and then squeaked with excitement, "A hostage! Tell me more!"

Her tone nettled Andrew but he managed a reply. "Smugglers," he said. Then he gave a quick explanation of what had happened.

"And the police are still looking for her?" Letitia asked.

"Yes, they are. That's why Mum asked me to be quick. She wants the phone free in case there's any news."

"Oh... oh yes. Sorry. I'll call again later," Letitia replied.

"I'll let you know what happens," Andrew said. The thought of what news he might have to relay got him all shivery again and his lip began to tremble. "Good bye," he managed to mutter before tears began to drip down his cheeks again. The phone was placed down and he stood there, his mind swirling with memories and emotion.

Letitia! Tantalising glimpses of her naked, of that glorious moment when she had given him his first real kiss. He shivered at the memories, then was disgusted with himself, both for having such lewd thoughts, and because images of Carmen in trouble kept intruding.

Poor Car. I hope she is alright, he thought.

It was only now that he realised just how much he loved his sister and how deeply he cared about her. Dreadful images of the smugglers throwing her overboard (or, even worse, of shooting her and tossing her body into the sea) or of them possibly doing things to her (his mind jibbed at the concept of rape, which he found utterly repulsive).

He began to pray, sitting quietly in one of the armchairs in the lounge room. Suddenly, the telephone shrilled next to him and he jumped with fright. For a breathless moment he was afraid to pick it up, lest it be bad news. But he could hear his mother coming along the passageway, so he lifted the receiver.

"Hello, Andrew Collins," he said, his mouth dry with fear.

"Inspector Carmody, Queensland Police," replied a voice. "Is Mrs Collins there?"

Andrew nodded, even though he was on the telephone. He was trying to read the man's voice to determine if it was bad news or not. Unable to decide he said 'yes' and handed the telephone to his anxious looking mother. The sight of the anguish in her eyes was almost more than Andrew could bear.

Oh please God! May it be good news, he prayed.

Heart in mouth with anxiety, Andrew watched his mother's expression and strained to listen as she answered. Then he saw her mouth open and he felt his heart tighten up. But she cried out in joy, "Oh thank God! Oh thank you!"

She turned to Andrew, but he had already guessed what she was going to say and his own heart was swelling so that he had trouble breathing.

"She's alive and safe," his mother cried. She then turned back to the phone and spoke to the inspector, her head nodding and saying 'yes' and 'please go on' and 'when?'.

Andrew found he was crying, hot tears of joy that trickled down his cheeks. He sat down and trembled with release. *Safe!* Then he tried to calm himself and act the 'stiff upper lip' that he thought would be appropriate for an admiral (or a pirate, or an ordinary seaman).

At last his mother put the phone down and turned to him. "A helicopter has located the boat. It is drifting near Low Isles. The policeman said that a paramedic had been winched down and that everyone on board is alright. Apparently, the motor has been damaged and the radio smashed, but the people are well. A Coast Guard launch is on its way there now and they should reach them within half an hour."

That cheered but puzzled Andrew. "But won't those smugglers still hold her as a hostage?" he asked.

His mother couldn't answer that. "The inspector did not explain," she said. She then turned to Andrew's father, who had arrived at the run from downstairs. "She's safe, Father. They are towing the boat into Port Douglas. Come on, get the car. We are going."

From their house to Port Douglas was only a 70-minute drive, even with the many bends in the Cook Highway. Along the way they went past Ellis Beach and across the spur above Simpson Point. As they drove along, Andrew stared out into the gathering dusk and relived the whole episode. Now that he knew Carmen was safe, he was consumed by curiosity to know exactly what had happened.

It was dark by the time they arrived, to find that the motorboat was just being towed in. They hurried along a jetty at the end of the marina and were just in time to watch. Andrew scanned the boats and the sight of Carmen's smiling face in a spotlight sent his heart pounding with relief. She waved and he waved back, then glanced at the other people in the motorboat and noted with surprise that they were not the smugglers.

What really annoyed Andrew then was the crowd of TV news people who were jostling for the best shot. Somehow that made it even worse. It was bad enough to be distressed without being gawped at and filmed by all these morbid strangers! Luckily his father and one of the policemen fended the TV people off and deftly handled their questions (Much to Andrew's admiration, he had never seen his dad perform under such stress).

By then both boats were made fast and Carmen gave him another big grin and waved. That helped calm Andrew.

She must be alright, he decided.

There were a few minutes of tearful greeting before one of several policemen took control. Andrew hugged Carmen and tried to hide the fact that he had been really upset. Instead, he looked over her shoulder in puzzlement as the other people were helped up out of the yacht.

"Who are they? Where are the smugglers?" he asked.

"Those people are off a yacht," Carmen explained. "The smugglers turned into pirates on the high seas and boarded it. They put the people on our boat and then sailed away. But not before wrecking the motor and the radio."

"Pirates!" Andrew exclaimed

His imagination conjured up images of a square rigger flying the Jolly Roger, cannon smoke billowing. Now that Carmen was safe, he allowed his mind to relax again and he was gripped by the drama of it all.

"What happened?"

She told him bits of it, in between answering questions from their parents, and from a paramedic, then from some plain clothes policeman. As they were urged along the jetty, Andrew saw Lt Cdr Hazard, Sub Lt Mullion (a chubby, motherly female OOC) and Petty Officer Evans hurrying in from the car park.

The cadet staff showed their enormous relief that Carmen was safe, and Lt Cdr Hazard apologised for placing Carmen at risk. It made Andrew feel even more affection and loyalty for them to see how much they cared. They explained that they had been phoned by the police and had come to help check what was missing from the boat.

Carmen, Andrew and the other people were bundled into cars and driven to the police station. Here, Carmen was given a hot drink, then taken into a room with their parents and asked a few questions. Andrew was left sitting in a draughty front waiting area, but he didn't mind. It allowed him time to relax and to sort out in his mind how he felt about things. After half an hour Carmen and their parents came out. She was then allowed to go home. By then she looked exhausted and was shivering, both with cold and with reaction. She was placed in the car and rugged up. While this was done, another TV crew arrived and Andrew felt his temper rise. Again his father fended them off, then made a phone call on his mobile phone.

When all was ready Andrew was told to sit in the front with his father so that his mother could sit beside Carmen. They then drove home. It was quite dark by then but when they came to those bits of the highway which ran along close to the sea Andrew stared out at it and again replayed the day's events. Only now he was able to allow his imagination some free reign and he started to fantasise how he could have rescued Carmen, of a desperate struggle on the boat.

Somewhere out there are the pirates, Andrew mused, staring at the dark sea under rolling dark clouds. In his mind he pictured the yacht sailing hard through the darkness; the searching aircraft; the hurrying patrol boats, guns ready...

* * *

At home, Carmen was bundled into the bathroom and then into bed. By then Andrew was feeling quite worn out himself and could sympathise with her. Before she was put to bed he joined her in the kitchen for a cup of hot Milo. Halfway through it she stopped chattering cheerfully and suddenly broke down and cried. Their mother hushed her, hugged and patted her till she calmed down, then hurried her to bed. Andrew was not allowed in to see her until she was settled.

As he went in to say goodnight, the telephone rang again, startling him. He ignored it and went to her bed.

"I'm really glad you are safe, Car," he said, and he meant it.

She was about to reply when their mother's voice called from the hallway, "Andrew! It is that boy from Townsville, Martin someone-or-other."

"Martin Schipholl," Andrew replied. He turned to Carmen. "Letitia rang this afternoon, wanting to talk to you. I will tell Martin you are safe and she can ring tomorrow."

"Oh, Letitia," Carmen said, her tone mildly disapproving, but also somewhat surprised.

Andrew knew that Carmen did not really like Letitia and thought she was a bit of a tart. That saddened and annoyed him, but he also knew that part of the reason was that Carmen cared deeply about him and did not want to see him get hurt.

"Good night, Sis. Sleep well," he said. He bent and gave her a peck on the cheek, then hurried out to the phone before he became teary again.

"Hello, Andrew Collins speaking," he said.

Martin's voice came to him clearly. "We saw it on the TV. Is Carmen really safe?"

"Yes, she is," Andrew replied. "She's home in bed."

"Thank God for that!" Martin replied. Andrew could tell by his tone that he really meant it and it made him like Martin even more.

"Thanks, Martin. I'll tell her you rang," Andrew replied.

"Can you tell me what actually happened?" Martin asked.

"What little I know," Andrew replied. He then gave Martin an account of the afternoon's events.

Martin listened carefully and asked a couple of intelligent questions. Then he said, "This probably isn't a good time to ask. I'll ring again tomorrow night."

"To ask what?" Andrew queried.

"What you and Carmen were doing over the Easter Holidays," Martin replied.

Easter was only three weeks away. Andrew shook his head. "Nothing special planned, why?" He imagined that he was going to be asked if they were coming to Townsville.

Martin answered, "My parents are organising a camping trip to Endeavour Island for a week and they wondered if we would like to take a few friends, so we thought of you and Carmen."

The idea had instant appeal. Images of Letitia walking along a sun-drenched tropical beach in her bikini (or less!) flitted across Andrew's mind.

"Sounds great, but we will have to ask Mum and Dad," Andrew replied.

"Do that and then ring me so we can work out the details," Martin replied.

Andrew hadn't wanted to admit his ignorance, but he made himself ask, "Where's Endeavour Island?"

"Off Cardwell. It's a 'high' island covered with jungle," Martin replied. "Named after Captain Cook's ship," he added.

Now Andrew could place it, and even knew what Martin meant. Many islands off the Queensland coast were really the tops of mountains which had been partially submerged after the sea level rose at the end of the last ice age. He knew that the others, the 'low' islands, were just flat sandy things which had built up on coral reefs and then been stabilised by vegetation taking hold. There were several near Cairns: Green Island being the most famous. Then he thought of others: Low Isles, near where Carmen had been rescued, Michaelmas Cay, Upolo Cay.

"Sounds good, but if it involves sailing and small boats Mum and Dad mightn't be too keen after today," he replied.

That got Martin all thoughtful. "I suppose so," he replied. "Well, ask anyway please. I'd like you to come."

That comment sent a warm glow through Andrew. He knew he had good friends in Cairns but it was nice to know that other people liked him as well. It made him determined to persuade his parents. But he did not ask straight away, reasoning that it was the wrong time.

I'll do some thinking first, then see if Carmen wants to go, he decided. So he went off to his room and dug out an atlas. A quick check showed no sign of Endeavour Island. *Too small to be named probably*, he reasoned, noting a whole cluster of islands off the coast between Cardwell and Innisfail.

He decided he needed a marine chart and resolved to ask Lt Cdr Hazard when he saw him next.

That turned out to be sooner than he expected. Lt Cdr Hazard called in at 8am the next morning on his way to work. By then the telephone had rung at least twenty times: friends of Carmen, friends of the parents, anxious relations, friends of Andrews.

Lt Cdr Hazard was only too happy to loan a chart. "Drop in after school at my shop and I will give you one," he said.

Then the phone rang again. Lt Cdr Hazard went to say hello to Carmen and Andrew answered the phone. It was his aunt Phoebe. While he was talking to her his mother arrived and he was glad to hand the receiver to her. He then said goodbye to Lt Cdr Hazard as he left. As soon as he had woken up Andrew had checked how Carmen was, but she had been asleep. Breakfast and the usual morning routine had then claimed him, so he now took the opportunity to see her before going to school.

"Hi, Sis! How are you?" he asked.

"Bit sore," Carmen replied, indicating a badly bruised cheek, neck and arms. "Who was that on the phone?"

"Just another curious relation. Aunty Phoebe in this case," Andrew replied.

"We've certainly got some curious relations," Carmen observed as their mother came in to join them.

"Curious! Most of them are downright bloody peculiar," Andrew replied.

He was thinking about some of his father's relations as he did. He knew there was a whole swag of them living in places like Daintree, Rossville and Cooktown but had only met a few. He actually thought his mother's branch of the family more normal.

Except dear old Aunty Phoebe!

"Andrew! Don't be horrible," his mother chided.

She then began to fuss about Carmen, who was not going to school. Andrew kept checking his watch and wished his mother would go so he could discuss the proposed trip to Endeavour Island with Carmen.

At last their mother left, but by then it was half past eight and Andrew knew he would be late for school if he didn't go soon. After quickly checking that their mother was out of hearing, he said, "Car, how would you like to go camping on an island for a week during the Easter holidays?"

"Is that what Martin asked you last night?" she replied.

That stumped Andrew. *How did she know that?*

"Yes," was all he could reply.

"Who else is going?" Carmen asked.

At that, Andrew began to blush. He could see that Carmen thought he was only interested because of Letitia.

"Martin and his sister and their mum and dad," he mumbled.

"Oh! His sister?" Carmen teased. Andrew blushed even more.

"Yes," he muttered. "Anyway, think about it. I've gotta go or I'll be late for school," he said. He hurriedly left the room.

That afternoon when he got home, he found there had been even more phone calls made, some of them by Carmen.

"We will go camping on this island if you want," she said.

Chapter 5

CAN'T WAIT!

Andrew felt his emotions surge. "That's great, Car. Do you think Mum and Dad will let us go?"

"They will. I asked Mum this morning and she said yes," she replied.

That really cheered Andrew. He had been half afraid to get his hopes up in case their parents said no. "What about Dad?" he asked.

"Mum said that Dad has to go to a business conference in Sydney that week and she had been thinking of taking us to visit Aunty Valda in Mackay but wasn't sure if we wanted to go, or if they could afford it. She said it was for us to decide," Carmen explained.

That put Andrew on a spot. He actually liked going to stay with Aunty Valda but they had done that the previous September; and she was only an aunty. In his teenage mind she could not compete with the fevered images of Letitia which now crowded his imagination. But he did hesitate and feel bad about it. "Mum might want us with her," he said, trying to ease is conscience.

To his relief, Carmen shook her head. "I asked her that. She laughed and said she doubted if we would enjoy being dragged around to visit all the rellies day after day."

"She's right there! Some of them are bloody odd." Andrew replied with feeling.

Gloomy memories of bored fidgeting during social calls to relatives whose names he could not even remember rose to stoke his desires to escape, to run free on a golden beach with a golden-haired Goddess.

Carmen laughed. "You should be more respectful of Aunt Phoebe. She's a lovely person."

"I'm sure she is," Andrew replied doubtfully. "So, I suppose we can now start organising things."

"Already done," Carmen answered. "I haven't lain here all day doing nothing you know!"

That peeved Andrew a bit but also relieved him. "Oh yeah! So what is the plan?"

"We all meet in Cardwell on the Monday."

"Why not Friday?" Andrew cut in, already feeling that two weeks was far too long a time to wait.

"Don't interrupt little brother," Carmen replied. "Monday. We then go out to the island by boat and camp there for five days, coming back on the Saturday."

"Is there a resort there? What do you mean by camp?"

"No, no resort. No buildings at all, other than a lighthouse," Carmen answered. "I checked on the tourist website. Camping is by permit only and the Schipholls have one. There are only a dozen people at a time allowed to camp on the island and the campsite isn't available till the Monday afternoon."

"A dozen. So we could be sharing with a mob of strangers," Andrew said, not at all relishing such an idea.

"Could be, but won't be. The Schipholls have invited a few others along to make up the numbers," Carmen answered.

"Who?" Andrew asked, his anxiety rising.

"Anne Maudsley. You remember Anne? She is the fair-haired navy cadet who sent you the card in January."

Andrew nodded. He did. *That might complicate things a bit,* he thought. At the time Anne had intimated quite strongly that she liked him. Then he shook his head. *No,* he told himself. *She is too much of a 'Plain Jane' and a 'goody goody'. She won't be any competition for Letitia.*

"Yes," he muttered. "Who else?"

"Jill Cooper and Mark," Carmen said.

"Now that might cause some problems," Andrew said.

During the January holidays he had been quite smitten by the lovely black-haired Jill, to the extent of vacillating over whether he liked her more than Letitia. His flirting with Jill had even led to Mark warning him off, and then to the two boys exchanging blows.

"Why?" Carmen asked. "You don't still think she likes you, surely?"

"Well, no, but..." Andrew replied. He was unsure what to say, and did not want his sister to guess the truth. "She doesn't approve of Letitia, and they could clash," he said.

"She doesn't like the way Letitia flirts and flaunts herself, you mean," Carmen said, giving a shrewd smile as she did.

"Yes, you know, how she... Letitia that is, and her mother both sometimes sunbathe," Andrew said.

Lurid memories of cycling along the driveway of the Schipholl's house to surprise Letitia and her mother, both of whom were lying naked beside the swimming pool, crowded his mind, causing him to blush.

Carmen laughed. "Oh, poor Andrew! Don't get your hopes up! You be sensible. Letitia's not the girl for you. You will only get hurt if you fall for her."

"Hummppf!" Andrew grunted. "Is anyone else coming on this camping trip?"

"Only Jacob," Carmen answered.

"Oh him," Andrew replied.

He was surprised that he hadn't thought of him already. Jacob was a Cadet Leading Seaman Carmen had met in January, but he didn't realise they were still in contact with each other.

"Yes, him," Carmen said in a challenging tone. Then she abruptly changed the subject. "How was school today?"

"Just ordinary," Andrew replied.

"Did people ask you about yesterday?" Carmen asked.

"Of course they did! It was all in the papers and on TV. I told them all that I know. Stephen Bell wanted to know why the smugglers didn't sell you into the white slave trade."

"Oh did he!" Carmen bristled.

"And Donna Hendricks said they should have tossed you overboard for the sharks," Andrew added.

"Oh did she! The jealous cow! I'll still beat her in every exam," Carmen said angrily.

"So, do we need tents and things?" Andrew asked.

"Yes. It will be camping. I've started making a list of what we need," Carmen replied.

She picked up a notepad from her bedside table and began reading aloud the things she had thought of. For the next twenty minutes the brother and sister discussed the things they might need and how they were going to cook their food. Andrew was astounded at the sheer quantity of gear and food Carmen had listed.

"We'll need a bloody truck, or a landing barge to get all this junk to the island," he said. "How do we get to Cardwell anyway?"

"Mum says we will have to go by coach," Carmen answered.

"That means we can't take very much," Andrew replied. For the first time he found he was profoundly ignorant about 'camping'. He had been on two school camps, but they had both been in buildings. So had the two navy cadet camps he had been on. In all his 14 years he had never slept in a tent.

"I will call Mrs Schipholl and ask what we need to bring. They may be bringing the big things like tents and stuff," Carmen said.

Andrew nodded and looked at his watch. "Good idea. You do that. I've got to ride to town to get a chart from Commander Hazard."

A few minutes later Andrew was on his way, pedalling his bicycle against the southeast trade wind. The effort made him puff and sweat.

Bloody wind! he thought. *Always against you when you're in a hurry!*

Twenty minutes later he was in Lt Cdr Hazard's shop. He ran a Ship's Chandlers. Lt Cdr Hazard asked how Carmen was, and then said, "Have you heard anything about the smugglers?"

"No sir, what?" Andrew asked, immediately interested.

"They sailed that stolen yacht into Newell Beach, just north of Port Douglas, and anchored her there. Then they went ashore. It seems they were met by someone with a car and were out of the area even before our boat had been found."

That peeved Andrew but he had to admit they sounded pretty clever. Now that the immediate fear and distress was fading, he was gripped by the sheer excitement of it all.

Pirates and smugglers, he thought, picturing himself swinging across from one sailing ship to the other through cannon smoke, cutlass in hand.

He said, "I suppose they will get away."

"Probably, but not for long," Lt Cdr Hazard replied. "The police seemed to know a good deal about them. Now, never mind the criminals, why do you need the chart?"

Andrew explained the camping trip. Lt Cdr Hazard nodded. "Endeavour Island, eh? Well, lucky you. I've never been there, but I've sailed past."

"What's it like sir?"

"About a kilometre long I guess, and perhaps as wide, no, a bit longer. A rocky ridge up the middle, some lovely little bays with sandy beaches, and areas of jungle and scrub. It's got a fascinating history."

That got Andrew's interest again. "Why sir? What happened?"

"Oh lots of things. I don't remember it all. You should dig out a few books and read up on it. From memory there are a couple of shipwrecks and one plane wreck, a haunted lighthouse; or is a haunted mansion? I can't remember which. It's too long since I read it all. Anyway, there have been a few murders there and there's quite a cemetery I remember someone telling me."

That surprised Andrew. He said, "Carmen told me there were no buildings on the island other than the lighthouse."

"I think there used to be a copra plantation. That was converted into a tourist resort, but something went wrong. I can't remember whether it was a cyclone or the bad reputation, but the venture failed and now I'm told it is all just ruins overgrown by the jungle," Lt Cdr Hazard explained.

As he heard this, Andrew experienced surges of growing interest. The island suddenly became much more attractive and sounded like an exciting place.

"Sounds more interesting than I expected, sir," he said. "I was wondering what we might do for a week."

Lt Cdr Hazard laughed and added, "You can always go treasure hunting."

"Treasure hunting! Now you're pulling my leg, sir."

Lt Cdr Hazard shook his head. "No I'm not. Real, ridgie-didge pirate treasure so I read."

At the word 'pirate' Andrew's interest soared. Even so he was still unsure if he was being fed a line as he suspected Lt Cdr Hazard was aware of his romantic streak and daydreams.

"Oh fair go, sir! There were never any pirates in the Coral Sea."

"No, maybe not, or at least not of the Captain Kidd and Blackbeard variety, although there were some grim goings on in the Nineteenth Century. No, the story I heard was that an English pirate named Bennett raided the Spanish colonies on the west coast of South America, Chile and Peru, then sailed away to stash his ill-gotten gains till the hunt died down. One story says he hid his loot on a place called Cocos Island, which is somewhere off Panama or Costa Rica. Another story says he sailed across the Pacific to Australia and buried the treasure here. Gladstone is the place most often touted as the likely location, but Endeavour Island has somehow gotten into the legend."

"When was this sir?" Andrew asked, his imagination fired by the imagery.

"Now you've got me. Ask your History teacher. Sometime around the end of the Napoleonic Wars, when those South American countries were trying to throw off Spanish rule anyway."

Treasure! Andrew thought, experiencing a real thrill.

Across the screen of his mind danced images of opening the rotting treasure chest in a cave full of skeletons; of the gleam of gold, the sparkle of precious gems.

"What book should I read, sir?" he asked, unable to mask his interest.

Lt Cdr Hazard laughed. "Sorry, I can't remember. I'm a ship's chandler, not a historian. As I said, go to the library or do a google search."

So Andrew hurried off, his mind seething with excitement. *Buried treasure! Pirate gold!* he thought. *Now, we must try to find that!*

At the municipal library Andrew was unable to find any books about Endeavour Island but he found one about shipwrecks off the Queensland coast. His mind still full of pictures of gold doubloons and pieces of eight he went to the computer catalogue and looked up 'pirates'. That yielded two more books. There were actually a dozen listed but the others were all out on loan. Satisfied he had enough to go on with, he made his way home.

He was just bursting to tell Carmen about the buried treasure but memories of past embarrassments over his failed enthusiasms made him hold his tongue. It took a real effort of will power and he was worried that Carmen was suspicious, but somehow he managed to stay silent.

She had been busy and was able to report that Mrs Schipholl had said they were only to bring their clothes, groundsheet and sleeping bags.

"They will provide the tents and cooking gear and so on," Carmen explained.

After dinner, brother and sister studied the chart. Andrew measured it and found that Lt Cdr Hazard's memory was accurate. The island was actually about 1.4 km long and about 800 metres wide. He was particularly pleased to note that there were several small islets and reefs close by.

"They will be fun to explore," he said.

As he studied the marine chart, Andrew found it wasn't quite what he needed. "We actually need a map, like the army cadets use," he said. "One with the land features in detail, the creeks and contours and so on."

"Could we get one?" Carmen asked.

"I suppose so," Andrew replied. "I'll ask Mr Conkey tomorrow at school during geography. He'll know."

Andrew bent back to peer closely at the chart. *Now, where might a pirate come ashore to bury his treasure?* he wondered. That got him thinking about prevailing winds and tides and so on. He placed his fingertip on the words 'Careenage Bay" *There, they might have beached their ship to scrape the barnacles off her bottom,* he mused.

Noting his interest Carmen queried, "What's there?"

"Oh! Oh nothing! Just reading the names," Andrew replied, silently berating himself for forgetting to hide his interest. Later, after he had done his homework, he went to his room and lay on his bed to read. By then he was fired with a desire to get to Endeavour Island as quickly as possible. The more he read or heard about it, the more there seemed to be to see or do.

And Letitia too! he thought as he lay in bed.

Chapter 6

ANTICIPATION

On Tuesday morning, Andrew and Carmen rode their bicycles to school together. Andrew could tell that Carmen was still a bit shaken by the incident but thought that the sooner she settled back into her normal life, the better. At school they separated, and Andrew sought out his own particular group of friends, particularly Blake and Luke Karaku. He also made a point of going to the library during the lunch break. He found this a disappointing experience. The library seemed to have very few books on North Queensland history and even fewer on pirates.

So Andrew settled to reading the ones he had obtained from the municipal library. He even read them in class when he should have been doing English or maths, but because he rarely gave any of the teachers trouble, and usually got very good marks, they hardly commented on it. Not having geography that day he did not make a point of asking Mr Conkey for an army map.

That chance came on Wednesday just before morning break. At the end of the geography lesson, Andrew waited so he could speak to Mr Conkey alone. To his mild annoyance, Peter Bronsky also waited behind. Andrew liked Peter, and respected his brain, as Peter usually topped the class, but just now he wished he would go.

Mr Conkey finished cleaning the board and went to gather up his books. "Yes Peter, what is it?"

Peter gave Andrew a self-conscious glance and held out some papers. "Here are the enrolment forms, sir."

Mr Conkey's face brightened. "Oh good! I'm glad you are joining."

Peter again glanced at Andrew and blushed. "Thanks, sir."

"So be on parade this afternoon and we will see about issuing you with a uniform," Mr Conkey said.

Peter nodded, then turned to Andrew with a half-embarrassed look. "I'm joining the army cadets," he explained.

"So I guessed," Andrew replied. He grinned and went on, "Don't

51

do it, Peter. There's still time. You should be joining the navy cadets instead."

Mr Conkey laughed. "Get away with you navy! What do you want, Andrew? Do you want to transfer from the navy cadets to the army cadets?"

Andrew also laughed. "Aw, sir! Get real! As my dad says, 'In the navy you always get a warm meal and a dry bed.'"

"Yes, if you are still afloat!" Peter commented with a chuckle as he made for the door.

Andrew struggled to find a smart comeback to that one but could only grin as Peter left the room. Andrew then said to Mr Conkey, "Could you help me find a map, sir, one of those topographic maps?"

"Which one?" Mr Conkey asked.

Andrew described the projected holiday trip to Mr Conkey. Mr Conkey nodded. "I need to look at a map register. We wouldn't have the one you want in our files. It's a bit out of our area, but I can tell you which map to buy."

"Can you buy them, sir?" Andrew asked. That surprised him as he assumed they were only issued by the army.

"Yes. 'Sunmap' sell them, so do Absell's Newsagency in Lake Street, plus a few camping stores, and so on," Mr Conkey answered. "See me after school and I will give you the map name and number."

"Thanks sir," Andrew replied.

He hurried out of the room and along the veranda in the direction Peter had gone. Seeing him had given him an idea. Peter was one of a group of four friends who were always going off on hiking expeditions. One of the group was Graham Kirk, who was in 9B and had been a navy cadet for a short while the previous year.

Graham's dad is a ship captain and has lots of books and charts, he thought. *Maybe he has something on Endeavour Island?*

Andrew saw three of the friends sitting in their usual place but noted that Graham was not there. Then he saw Graham walking over from the direction of the tuck shop to join them.

He looks a bit unhappy, Andrew noted.

Even before that he had felt a bit reluctant to approach them. It wasn't as though they were strangers. He knew them reasonably well, had even been quite good friends with Graham. But the memories of

Graham's absolute despair when he had learned he could never be a naval officer because his eyes weren't good enough rose up to haunt Andrew. He had spent hours floating in the sea after the floatplane crash trying to convince Graham not to just give up. During that time, Andrew had used every argument he could think of and they had exchanged some very intimate information. It had been a harrowing experience for them both, and for Ken, the paraplegic friend they were supporting. Even now, Andrew suspected Graham still contemplated suicide and that bothered him deeply.

He looks pretty miserable even now, he decided as he plucked up courage and walked towards them.

As he approached, the friends turned to look. Stephen Bell was the first to speak. "Ship Ahoy!" he called. "Hard a port! Pass the port!"

"Any port in a storm!" Andrew replied, for something to say.

"Is that why you navy blokes always have ugly girlfriends?" Stephen jibed.

Andrew snorted. "Huh! Get real! We always get the pretty ones."

Roger Dunning, the chubby one, who despite being a Year 8 was a member of the group, slid along the bench to make room for him. Andrew sat down opposite Graham. As he did, Andrew smiled and noted with surprise that Graham appeared to be struggling to hold back tears.

He looks like he's going to cry, he thought.

To change the subject, Andrew immediately asked Graham if his dad had any books on Endeavour Island.

"Endeavour Island? Where's that?" Graham asked.

Andrew described the location and the projected holiday trip. Despite his intense interest in the treasure story he made no mention of it, not wishing to be teased even more.

Graham nodded and said, "I'll have a look. Dad's away at the moment; won't be back till next month sometime."

Stephen asked, "Who's going to this Endeavour Island? Is it a navy cadet thing?"

Andrew shook his head. "No. Most of them will be kids from Townsville, and some parents." He named them.

Stephen grinned. "This Letitia, is she the blonde you met during the holidays?"

That both shocked and nettled Andrew. He had been careful never to mention any details like that. *I wonder who told Stephen?* he puzzled. But he blushed, tried to stop it, and blushed even more as lurid images of Letitia flooded his mind.

Stephen chortled. "Oooh it is! Look at the colour he's gone!"

Annoyed and embarrassed, Andrew asked, "How do you know about her?"

"I have my sources," Stephen replied, trying to sound mysterious and all-knowing.

Andrew was angry now. "Who?" he demanded.

"Arthur Blake told me," Stephen said simply. "But he only had the bare outline." Stephen nudged Graham and said, "Ya get it? The bare outline..."

With that Graham stood up and walked away. Andrew was surprised at the abruptness of his actions. He frowned and wondered if he had said the wrong thing.

Turning to the others he asked, "What's wrong with Graham? Did I say something?"

Stephen made a face and said, "Nah! He's just not happy because his love life isn't going very well."

Andrew glanced after Graham and thought, *I can relate to that!*

"Who is he interested in?" he asked.

"Little moll in Year Eight," Stephen replied. "Deslie Desmond, comes from Kuranda."

Andrew didn't know her so shook his head. *Poor old Graham,* he thought.

"What's the problem?"

"She likes him, but I reckon she's just stringing him along. She's a flirt and he just saw her talking to Lipman," Stephen explained.

"I thought he was going out with a girl from Kuranda named Esme?" Andrew said.

Stephen shook his head. "Nah! They broke up. This Deslie's the new attraction."

At that moment, the conversation was ended by the ringing of the bell. Andrew hurried back to class. On the way he passed Arthur Blake. He was a bit annoyed with Blake but could guess how he got the story. Blake was a navy cadet and knew some of the Townsville cadets.

One of them must have told him, he thought. So he asked.

Blake looked surprised, then a bit sheepish. "Mark," he replied.

"Thanks a lot!" Andrew snapped. Inside he seethed.

Bloody Mark! Trust him.

"Hey, don't get stroppy with me," Blake said. "Everybody knows the story. It's no secret."

That made Andrew blush and feel even more upset. He had images of other navy cadets sniggering behind their hands, whispering tales about what he and Letitia might have done, when in fact they had done very little. Nodding to let Blake know he was still a friend, Andrew hurried on to class.

After school, Andrew made his way to underneath C Block, where the army cadets had their Q Store and office. Mr Conkey wasn't there yet so Andrew stood to one side watching the army cadets milling around before their weekly 'Home Training' parade. Their school was one of the few which had a cadet unit and Andrew knew it was only because Mr Conkey gave the time and effort to organise it.

While Andrew stood watching, he was joined by Kit Walker, the smallest student in his class and also the smallest cadet in the navy cadets. As he did, they were teased by the army cadets that knew they were both navy cadets. Most added a few smart comments to either put down the navy cadets or to boast about how much better the army cadets were. One even suggested they transfer from the navy cadets.

Over to one side Andrew noticed Graham and Peter, both in school uniform. They were talking and as Andrew watched Peter gestured towards the assembling cadets and Graham shook his head, then walked away. As he went, Andrew felt a stab in his heart at the look on his face: half hope, half despair.

Poor bugger! He is hurting alright, he mused. Once again, anxiety over Graham's previous talk of suicide came to bother him.

Peter walked over to join Andrew and Kit. "Hi Andrew! Changed your mind have you" he joked.

Andrew smiled. "Fat chance!" he replied. Then he nodded towards Graham's departing back. "Were you trying to persuade Graham to join?"

Peter gave wry smile and nodded. "Yes, I was."

"He should. He needs something," Andrew said, but he could not bring himself to betray Graham's confidences, even to so good a friend as Peter.

At that moment, Mr Conkey appeared, now wearing his army uniform and the rank badges of a captain. He saw Andrew and smiled, then called him over.

"Just wait till I get this show on the road," he said.

"That's what my dad said the army was like, sir," Andrew replied. "Just like a circus only more tents."

Captain Conkey snorted, then laughed. "Cheeky bugger! Do you want these maps or not?"

Andrew said he did. Kit gave a grin at that and went on his way. Captain Conkey again asked Andrew to wait, gave orders to some older cadets and to a couple of teachers who were also transformed into army officers, then went into the cadet office for a while. He came out a few minutes later with a map and showed Andrew the location diagram among the marginal information.

"That's the one you want. Write down both the name and the number."

Andrew did so, then thanked Captain Conkey and quickly left, aware that he was now just in the way while the cadets were called on parade. For a few minutes he stood at the side of the grass quadrangle and watched the army cadets conduct their company admin parade, interested in the differences in drill and procedures, then he went to the bike racks.

An hour of riding around town and calling at various shops at last secured him a copy of the 1:50 000 scale topographic map he wanted. It was much more detailed than the naval chart and Andrew studied it with satisfaction before rolling it up and riding home.

At home he settled to do his homework, then began reading. That evening he read *Treasure beneath the Sea*. He found it interesting enough and got him thinking about learning to be a diver, but it had nothing about either Australia or any pirate named Bennet. Before going to bed he sat and studied the new map, thinking of places to explore, and wondering where a pirate ship might anchor.

Out of the South East Trade wind, he mused, again eyeing Careenage Bay.

His eye caught the name 'Wreck Bay' and that got him interested.

The symbol for a shipwreck was marked close in to the beach on a coral reef, but there was no name next to it.

I wonder what ship it was? he thought as he went to bed.

He then lay in bed thinking about the island, then about pirates, and wrecks, and then about rescuing Letitia from pirates. From there it was only a short step to fantasising about Letitia and to imagining what she and he might possibly do. Then he got all ashamed and guilty, knowing there was no way he would do any such things. They were all too 'adult' and serious and he had no intention of wrecking his life.

But Letitia was among his dominant thoughts the next morning. *Oh come on holidays!* he thought. His urges surged in him like an itch he could not scratch and he fairly squirmed with unfulfilled desire. Then he became even more guilty as he knew that Anne really did like him and had been saying as much by writing and telephoning. But she didn't set the pulses racing in the same way as Letitia!

That got Andrew wondering how he could gently put Anne off without hurting her feelings. *Maybe I could hint to Martin that she doesn't come?* he thought. But that just made him feel worse, and he knew Carmen would see through the plot instantly. *And with Jill being there as well there might be a fair bit of tension in the group. I don't think that it is going to work.*

School seemed to drag. This was made worse by having assignments due. *And exams start next week,* he thought irritably. He did not want to waste time studying, he wanted to read as much as he could.

Even the reading was frustrating. He found a well-illustrated book called *Pirates and Buccaneers* by John Gilbert which was a good general history but again it made no mention of Australia or of Bennet. His mother tried to help by bringing home *The Chronicles of Captain Blood* by Rafael Sabatini. Andrew did not hurt her feelings by pointing out that it was a novel. Even so he read that on Friday and while he loved the style and the romance, he was left with a feeling that the author knew little about ships and just used them like pieces of stage machinery.

He makes it all sound a bit too easy, Andrew mused, his mind roving over the more technical stories about sailing ships that he had read by Patrick O'Brian or C. S. Forester.

Once again, Andrew considered asking Graham. Even though he feared another rebuff he decided he would and went looking for him at lunchtime. He found Peter, Stephen and Roger in their usual places but no Graham. The three friends looked quite gloomy.

"What's wrong?" Andrew asked. "Where's Graham?"

Stephen answered. "Kept in. He's in trouble with old Mr 'Buggermaster'."

"What for?"

"Lorna drew a crude drawing of that Tarzan bloke and gave it to him and Burgomeister saw it and blamed him," Stephen explained.

Andrew shook his head. He knew just who Stephen was talking about. For weeks now stories had been circulating about a naked madman who lived in the jungle near Kuranda. 'Tarzan', as he had been nicknamed, was held responsible for several rapes. Andrew now learned that Graham had apparently seen him the previous weekend. He also understood that Graham was the sort of person who would take the punishment rather than dob in a friend.

For a while they discussed Tarzan and then Andrew took himself to the library and searched the internet for information on pirates. To his annoyance, he found there was too much and much of it poorly written or of doubtful accuracy. Again he found nothing on Bennet.

Friday evening meant Navy Cadets. In some ways Andrew was not keen to go as it brought back quite forcefully the painful memories of the previous weekend. But it was also a familiar and reassuring place with good friends. As it was only a few weeks to Anzac Day much of the training session was taken up with drill, mostly marching. They also cleaned out the boats and checked and re-stowed all the boat gear.

Saturday was chores at home. On Sunday Andrew decided he would go over to Graham's house to ask about books. However, on arrival he was met by Graham's little sister Kylie, who was obviously annoyed by something. "Graham's not here," she said. "He's gone to Kuranda."

"Kuranda?" Andrew replied, quite surprised.

"Yes," Kylie replied, but she did not enlighten him.

Andrew left it at that and went home, to read more of his old favourite: *Treasure Island*.

Enlightenment came on Monday at school. Once again, Graham was not with his friends (He had a week of detention for the drawing).

It was Stephen who explained. "We rode our bloody bikes up to Kuranda. Bloody hell! Never again."

"Kuranda? Why?"

"That's where Deslie and Lorna live," Stephen explained.

Andrew nodded. He now knew who Deslie was and thought she was a pretty little thing. *But not a patch on Letitia.*

Instead, Andrew rode over to Graham's after school. This time he was lucky. Graham was home and seemed to be in a happy mood.

"Hi Andrew, come in. What do you want?"

"Remember me asking about books or charts on Endeavour Island?" Andrew replied.

"Oh sure. Let's go and see what we can find," Graham replied. He led the way through to a large bookshelf in the lounge room and began to scan the titles. After a minute he pulled out a book, then a second one. He passed these to Andrew, who read the titles: *Ships in the Coral* and *Coasts of Cape York.*

"You were interested in pirates too, weren't you?" Graham asked.

Andrew nodded and felt foolish. Graham did not seem to notice and pulled out a very old encyclopaedia: *Newnes Pictorial Knowledge, Volume 8.*

"I've got a couple of books of my own too," he added.

He led the way back out to his bedroom, the enclosed front veranda of the 'Old Queenslander'. Here he dug around and produced a couple of books.

As he did, Andrew could not help noticing a half completed model sailing ship on the side table. He knew that Graham had a very large collection of scratch-built ship models. Half of the downstairs area of the house was enclosed and was the 'ship room'.

For a moment he bent over and studied the model, then said, "That's a great model Graham. It's an Eighteenth Century frigate, isn't it? What's her name?"

"The HMS *Artemis* of 1805," Graham replied, going red.

"You are doing a really good job on her," Andrew said, noting Graham's embarrassment. Then he asked, "Have you thought about coming back to navy cadets?"

The moment Andrew asked this he wished he hadn't as he saw a look of pain cross Graham's face, which then went all stiff and wooden.

"No," he replied.

There was an embarrassed silence. Andrew groped around for something to say and then noted that the ship model had a full hull. All the other models of Graham's he had seen were 'waterline' models, designed to be pushed around the floor in games.

He asked, "Is this model being made to float?"

Graham nodded. "Yes. It's for a race against a model Peter Bronsky is making."

"That will be interesting," Andrew commented, again studying the careful craftsmanship of the model. "When is the race?"

"When both models are finished. Not till after the holidays probably," Graham replied.

"I'd like to watch," Andrew said. "Let us know when it is please."

At that, Graham grunted and nodded and Andrew decided he was embarrassed about it.

Probably thinks people reckon he is a little kid to be playing with toy boats, he thought, comparing it with the looks he sometimes got when he forgot himself and made some daydream imaginings public.

To change the subject he asked, "Which of these books is best?"

Graham touched a little old hardcover book with no dustcover. "That one. It's not about Australia though. It's just a novel. I thought you might like it."

Andrew did. It was by R. M. Ballantine and was over a hundred years' old and titled *Pieces of Eight.* It was about a treasure hunt in the Bahamas and Andrew loved it.

What a little gem! he thought happily as he put it aside the next afternoon. It really got his romantic mind working and he happily daydreamed for a while.

Then he was even more thrilled to find that the old encyclopaedia had a short chapter on Bennet. The picture caught his eye. THE TREASURE OF COCOS ISLAND the title read. Beneath it were a line of pirates walking up the beach from their boats, the treasure chest slung from an oar between two pirates and the captain following, pistols in his belt. A brig rode at anchor out on the sea and palm trees along the beach gave it a tropical flavour.

Heart beating a little faster Andrew read the short story. It said: 'In 1818, a British pirate, Bennet Graham, or Benito Bonita, as he preferred to call himself, buried loot taken from Peruvian churches on Cocos Island.'

There was more detail but that tended to lower Andrew's spirits as all the mention of buried treasure was on Cocos Island and there was absolutely no mention of Bennet Graham coming to Australia, in fact no mention of Australia in the whole chapter.

It must be just a rumour that has got out of hand he decided.

But it had been good reading all the same. Having done his homework and studied for his exams he settled to reading *Ships in the Coral* by Hector Holthouse. He found it fascinating and had trouble putting it down to go to bed. Reading it took up all his spare moments for the next two days.

Amazing! he thought as he finished. *I had no idea there were so many shipwrecks and missing ships off the coast of Queensland.* It fired his imagination even more.

"Here Carmel, read this," he said, offering her *Ships in the Coral*. "It will just boggle your mind how many shipwrecks there have been on the Barrier Reef."

Chapter 7

AT LAST!

Two days later, Carmen closed the back cover of *Ships in the Coral* and looked out her bedroom window.

Andrew was right, she thought. *There have been just an amazing number of shipwrecks in the Coral Sea.*

For a while she sat and thought about what she had just read. Some of the dramas had been a bit too close to the bone emotionally, especially the stories about women being shipwrecked or kidnapped.

She sat and tried to imagine what it might have been like to be cast away after a shipwreck back in the early days of exploration and settlement. That made her feel quite uneasy as she pictured herself being taken prisoner by wild Aborigines, her clothes being torn off, her body examined, touched...

That got her wondering again. She knew she was becoming more and more tense as the holidays grew slowly closer. Partly it was emotional reaction to the frightening experience she had been through but mostly it was mingled apprehension and excitement. Boys had not been a big factor in her life up until January, even though most of her classmates were apparently obsessed with 'relationships' and 'love'. Then she had met Jacob Edwards.

Into her mind swept the picture of when she had first seen him: the white teeth smiling in the handsome, tanned face, the strong arms, muscles rippling as he lifted a heavy box. It had helped that they had navy cadets as a common interest, and that they both liked sailing. Talking about that had helped them over those first few nervous days when both were aware of each other. It had certainly been a real boost to Carmen, who otherwise felt very shy.

She had been astonished at her own reactions. Normally she just treated boys with tolerant disdain and bossed them around, but suddenly she had felt tongue-tied and become anxious to be near Jacob, to see him, for him to look at her. At the time she had thought it must be true love. Now she smiled and sighed.

Oh, I hope so!

She picked up another book. This was one her Aunty Edith had sent her in the mail when she had told her about the holiday plans. *Island that we Knew* was its title, by a lady named Busettin, a Mackay local, Aunty Edith had said. Carmen lay back and began reading, and was soon absorbed. The story was a very personal one but all the more gripping for that because it was exactly what Carmen could relate to.

She enjoyed the book so much she finished it in a day and a night. Then she gave it to Andrew, who was still scratching around for information about pirates. In fact she found him reading *Treasure Island* again. He had two copies, one a hard cover edition with no illustrations and the second a much smaller one, with as much space devoted to colour pictures as to the words. It was obvious this was Andrew's favourite version, and she could see why. The artwork was superb, the drawings accurate and colourful. Even the pictures of the ships looked right, the set of the sails matching the scend of the waves, the details of rigging being technically correct.

Poor old Andrew, she thought as she left him. *He is such a romantic. He was born in the wrong century.*

She knew he was embarrassed when people realised he was dreaming about pirates and sailing ships. Then another twinge of concern caused her to worry about Andrew being silly over Letitia.

She's not the girl for him, she thought. *She's just a... a...*

She struggled to find a polite way to say 'tart'. Memories of Andrew's eager excitement in January got her even more worried. There was no doubt that Andrew had learned more about girls in that month than in the preceding thirteen years.

And saw more of them too! Carmen told herself, giving a wry smile as she did.

She wasn't exactly a prude, but she had rarely seen Andrew with no clothes on and he certainly hadn't seen her in the last few years. But in January he had got a few eyefuls of Letitia, who had several times pranced around with only a skimpy bikini on.

Poor Andrew. I thought his eyes would pop out, Carmen thought.

She shook her head at the memory, and blushed at her own scandalized embarrassment. It wasn't that she did not know the basic facts of life, but she had never felt any real interest in sex as such.

Love is what matters, she told herself.

That got her thinking about Jacob again. He had made no improper advances, but they had certainly kissed with real passion and several times she had tingled with thrill when his hands had strayed close to her 'forbidden zones'. Carmen had never allowed any boy to do more than kiss her and she now wondered if she would allow Jacob a bit more, and whether she was comfortable with that. It was certainly a worry, but she knew she was anxious to meet him and to see just how she felt.

It will be ever so romantic on a tropical beach in the moonlight, she thought, hugging herself in anticipation.

But there was another week to go, and it just seemed to take forever. Saturday was Navy Cadets and again she was glad to go, if only to be with her friends. Once again, the program was mostly drill and ceremonial training to get ready for Anzac Day. Carmen enjoyed that. She knew she could do the drill well, and she also told herself that she looked very attractive in the white dress uniform.

Sunday was spent studying for exams and finishing assignments. The work done to her own satisfaction Carmen settled to reading *Robinson Crusoe*. Andrew, she noted, was now reading a book called *A Coral Island*.

I must read that after him, she thought.

However, she never found the time. At school on Monday exams began and she spent all her spare time reading. She also listened to the latest gossip about Graham and Stephen. They had both gone to Kuranda for the weekend by train and once again Graham claimed to have seen the naked wild man nicknamed 'Tarzan'.

"Graham is getting a real bee in his bonnet about him," Andrew said. "I worry about him sometimes."

Carmen knew how Andrew had helped save Graham from drowning but only nodded and did not pass on the real gossip, which she had overheard from two Year 8 girls. Apparently, Stephen and three of the Kuranda girls, including the object of Graham's adoration, Deslie, had gone 'skinny dipping' at the Barron Falls.

"They will get raped by that Tarzan creep," one of the girls had suggested.

At that, Carmen had shuddered and her whole body seemed to squirm with revulsion. The previous week it had been a major news item that

Tarzan had snuck out of the bush at Buchans Point, at the southern end of Ellis Beach, and raped a woman who was sunbathing. A swirl of conflicting emotions had mixed in Carmen's head when she heard that. Part of her had censoriously said, 'serves her right for behaving like that', while another part felt deep concern and sympathy. Then her own memories of being taken hostage, with the fears of possible rape and murder at Simpsons Point, which was only a few kilometres further north along the coast, made her shudder with deep emotion.

How would I cope? she wondered, trying to picture her own reaction to being raped. *Would I fight, or freeze up in fear? And what would I do if I survived?* It was frightening and distressing to think about. *I will be careful to avoid such situations,* she decided.

Which got her thinking about Jacob again, and whether he would protect her. *Or might he be the man trying to do it?* she wondered. She knew full well that most rapes were 'date' rapes.

Talking on the phone to Jacob helped calm these anxieties. She never mentioned them of course and always made sure her conversations were bright and cheerful. He sounded so pleased to hear her each time that she felt uplifted, then impatient.

Oh, will the holidays never come! she fretted.

There were also phone calls to the others in Townsville, particularly to Anne Maudsley. Carmen really liked Anne and hoped that Andrew wouldn't hurt her feelings by being silly over Letitia. And Letitia was very much in her mind of Monday morning. Once again, Tarzan had struck, this time seizing a Swedish tourist who was swimming at Crystal cascades. The girl had managed to escape and get to safety, but hearing about it caused Carmen to picture Letitia flaunting herself and inviting just such a situation.

I hope she doesn't do anything to embarrass people and to upset things, she mused.

Tarzan was one of the topics of conversation, in between exams. It seems that Graham Kirk had again claimed to have seen him standing beside the railway to Kuranda at a place called Glacier Rock. On hearing that Carmen raised her eyes and stared into the distance. Glacier Rock she knew well. She saw it almost every day of her life. It was a prominent granite outcrop in the jungle just to the left of the gash in the mountains which marked the Barron Gorge.

With an effort she shook off her distressing thoughts, which had wandered back to rapes on beaches, then to smugglers taking her hostage.

"It's over. You are safe," she told herself.

By an effort of will power she changed her thoughts to study and took out a book to read. That helped. Physics was the next exam and she wanted to do well.

She thought she did, but now the approaching holiday was starting to cloud all her thinking. Time alternately dragged and hurried. There were more exams but also the beginning of packing. Not that there was much to pack. It was a beach holiday, and old clothes and bathers were the main items.

The last couple of days just seemed to go on for ever until she was a fever of impatience. She phoned Jacob every night and told him she was really looking forward to seeing him, and she meant it. An almost physical hunger now gripped her and she had trouble sleeping. But at last it was over. The last day of school dragged to a close and she hurried home, bursting with impatience and relief.

Soon, she told herself.

Chapter 8

CARDWELL

11:30 am, Easter Monday.
Cardwell, North Queensland.
A typical April morning. The air temperature already 30 degrees Celsius and the humidity approaching 90%.

Andrew wiped perspiration from his face and looked out to sea. *Humidity 90%, eh?* he thought. *From the look of those grey clouds hanging over the sea it will soon be a hundred percent.*

Andrew and his sister Carmen were seated under a shady tree at the beach end of the long concrete pier leading out over a hundred metres of black mud to where the tide was still on the ebb. He was engrossed in reading *Treasure Island.*

After a while he slipped a bookmark into place and closed the book, then stared out to sea to where distant islands dotted the horizon.

"I wish it was Treasure Island we were going to instead of Endeavour Island," he commented.

Carmen smiled and nodded. She knew that her little brother was a hopeless romantic. He had a passion for sailing and loved to read stories about the old square-rigged sailing ships.

"Well I don't think we will meet any pirates on this holiday," she said.

Andrew grunted, then gestured with his head towards a one-legged man using a crutch who was hobbling along the pier towards them.

"Oh, I don't know, I reckon this joker could pass for Long John Silver."

Carmen glanced towards the man and found herself staring at a face which struck her as looking truly villainous. The man was middle-aged, with grey hair and a thick bristle of unshaven stubble. His skin was deeply lined, and tanned dark brown by the sun. His clothes were faded grey and ragged. He even had a big gold earring in one ear. The only apparent concession to the modern age was that he had an artificial leg made of tubular steel.

At that moment, the man glanced at Carmen and their eyes met, then locked. For an instant Carmen was unable to look away and she felt a stab of emotion that she could only label as alarm, if not actual fear. The man gave her such a hostile glare that she hastily looked away. For a moment she feared he was going to stop, but he stumped on past her and off along the pathway towards the shops across the road.

"Strewth! All he needed was the black eye patch and the parrot," Andrew muttered as the man passed out of earshot.

"A nasty looking piece of work," Carmen agreed.

Andrew glanced at his watch and then snorted impatiently. "Oh, I wish they would hurry up. They said eleven o'clock," he said. 'They' being their group of friends from Townsville. Andrew and Carmen had travelled south for 200 kilometres from Cairns, arriving an hour earlier. The others were coming from Townsville, 160 kilometres to the south. Andrew and Carmen had travelled by coach but their friends were being driven by Mr and Mrs Schipholl.

As Andrew sat there, images of the golden-haired and very busty Letitia rose to the top of his consciousness, pushing aside the image of the other girl he was waiting to see: Anne Maudsley. Memories of the brief holiday romance, with its tantalising promise of more to come, now got Andrew fidgeting with what could only be described as intense sexual tension, allied to a strong sense of guilt, as he knew he should not be thinking about Letitia.

She deceived you and dumped you, don't forget, he reminded himself.

He had a vivid flashback to that last day when Letitia had walked in with her arms around a youth named Johno. Johno had been away on holidays and Andrew had felt very hurt. The pain now returned, in a surprisingly sharp stab. What bothered Andrew a lot was the niggling doubt that at least part of the pain was jealousy.

Think of Anne, he told himself.

It had been the much quieter and much nicer Anne who had then written to him and who was now on her way to be with him. Anne was the same age, a pleasant girl with freckles, blue eyes and mousy fair hair. He had written back to her, sent her a dozen e-mails, and spoken to her on the telephone at least once a week during the intervening two months. Now he wondered how he felt about her.

But, in spite of his best efforts, thoughts of Letitia crept back in. Partly this was because of the physical contrast. Anne was pretty and had a nice figure, but Letitia was an outgoing blonde with a very large bosom. Just the memory of her made Andrew's mouth go dry with lust, causing more twinges to his conscience.

Letitia had been someone quite outside his previous experience and a number of times he had found himself in situations which had almost moved from passionate to sexual. That Letitia was two years older and obviously much more experienced had been both a source of jealous pain and comfort. She and her parents also often went without clothes at home, a source of severe embarrassment to Martin Schipholl, and of fascinated amazement and interest to Andrew.

The whole holiday in Townsville had been an eye-opener to Andrew in more ways than one. He had found that he was deeply disturbed by Letitia's extravert behaviour. He had also found his own moral values severely tested, as he was a strong believer in not hurting anyone just for your own pleasure. Now he wasn't so sure as he found his mind frequently wandering to the 'almost' and 'maybe' situations with Letitia. He spent half the time being disgusted by his own weakness at thinking such thoughts, and half the time fantasising about possible passionate scenarios.

What really bothered Andrew deep down was the fear that he might actually be a weakling and that, if really tempted, he might give in to his evil thoughts. He was fully aware that some boys his own age were already having sexual relations with girls and that grieved him deeply. Not that he was a religious bigot. It was just that he believed that love was something sacred and not to be sullied that way. Which was why he had been so tormented over jealousy about what Letitia might have done. There was even a part of his mind that occasionally tossed up terms like 'tart' to describe her.

So now he sat waiting, his mind and body being stirred by very mixed loyalties, desires and physical passions. He knew that part of him wanted to have sex, to enjoy the experience, to prove he could do it- to prove he 'was a man'. Yet he was also strongly aware that he wanted to stay strong and moral. It was this conflict that now deeply troubled him. But when the invitation to join the Schipholls for a week of camping on Endeavour Island had arrived he had experienced such an intense surge of excited desire to see Letitia that he was ashamed of himself. He knew that secretly he hoped to see her naked, and that he yearned to touch her bare skin, as he several times had.

Memories of those glorious moments crowded his mind and he found to his dismay he was actually breathing faster and that his fingers were tingling with frustrated desire. The mounting excitement caused him to perspire even more than the high temperature and humidity warranted. In an effort to regain control of his thoughts and body, he turned back to reading his book.

It took an effort, but this worked to some extent. At least his arousal slowly subsided so he could stand up when Carmen called him to come and look at a distant boat. As a navy cadet he was genuinely interested in boats and studying the few craft that dotted the sea also helped keep his thoughts off Letitia.

Carmen turned from studying the sea to look back towards the road. She suddenly pointed and let out a cry, "Here they are!"

Andrew felt his heart rate instantly shoot up and his throat constrict. He found it hard to focus his eyes and he gulped several times without realising it. Carmen noted these reactions and they both troubled and amused her. In January she had several times warned Andrew not to fall for Letitia lest he get hurt. She had also been worried that Letitia might persuade Andrew to do things he would later regret. That same concern remained.

Two cars had stopped nearby and out of them climbed six teenagers and two adults. The teenagers began walking over towards them. Most obvious among the group was Letitia. Her golden air shimmered in the sun and her curvy body and clothes both made her stand out. Anne and Jill both wore jeans and long-sleeved shirts, but Letitia wore a short wrap-around skirt and a short cotton top which left her mid-rif and most of her back bare. Two thin straps tied behind her neck indicated she wore her bikini underneath it.

Watching Andrew's eyes hungrily take in Letitia's voluptuous form caused Carmen to bite her lip. *Maybe this holiday wasn't a good idea,* she told herself. She began worrying about how to protect Andrew from himself.

But her own consciousness was split. She was also expecting someone she thought she was in love with- Jacob Edwards. Now she saw him walking towards her, his handsome face creased by a huge grin. Until the previous January Carmen had never been 'in love'. Then she had met Jacob during a visit to the Townsville naval cadet unit, TS *Coral Sea*. Jacob was a rank ahead, being a Cadet Leading Seaman and was also doing Year 10 at high school. Jacob had Aboriginal heritage and it gave his skin a delightful tanned appearance. With his curly back hair and infectious grin Carmen thought he was a charming person.

The other two girls were a contrast. Both were 14 and pretty but Jill was slender and black haired while Anne was more rounded and leggy. The boys were so similar they might have been brothers, except that Martin Schipholl's eyes were blue and Mark Swain's brown. Mark and Jill were boyfriend and girlfriend and had been for some months.

Andrew thought Jill looked very 'cool' and classy. In January he had been strongly attracted to her, to the extent of coming to blows with Mark and of being torn over which girl to choose. However, Jill had settled this by staying with Mark. With an effort of will Andrew forced himself to take his eyes off Letitia and Jill and to look at Anne. As he did, he was struck by her cheerful smile and pretty eyes. A wave of relief surged through him.

It is going to be alright, he told himself.

Anne stopped and they exchanged awkward smiles. Andrew was so flustered he was unsure about what to do next. He had never even held Anne's hand, much less anything more intimate, so he was reluctant to be forward and try to kiss her.

Take it steady, he decided as shyness overcame him.

Anne stood and looked happily at him, then held out both her hands. "Hello Andrew," she said.

What a lovely voice, he thought as he took her hands. Intense awareness of how warm and nice those hands felt surged through him. Again he was reminded of how pretty she was. Anne then turned and gave Carmen a friendly hug.

When Letitia reached them, Andrew was even more flustered about what to do. Letitia quickly settled this by wrapping her arms around his neck, pressing herself hard against him, and giving him a big kiss on the lips. This sent Andrew into a state of delight, scorched by embarrassment and concern.

Anne is watching, and Letitia's parents are just up there, he thought anxiously. *I don't want them to get the wrong idea.*

Carmen watched this greeting with amused concern, then faced Jacob and had exactly the same worry. However, she went all shy and could only smile and nod. Jacob also seemed more reserved and merely said hello and made it plain he was glad to see her. Since January they had spoken on the phone a few times and exchanged a dozen letters, so Carmen thought she now knew him fairly well. Despite this she was still unable to just relax and be natural.

After Letitia released a crimson Andrew there was a general greeting session, with handshakes and hugs. Once again, Andrew was stuck by Jill's loveliness, but he was also very aware of the anxious, mildly hostile look on Mark's face, and of Letitia's presence, so he just said hello to her and acted casual. He shook hands with Martin, who he was genuinely glad to see, and then with Mark. As they did, the two boys exchanged cautious glances.

Mark hasn't forgotten that fight, Andrew thought. *And he looks very anxious.* That made him glance at Jill again and he gave a wry grin. *And I don't blame him for being worried and jealous. Jill is really pretty.*

Mr and Mrs Schipholl came walking across from where the cars had been parked. Mr Schipholl was a hairy bear of a man with a pot belly and cheerful smile. He was half bald and could not be described as handsome. Mrs Schipholl was a blousy blonde. She was just on the edge of being chubby but was still very curvy and attractive.

The adults exchanged cheerful greetings and Mr Schipholl apologised for them being late. "My fault. I hadn't got the gas bottle filled so we went via the shop," he explained.

"Doesn't matter," Carmen replied. "We've only been here an hour, and we weren't bored." She gestured to Andrew's book.

"What are you reading Andrew?" Martin asked. He tilted his head to read the title. "Oh, *Treasure Island.* That's a great yarn. I haven't read it for years though."

"It's a kid's book, isn't it?" Mark said.

Carmen detected the challenge in Mark's voice and at once stepped in. "It's one of the classics," she said. "I think Robert Louis Stevenson was one of the greatest authors ever."

"Never mind books," Letitia interrupted. "I'm hungry. Can we have something to eat?"

"You had better hurry up," Mrs Schipholl said. "We have to garage the cars and then organise with the man who owns the boat to take us across to the island."

"I'll go and check on that now," Mr Schipholl said. "You others go across to that cafe and eat." He indicated a MOBIL Roadhouse on the other side of the main road.

Letitia set off, leaving Andrew slightly flustered. He turned to Anne and met her eyes. *I hope she doesn't think I still like Letitia?* he thought. Now that she was with him, he realised how much her really did like her.

"We eating too?" he asked.

Anne smiled and nodded, then started walking. Andrew walked with her, yearning to hold her hand but much too scared to risk a rebuff, or to spoil things by going too fast. Alas for good intentions. As he followed Letitia across the car park Andrew found his eyes drawn to her. Her curvy female shape was clearly outlined in the thin cloth of the wrap-around skirt she was wearing. The rhythmic movement of her walk he found very noticeable, and it was with some difficulty he dragged his eyes away to focus on the road safety problem of crossing the busy road. Now that Letitia was physically present and visible he found all his earlier resolve being swept away by rapidly increasing desire.

Andrew found his eyes exploring Letitia, noting the lovely curve of her hips and the glimpses of roundness in all the right places. He recognised her bikini top as the skimpy yellow one which had granted him (and everyone else) such delightful glimpses in January (*Well, more than glimpses really,* he mused). Heated memories surged in his brain. The result was Andrew experiencing an embarrassing surge of arousal as he walked along.

But no-one was looking at him, their interest being on Letitia. That she was aware of the way male eyes followed her was obvious, even to Andrew.

What a tease she is, he told himself, *But bloody hell! Isn't she fabulous!*

The others followed them into the roadhouse cafeteria and there was a bout of noisy ordering after which they stood around talking while they waited for the food to be prepared. Jill and Anne seated themselves at a nearby table and Andrew joined them. Letitia stood and talked to them. Mark and Martin stood looking at postcards and Carmen and Jacob sat at another table, deep in conversation.

Andrew eyed Jacob with some concern. *He seems to be a nice enough bloke,* he conceded, *but I hope he doesn't break Carmen's heart. Or worse,* he added.

Letitia wandered off to look at some tourist souvenirs. Andrew was then able to admire her better, and less obviously. Then his enjoyment was spoiled. A man sidled over to stand next to Letitia and spoke to her. He was in his early twenties and had a long, thin face. His hair was long and plaited into a waist length pigtail. From each ear dangled large gold ear-rings. He looked very fit and muscular, his biceps bulging below torn-off short sleeves. Andrew took an instant dislike to the man and was peeved to see Letitia return his smile and answer him.

Anne gestured towards Letitia and said, "Who's that talking to Letitia?"

Jill looked, then shrugged. "Her boyfriend?" she suggested.

That really hurt Andrew. *I thought that was Johno,* he told himself. But deep down he suspected that she probably had more than one. *Still, she doesn't have to be so friendly to strangers,* he thought irritably.

Mark and Martin joined them and Jill pointed to Letitia. "Who's the guy with the gold earrings talking to your sister?" she asked Martin.

Martin looked, then made a sour face. "Some creep. I wish she wouldn't talk to every bugger who ogles her."

And the man was ogling her. That got Andrew really anxious and jealous. *That bastard is positively leering down her front and she is still being nice to him,* he fumed.

It was a real relief to Andrew when the girl behind the counter called Letitia over and handed her a hamburger. The man said something to Letitia that made her giggle and she called, "Bye, have a good time fishing," as the man turned away.

When Letitia joined them, Jill asked who he was. Letitia shrugged. "I don't know. Just some smooth operator hoping to get lucky I guess," she replied.

Letitia's air of worldliness did little to ease Andrew's emotions and he watched resentfully as the man left the cafeteria. Then it was his turn to go to the counter for his hamburger. While he ate, he talked to Jill and Anne and pushed the incident out of his mind.

After the meal it was all a bustle of activity. They made their way back across the road to the cars. By then all the camping gear had been unloaded by Mr and Mrs Schipholl. Mr Schipholl pointed to a small motor launch at the far end of the jetty and instructed them to carry all the gear along to it.

"The owner is Mr Bulkington. He will show you where to stow it," he instructed.

Andrew slipped his book into his haversack and swung this onto his back. The group set to work lugging bags and bundles and boxes along the 100 metres of pier. While they did this Mr and Mrs Schipholl drove off to garage the cars. It was hot work carrying the luggage in the blazing tropical sun and Andrew found he was sweating heavily before it was done. He and Carmen collected their own modest bundles and carried them along as well.

The motor launch was an old wooden half-cabin about nine metres long. It was tied up at the bottom of a set of concrete steps which led down to below high-water level. Andrew was quite surprised at how high the pier stood at low water and noted that the water was so shallow the launch was nearly aground on the glutinous black mud that made up most of the foreshore. It was only a small boat, the freeboard aft about half a metre, and he hoped it was seaworthy enough for the trip. Tethered astern on a painter was a 4-metre aluminium dinghy with a small outboard engine. This, Andrew presumed, was the small boat they were hiring for the week.

As he was interested in all things nautical, and having the ambition to become a naval officer, Andrew experienced a peculiar sense of thrill as he stepped from the solid concrete onto the gently rocking launch. It wasn't exactly embarking on a big ship, but he still liked to be afloat. In his mind's eye he conjured up famous pictures he had seen: Nelson embarking for his last voyage; Admiral Cunnigham stepping into his launch beside the battleship HMS *Warspite*; Henry Morgan, sword in hand, directing a ship's longboat full of pirates towards a palm-fringed shore. It was all romantic stuff, and he began to construct a secret daydream of his own great voyage of... of...

He bit his lip and wondered. Was it to be a voyage of exploration, or of being a roving buccaneer?

The interior of the tiny cabin smelt badly of oil, diesel, paint and fishy odours, so Andrew moved himself to sit near the stern on the starboard side where he could get plenty of fresh air. He helped Anne stow her bags and she then seated herself on his left. Martin and Mark stowed the luggage in the cabin, then joined him. Jill and Mark seated themselves opposite and Martin sat on Anne's left near the stern. Carmen and Jacob made their way up through a small hatch on the port side onto the small foredeck. Andrew had been hoping Letitia would sit next to him, but she also clambered onto the foredeck and sat down. Andrew half-expected the owner would tell her to move and was irritated to notice that all he was doing was looking at her with what looked like a lascivious gaze.

Bloody dirty old man! he thought angrily.

To divert his thoughts Andrew looked over the side and studied the purple and grey coloured crabs clinging to the barnacles on the concrete piles.

The tide is coming in, he noted. Then he mentally rebuked himself for not getting a copy of the tide tables. *We might need them,* he thought.

Then he was further annoyed to hear a man call out. Andrew turned to see and saw that it was the young man with the pigtail and gold earrings. He was in a small aluminium dinghy with an outboard motor and was puttering past, heading out towards a large luxury motor launch anchored in deeper water. To his chagrin Andrew saw Letitia return the man's wave.

Mr Gold Earrings grinned. "You should be the figurehead babe!" he yelled.

"In your dreams!" Letitia called back with a laugh.

The man laughed and grinned, then turned to steer his boat. Andrew quietly fumed and wished Letitia wasn't such an exhibitionist. At the same time he could only agree with the man. *She would make a great figurehead.* He found his thoughts turning to fantasies of possibly seeing Letitia with not much on and that caused him to squirm with arousal.

After a twenty minute wait the Schipholls arrived. They loaded more stores into the dinghy, then climbed aboard and seated themselves at the stern.

"Okay, that's the lot," Mr Schipholl said. "We can get going now."

The boat's owner grunted and spat over the side, then turned a key to start the engine. As it spluttered into smelly life and sent a swirl of muddy water out astern Andrew felt a surge of real excitement.

Endeavour Island, here we come, he thought. *I wonder what it will be like?*

Chapter 9

ENDEAVOUR ISLAND

The 'Hispaniola' sets sail, Andrew told himself as the motor launch drew away from the pier.

His pulse quickened with excitement, and he leaned out to see more clearly where they were going. Now that they were actually afloat and under way, he felt much happier. Even the smelly interior of the launch, and its obvious age and doubtful seaworthiness, ceased to bother him. He sniffed the sea air, then breathed deeply and sighed with pleasure.

The motor launch threaded its way through half a dozen anchored small craft: two trawlers, a small cabin cruiser, two yachts, and the large, white-painted luxury motor launch. To Andrew's relief, there was no sign of the man with the ponytail and ear-rings. His dinghy was moored alongside one of the yachts, but the man was not visible.

Martin indicated the luxury launch. "That would cost a pretty penny to run," he said.

Andrew studied the vessel and nodded. "Be all of twenty-five metres long," he remarked.

"Speaking of pretty, are those two girls sunbathing on the foredeck of that boat?" Mark said.

Andrew shielded his eyes from the reflected glare of the sun. "Yes."

Two girls, or women, lay on the fore deck of the luxury cruiser. To Andrew's eyes they appeared to be naked, but he did not want to say so. Nor did he want Jill or Anne to think he was interested in such things.

I don't want them to think I am a perve, he thought.

To avoid any such suspicion, he deliberately looked out through the other side of the boat.

The launch headed steadily out to sea, rocking slightly on an almost glassy sea. Andrew studied the ocean and the sky, noting the low, grey clouds which took up half the horizon.

We will get rained on soon, he decided.

It was still very humid, and he wiped sweat from his face. Mrs Schipholl insisted they all put on more suncream. Despite loathing the feel of it Andrew did so, well knowing from painful experience that he would look like a cooked lobster by midday if he did not.

Mrs Schipholl made her way up onto the foredeck to insist that the people there also put on sunscreen. Through the front window Andrew was able to watch Letitia begin to apply it. She had only just begun to do so when a shower of rain swept towards them. This led to Letitia, Jacob, and Carmen hastily retreating to the shelter of the half-cabin. Letitia came and squeezed in between Andrew and Mark, much to Andrew's enjoyment.

"You still reading?" she asked, indicating the book on Andrew's lap.

Andrew shook his head. "Not now. I'm enjoying the trip."

The rain now began in earnest, quite a few drops splashing in. Andrew had to hastily cover his book and put it back in his haversack. He picked it up and kept in his arms as water began to swill and trickle across the deck. When the cold drops first hit them, Letitia had squealed and done a lot of squirming but now she snuggled in against Andrew.

"That's cold!" she cried.

Andrew laughed and put his hand out into the rain, then wiped his face. It felt very refreshing. The rain shower quickly passed, the boat moving back into blazing sunshine. Carmen now took out a chart and began alternately studying it and peering out through the front.

"Are we nearly there?" Letitia asked.

Carmen shook her head. "Not even a quarter of the way."

"Which one is Endeavour Island?" Mark asked, indicating the scattering of islands across the horizon.

Carmen frowned with concentration and looked out, then shook her head. "I don't think you can see it yet."

"You can't," commented the motorboat's skipper. "It is behind that biggish island straight in front of us."

"So what are all those islands?" Jill asked.

Carmen pointed to starboard. "That really big island is Hinchinbrook."

"I know that," Jill said. "We stayed at a resort on it once."

"So that is Hecate Point we are just passing now," Carmen went on. "That is the closest part of Hinchinbrook, except it has another long arm. You can just see its most northerly point now, that little hill at the end of that long flat bit. That is Cape Richards."

"I think that's where we went for that holiday," Jill commented.

Carmen pointed ahead. "So that big island is Gould Island. The smaller ones to the right of it, I mean to starboard, the ones just visible on the horizon, are the Brook Islands. The islands you can just see in that rainstorm away off over the port bow are the Family Islands and the biggest one you can see to the north is Dunk Island."

Andrew took all this in and carefully studied the chart. He was quite amazed at how many islands littered this section of the North Queensland coast. They were, he noted, all 'high' islands, not coral cays. They all seemed to be thickly clad in vegetation.

The launch master pointed. "That's Endeavour just coming into view now," he said.

Andrew moved to get a better view. That first glimpse of the island he found quite gripping. Having studied the map and chart he knew what to expect: another high island. It certainly looked that.

"It looks pretty rugged," he commented on observing the boulders littering the steep ridges on the side facing them.

The island was still about ten miles off he judged. At that, distance the vegetation was not clear, a bluish haze obscuring detail, but the larger rocks were obvious.

"How big is it?" Martin asked.

Carmen answered that. "Just over a kilometre and a half long from north to south and a bit over a half from east to west."

"That sounds quite big," Mark commented.

"It will do us for a week, I'm sure," Mr Schipholl replied.

"Why is it called 'Endeavour Island'?" Jill asked. "Does it have anything to do with Captain Cook's ship?"

Andrew had the answer for that, having done some reading during the previous week. "Yes. It is named after it. The highest point is called Mt Gore after one of the lieutenants."

"Did Cook land there?" Mark asked.

Andrew shook his head. "No, he just sailed past. As far as I can determine, the first recorded landing was by a survey party from the British gunboat HMS *Pelorus* in 1839."

"What about the Aborigines?" Letitia asked.

"They certainly visited the island, but we don't know their names," Andrew replied.

Jacob said, "I read that the next people to land were from the British-

India Line ship, *Hyderabad*, in 1852. Apparently, the ship's master died from some illness."

"Appendicitis," Andrew interjected.

"Whatever. Anyway, before he died, he expressed a wish to be buried on land so his body was interred just back from the beach at Fishermans Bay," Jacob explained.

"You mean there is a grave there?" Anne asked, her face showing some anxiety.

"There's a whole cemetery," Jacob replied.

Mark nodded. "And the captain's ghost walks the beach on the full moon," he added.

Anne looked horrified. "Oh it does not!"

"Does so," Mark replied, but Andrew saw he was struggling to hide a grin.

"It does not," Andrew said. "Don't believe him, Anne. He's just making it up to scare you."

"Are you, Mark?" Anne asked.

"No. Well... yes," Mark admitted.

Jacob now fuelled Anne's fears. "There are enough dead bodies on the island to provide a dozen ghosts though."

Once again, Anne looked anxious. "Why? Who has died there?"

"I read that back in the Nineteenth Century there was some sort of mutiny on a sailing ship and that most of the crew were murdered," Jacob said.

Andrew nodded. "I've got a book in my bag which tells us what happened," he said. "They were mostly Melanesians who were the crew of a 'Blackbirder'. I can't remember the details."

"Didn't an American bomber aircraft fly into the side of the island back during World War Two?" Mr Schipholl asked the launch master.

"Certainly did," Mr Bulkington replied, shifting a smelly pipe to the other side of his mouth. "My dad showed me the wreck when I was a kid. It's right up on the north slope of Mt Gore. Not much left though. Made a terrible mess. Killed the whole crew."

"Are they buried on the island?" Carmen asked.

Mr Bulkington shook his head. "Nah. The Yanks took the bodies back to America. The people in the cemetery are just fishermen, a few cholera victims, a lighthouse keeper, and a fellow who committed suicide when the old plantation was being run as a tourist resort back in the nineteen fifties."

"Plantation?" Carmen asked.

"Yeah, coconuts. Not much of one though. The island is too small," Mr Bulkington replied. "There are a few ruins but not much. It was all built of timber and corrugated iron you see, and it has mostly rotted or rusted away."

Andrew had seen the ruins marked on the map and was very keen to explore them. Hearing there wasn't much to see dampened his enthusiasm, so he said, "Isn't there supposed to be a pirate treasure hidden there?"

"Oh pirate treasure!" Martin guffawed. "You read too many stories Andrew. There were never any pirates in this part of the world."

Andrew blushed and tried to think of a reply. He was saved by Mr Bulkington who turned to fix Martin with a disapproving glance.

"Don't you sneer young fella. My dad believed the story. We even went looking a couple of times."

Martin blushed but stubbornly asked, "What pirate?"

"Fella named Bennet Graham, an Englishman," Mr Bulkington replied. "Back around 1820. He raided Spanish ships and towns on the west coast of South America, then sailed off to hide his ill-gotten gains so he wouldn't be hung for piracy."

"Wouldn't they hang him anyway?" Carmen asked.

"The Spanish would have for sure, and I suppose the British might have if they could have caught him with the loot," Mr Bulkington replied.

"But why would he come here to do that?" Jordan asked.

Mr Bulkington shrugged. "Might've been the first bit of British territory he came to on this side of the Pacific, and not too far from Sydney."

Andrew became restless and wasn't convinced, even though he wanted to believe. "I read about him. But the book I read said he hid his treasure on Cocos Island."

"But that's even further away," Jacob protested. "Why go all the way to the Indian Ocean?"

"No, not that Cocos Island," Andrew replied. "There is one in the Gulf of Panama too."

"It sounds a bit unlikely to me," Mr Schipholl commented. "But it should still make it a fairly interesting holiday. We can go treasure hunting during the day and watch the ghosts at night."

"Oh don't say that!" cried Anne.

"Sorry," Mr Schipholl replied.

While they had been talking, the launch had drawn abeam of Gould Island. Beyond it was only Endeavour Island and a few small outlying islets. Andrew again leaned out to look at Endeavour Island. He could now see all of the southern side and the vegetation was showing as a mixture of greens above a coast made up of alternating black rocks and white sand. To him the place had now taken on exactly the aura of mystery and romance he had dreamed off.

Pirate treasure, he thought. *This will be great fun.*

Noticing a small, well-thumbed booklet of tide tables on the bench above the wheel Andrew asked if he could look at it and then spent a few minutes studying them and memorising the tides times for the week.

Another shower of rain swept across, hiding the island from view. With the rain came some wind and the launch began to pitch as it shouldered its way into the small waves. Spray was thrown up by the bows and came sheeting back to wet their backs. Letitia shrieked and snuggled in closer to Andrew. He was experiencing mixed emotions. One he was reluctant to admit was fear.

I hope this old tub is seaworthy, he thought anxiously, glancing nervously at the white caps.

He began wondering if he could swim all the way back to Gould Island, now several miles astern. He looked around to see if he could locate the lifejackets, just in case, but could see no sign of them. However, he hid his qualms as he wanted people to think he was an experienced and hardy seadog. Seeing that Mr Bulkington was steering with one hand and filling his pipe with the other, apparently quite unconcerned, Andrew tried to reassure himself.

On looking astern to study the way the dinghy was handling being towed in those conditions Andrew was surprised to see Anne leaning over the taffrail. Carmen was holding her.

Seasick! he thought in astonishment. Then he noted that Jacob was looking very quiet and had gone a funny colour. *He's a Leading Seaman. He couldn't get seasick!* Andrew thought in amazement.

After a few minutes Anne sat up. She looked quite miserable, and her face had gone very pale, so that her freckles stood out clearly. Then she twisted to heave over the stern again.

Poor kid, Andrew thought.

As surreptitiously as he could, he studied the others to see if any others were suffering. None appeared to be although Jill was very pale and quiet.

The squall passed and they came out into sunlight again. Ahead of them the curtain of rain drew off to port to reveal Endeavour Island now only a couple of miles away. For something to do Andrew asked Jacob for the chart he was holding. Using that he orientated himself. He noted that about half a mile to the east of the main island was a small, rocky islet. It was steep sided and crowned by what appeared to be grass and small bushes.

Firefly Island, he noted. *Then the Challenger Passage. I'll bet they were British warships.*

He knew that many of the islands and coastal features along the east coast had been named by the Royal Navy people in the 19th Century. The eastern tip of the island was a similar rocky headland clothed in grass.

Oyster Point, Andrew noted. *So that beach must be Fishermans Bay where we are going camping.* Then his eye travelled down a long, rugged ridge from the highest point to a rocky headland on the western side of Fishermans Bay. *That will be Snapper Point, and that steep little rocky island beyond is Schooner Rock.*

Now that they were close, Andrew found his excitement mounting and he took in every detail he could. The chart told him there were other bays with sandy beaches but he could not see them from that angle. The beach at Fishermans Bay certainly looked appealing, a strip of clean white sand with a wall of dark green vegetation behind it. In contrast the headlands and the long ridge running up to Mt Gore were covered with grass, rocks and dry scrub.

Martin leaned over his shoulder to look, then said, "This is going to be great. A whole island to ourselves for a week."

Mr Schipholl shook his head and pointed to where a small timber jetty could now be seen. Close beside it was what could only be a boat.

"I don't like to spoil your fun, but we will have to share the island. In fact, I'd say there are other people there now."

"That's a shame," Jill commented. "I was looking forward to being on a desert island."

Mark grinned and pointed at Firefly Island. "We can drop you off on that little one over there," he suggested. "It doesn't appear to be inhabited."

"Oh poo to you!" Jill cried, then laughed.

Andrew had experienced a definite drop in enthusiasm on noting the other boat, but he knew that they had been required to apply for a camping permit.

"Only twelve people at a time are allowed to camp here aren't they Mr Schipholl?" he asked.

"Yes. It's part of the marine National Park and we have to remove all our rubbish."

"There will be fishermen and day-trippers too," Mr Bulkington added.

By this time they were inside the sheltered water of Fishermans Bay and Andrew was enchanted. It also looked exactly like he imagined Treasure Island to appear. The colour of the water changed from a dark green to a bright blue and then to a very pale green. This rapidly faded to be translucent. The water was crystal clear and the bottom appeared to be white sand.

Letitia looked down. "I can see the bottom!" she cried in surprise.

They all glanced over the side. Anne let out a gasp of delight. "Oh! Look at all the fish!"

Andrew glimpsed flitting shadows, then turned his attention back to the beach. About a hundred metres along to the left he noted what appeared to be the shallow mouth of a small creek.

That looks great! he thought. *I'm going to enjoy this.*

The launch slid in along beside the small timber jetty and the propeller stopped.

"Well, here we are," Carmen cried happily.

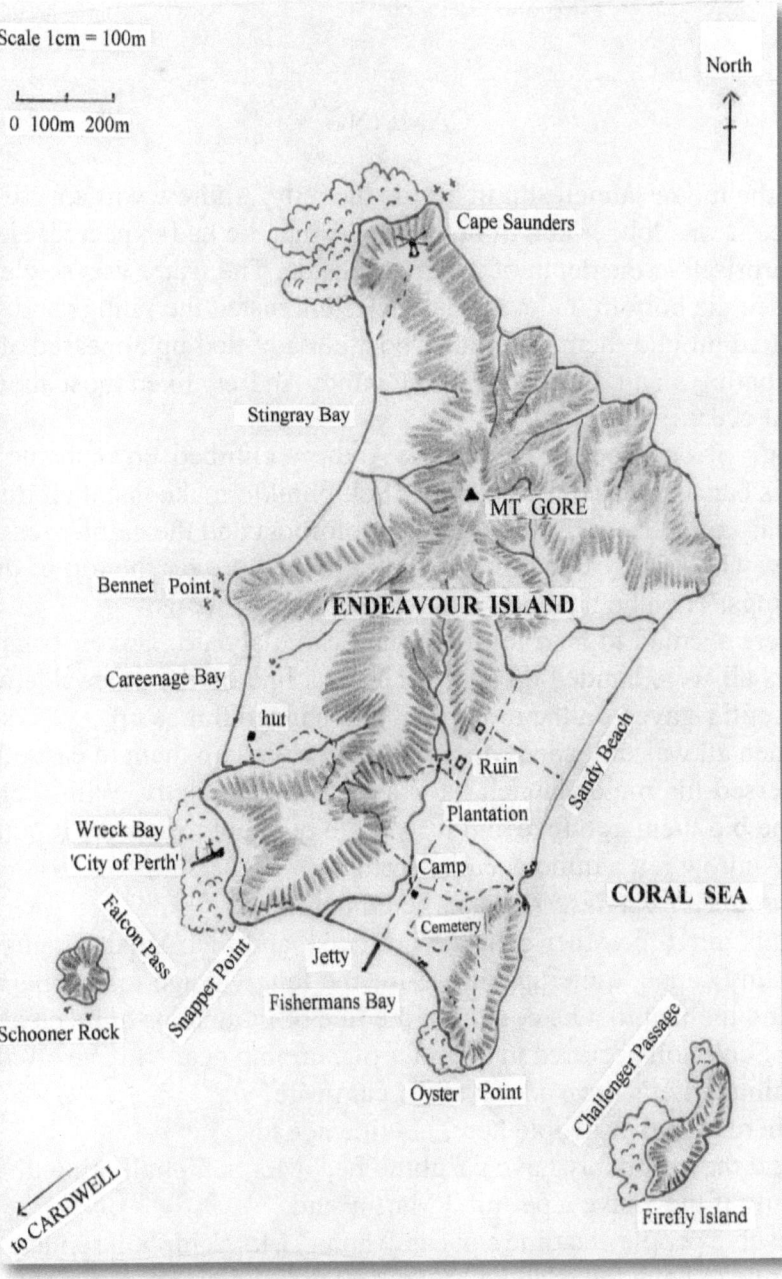

Scale 1cm = 100m

0 100m 200m

North

Cape Saunders

Stingray Bay

MT GORE

ENDEAVOUR ISLAND

Bennet Point

Careenage Bay

hut

Ruin

Plantation

Sandy Beach

Wreck Bay
'City of Perth'

Camp

CORAL SEA

Cemetery

Falcon Pass

Snapper Point

Jetty

Fishermans Bay

Schooner Rock

Oyster Point

Challenger Passage

to CARDWELL

Firefly Island

Chapter 10

CAMPING

As the motor launch slid in beside the jetty, Andrew was surprised to see it was longer and in better repair than he had expected. He was also surprised at the depth of water alongside. The water was so clear he could see the bottom in detail. Barnacles encrusted the pilings and small fish flitted around them. The other boat already tied up appeared almost to be floating on air. It was one of the things Andrew liked most about the tropical ocean.

Work at once began to unload. Andrew climbed up onto the jetty with his bag and was directed by Mr Schipholl to make fast their dinghy. This was untied from the stern of the motorboat and the painter tossed to Andrew. He quickly tied a bowline and looped it over the top of one of the pilings. Then he bent down to help with other items.

There seemed to be a lot more than came aboard. Boxes, bags, and bundles all were handed up and placed in a line on the other side of the jetty. Letitia stayed on the motorboat and handed things up.

When all was unloaded Mr Bulkington called on them to cast off and he reversed his motor launch back away from the jetty. With a cheery wave he bid them goodbye and turned the boat out to sea. As it puttered away, Andrew felt a quite peculiar thrill.

Marooned on a desert island, he thought.

In his mind the other boat did not exist, and their small dinghy was only a tiny canoe, quite unsuitable for the long voyage to the mainland (ignoring the fact that he could see the line of mountains quite clearly).

Mr Schipholl gestured to the litter of camping gear. "Leave all of this for a minute. Let's have a look at the campsite."

"There are other people here," Letitia added.

"And they probably have a right to be," Mrs Schipholl replied.

"Only if they have a permit," Martin said.

"Twelve people at a time can camp here," Mrs Schipholl replied. "We can't hope to have the island all to ourselves."

"Be nice if we could," Andrew added.

"Yes, now let's look around," Mr Schipholl said. He turned and led the way along the jetty past the motor launch.

Several fishing lines were set and Andrew had to step over a tangle of lines and a litter of fish scales and heads.

Bloody grubs! he thought. *I'll bet I don't like them.*

And nor did he. They met the other people almost at once. At the end of the jetty, a sandy foot trail led in under the trees. Beside it was a large sign reminding people the island was a National Park and of the conditions required to camp or fish. Next to that was a concrete block barbeque and fireplace with a stack of split firewood beside it. Two concrete picnic tables with seats stood nearby. The trail then passed in through the trees for fifty paces, curving slightly. On the right was a thick tangle of bushes and dry scrub, and on the left a forest of large trees with a litter of dry leaves and twigs under them. Next was a clearing with a concrete block toilet on the right and another barbeque and picnic table on the left. The people were seated there.

There were six of them, two men in their thirties, a woman of the same age, and three young children ranging in ages from about five to ten: a boy and two girls. The people all gave them an unfriendly stare and the children were openly hostile. Andrew's first glance settled his opinion. Both the men were holding cans of beer and there was a litter of empty cans on the ground around their folding chairs. The woman was also drinking, and she was smoking as well. The children had been noisily arguing over who was to eat the remaining sausages on the barbeque, but they now fell silent.

Mr Schipholl smiled and raised a hand in greeting. "Hello," he said, eliciting a couple of nods and half-hearted grunts in reply.

A sign indicated that the area beyond the table was the camping ground. As they walked towards it one of the men called out, "You need a permit to camp on the island."

Mr Schipholl pulled a piece of paper out of his pocket. "We've got one thanks," he said, his voice hinting that the others should produce theirs too.

That had the effect of silencing the man and he gave a surly nod and sucked at his beer. It all made Andrew feel unhappy and he wished the other people weren't there. His resentment was fuelled by the way the two men ogled at Letitia.

The group walked another 25 metres into the clearing. Three large Banyan trees and open rainforest surrounded it and the Banyans provided shade for the whole area. On the far side of the clearing on the left was a creek.

The creekbank was an instant magnet and the teenagers were soon looking down from it. It wasn't much of a creek, only knee deep and two or three paces wide but the water was crystal clear and flowing over a sandy bottom, so it looked very inviting. The creek flowed through a shallow dip a few metres deep. On the far side was more rainforest, proper tropical jungle this time with vines and ferns.

Carmen swept her hand around. "This will be nice," she said happily.

"Except for those people back there," Andrew replied.

"Oh well, can't have everything," Mr Schipholl said. "Now, let's carry our gear in."

They walked back to the jetty. On the way they passed the people and Andrew noted that the children were not there. They were out on the jetty bending over the piles of camping gear. As soon as they saw the group returning, the children tried to pretend they were just checking their fishing lines.

"Oh dear! I hope we don't have to guard our camp all the time," Mrs Schipholl commented.

That was an unpleasant thought. Andrew felt a surge of resentment at the other people and glared at the children, who returned insolent stares.

"You guard the stuff here, Car," he said as they reached their camping gear.

Carmen agreed and seated herself on the jetty. The others all picked up as many bags and bundles as they could manage and set off back. Lugging the gear turned into an uncomfortable chore with the need to pass back and forth across the unfriendly gaze of the drinking adults and evident hostility of the children.

As Andrew returned for the last load, he said to Mr Schipholl, "What about our boat?"

Mr Schipholl shook his head. "They wouldn't touch it, surely. We know who they are." He indicated the registration number of the motor launch.

Andrew wasn't so sure and felt a distinct sense of unease. However, there was nothing for it, so he walked back to the campsite with another armful of gear, again noting how the men's eyes followed Letitia's wiggling form.

Dirty old buggers! he thought resentfully, his anger increased by the knowledge that he was a hypocrite as his own eyes had been doing exactly the same thing.

The other people were then forgotten in the excitement of setting up camp. There were five tents, and these were placed in two lines. Mr and Mrs Schipholl placed theirs on the downstream side of the clearing beside the table Carmen and Letitia erected theirs on the creek bank on the upstream side. The other three tents were placed under the Banyans opposite. Anne and Jill went nearest the toilet. Martin and Jacob went in the centre of the line and Andrew and Mark at the end of the line opposite Carmen and Letitia.

Andrew wasn't really happy sharing with Mark, and secretly had wanted to camp close to Letitia but he decided it didn't really matter.

We won't spend much time in the tents, he thought.

Putting up the tents was a lot of fun. Hoisting a large blue plastic 'fly' up under the branches of the middle Banyan so that it also covered the picnic table was harder but to a group of Navy Cadets was a simple chore. Then the gear was stowed in the tents.

Mrs Schipholl then said, "Now that is done, let's eat."

That was a popular decision. Andrew found he was quite hungry and certainly needed a drink. Gratefully he accepted a large cup of cold fruit juice. He then seated himself at the picnic benches. Anne came and sat next to him, giving him a shy smile as she did. That made Andrew feel a heel as he had been busy ogling Letitia. To compensate, Andrew now devoted all his attention to Anne, talking about school and the car trip.

The sun had now come out with full force and Letitia wiped perspiration from her brow and said, "It's hot! Let's have a swim."

"Good idea, let's get changed," Carmen agreed.

Mrs Schipholl pointed to the concrete block building. "I think the end section of that building is a change room."

Andrew looked and saw that the building was the usual mirror image, male-female structure except that the end section closest to the two entrances had no roof. Both entrances were side by side and just in front of them, on the seaward side, were a concrete slab and a single waterpipe with a shower rose on it.

For rinsing off the salt after the swim and before you go in to change, he thought.

There followed ten minutes of to-ing and fro-ing, with much giggling and laughter. Andrew already wore his bathers under his shorts, but Jacob had to change. Letitia likewise just peeled off her skirt and top to reveal her skimpy bikini. As before, Andrew could only gape and wonder how her parents allowed it. But he knew, as Mrs Schipholl peeled off her jeans and unbuttoned her long-sleeved shirt to reveal a very similar bikini. Mr Schipholl shrugged off his clothes to stand in a pair of old shorts.

Seeing Mr Schipholl's very hairy body made Andrew feel uncomfortable and embarrassed. Knowing that both parents were nudists at home did not help.

I hope they aren't going to embarrass us, he thought. Already he had noticed a couple of glances from Jacob, indicating his disapproval.

The other girls then returned from changing. Andrew tried to pretend he wasn't interested but made a careful study of them. Carmen wore her usual dark green one-piece which made her look very shapely and attractive. Jill wore a dark blue one-piece that was even more modest, and which hid more than it revealed. Anne wore a bikini, but it was a quite modest white one. Letitia's was the opposite and revealed more than it hid, the top being just two triangles of cloth.

Andrew studied Letitia and shook his head in wonder. Then he became ashamed, and he forced himself to look elsewhere. By then the other three boys had arrived, all wearing shorts of varying lengths. They stood talking, their eyes flicking continually over the girls with interest and approval.

Mrs Schipholl noted this with an amused smile. "Well then, if everyone is ready, let's go."

"Should we leave anyone to guard our camp?" Mark asked, nodding his head towards the other people, who could just be seen through the trees.

"No. We can't do that all the time," Mr Schipholl said.

Carrying towels and bags they trooped back along the track to the beach. On the way past the other people Andrew noted that only the two men were there, their eyes following Letitia's every move. To Andrew's annoyance, Letitia seemed to wiggle even more than usual.

She's doing that deliberately, the show-off! he thought.

On reaching the beach there was more embarrassment. The woman was there with the three children, the youngest two of whom were naked. The little boy of about three was running around looking for seashells while the girl of about five or six was busy digging a hole in the sand. The older girl gave the group a hostile glare and then looked away while the mother simply ignored them.

Jacob glanced at the naked children and Andrew noted the corners of his mouth tighten in disapproval.

He doesn't like seeing that, Andrew mused. Personally it did not bother him at all, and he knew that Carmen had no problem with little children running around in the nuddy. *She thinks it is perfectly natural.*

Andrew's attention was then taken by Anne. She was walking beside him and gestured to the sea.

"Isn't it beautiful?" she said.

"It certainly is," Andrew agreed. He stood there feeling tongue-tied and anxious about how to please her.

Anne helped. She reached into her shoulder bag and produced a tube of sun lotion. "Would you rub some on my back please?" she asked.

Andrew could only nod and take the tube. Anne turned her back to him and he squeezed out some cream and very gingerly dabbed it on her shoulder blades. As he did, he noted that her skin was quite fair and sprinkled with freckles. It felt nice to touch and he began to use his whole hand to smear the cream across all the exposed back. Anne took the tube from him and began applying it to her front.

As Andrew worked, he saw Letitia begin rubbing a sun lotion on her front. He found it hard not to stare and was aware that he was very interested. By then Andrew was faced with the dilemma of how far down Anne's back he rubbed the cream as his hands were now close to the top of her buttocks.

I had better stop, he decided, not wanting to offend Anne in any way.

"Rub some on my back now, please," he asked her.

He turned and Anne began to do so, her hands feeling very smooth and cool. As she did, Letitia held out her lotion bottle.

"Who would like to rub some oil on my back please?"

Andrew knew he badly wanted to do that but did not dare suggest it with Anne ministering to him. A glance showed Mark shaking his head but also looking interested.

He wants to as well, Andrew decided, but with a scowling Jill standing beside him he was not game either. *And Jacob looks like he doesn't approve of the whole deal,* he decided.

When nobody offered, Letitia pouted and said, "Oh well! Somebody please. What about you, Andrew?"

That put Andrew on the spot, and he could only shake his head and hope it didn't upset Anne. Letitia then offered the bottle to Jacob, but he pursed his lips and shook his head. Carmen then stepped forward.

"I will," she offered.

Letitia opened her mouth to say something but then closed it and handed over the bottle. Carmen then stood and smeared the oil over Letitia's back. By then Mr and Mrs Schipholl had liberally smeared each other with cream.

Mrs Schipholl held up a bottle which she took from her shoulder bag. "This is vinegar in case anyone gets stung by a jellyfish," she explained. "You children keep an eye out for them."

Andrew certainly needed no prompting to do this. As a North Queenslander he was very conscious of the danger marine stingers posed during the warmer months. In fact, he was chary of swimming in the sea at all and made a careful scrutiny of the bay, scanning for any sign of a shark or similar predator.

By then Mark and Martin had waded in and begun splashing about. As the girls walked down to join them, Mark started splashing Jill and Letitia. This immediately developed into a general water fight. Andrew quickly waded in, being surprised at how cold the water still was. As the friends splashed each other, Andrew could not help watching Letitia as she joined in. It made him feel physically hungry and he felt a distinct yearning to grab her.

This urge was turned to festering jealousy when Mark grappled with Jill and ducked her. She appeared to enjoy this and made only perfunctory protests. Mark then remained with his arms around her. Letitia continued to splash and jump around, and Andrew formed the strong impression she was taunting him in the hope he would also grab her. He certainly wanted to, but forced himself to turn to Anne and half-heartedly splash her till she lowered herself to her neck. They then knelt in the shallow water to talk. Carmen and Jacob both subsided without any physical grappling and that made Andrew wonder.

The water fight died away and the friends swam around or talked, enjoying the coolness of the water. Andrew stayed in the shallows and remained tense, both out of fear of marine creatures and from awareness of the girls. His eyes continually swept the surface of the water, then flicked to Letitia before returning to Anne's face.

"This place is really lovely," Anne commented, her blue eyes sparkling with pleasure.

"Yes, it is," Andrew agreed, thinking that Anne was as well.

She's not such a 'Plain Jane' at all, he decided, admiring her nicely shaped body and lovely long legs.

Without any conscious decision, the group slowly swam and drifted along the beach away from the jetty. The shady trees and mouth of the small creek seemed to draw them like a magnet. It was certainly the most beautiful part of the bay. As they did, Andrew slipped into a daydream, imagining the pirates rowing in to the beach in their long boat, then leaping out to splash up into the mouth of the creek.

They'd be checking for fresh water, he thought.

Then his imagination took the pirates up into the shadows under the trees, muskets ready in case of attack by wild savages. Happily he joined the others as they waded ashore and strolled along the damp foreshore into the shade of the trees.

The creek was only ankle deep, but the water was even colder and felt very refreshing. The stream flowed out into the bay through a miniature delta of sand which was obviously demolished at every high tide. Inland it curved out of sight among the large shady trees.

"Let's explore," Martin suggested, pointing up the creek.

Chapter 11

EXPLORATION

Explore! The idea had instant appeal.

Once again, Andrew's imagination took over and he saw himself leading a group of navigators up into the jungle. Images of Captain Cook, in company with Sir Joseph Banks, several seamen armed with pistols and cutlasses, and a detachment of red-coated marines with white cross straps, three-cornered hats and carrying muskets filled his mind. In the shadows he saw the cannibals lurking, waiting their moment, arrows (poisoned arrows of course) notched to their bow strings.

Mrs Schipholl, who had unrolled a beach towel nearby, called to them, "You children don't go far. And be back by three o'clock."

"Yes Mum," Martin called.

For a moment Andrew's romantic images retreated, to be replaced by interest in the girls. *Everywhere I look there are lovely sights,* he thought, his eyes sweeping over the girls in their swimsuits.

Ashamed at this, he hurried to the front and made a conscious effort to thrust such thoughts from his mind. Again picturing the painted savages in the jungle, he advanced, this time as an armoured 'Conquistador', sword in hand, to search for El Dorado in the steaming tropical jungles.

Except he thought the jungle was cold. As soon as they moved into the shade, he almost shivered. Not only was the creek water cold but the breeze off the bay cooled the drops on his skin. The creek was mostly easy to walk along. It was only ankle deep in most places and had a fine, sandy bottom. Only an occasional dangling vine or fallen tree obstructed their path. Up on either side was jungle, but Andrew had enough experience of that to judge that it was not the really dense tropical rainforest of the coastal mountains but rather a drier, more open version of it.

The creek curved to the right and Andrew was able to judge that it would lead them back to their campsite. It did this rather more quickly than he had anticipated. The only new discoveries were a waist deep pool where the current had scoured out at a bend, and an obvious foot track which led across to the west from near the last tent.

Andrew turned to follow this track but as he reached the top of the bank Carmen called him back.

"We don't want to get far away from the camp," she said.

Reluctantly, Andrew turned back from the belt of jungle, beyond which he was getting glimpses of a rugged, scrub-covered ridge. The high ground seemed to beckon him on but all he could do was shrug and turn to follow the others.

We will explore that way tomorrow, he told himself.

Instead, he went up the foot track to the barbeque area near the parent's tent. As he did, he found himself close behind Letitia. His eyes seemed to be drawn to her body by a magnetic force. As she went up the slope he stared at her lovely female shape. Fascinated, yet afraid someone might see him looking, he averted his gaze and tried to think of something else.

* * *

In this he was only partly successful. Carmen, glancing back from the top of the bank, noted Andrew's shaking head and flicking gaze and bit her lip with concern. Already she had observed signs that Andrew was very interested in the sight of the girls in their bathers, and it had her both amused and mildly worried.

"Poor Andrew!" she muttered.

She could also see that both Mark and Martin were frequently eyeing the girls and that both were obviously very interested. What puzzled her a bit was watching Jacob's reactions to the girls. He did not seem to continually glance at them, not even at Letitia. Rather he appeared to deliberately look away.

Maybe he doesn't approve? she wondered.

That puzzled her as Jacob had spent a day at the beach with them in January and he had seemed quite a normal male then. It had been Martin who had been most obviously embarrassed, mainly, she suspected, because his mother had worn a skimpy bikini that did not really suit her chubby build.

Carmen glanced at Jacob and felt the familiar flutter of her own emotions, noting the ripple of muscles under his smooth, bare skin. She considered Jacob to have a near perfect male body, trim waist, broad shoulders, strong arms and well-muscled legs.

As the group reached the tents, she stopped them. "Are we going back to swim, or going exploring?" she asked.

Mark answered. "Explore. We can go swimming anytime."

The others nodded agreement, so Carmen said, "Then we had better get dressed. At least something on our feet."

Acting on this advice, she went to her own tent and pulled on a hat, jeans, a long-sleeved shirt and sandshoes. She also picked up her small daypack and a water bottle. Letitia came and reached in to get sandshoes.

Carmen found herself staring straight into Letitia's cleavage. Blushing, she averted her eyes.

"You might need a shirt at least, or the sun will cook you," she suggested.

Letitia shook her head. "Nah! Some suncream will do. I came here to get a good tan."

Unwilling to press the issue, Carmen did not argue. She made her way out and had a drink while the others got ready. Jill and Anne both dressed in long trousers and tops and Anne added a large straw hat while Jill donned a cap and sunglasses. Jacob also dressed fully and also put on sunglasses. Mark and Martin both put on shirts and sandshoes, but Andrew only pulled on sandshoes and a cloth hat.

"You'll get sunburnt, Andrew," Carmen warned.

He ignored her and set off along the sandy path through the cottonwood trees. A sign told Carmen that this track led to the old cemetery. The others followed, chattering happily.

It was no great distance, 50 metres at most. They came out into a flattish area of sun-dried, brown grass on sandy soil. A dozen or so tombstones dotted the area, among a rough grid of sandy foot tracks. On the far side of the old cemetery was the rocky, grass-covered hill that ended in Oyster Point. To the right was a line of Banyan Figs along the top of the beach. There were a couple of graves under them, including a substantial monument surrounded by a rusty iron fence. On the left a track led through a gap in the scrub between the end of the hill and the edge of the scrub to another beach.

Sandy Beach, Carmen reminded herself, studying the map she had taken from her daypack.

The group walked to the nearest headstone and stood around it. To Carmen's surprise, the stone was properly made with the name of a

Townsville stonemason on it. The lettering was inlaid and still easy to read. It read:

FREDERICK WILLIAM BUSSEY
1867- 1932
From earthly paradise to Heavenly Paradise

"Amen to that!" muttered Jacob.

"Who was he?" Mark asked.

Carmen consulted the notes she had prepared on the island. "He bought the island back in 1887. He was the man who set up the copra plantation," she explained.

"What's copra?" Anne asked.

"Dried coconut I think, or maybe it's the coconut oil," Carmen replied. She didn't know for sure and nor did anyone else.

They moved on to the next marked tombstone. This was of a little girl; Flora Bussey, aged three. On reading that Carmen shook her head and sighed.

"Oh, how sad!"

"Poor little mite," Anne agreed.

"Lots of children died young in the old days," Jacob said. "We did a class excursion to the old West End cemetery in Townsville, and it is just full of kid's graves."

For a few moments Carmen stood there, vaguely aware she was perspiring in the hot sun, and of the reflection of heat and sunlight from the sandy soil. Into her mind came images of the grieving parents grouped around the grave as the tiny coffin was lowered in.

There probably wasn't even a priest to administer the burial service, she thought.

Deep inside she knew she was scared of having to ever face up to such a bitter reality. So far her life had been free of any close tragedies and she mentally steeled herself in anticipation.

The next grave was also a child, from smallpox at age six.

"Lots of diseases they couldn't treat in those days," Martin commented.

"Or women died in childbirth," Jill added, pointing to the next grave, a young woman of only 19 named Dorothea.

That also saddened Carmen, as well as making her anxious. For a few moments she wondered what giving birth might be like and whether she wanted to put herself through such an ordeal. Then she shrugged and knew it was a natural instinct and that, if she met the right man, she would gladly face that reality.

That thought caused her to glance at Jacob. For a moment their eyes met and she experienced a sudden pang of sadness. There was no spark there, no burning hint of being a kindred soul.

He isn't the man for me, she thought, somewhat shocked by her own insight. Then doubts assailed her. *I'm being silly. I don't really know that,* she mused, still wanting to find romantic love.

Hoping things would turn out as she hoped she smiled at him and moved to stand beside him.

The next group of graves were fenced off and marked only by rusty iron markers with numbers on them. A small sign erected by the National parks and Wildlife Service explained that these were the graves of people drowned in the wreck of the three-masted barque *City of Perth*. It read:

Driven onto rocks in Wreck Bay at night during a storm in 1888. 29 out of 105 on board perished. Only a few bodies could be identified.

"That's the wreck marked on the map," Andrew said, his eyes alive with interest. "I think Wreck Bay is over that way." He pointed west over the ridge beyond the camp.

"It is. Just around Snapper Point," Carmen said, showing the map.

"We must look at it," Mark said.

"We will," agreed Martin.

"What's a barque?" Anne asked.

Martin and Andrew both answered at once. Anne turned to Andrew, who explained, "A three-masted ship which is square rigged on its foremast and main mast but only fore-and-aft rigged on the mizzen mast."

Anne nodded, and Carmen wondered if she had really understood. She knew Anne was also a navy cadet, but she was only a 'First Year' and it wasn't the sort of knowledge taught at cadets, being quite archaic. Out of the side of her eye Carmen watched how Andrew was treating Anne, concerned to note that he seemed to be virtually ignoring her, his eyes continually flicking to Letitia.

The next group of graves, with a low stone monument, were to five people who had died of cholera while travelling on a steam ship from Hong Kong to Brisbane back in 1907.

The group moved down to the large monument under the Banyan Fig at the top of the beach. Carmen found it a relief to get into the shade. This grave turned out to be that of Captain Herbert William Simpson, Master of the British-India Line ship *Hyderabad*. He had been buried in 1852.

"This was the first grave on the island," Carmen said.

"I read about him," Andrew said. "He got sick as his ship was sailing north along the coast and he made a dying wish that he not be buried a sea. So when he died, they buried him here. The monument was erected years later by his family."

Carmen leaned down and noted the name of a Sydney stonemason at the bottom of the ornate headstone. Mark said, "Is he the one who is supposed to be the ghost that roams the cemetery at night?"

Anne looked anxious and Jill paled. The comment annoyed Carmen but before she could speak Jacob said, "No. I read that there was a murder and a suicide here in the 1930s."

"I wonder where their graves are?" Martin said, looking around the rows of headstones.

"Probably not here at all," Jacob answered.

Jacob gestured at the remains of a fence. "If this is consecrated ground, you know, religious stuff, then they wouldn't have buried a suicide here. In the old days they were buried in unmarked graves and without the benefit of any religious ceremony."

"Oh that's a bit harsh," Anne cried.

"That's how they viewed things. Suicide is against God's laws, so they didn't deserve to go to heaven. It is also a cowardly act," Jacob replied sternly.

Carmen looked at Jacob and bit her lip. He was suddenly revealing a religious side she had not realised existed. An argument on the rights and wrongs of suicide began but was stopped by Martin saying, "So what about the murder victim?"

Jacob again shook his head. "The body was probably taken away by the police for a postmortem. They wouldn't bring it back unless the family wanted it here."

"It will be his ghost that roams around then," Mark joked.

Seeing Anne go pale caused Carmen to snap angrily, "Oh stop your silly talk about ghosts, you boys! We don't even know if there was a murder. It is all just rumour. Anyway, there are no such things as ghosts."

"There are of course," Jacob quietly contradicted her.

"Oh there are not!" Carmen snapped, half annoyed, half frightened.

Jacob shrugged. "Well, my religion insists there are, you know: Father, Son and Holy Ghost?"

That stumped Carmen and she could only shake her head. It was Martin who answered. "That's not the same thing as we mean," he said.

Jacob gave him a hard look and said, "Are you sure?"

"Well... er... er... no," Martin replied. "But you know what I mean: the headless horseman type of thing, or the misty lady with a lantern who stalks around old houses on the moors at night."

"There are probably ghosts wherever people have died without absolution," Jacob replied.

Mark tried to laugh. "Wouldn't be many of them around here."

"What about the crew of that schooner who got hacked to death by the Kanakas?" Andrew said.

"What crew? What schooner? What happened?" Martin asked.

Carmen was now quite annoyed by the turn of the conversation, which she could see was causing Anne and Jill to both look anxious. Even Letitia was casting nervous glances around.

She flicked open her notes and said, "It's in here. In 1879 the schooner *Flying Scud* was returning from a 'Blackbirding' voyage to the Solomon Islands."

"A black what?" Mark asked.

"Blackbirding. They needed workers for the new sugar plantations, so they went to the islands of the South Pacific and recruited them," Carmen explained. "They were supposed to be indentured labours signed on, on a contract, but I've read that there was often a lot of trickery and deceit involved."

"Most of them couldn't read or write," supplemented Andrew.

Carmen went on, "And sometimes the Kanakas, that's the name they called the South Sea islanders, were just taken by force, at gunpoint."

"But wouldn't that be slavery?" Jill asked.

"Probably," Carmen agreed. "It was certainly illegal."

"But wasn't slavery abolished in the British Empire?" Anne said.

Andrew answered that. "It was, back about 1803. But this part of the world was a long way from England and law and order. That's why the Royal Navy had a flotilla of gunboats stationed here for most of the Nineteenth Century."

"So what happened to this schooner?" Jacob asked.

Carmen read from her notes. "She was damaged while passing through the Great Barrier Reef and began taking in water. She arrived off Endeavour Island in a sinking condition and was beached in Careenage Bay. Somehow the Melanesians, that's the Kanakas, broke free. They murdered all of the crew except the cook, Ben Watson, who escaped into the jungle. The Kanakas then made canoes and stripped the wreck of everything useful, before sailing away. Old Ben then lived a 'Robinson Crusoe' existence for five years before being rescued by a passing Trochus Shell lugger. By then he was quite mad."

"Charming!" Mark commented.

Martin looked thoughtful. "So there would be plenty of unquiet spirits there who hadn't made their peace with God," he added.

"Oh stop talking about ghosts!" Carmen flared. "Let's go up onto the hill there and see what the place looks like."

Without waiting to see if the others followed, she set off along a faint foot trail which led off from the seaward side of the cemetery. The trail led along the top of the beach past an outcrop of rocks, then past a very distinctive clump of three pandanus palms. From there it led up onto the dry, grassy slopes of the hill.

To her relief, the others followed. She walked so fast that, by the time they reached the base of the hill, she was perspiring freely. It was stiflingly hot in behind the hill out of the breeze.

As they climbed up the rough track, the sound of an aircraft's engine came to them. Martin pointed to it, well out to sea and off to the northeast.

"One of those Coastwatch planes," he commented.

Carmen saw it then, a tiny red and white, high wing, twin engine thing. For a fleeting moment she had an image of just such a plane circling the damaged motorboat near Port Douglas and she shivered. For just a moment a chill seemed to reach out of the heated tropical air. Then she thrust the thought from her as the plane droned on its way northwards.

Instead, she concentrated on making her way up over a stony section of the track towards the crest of the hill.

Chapter 12

FANTASIES

As he climbed to the top of the hill, Andrew's imagination conjured up a fantasy about the 'Blackbirders'. He saw himself as one of the crew of a trading schooner back in the 19th Century.

I am the mate. We are ashore looking for trade, he thought, picturing several other white men with him, guns in hand, *and the warriors are attacking us. They are big men: savage cannibals wearing grass skirts, feather headdresses and shark teeth necklaces. They are armed with spears and knives and are howling for our blood. We have battled our way clear of the village and up the hill.*

He pictured the screaming pursuit, then imagined firing his revolver to shoot down a huge warrior who had suddenly scrambled up over a rock.

Got the blighter! he told himself, mentally wiping sweat from his brow.

Another cannibal sprang into view and raised his spear. Just in time Andrew saw him and fired his pistol.

We had been surrounded on their ceremonial execution ground, he told himself, changing the cemetery to suit in his mind's eye.

Instead, of tombstones he pictured rows of posts surmounted by sun-bleached skulls. By then the group had reached the top of the hill. Andrew paused and looked around.

Now, he thought. *Where is our schooner and which way do we go to get to here?*

His sailor's instincts told him the schooner would be anchored in Fishermans Bay, to be in the shelter of the hill. He looked that way and found it a very pretty sight. The white curve of the beach lay almost below them, the jetty in plain view. Also in plain view were two people lying on towels on the beach. They were in a small strip of sand at their end of the beach near three pandanus palms. This was partially blocked off by an outcrop of rocks so that it would not be visible from the shore end of the jetty. It was at least a hundred metres from where Andrew stood: just too far to make out details, but to his eyes they appeared to be naked.

Is that Mr and Mrs Schipholl? he wondered.

It was just too far to be sure but from the anxious look on Martin's face he suspected that was the case.

Anne was thrilled by the view. "Isn't it all beautiful!" she cried, pointing to the bay and islands set in the sparkling sea.

Jill nodded. "I love the way the water changes colour," she said.

It did too, Andrew observed. He could clearly see the sandy bottom of the bay. Close in to the beach it looked almost white, shading off into a pale green, dark green and then to dark blue in the deeper water, particularly in the strait between the next point (Snapper Point?) and a small rocky island.

"Is that Snapper Point?" he asked Carmen, seeing her take out her map.

Carmen nodded. "Yes, it is. And that is Schooner Rock. The strait between them is called Falcon Pass. Wreck Bay is just around the other side of Snapper Point."

Andrew noted the brown smudgy shades in the water off Snapper Point that indicated coral reef.

"Looks a bit dangerous that area," he observed. "There are a few rocks and reefs there."

"And a strong current through the pass," Mark added.

That was true. Andrew now noticed the swirls, streaks and turbulence that indicated a strong flow.

"That would have been no fun navigating in a sailing ship," he commented.

"Might not be so bad when the tide is on the make," Carmen suggested.

As always, Andrew was a little amazed at how his sister could be so acutely aware of such nautical things as the tide. But he saw that she was right. From memorising the tidal pattern for the week he knew that the tide was now on the ebb.

"Those other people are leaving now," Jill said, pointing to the distant jetty.

"Good!" Mark growled. They all stood and watched as the other group loaded their motorboat and then cast off. As the visitor's launch headed out of the bay Andrew noted the two figures on the towels both move.

They rolled over and sat up and Andrew was now sure they were the Schipholls. To his own embarrassed shame, he found himself straining his eyes.

Out of the corner of his eye, Andrew saw that Martin was also looking at his parents. His face was mottled red.

Either sunburn or he is embarrassed, Andrew decided.

To save his friend from embarrassment, he turned and looked out towards the open ocean. The sight of the upperworks and cranes of a large ship on the horizon gave him the excuse he needed.

"Look, there's a big ship out there, hull down," he said.

The others all turned and followed his pointing finger with their eyes. Mark spoke first. "Container ship, heading south," he said.

Andrew studied the distant ship and then the far horizon. More rain squalls were building up out to sea, but the weather seemed to have cleared up in their vicinity. He turned and studied the shoreline below him, his gaze moving northwards from the rocks and coral reef at the end of Oyster Point and then around to the north.

Jill pointed to the rocky island a few hundred metres to the southeast. "What is the name of that island again?" she asked.

Carmen answered. "Firefly Island. And that is the Challenger Passage between here and it."

"Would fireflies live on a place like that?" Anne asked. "I thought they lived in the jungle."

"They do," Jacob said. "I think the island was named after one of the British gunboats that surveyed the area a hundred and fifty years ago."

Andrew considered that and agreed. He said, "The *Challenger* was certainly a British warship. And there was a gunboat named the HMS *Fly*. Thats the ship the Fly River in Papua is named after."

"It's hard to imagine people from the other side of the world having any interest in this part of the world," Anne commented.

"Just as well they did or you wouldn't be here," Jacob replied with a chuckle.

"Why? What do you mean?" Anne asked.

"Where do your family come from?" Jacob asked.

"Townsville and Sydney," Anne replied.

Jacob snorted. "Yes, but before that. With your skin and hair you can only be European in ethnic origin."

Andrew glanced at Anne and knew what Jacob meant. Anne had fair hair, blue eyes and freckly skin. He also noted Carmen give Jacob a quizzical glance, almost a frown.

Anne nodded and said, "Oh yes. I see what you mean. Most of my great grandparents or grandparents came from England."

Andrew had now returned to his daydream. The mention of race had got him feeling guilty about the idea of battling with cannibals in the South Seas. He knew that had not been a respectable job, even back then. Feeling somewhat ashamed at his immoral and selfish thoughts, he changed the daydream. Instead, he considered the idea of his schooner being named the *Flying Spray*, a sister ship.

And the 'Flying Scud' is commanded by my wicked brother, he thought. *So I am innocent, and the cannibals have mistaken my ship for his and are attacking; even though I came to make friends.*

That led to ideas about being a peaceful trader, or about having brought Christian missionaries to the area. That opened up a whole new set of ideas.

Yes, missionaries. And one is a lovely young woman, and they are going to be killed and eaten by the cannibals and I have arrived just in time to rescue them.

He resumed his fantasy about fighting off the savage hordes, of running out of bullets and of heroic hand-to-hand fighting using spears and knives, all the while edging closer to where their boats lay waiting on the beach.

He looked to decide exactly where the boats were beached. In doing so he noted that Mr and Mrs Schipholl were still on that other beach.

Oh I don't want the others to notice! he thought anxiously.

Andrew was very concerned and glanced sideways to see if any of the others had noticed. To his dismay, he saw that Carmen was also looking, as was Anne. Carmen gaped and then must have noted his glance as she blushed and quickly turned.

In a firm voice she said, "Let's go this way."

She led the way northwards along the crest of the ridge. Andrew burned with shame and a few hasty glances showed him red faces and cheeks on Martin and Anne as well. Jacob did not seem to have noticed but Mark was grinning and Letitia kept glancing back.

Out on the seaward side of the hill Carmen stopped. This gave them a wonderful view along the sweep or Sandy Beach to Lookout Point. Andrew noted the flat coastal plain between the beach and the base of Mt Gore. The plain was a riot of vegetation but the hundreds of coconut palms growing in regular rows still showed where the old copra plantation had been.

It was easy walking down the long spine of the hill. There was a rough walking track, and the ground was as much bare rock as dirt. There were a few stunted trees and some rough, prickly bushes but mostly the vegetation was just tussocks of tough grass. The northern end of the hill became very rocky, with large granite boulders. The beach at Fishermans Bay was now hidden by trees so Andrew was able to focus on the scenery ahead. He noted that the boulders led right down to the southern end of Sandy Beach. Right at the bottom of the hill was a small area of beach about 50 paces long, shut off from the main beach by two large boulders. A foot track led up around the shoreward side of the boulders.

Jill gasped with delight. "What a lovely little beach!" she cried.

"Certainly nice and secluded," Letitia added.

At that, Andrew had instant fantasies of Letitia walking nude along the little beach. That got him aroused and ashamed. His daydream about fighting off hordes of black savages slipped right out of his head. He surreptitiously eyed Letitia. The sight was enough to make his mouth go dry with lust.

"I wonder if it's got a name?" Anne commented.

Carmen studied her map and then shook her head. "Too small to show on this map," she replied.

"It's such a beaut spot it needs a name," Martin said.

"Pirate Cove," Andrew at once suggested.

Carmen laughed. "You and your pirates!"

Anne looked around. "More like Secret Cove."

"That's a good name," Mark said. "I like it."

"Secret Cove it is then," Carmen agreed.

None of the others objected so she continued walking. Twenty paces took them around the inland side of the boulder. This put them at the junction of three trails, and at the southern end of Sandy Beach. One trail led back towards the cemetery and camp. Another went off into the overgrown coconut plantation, angling inland from the beach. Andrew noted that the wind was now stronger and that quite a respectable surf was blowing in to break along Sandy Beach. It confirmed his instinct that the sailing ships would have anchored in Fishermans Bay.

Too exposed to lie offshore here, he thought. *And dangerous; a lee shore.*

He was about to walk north along the beach when Carmen called to him.

"Time we went back to camp," she said.

Then she turned and led the way back inland. The track was easy walking, mostly sand with bushes and grass on either side and a few small trees. Within a couple of minutes they were back at the cemetery.

As they walked in from the beach, Andrew's imagination was hard at work. Now he wore a white naval officer's uniform. In his hand was a revolver. It was the 1870s and a line of armed naval ratings with rifles and webbing followed him.

The missionaries are kept prisoner in the cannibal's village, he told himself. *They are tied to stakes and the ceremony to kill and cook them is about to begin. We have landed at the small beach by boat from our gunboat and are sneaking in to rescue them.*

His first images of the missionaries' daughter had Anne's face and had her wearing a long white dress. However, Anne's image quickly changed to Letitia's. For a few seconds he visualised her voluptuous form squirming against the ropes as she tried to get free. Among the crowd of chanting natives he imagined curvaceous native girls wearing only grass skirts. He gave an involuntary sigh and felt the lust surge in his veins. Then a wave of shame swept over him and he bit his lip.

I shouldn't think such lewd thoughts, he told himself.

But it was very hard not to think such thoughts with Letitia's hips wiggling only metres in front of him!

By then they were back at the toilet. Andrew saw Carmen looking anxiously around and particularly to her left, towards the beach.

Is she worrying about seeing the Schipholls, he wondered.

* * *

Carmen was. She had no particular objection to nudity except in so far as it might offend or embarrass people. Nor was it something she would choose to do herself, feeling an instinctive inhibition. There was also, at the back of her mind, a tiny doubt that Jacob might have some strong feelings on the subject. She was sure he hadn't seen Mr and Mrs Schipholl on the beach, which was a relief. It had been such a surprise she had simply stared in fascinated amazement until she became aware of the others. Then she had been ashamed of herself and had hurried them away. The last thing she wanted at that moment was an embarrassing incident. To her relief, the Schipholls were nowhere in sight.

She turned to Letitia and said, "Letitia, find your mum and dad and tell them we are back at camp. It is time to start cooking tea."

As she watched Letitia walk off towards the jetty, Carmen noted Andrew staring after her. She also noted that Anne was aware of this and looking unhappy.

Oh dear! she thought. *What can we do about this?*

Unable to think of any plan, she diverted their attention by ordering everyone to get ready for tea.

"Who will light the fire?" she asked.

Jacob volunteered and Mark offered to help. Andrew was told to wash down and clean off the picnic table under the fly. Anne said she would help him and that pleased Carmen.

Anne obviously isn't just going to give up, she thought.

A few minutes later, Mr and Mrs Schipholl returned. Carmen was relieved to see that Mrs Schipholl now wore a long-sleeved shirt. Carmen could only shake her head and hope there would be no problems. To keep things moving, she asked the parents who was to do what.

Mr Schipholl took charge. "I'm the cook tonight," he said.

He directed her to collect cooking utensils from a cardboard carton and sent Letitia to get meat from an eski. By then Jacob and Mark had collected kindling and arranged it in the fireplace. Matches were found and the fire lit. Mr Schipholl scraped down the blackened and much used barbecue plate and then poured vegetable oil on. Soon the tantalising aroma of frying steak and onions began to tease their nostrils.

While the cooking was going on, Andrew and Martin sat to one side. To Carmen both seemed to be at a bit of a loose end.

She said, "Andrew, you and Martin go and check on the boat."

"Should we pull it right up onto the beach?" Andrew asked.

Mr Schipholl answered that, in between turning a sizzling steak. "No. We will only do that if there is a change in the weather. Just make sure the lines are securely fastened and long enough so she doesn't get hung up or dragged down by the tide."

Andrew and Martin walked off towards the beach. Anne stood and watched, obviously unsure of what to do. Jill moved to a seat and just chatted. With nothing else to do Carmen joined her. Mrs Schipholl went to her tent and re-appeared a few minutes later with a small radio and a book.

"We need to listen to the weather reports several times a day," she explained. "We don't want to get caught by a sudden change."

The weather provided a topic of conversation for a few minutes. But then a silence settled on the group. Carmen became anxious and wondered what she could talk about to ease the social situation. The history of the island seemed to her to be a suitable topic, so she dug out her notes and began to talk about the plantation and the tourist resort that had been built during the 1920s.

Andrew and Martin returned and sat on folding stools, waiting for their dinner. By then the breeze had dropped and the afternoon sun was lighting up only the top of the hill beyond the cemetery.

What a beautiful evening, Carmen thought.

She knew that the temperature and humidity were both still too high to be comfortable for tourists from Sydney of Melbourne but to her it was just right.

By then the steaks and sausages were cooked and the children lined up to get theirs. Carmen had two sausages on a bread roll, adding some tomato sauce, cheese, tomato and onions to it. It tasted delicious and she sat and happily munched away while the twilight set in. Mr Schipholl switched on a couple of battery lanterns and their bright light quickly blotted out the features under the trees within about 20 paces. This made it seem darker than it actually was. This was made apparent by the brighter light out over the sea.

Dinner over they cleaned up. Carmen did her fair share, collecting scraps and securing them in a plastic garbage bag which she tied securely with a wire twist-tie. That done there was a short discussion about what to do next.

Mr Schipholl settled that. "We are going out onto the jetty to do some fishing."

"Can we go swimming?" Mark asked.

"Definitely not!" Mr Schipholl replied. "Swimming at dusk and in the dark is very dangerous. That is when the sharks really like to bite."

"And if you get into difficulties and go under you will be hard to find," Jacob added.

As Carmen didn't have any desire to go swimming, she was content with that. She placed her eating gear in her tent and collected her fishing line. Then she stood waiting till Jacob joined her. For a few minutes she thought he wasn't going to but then he moved over beside her. Andrew, Martin, and Mark had already gone, leaving the adults and girls behind.

What Carmen was hoping for now was a bit of romance, so she deliberately lingered until the Schipholls and the other girls had started off towards the jetty. To her secret disappointment, Jacob did not seem to realise that she had delayed intentionally and he urged her to hurry to catch up. Feeling slightly miffed, she walked beside him out from under the trees and onto the jetty.

The transition was abrupt and uplifting. There were still signs of the sunset and the sky still had a bluish tinge but the first stars were already showing. Carmen knew that the moon had come up about half an hour before and that it was a full moon, but it was still hidden from them by the bulk of Oyster Point. Even so its light was already replacing the daylight, gently flooding everything with a silvery glow. The bay and the islands beyond seemed to take on a magical luminosity. The sheer tranquillity and beauty of the scene took Carmen's breath away.

Oh! I wish Jacob and I were the only people here, she told herself, then blushed at her own temerity.

Thinking about romance caused her to tingle in a way she wasn't used to, but which she recognised as arousal. Several times she sighed with the pleasure of the situation as she and he strolled out along the jetty to join the others.

The tide was well on the make and the boys were already hard at work, casting hand lines baited with small prawns. Still hoping that Jacob would make a romantic move, Carmen sat down beside him, deliberately 'accidentally' bumping him a few times. To her annoyance, he seemed not to notice and set to work to bait a hook and then to cast his fishing line in. Fishing did not interest Carmen, so she just dropped hers over the side, fastened the line to a cleat and hooked the hand reel onto that, then sat and relaxed.

Fishing was not a success. Nobody caught anything, although there were many nibbles and false alarms. Carmen didn't care. She just enjoyed sitting there and staring down into the sea. As the moon rose it lit up the water so well that she could see the dark, shadowy shapes of small fish flitting below her, silhouetted against the sandy bottom. A gentle breeze sprang up which she found most refreshing.

"Isn't it beautiful?" she commented, nudging Jacob. "I love the way the waves look all silver and black in the moonlight."

"Huh? Yeah," Jacob agreed, but he showed no real interest. Indeed he seemed somewhat annoyed at not catching anything.

Carmen thought she could have sat there all night, being soothed by the gentle, rhythmic swash of the small waves on the beach. Her eyes roved across the millions of stars lighting the sky, to the dark shapes of the other islands, then to the rugged bulk of Mt Gore and Snapper Point. In the moonlight they looked even more rugged than they did during the day.

I really feel like knowing I am on an island, she thought, hugging the feeling of isolation to herself.

At last the boys tired of their lack of success and Mrs Schipholl suggested supper and an early bed. They agreed to this with alacrity and lines were rolled up. Once again, Carmen deliberately went slow and ensured that she and Jacob were the last to leave the jetty. She was sure that Letitia and Anne both understood what she was doing but just as obviously the boys had no idea.

Nor has Jacob! she thought. *What do I have to do? Tell him straight out?* she wondered.

But there was no way she was going to be that forward. Instead, she made sure she 'accidentally' brushed against him a few times as they stood up and strolled back along the jetty.

But it was to no avail. Even though their fingers touched he still did not take the hint. Instead, he moved to walk further away from her.

Oh poo! she thought irritably as they rejoined the others at the campsite.

While Mrs Schipholl heated water on a gas stove, Carmen took the opportunity to go to the toilet. This was a bit spooky in the dark and she used her torch to light the way. Later she sat with the others and sipped hot, sweet Milo and chatted about the day and the island. It was nearly

10pm by then they were urged to bed. After a last hopeful smile at Jacob, Carmen went to her tent.

Here she was confronted by one last challenge for the day. Letitia crawled in and proceeded to strip off. As she tossed her T-shirt aside and began undoing her bikini top, she said, "You don't mind if I just sleep in a big T-shirt do you? At home I always sleep in the nuddy."

"No," Carmen replied, turning away and flushing with embarrassment. Then an impish idea came to her. "What if there is a fire?"

Letitia giggled, then said, "Then the boys will get even hotter!"

Carmen giggled as well, but with embarrassment as much as anything. Sliding down into her lightweight sleeping bag she rolled on her side away from Letitia.

"Good night," she said.

Letitia answered but then spent a few more minutes squirming and fidgeting while she found her other T-shirt and tugged it on.

For a time Carmen lay thinking, wondering how she might progress her friendship with Jacob, and just how far she might want it to go.

Chapter 13

THE PLANTATION

Andrew woke in the early hours and looked about him. It was still dark, with a strong dapple pattern of leaves and moonlight. His watch said 3am.

What woke me? he wondered.

Feeling unaccountably anxious he lay still and listened. But above the murmuring swash of small waves on the beach and the breeze in the leaves he could hear nothing. For quite a while he lay there, listening and puzzling over whether he really liked Anne or not. He at least knew he wasn't in love with Letitia.

That is just lust! Thinking about it made him blush with shame.

For at least an hour Andrew lay in his sleeping bag wondering what life and love might be like. At last he slipped back into a disturbed sleep, to wake feeling tried and grumpy when voices penetrated his consciousness. It was Jacob and Martin. They had already been out to the jetty and had returned with two whiting large enough to eat. It was full daylight by then, so Andrew slid out of his sleeping bag and sat up. Next to him Mark groaned and opened his eyes.

"What is it?" he muttered.

"Cannibals attacking," Andrew replied. He pulled on his gym boots and crawled out of the tent to greet the others. "What's the weather like?" he asked, although his skin told him it was already hot and humid.

"Might rain. A few showers out to the east," Martin replied.

Mr Schipholl suddenly called to them from inside his zipped-up tent. "Shut up and go back to bed you bloody kids! It's only six o'clock."

But it was no good. The girls now woke up as well and began talking. Andrew looked around as Carmen pushed back the flap of her tent and looked out. As she did, Andrew was able to see in and was granted a tantalising glimpse of Letitia. Carmen crawled out and allowed the tent flap to drop back into place. Andrew shook his head, ashamed at his own weak desire to see more, and hoping no-one had noticed. He found it a relief to go to the toilet and then help get breakfast ready.

Breakfast he enjoyed. They ate Weetbix with butter and honey, drank fruit juice or coffee and nibbled at various fruits Mrs Schipholl had brought along. After that there was a discussion on the day's plans. This was fairly easy to decide as the word 'Ruin' on the map beckoned with an irresistible lure.

Carmen read to them the brief outline of the plantation's history and they spent about twenty minutes getting ready: filling water bottles, dressing and going to the toilet. Mr Schipholl insisted they all wear long trousers and strong footwear in case they had to walk through weeds or long grass.

"I don't know if there are any snakes on the island," he commented, "But it is better to be sure than sorry."

He also took out his mobile phone and briefly turned it on to check its 'service'. Reception was weak but he hoped sufficient.

Andrew dressed in long blue trousers and an old blue work shirt with long sleeves. An old felt hat and gym boots completed his attire. In his own mind he buckled on an imaginary belt hung about with pistol holster, sword and various survival items. His real belt only had a small, but very sharp, pocketknife in a small leather pouch.

We are going to hack our way into the trackless jungles of the interior to rescue the maidens before they are sacrificed to the evil god of the cannibals, he thought.

The notion of finding an overgrown Maya or Aztec temple in the jungles of South America was a nice romantic fantasy. But within 50 paces he felt silly because the National Parks people had recently mowed the old road leading to the ruins and it was a wide and gentle path that a toddler could have followed.

After passing through a belt of tangled dry scrub, the group found itself in the old coconut plantation. The trees were now all fully grown and towered up for fifteen to twenty metres to their palm crusted tops. The coconut trees had been planted in straight rows and this allowed long views in all directions, hampered only by secondary growth that was now growing up. Underneath the palms was a thick tangle of weeds, ferns and spiky bushes, mostly about waist high but in places thrusting up as fully grown rain forest trees.

"The National Parks people are going to remove all these coconut palms," Mr Schipholl said, gesturing to the plantation around them.

"Whatever for?" Anne asked in astonishment.

"Because they aren't native Australian trees," Mr Schipholl replied.

Andrew was amazed. "But surely coconuts have been growing along the coast since before Captain Cook sailed past in the *Endeavour*?"

Mr Schipholl gave a wry smile. "Undoubtedly. But that is the policy, or so I heard."

"But that's ridiculous!" cried Mark. "In that case they would have to remove any other things that aren't Australian natives, like mango trees, and paw paws and all those fruit trees."

"And us!" Anne added. "We weren't here before Captain Cook either."

"Maybe not a bad idea," Jacob commented.

There was a moments silence before the implication sank in. Then Letitia retorted, "Now that is ridiculous. I was born in Australia, and so were my parents."

Martin snorted. "Don't forget that the Dutch discovered and charted three quarters of Australia before Cook. He only had to fill in the fourth side and it wasn't too hard to guess where that might be."

"Oh piffle to you!" Anne replied, but then trilled with laughter.

Mark looked puzzled. "What do you mean Martin?"

"Oh Mark! Didn't you pay attention in school? A Dutch explored named Willem Janz in a ship named the *Duyfken* sailed down the west coast of Cape York Peninsula in 1606. That's a hundred and fifty or sixty years before Cook."

"And the Dutch charted all of Northern Australia and Western Australia, right around to the Great Australian Bight," Carmen added.

Jacob grinned. "And ran into it a few times too," he added.

Mr Schipholl now joined in. "Never mind Captain Cook and the British, the First Fleet and so on. Australia was going to be settled back then anyway, because of world strategy, the power play between the great powers."

"What do you mean dad?" Martin asked.

"Britain and France were at war much of the 17th and 18th Centuries and were competing for command of the sea. If it had not been the British it would have been the French," he said.

Anne looked doubtful. "You think so?" she asked.

Mr Schipholl nodded vigorously. "Don't forget that La Perouse turned up at Botany Bay with two French warships just two days after the First Fleet had arrived back in 1788. That's no coincidence and a very close thing."

Andrew agreed. "It was naval strategy alright. Our History Teacher, Mr Conkey, said that the First Fleet was sent to set up a naval base and to deny the area to the French. It was commanded by a naval officer, Captain Arthur Phillip, it had marines to guard the place, not soldiers, and two warships stayed. The convicts were just the workers to build the naval base."

Mr Schipholl nodded. "That's right. And within a week the First Fleet was split and some sent to occupy Norfolk Island," he said.

"Norfolk Island! Why would they do that?" Anne asked.

"Because it was to windward of the east coast of the continent," Andrew answered. "In the Age of Sail being upwind gave a huge tactical advantage."

"That's right," Mr Schipholl added. "It was why the British clung on to lots of islands off the coast of places: Bermuda, Barbados, and so on."

"Captain Cook also reported there were huge pine trees on Norfolk Islands that might be suitable for ship's masts," Martin put in.

"Yes, but it turns out they weren't," Andrew agreed.

Jacob made a face. "And if the French had got here first, they would probably still be here. They still own all those islands out on the Pacific."

"Do they?" Letitia asked in surprise.

"Letitia!" Martin cried. "Yes, they do: New Caledonia, Tahiti, and lots of small islands right out in the middle."

"Oh, I didn't know that," Letitia replied. "I know where Tahiti is. That's where the hula girls come from in their grass skirts. But where is New Caledonia? I've heard of that."

It was Carmen who answered. Pointing out to the east she said, "That way. It is nearly as close to us as Brisbane is; just the other side of the Coral Sea."

Distracted, Andrew saw something and pointed. "Is that the ruin I can see?"

It wasn't, but as they came to a line of mango trees, they saw beyond them a low hill covered by a grassy lawn of buffalo grass, also recently mowed. Along the edge of the lawn to their left were a row of five concrete slabs, some with the remains of timber framework and a few broken panels of 'fibro'. In the middle of the lawn, among a riot of purple and maroon Bougainvillea flowers, was the 'ruin', now only a few concrete stumps and a brick chimney.

"They'd better pull out all this buffalo grass," Mark commented sarcastically.

"And that bougainvillea," Carmen added.

"And those orange trees, or are they lemons?" Letitia said, pointing to the left, where the lawn sloped down towards the creek.

Jacob gave a half-smile, half-sneer but made no reply.

Oh dear! Andrew thought. He noted an anxious little smile on Carmen's face and felt sorry for her.

They moved to study the remains of the plantation house. It had once been a bungalow of considerable size but all that remained now were rows of low concrete stumps and the front steps, also concrete. On a post in the middle of the lawn was an information sign. This included a picture of the house as it had once been, the writing and print protected from the weather by a plastic cover. The house had been surrounded by gardens and verandas and it had a very gracious and comfortable look to it. The building had been constructed of timber, but this had obviously been burnt or removed. The only other sizeable remains were of a brick fireplace and chimney at the rear.

"What on earth would they have wanted a fireplace for here in the tropics?" Anne said.

"For cooking," Mr Schipholl replied. "That was probably the kitchen."

The thought of cooking food by burning wood held all their thoughts for a few moments, so used were they to cooking by electricity or gas.

"No microwaves then," Mrs Schipholl added.

They strolled around to the back lawn and found the remains of several more structures. Two had obviously been the toilet and one looked like a storehouse or shed. Down a short path was a substantial shed made from concrete. It had a steel door which still hung on rusty hinges. This was pushed open to reveal an old pump and motor and several pipes.

"The water supply," Martin suggested.

"But why such a strong shed?" Mark wondered.

"Possibly a cyclone shelter?" Jacob said.

To them that made sense. As North Queenslanders, they had all grown up with the annual summer threat from cyclones. Hurricanes, the

Americans called them, except that here in the Southern Hemisphere they rotated in a clockwise direction. Andrew had only ever been on the edge of one, none having struck Cairns directly in his lifetime, but he still felt a chill of fear.

The path continued downhill for another 50 paces to the creek. This was the same creek which flowed past their camp. The creek was in the bottom of a small, deep-sided valley. Here it was rocky and fast flowing. Just upstream of where the path crossed it was a small concrete dam which held back a deep pool. Beyond that was a boulder-choked gorge overhung by jungle.

The idea of a swim was canvassed by Letitia but overruled by her parents. "Let's explore first," Mr Schipholl replied.

They returned to the front lawn. As they were now facing the other way, Andrew saw with surprise that the ruin was actually quite high up on the end of a low spur of Mt Gore. From where they stood, he was able to see out over the tree tops to the sea. They were granted a beautiful vista of ocean dotted with islands.

"Very pretty!" Carmen cried. "I can see why they picked this spot to build."

"Well away from the sea in case of storm surge, too," Mr Schipholl added.

The group admired the view for a few minutes, then went back down onto the old vehicle track. This continued on northwards past the front of the house and through a line of crotons, orange trees, and other bushes. Beyond these the track emerged in another open area of lawn. This was not as well kept and was spotted with weeds and grass seeds. Over on the left, against the wall of jungle at the base of the mountain, were the remains of a long, low building. It had once had a timber veranda all along its front and enough remained to show it had been some sort of accommodation. There were a line of empty doorways and windows among the rotting and broken timber frames.

"This was the old servant's quarters," Mr Schipholl explained.

They strolled on along the track until it did an abrupt right turn and went east. An overgrown clearing went on northwards towards a distant ridge, indicating it had once been a road or track. Now only a narrow, mowed lane went towards the sea. A couple of hundred paces walking down a gentle slope through the overgrown coconut plantation brought them out on the beach. It was more or less where Andrew had expected, about halfway along Sandy Beach.

By looking to his right he could see the large boulders at the secret cove they had visited the previous day. For a few minutes they stood on the beach admiring the view. The breeze was quite strong, and the waves were just too big to make for comfortable swimming. In the distance Andrew could see more islands. Out to the southeast he noted a line of rain showers drifting in from the sea.

By common consent they turned left and began strolling along Sandy Beach, heading northwards. The beach ended about half a kilometre ahead at a rocky headland. This was the lower end of a ridge which ran down from the top of Mt Gore. As they strolled along, Andrew walked between Anne and Martin. Letitia, Mark, and Jill followed, then Carmen and Jacob, with Mr and Mrs Schipholl bringing up the rear.

"We are going to get wet," commented Mark, indicating a shower sweeping towards them.

"So what?" Martin replied.

Andrew could only shrug and agree. It was only summer rain. "It will cool it down a bit," he added, well aware that he was perspiring in the humidity.

The rain was surprisingly cold when it did arrive. Letitia let out a few squeals and there was some surprised muttering but then they just walked on. A few minutes later the shower passed and the sun came out again, its force seemingly redoubled.

Carmen got the conversation going again by speculating whether they would be able to see the lighthouse on Cape Saunders from up on the point. They couldn't. Ten minutes of scrambling up over rocks and through tough tussocks of grass and prickly bushes had them on Lookout Point. From here they could see much of the north coast but it was just a jumble of steep, rocky slopes plunging down into rough water studded with hundreds of rocks.

Once on top of the headland, Andrew made a careful study of the sea and distant islands. He noted the masts and superstructure of a large freighter heading northwards, then had his attention attracted by the drone of an aero engine. It took him a while to locate the plane but at last he spied it, well out to sea and also flying north. From its red and white colouring he thought it was one of the Coastwatch planes but wasn't sure.

Martin set out to try to make his way to the next headland in the hope of seeing the lighthouse. The others followed. This necessitated clambering down and around many large rocks and through clumps of vegetation. By the time they reached the base of the cleft between the headlands it was obvious to them all that it was not going to be easy.

Mr Schipholl called out from behind them, telling them to stop. "This is no good," he said. "If someone slips and injures themselves we will have a devil of a job getting them out. I don't feel like phoning for a rescue helicopter. We will go back."

There was some reluctance on the part of Martin and Mark, but Andrew knew it was a sensible decision. They turned and began picking their way back up the rocks. In doing so they became strung out. Andrew found himself following Anne, and with Letitia behind him. As he scrambled up a large rock, she called out to him.

"Wait for me, Andrew. Give me a hand up."

Andrew turned and reached down, offering her his hand. She took it and the touch sent a tingle through him. She climbed up beside him, moving so close that her legs and arms brushed against his. The feel of her skin sent another pulse of excitement through him. She gave him a smirk which told him she knew what effect she was having.

Suddenly she leaned over, pressing against him. "Thanks," she muttered, giving him a kiss on the cheek.

Andrew was so surprised that he could not react. He was aware that the touch was setting him on fire but that was nothing compared to the shame that flamed when he glanced around and saw Mark and Jill coming into view with Carmen behind them.

For a moment he met his sister's eyes and then another hot wave of shame swept through him.

Chapter 14

GETTING HOT

Carmen saw the blush mottle Andrew's cheeks even as he pulled back from Letitia.

Oh dear! she worried. *Did she start that? Or was it Andrew?*

Andrew and Letitia moved apart and continued climbing up the rocks. Behind her Carmen heard Jacob climbing up. She hoped he hadn't seen, sensing that he would not approve. Then she found the same problem that Letitia had; the rocks were just a bit too big for her to comfortably climb. So she indicated that Jacob go ahead.

"Give me a hand up," she said.

By then Letitia, Andrew, Mark, and Jill had all vanished from view. She thought Martin was still behind somewhere, but she could not see him either. With a guilty start she realised she was hoping to do exactly what she had just seen: steal a quick kiss while nobody was looking. Then she gave a wry smile, even as she reached up to take Jacob's offered hand.

That's if Jacob will be in it, she thought.

His hand felt nice and his eyes met hers as he hoisted her up. For a second she stood very close to him, their clothes brushing together.

Now! Do it now! Kiss me! she thought.

Whether she was urging herself on, or silently willing Jacob to act, she wasn't sure. For just a moment she thought he might, but then he released her hand and turned to keep clambering up the rocks.

Feeling slightly disappointed, Carmen followed. *Maybe tonight?* she wondered.

On top of the headland she found most of the others. Mr and Mrs Schipholl had already started down the other side and Letitia and Andrew were following them. Jill and Mark stood side by side looking along the beach, while Anne and Martin sat staring out to sea.

Oh there's Martin. Jacob and I could have lingered for a quick kiss, Carmen told herself. Then she noted that neither Martin, nor Anne, looked very happy. That got her worrying again.

121

"Come on you two, back to camp," she said.

They both looked and nodded, but neither said anything. However, they did stand up and follow. It took only a few minutes to climb back down to the beach.

Just as well we did come back, Carmen thought as another rain shower swept over them, making the rocks slick and dangerous.

The group straggled back along Sandy Beach in pairs: Mr and Mrs Schipholl; Andrew and Letitia; Mark and Jill, then herself and Jacob. Martin and Anne brought up the rear, walking slowly and talking quietly. It was obvious to Carmen that the relationships within the group were being subtly rearranged.

I just hope there aren't any bust-ups or ill-will, she thought anxiously.

It wasn't till they were past the side track to the ruin that Carmen realised that they had not turned off. Instead, Mr and Mrs Schipholl led the way south to the rocks at the end of the beach. Here they climbed up around them and waited at the point where the three tracks met.

As Carmen and Jacob arrived, Letitia wiped perspiration off her face and pointed to Secret Cove. "What about a quick swim? I'm melting," she said.

Mr Schipholl nodded. "Alright, but don't go out far. The seabed shelves much more steeply here and there will be an undertow with these waves."

Carmen would have preferred to wait to swim in the shallower and more sheltered waters of the bay, but as the others all thought the idea of a swim a good one she also began to undress. She had her bathers on underneath her shirt and trousers, so it was no problem. Likewise, Anne and Jill could just strip down to swimmers and the boys either wore their bathers underneath or went off among the bushes to change. But not Letitia. She took her bikini top out of her small bag and just turned her back and peeled off her T-shirt, then proceeded to tie on the top.

Carmen coloured with embarrassment but could not help admiring both her nerve and her lovely shape before turning away and walking down the beach. As she did, she saw Andrew staring at Letitia with a look that worried her; and Jacob staring with a hostile frown, which worried her even more.

The water was colder than Carmen expected, and she found it very refreshing. As always, she was surprised at how salty it was, and at how strong the currents were. The waves weren't as big as further along Sandy Beach, but they were big enough to sweep her off her feet and roll her up the sand. As she regained her feet and wiped the water from her eyes, Carmen saw that Letitia was now walking down the beach, still tying up her bikini top as she did. Mark stood nearby, staring.

Jill looked to be really angry. "You could get changed in private!" she snapped at Letitia, though Carmen suspected her real anger was directed at Mark.

Letitia just shrugged and ignored her, then ran into the surf. Carmen glanced at the Schipholls to see what they thought of the incident, but they were busy splashing in the waves and appeared not to have heard. When they did come up, Mr Schipholl had his arms around Mrs Schipholl. The two adults seemed to be quite unaware that they were making a bit of a spectacle and went rolling over in the waves with much chuckling and giggling. To Carmen it looked normal and loving, and she experienced a deep hope that her own future husband might be as physically affectionate.

Then Letitia made a show of herself again. She tried to ride a wave in but was dumped by the surf. As she struggled spluttering to her feet, Carmen noted that one of Letitia's breasts had escaped from her bikini top. Letitia apparently did not notice as she stood up, spluttering and giggling.

"Letitia! Don't be so rude!" Jill snapped.

Letitia looked puzzled, then glanced down. With a hurt and hostile look on her face, she reached up and thrust the offending breast back into the cloth.

"What's wrong with you? It's only a tit," she retorted.

Jill went red and pursed her lips. "I don't like seeing that," she snapped.

"So why did you come to the beach then?" Letitia cried angrily.

Mr and Mrs Schipholl stopped hugging and turned to see what the trouble was. Mrs Schipholl stood up and waded over, adjusting her own top as she did. Carmen had to shake her head.

I can see where Letitia gets it from, she thought.

"Now, now, children. Let's not fight," Mrs Schipholl said.

Jill, sensing that she did not have an ally in Mrs Schipholl, and now blushing furiously, said, "I would prefer if Letitia didn't... didn't... expose herself."

Mrs Schipholl nodded, while absent-mindedly adjusting her own bathers. "Fair enough. Letitia, behave yourself. Don't upset Jill and the others please." She looked from one to the other. Both Jill and Letitia eyed each other. Letitia at last nodded. Mrs Schipholl then said, "Good! Now let's get back to camp. It's time for lunch. You can have another swim this afternoon."

The group picked up clothes, towels, and bags and set off along the track to the cemetery. No-one made any attempt to change back into their clothes. A few minutes later they were back at their camp. Carmen found that a bit of a relief. She had a big drink and went to the toilet and changed back into shirt and jeans, then sat and helped Mrs Schipholl prepare lunch: cold meat and bread.

"What are we doing this afternoon?" Martin asked.

"Fishing," Jacob at once responded.

"Another swim," Letitia said.

She was still wearing only her bikini and Carmen felt sure she was doing that out of stubborn defiance.

"I want to visit the wreck," Andrew said.

"What wreck?" Martin asked.

"An old sailing ship named the *City of Perth*," Andrew replied.

Martin frowned. "Sailing ship? When was it wrecked?"

Carmen could answer that. "It was the one that half the people in the cemetery came from. There was a sign there, remember? The wreck was in 1888. I think something like seventy or so of the hundred and five on board were drowned in the wreck."

"Oh yeah, I read that," Martin answered.

"1888! That was a long time ago. There wouldn't be much left after all this time," Mark commented.

Mr Schipholl, now clad in loose shirt and baggy shorts answered. "Oh yes there is. The ship was made of iron and most of the hull is still there. Last time we were here there were even a few of the old rolled iron masts sticking up."

Mark nodded. "Oh, iron. I assumed it would have been made of wood," he replied.

Anne looked puzzled. "But doesn't iron rust?" she asked. She now sat beside Andrew, wearing a lovely floral shirt.

Mr Schipholl frowned and scratched his head. "Yes, well. Now I'm no chemist, and metallurgy isn't my thing, but I seem to remember reading that some of the old iron was very resistant to rusting. It must be, for this thing to last this long."

"How did it get there?" Jill asked.

Carmen answered that. "Driven ashore during a storm."

The wreck, and the afternoon's program, provided them with neutral topics which carried them through lunch. There was then a short period of preparation while bags were packed with drinks, towels and fishing gear. Then the group set off. First, they strolled to the jetty to check the boat.

At that, point Mr Schipholl said, "I think we will take the boat and meet you there. It is low water at about fifteen hundred, but I am not sure if it is low enough for you to walk out to the wreck. If it isn't we can ferry you out in the boat."

"You just don't want to walk," Martin replied.

His father grinned. "That too, and I want to do a bit of fishing."

Mr and Mrs Schipholl, now covered from head to toe with hats, long sleeves, long pants and shoes pulled on life jackets and climbed down into the boat. Martin cast off the painter and the group then strolled back to the beach while the boat got under way. Mr Schipholl motored slowly out into the bay and then took up his fishing rod. The others turned left and walked west along the beach. They were in no hurry and Carmen enjoyed herself strolling along, scanning the beach and shallows for seashells and marine curiosities.

They had to wade the mouth of the creek and most took off their sandshoes or gym boots to do so. The water was so shallow that it barely wet the bottoms of their jeans. Carmen was again surprised at how cold it felt, and she bent down and rinsed her face. Feeling quite refreshed and happy she strolled on, frequently stopping to pick up pieces of coral or shells.

"Don't forget this is a marine national park," Jacob reminded her.

Carmen knew that and was well aware it was illegal to remove such things, but it peeved her slightly to have Jacob point it out to her.

After wading the creek, Mark, Jill, and Martin continued on wading, splashing along in the shallows. The tide was definitely on the ebb and there was hardly any surf, just small waves that rippled in gently, knee high.

Suddenly Mark jumped up and cried out and Carmen looked in time to spot a disturbance in the shallows just in front of him. The surface boiled in places five metres apart and little spurts of sand swirled up from the seabed. She did not see what had caused it but could guess.

"Stingray," Mark said, staring carefully into the shallow water.

"You had better be careful," Jacob cautioned. "It will be no joke getting you to hospital if you stand on one and get jagged."

Carmen could only agree. She had seen many stingrays over the years but so far had been spared seeing anyone stung. Despite that, she was well aware that the flat 'bottom' fish with their sharp and poisonous spine at the base of their long, thin tail, were a creature to treat with respect and caution.

Soon after that, Martin almost stepped on another. This time Carmen glimpsed the flash of silver-grey as the ray sped off to deeper water.

"I think you should walk on the beach," she said.

They did so, all now peering into the shallows in the hope of seeing another stingray. It wasn't only stingrays that were worrying Carmen. The possibility of poisonous jellyfish, even this late in the season, was very much on her mind. Tropical seas, she knew, looked lovely and were full of beautiful wonders, but they also teemed with unpleasant and deadly creatures: stonefish, blue-ringed octopi, sharks, sea snakes, jelly fish, moray eels, poisonous seashells. She shuddered at the catalogue of potential horrors which flitted through her mind.

At the end of the beach, they climbed up onto a rough foot track that led around the rocks at the end of Snapper Point. It was easy going but very hot. Carmen found she was sweating profusely. The sky had cleared so that there wasn't a cloud in sight and the breeze had dropped so that the sea was almost flat. A misty haze obscured the mainland and distant islands. Schooner Rock now stood up sharp and clear, looking far more jagged and steep than before.

The boat with the adults in it puttered into the Falcon Pass, Mr Schipholl clearly visible fishing and Mrs Schipholl reading, sheltered by an umbrella and a large straw hat. To Carmen it all looked very peaceful and she sighed, wishing Jacob would make more conversation and show more interest.

To her mild annoyance, his eyes seemed to be more on the sea than on her. Then he cried out and went scrambling down over the rocks.

"Oooh! Look at those beauties!"

Those beauties were several large fish which were feeding in close to shore. From above they were quite visible in the clear water.

"What are they?" she asked as she climbed down to look.

By then the fish had taken fright and flitted off into the shadows under the rocks, or into deeper water. Nobody else had seen them so she was left none the wiser.

Andrew, Mark, and Jill had continued on and they now stood on the highest point of the track, right at the end of the point. Andrew turned and called back, "There's the wreck! Come on! The tide is right out and we can reach it easily."

Carmen and Letitia at once hurried on, leaving Jacob and Martin to follow. As she reached the top of the rocks, Carmen paused and gasped with delight. Below her stretched a small bay, perhaps a hundred metres from one point to the next. Almost all of the inside of the bay was brown, indicating coral or rocks. Standing high on this, its bows almost on the beach, was the black and brown remains of the rusting shipwreck.

"What a great shipwreck!" Andrew cried with delight.

He set off down the rocks as quickly as he could safely climb.

Chapter 15

THE WRECK

Andrew stood on top of a rock and looked down into the bay. The moment he saw the wreck his spirits soared. It was a real wreck and looked like one; and it was plainly of a sailing ship. He could tell that by the shape of the hull and the remains of the bowsprit which still protruded from the bow. Instantly his imagination took hold. His eyes and brain recognised the ship as having been a 19th Century type; a clipper or three masted barque, but in his mind's eye she was much older, the Spanish galleon driven on the rocks after the storms had scattered the Armada.

And most of her crew are still alive and are armed and determined to prevent us capturing the treasure, he thought.

He would have preferred to remain up in the rocks for much longer, to savour this treat; and then to creep from rock to rock, pretending to be sneaking down to make a surprise attack. However, the others went hurrying down the rough track towards it, so he had no real choice but to follow.

As he got closer, his initial impression changed. At first the hull had appeared to be black and intact, but as he got closer he saw that the old iron was in fact heavily corroded with yellowish and ruddy rust flakes visible. To his great disappointment, he saw that the lower plates of the hull, up to what was probably the usual high tide level, were mostly missing, and that the upper hull was held up on the remains of the iron frames and concretions of marine growth.

When he reached the beach at the base of the rocks, Andrew stopped and carefully studied the wreck, now only 50 paces away. From that distance it looked very much larger than he had thought, towering well above him. Its bow was only a dozen metres from the beach, the stump of the iron bowsprit pointing directly inland. To his real delight he saw that the remains of two lower masts were still visible, although both were now lying broken across the bulwarks.

"A sailing ship alright," he muttered

He noted that there was no sign of a propeller and then saw the rusting remains of the 'chains' and 'channels' which had secured the shrouds and backstays. Still marvelling, he joined the others in the shallows near the almost vertical cutwater.

Carmen held up a hand. "Watch out for stonefish," she cautioned as they waded out to the remains.

The tide was just low enough for them to do this with the water only reaching up to their knees in places.

"Try not to stand on any coral," Jacob added. "That kills it."

Wading on the small areas of sand between the clumps of coral, Andrew made his way right out and put his hand on the rusting iron of the bow. It felt dry and flaky and pieces broke off, either adhering to his skin or dropping into the water. All he could do for a minute or so was stand and stare up, taking in the lines of the hull and all the details that spoke of days gone by and the way men used to do things.

An old quote came into his mind. "Wooden ships and iron men," he said, before realising that it was actually an iron ship. "This ship was the real McCoy, the transition from timber construction to iron and steel."

He had enough knowledge of the history of ships to know that it had probably already been technologically doomed even before it was built. By then there were already iron steamships at sea. He gave a nostalgic sigh, his thoughts tempered by the idea that maybe the good old days hadn't been quite so good.

Bloody hard work, and very dangerous, he told himself.

Mark reinforced this by saying, "They almost made it to the beach. You'd wonder how so many got drowned."

"In the waves," Carmen suggested. "If it was a cyclone the waves might have been enormous."

"But this is the sheltered side of the island," Jill pointed out.

Carmen shook her head. "Not if it was a cyclone and its eye was to the south of them. In that case the wind and waves would have been driving straight into this cove."

"Was it a cyclone?" Anne asked.

"Don't know," Carmen replied.

For a few moments Andrew stood in the shallows, staring back at the beach and trying to picture the dreadful event. In his own imagination he was strong enough to swim through the raging surf, though deep down he knew that was just fantasy.

Then I'd secure a line to those trees up there, before swimming back to rescue...

His thoughts were distracted by Letitia wandering in front of him. They began wading slowly along the starboard side of the wreck, peering in through the gaps where hull plates were missing. Andrew carefully studied the shapes and angles of the frames and then ran his fingers along the seam between two iron hull plates. Very slowly he rubbed at the rounded head of a rivet. He had read about ships being riveted together but had only ever seen it in photos. Now he was amazed at the thousands of tiny round bumps which studded the outer hull, holding the plates to the frames and to each other.

"Amazing!" was his comment. All he could do was marvel at the work involved to make such a thing.

Anne suddenly pointed down and gave an exclamation of surprise. "Ooh! Look at this little clam shell!"

Andrew carefully skirted a clump of coral and weeds and joined the group, who stood in a circle looking down. He saw that Anne was right; it was a tiny clam. They were things he had seen before but he was still fascinated. This one was only about three centimetres long but appeared to be a perfect miniature of the full-grown clam. It had the same scalloped lips with their interlocking, curved edges, and the same corrugated exterior. The only real difference was that the flesh inside was a bright purple colour, whereas in the older clams it tended to be a sort of grey-green or brown.

"Can it bite?" Anne asked, crouching down to look more closely.

Mark laughed. "Stick your finger in and find out," he suggested.

Jacob shook his head. "Don't. You could get a scratch and scratches from coral and marine life often get infected very quickly," he warned.

"I didn't know you were an expert on fish and things," Martin said to him.

Jacob shrugged. "I do marine ed at school, and biology."

"Don't clams grow really big?" Martin asked him.

Jacob nodded. "Yes, they do. They can grow to be over a metre long."

Mark laughed. "They are the ones you see in the movies that snap shut on a diver's foot so that he drowns."

Anne looked horrified. "Oh! They don't do they?"

Jacob shook his head. "There's no real proof. I read somewhere that is just rumour. But you could get caught. The big ones get slow at closing I read."

"Here's another clam," Letitia said.

"Oh yes," Carmen agreed. Then she gasped. "Ooh! Look! There are dozens of them."

Now that Andrew looked more closely, he was amazed they hadn't noticed them earlier. The reef was dotted with dozens of baby clams. The biggest was about twenty centimetres long and had its jaws wide open. The bi-valve mouth was plainly visible.

Letitia bent over and swished water into it, causing the clam to contract to half-shut. That made her giggle, so she did it to a couple more. Then she gasped and cried out in disgust.

"Eeergh! What's that horrible thing?"

Jacob answered her. "A sea slug," he replied. "Sometimes called a Sea Cucumber or Beche-de-Mer. Asians dry them and eat them."

Again Letitia expressed disgust and wrinkled her nose. "What's this thing?" she asked.

Andrew splashed over to look. His eyes followed her pointing finger and he saw a small wriggling thing. His first thought was that it was sea snake, which he knew might be deadly. Then he saw the flattened body shape and the head.

"It's a baby moray eel," he replied, looking up.

Their eyes met and he found she was studying him with a quizzical, half-amused gaze. "Is it dangerous?" she asked.

Andrew shook his head. The moray eel was only as thick as his finger and 15 centimetres long. "No, it's only a baby," he replied. "A full-grown one is a metre or more long and has a vicious bite, or so I've heard."

Letitia leaned further forward to get a closer look at the eel, which began backing under a piece of coral. Andrew's eyes were drawn to the way her breasts bulged.

Bloody hell! he thought. *She will spill out of that top if she isn't careful!*

He wasn't the only one. Jill called sharply, "Letitia! Andrew is just there."

Letitia looked at her but stayed bent over. "So?"

"He can see everything the way you are exposing yourself," Jill replied heatedly.

"I'm sure he doesn't mind," Letitia replied. "Besides, my mum said, 'if you've got it, flaunt it. You are only young once'."

"That's disgusting!" Jill snapped.

"I don't like it either," Jacob added.

Letitia now straightened up, her neck and face going red, but whether from anger or embarrassment Andrew could not tell. He was certainly blushing himself. For a moment Letitia stood, mouth open and hands on hip, her eyes blazing. Then she snapped her mouth shut and turned towards the beach. Without a word she splashed past a blushing Anne and a wide-eyed Mark.

Martin looked very embarrassed. He glanced at his sister, then out to sea. Andrew followed his gaze and saw that the boat with the Schipholls was drifting just out past the edge of the reef. It was too far away for them to have heard and they appeared to be engrossed in fishing. Andrew badly wanted to follow Letitia but could not think of any plausible excuse that would not make obvious his desires, so he resumed studying the hull of the wreck. The others followed him.

He made his way to the very stern and stood staring at the barnacle encrusted stern post and frames. The rudder had been wrenched off and was nowhere to be seen but the badly distorted pintles on which it had been hung were still in place. Andrew looked up, admiring the curving sweep of the hull plates up to the overhanging counter stern.

Nice lines, a real ship, he thought.

The Schipholls called out and waved and the group waved back. By then they were standing in thigh deep water and the odd, rippling wave surged up to almost waist deep, soaking their clothes. Andrew didn't care. His old shorts were meant for that, but Anne and Jill began to grumble.

Andrew waded out into even deeper water, stepping into one sandy hollow that was waist deep. A wave went up to his chest. What he wanted to see was the full run of the hull from a distance. What he also saw were several small crabs and a spiny sea urchin, which he carefully avoided. When he was 50 paces from the wreck and close to the edge of the reef, which was clearly marked by the change of water colour to a dark green, he turned. For several minutes he stood and studied the old ship, picturing her as she might have been with masts still standing and all sail set.

The Schipholls were only 50 metres away and he spoke briefly to them, asking how the fishing was. As he did, he heard the growing drone of aero engines. It came from his left, so he turned, just in time to see a red and white, twin-engine plane come low around Snapper Point. It was only a few hundred feet up and turned to fly between the island and Schooner Rock. Faces were clearly visible at the aircraft's windows. So was the writing along its side. Coastwatch, it read. The plane kept turning and went on around the next small point and vanished northwards.

They were checking who we are, he thought.

For a few moments he remembered the awful incident at Simpson Point. Then he forgot about it as a larger than normal wave almost lifted him off his feet.

The others began making their way back along the port side of the wreck towards the shore. Andrew scanned the beach looking for Letitia. He saw no sign of her and wondered where she had gone.

Back to camp probably, he surmised.

He began wading slowly after the others. As he did, he looked up at the rounded, overhanging stern counter of the wreck. For a few moments he imagined he was swimming, knife between his teeth, to try to recapture the ship from the pirates. Then the flurry of a stingray near his feet shifted his thoughts back to the present. Slowly he made his way along, looking alternately at the marine life, then at the wreck.

Carmen called to him from the beach. "Come on, Andrew! You can always come back again."

Reluctantly, he sloshed ashore to join the others on the sand. Martin asked, "Where to now?"

"I want to go fishing on those rocks back there," Jacob replied.

"More exploring first," Andrew said. He pointed to the left. "I want to see what Careenage Bay looks like."

"What's a careenage?" Anne asked.

"A place where ships can be placed on the beach at high tide so you can work on their bottom at low tide," Andrew replied. Without thinking he said, "It's the sort of place pirates would have beached their ships to repair them."

"Pirates!" scoffed Jacob. "What pirates? This is North Queensland, not the Caribbean."

Andrew flushed and wished he hadn't let his daydreams be so public. To save his pride, he said, "There was so. You heard the man on the launch telling us about that pirate Benito Bennet. He might have come here to repair his ship. He would have needed a secret careenage after crossing the Pacific." (*And to bury his treasure,* he added in his mind.)

"Can't it wait?" Jill said, fanning herself with her cloth hat. It was now very hot and still and they were all sweating and looking flushed.

"It's just over those rocks," Andrew replied, pointing to the small rocky headland a hundred paces away.

"Oh alright! But then I'm going fishing," Jacob replied.

Andrew set off, leading the way. Somewhat reluctantly the others followed. It was hot, he conceded, but explorers shouldn't be daunted by that sort of thing. Hardships were part of the deal.

If it was easy there'd be no achievement, he told himself.

The point was low and short and even as he climbed over the rocks Andrew began getting glimpses of the next beach and of the next point.

"That next headland is Bennet Point," he told himself. "So why would it be named that unless Benito Bennet actually did come here?"

It made sense to him and fired his imagination. Then the idea came to him that the pirates might be there at that very moment, with their ship heaved up on the strand. With that in mind he chose a route which allowed him to keep as much under cover as possible. Without making it too obvious to the others that he was playing a game he made his way over the rocks.

As the beach came into view, he changed his story. No pirate ship was visible, but there was a small boat pulled up on the sand beside a tiny creek.

Long John Silver has come ashore with just two men and Jim Hawkins to dig up the treasure. I must hurry to save Jim, or he might be shot along with the other sailors.

Andrew believed that pirates always shot a man and left his body in the hole with the treasure so that his ghost could help guard it.

Careenage Bay was about half a kilometre long, a gentle curve of white beach ending at Bennet Point, the next rocky headland. At the top of the beach was a line of trees and bushes, mostly She Oaks. Inland of that appeared to be a small coastal flat, then the steep, jungle-covered slopes of Mt Gore. The grey of huge boulders showed here and there among the jungle, even up near the top of the mountain.

That looks pretty rough, Andrew thought, revising the idea of climbing the mountain.

Still pretending to be playing pirates, Andrew clambered around behind another large boulder and stepped out onto the beach near where the small boat lay. For a moment he could not believe his eyes and he just stood and gaped. Then the scene registered. Letitia was standing topless in front of a man! She was standing sideways and was obviously posing. The man wore only a pair of very brief nylon bathers and a cloth hat and had his back to him. What first registered in Andrew's consciousness was that the man had a solid build and very tanned skin. Next, he noted with a pulse of dislike, that the man's back and legs were very hairy.

That Letitia was posing and not in the least concerned and not in any apparent danger was immediately obvious. She was standing casually chatting with the man. The man, who looked to be in his late thirties or early forties, was holding a sketchbook and a pencil. Nearby on a small table was a palette and a paint brush and beside Letitia was an easel holding a painting.

An artist, Andrew deduced, even as his horrified mind raced. *I must stop the others,* he thought, hoping to save Letitia from any trouble.

With that in mind he turned, his mind groping for some plausible explanation. To his dismay, he saw Carmen and then Jill both step out from behind the same boulder.

Chapter 16

ATTITUDES EXPOSED

The first thing Carmen saw as she stepped out from behind the boulder was Andrew's face. Even as the anxiety, even distress, on it registered in her mind, she saw Letitia and the almost naked man. Her reaction was also to prevent all the others seeing them too. That hope was dashed instantly. Even as she began to turn and tried to choose words to use, she heard Jill's shocked gasp.

The man heard the sound and half turned to look. Other details of the man registered: brown eyes, brown hair, a very hairy chest and arms, thickening about the waist with middle-age spread but obviously still fit and muscly. Then Carmen's eyes took in the sketch book and noted that the man had already produced a very good likeness of Letitia.

To sketch that well in such a short time means he has real skill, she thought.

Beyond the man was a painting on an easel. One glance told Carmen that the man was a real artist. The painting was a seascape of Careenage Bay and even half completed it was obviously quality work which showed that the man had both technical skill and artistic knowledge. Under other circumstances, she felt she would have really admired the work and sensed that it was the sort of picture she would like to have hanging on her lounge room wall.

Her attention now shifted to Letitia who had also spun round, folding her arms over her front and looking annoyed as she did. More shocked comments including a 'bloody hell!' from Mark and a sharp intake of breath by Jacob told Carmen that there was no way to avoid a scene.

She was not the only one who thought so. Jill at once snapped, "Letitia! Cover yourself. The boys are here."

Letitia's defiant response was to move her arms slightly to reveal more. "So what? They don't mind."

"I do!" Jacob cried, causing Carmen to glance anxiously at him.

Jill returned to the attack. "Cover up, you disgusting cow!"

"Don't call me a cow!" Letitia cried angrily, moving her hands to her hips and revealing all her front. Carmen stared and thought how apt the 'cow' term was. Letitia went on, "You're just jealous because yours aren't very big."

"How dare you!" screamed Jill. She shook with rage and took a step forward. Carmen reached out and restrained her.

"Cover up!" Jacob ordered.

"No! You go somewhere else," Letitia replied, her hands now clenched into fists on her hips.

Carmen tried to mediate. "Letitia, please!"

"Oh, for God's sake!" Letitia cried. "They're only tits! Everyone's got them, except that some have bigger ones than others." Once again, she cast an insulting glance at Jill's bosom.

Carmen thought that Jill would explode but it was Jacob who strode forward. He raised one hand and boomed, "Cover up and hide thy shame woman! Remember the Word of the Lord! When he cast us out of the Garden of Eden, he commanded us to be modest and to hide our nakedness! Now heed the Lord's word!"

Carmen heard that statement like a revelation. She dimly thought that there was something like that in the Bible, but now she knew with absolute certainty that she could never have a relationship with Jacob.

He is a fanatic, a bigot! she thought.

Sadly she realised that he was not likely to be very tolerant, or to have much compassion or kindness, much less forgiveness.

The sheer vehemence of Jacob's speech stunned them all. Even Letitia looked shocked. She glared in embarrassed defiance.

"Stick it up your bum!" she shouted angrily.

She then turned and began walking away, snatching up her bikini top as she went. A few moments later she had waded the shallow creek where the boat lay and was lost to sight among the trees.

Carmen now became aware that the man was staring at Jacob with a look of cynical challenge on his face. The artist did not look at all afraid, but he did hold his sketch book in front of him to keep himself covered. He turned to Carmen and Anne and gave a slight bow.

"Pardon me, ladies. I did not know I was going to receive guests, or I would have been more prepared. You are the first people I have seen in a week."

That caused Carmen to experience the feeling that it was them who

137

had intruded. "We thought we had the island to ourselves," she answered lamely.

Jacob now turned on the artist. "Get properly dressed!" he ordered.

The artist returned a steely look. "Get stuffed! I was here first. If you don't like it, then clear off!"

"It is against God's law!" Jacob ranted.

"I might belong to a different religion," the artist replied, giving a sardonic smile as he did.

This plainly infuriated Jacob, as he actually spluttered, before snapping, "It is not decent, and there are girls here."

"Sorry ladies," the artist replied.

Carmen decided that his accent wasn't Australian. *English maybe?*

He went on, "As for you mate, leave me in peace."

Jacob was obviously in the grip of strong emotions, but even so he wasn't willing to tackle the artist. The artist clearly wasn't afraid of him and quite calmly stood his ground.

Jacob tried another tack. "You need a permit to camp on this island."

The painter raised an eyebrow. "How do you know I'm camping? Anyway, I have a permit." Then he gave an amused grin and gestured, "But not on me at the moment."

Carmen had to smile at that one. She found she didn't exactly like the artist but thought he seemed sane and pleasant. Jacob obviously didn't.

"You shouldn't get young girls to undress and expose themselves," he snarled, gesturing in the direction that Letitia had gone.

Now the artist showed a hint of anger. "I didn't! I was minding my own business when she walked up from behind and started talking to me. It was her suggestion. She asked me if I would draw her, and she just took off her top. Anyway, she didn't look like a young girl."

"She is underage. It is against the law!" Jacob snapped back.

Martin now spoke up. "No she's not. She's sixteen."

Jacob turned an angry glare on him. "Don't place your sister at risk."

"Thou shalt not bear false witness!" retorted Martin.

For a second Carmen thought Jacob was going to lose his temper and strike Martin. Being mocked in that way caused his face to suffuse with rage and for a moment he was incoherent.

Then he spluttered and gestured towards the artist, "I will tell the police about this... this pervert!"

Now the artist took a step forward. "You call me that again and I'll knock your block off! Now get off my part of the island."

Carmen now decided it was time to go. *There will be a real fight in a minute*, she thought anxiously. She reached out and took Jacob's sleeve.

"Come on, let's go," she said.

"We cannot leave Letitia here with... with this... this... man," Jacob choked.

"She's not here," the artist replied flatly. "I reckon she has gone along the track that goes up over the ridge there. Now please go."

Mark also plucked at Jacob's sleeve. "Come on, Jake, let's go back to those rocks and do some fishing."

Reluctantly, Jacob began to move away. Andrew looked pained. "But I wanted to see the lighthouse," he said.

The artist pointed behind him along the beach. "You can see it from the point there."

Carmen was in a quandary. She thought she had better follow Letitia. Jacob and Mark had both moved back to the rocks and Jill joined them.

"Are you coming?" she called to Carmen.

Carmen shook her head. "I will follow Letitia. See you back at camp. Come on, Andrew."

"Aw! I wanted to see the lighthouse," Andrew said.

Anne stepped over. "I'll come with you Carmen."

"I'll go with Andrew," Martin said.

That surprised Carmen. She had assumed Martin would come with her to find his sister. "What about Letitia?" she asked.

"She can look after herself," Martin replied shortly. He turned to the artist. "Do you mind if we go along to the next point?"

"Not if you aren't going to make a fuss," the artist replied.

That jibe caused a snort of anger from Jacob, but he then turned and vanished back among the rocks, followed by Mark and Jill. Martin just shrugged and Carmen knew he was embarrassed. It also made her consider her own attitudes and she found she didn't really care how people were dressed, as long as it wasn't some sort of offensive suggestion or assault.

Andrew and Martin hurried past the man. Carmen went the same way, Anne following her. To Carmen's surprise, Anne stopped and spoke to the artist, who had turned to keep himself covered.

"Are you an artist?" she asked.

"Yes miss," the artist replied.

Carmen stopped and saw that Anne was pink from embarrassment (or was it just sunburn?) She said, "I'm sorry about all that unpleasantness."

The artist shrugged. "As I said, I thought I had this side of the island to myself."

"We are camped over at Fishermans Bay," Carmen explained.

"May I look at your painting?" Anne asked.

The artist bowed and indicated she might. So Carmen walked over with Anne to study the painting. It was, as she had suspected, quality work.

"You are a real artist," she said, as a statement rather than a question.

Again the artist bowed. "Yes miss. London Academy of Fine Art."

"You're English?" Anne queried.

Again the artist bowed. "Yes miss. James Mason, from Stafford. I am sorry we haven't been introduced."

Anne smiled. "I'm Anne and I love this! You paint really well," she enthused, indicating the painting.

Carmen could only agree. The artist had captured the tropical light so that it looked just right, the sparkle of sunlight on the sea, the green tints in the water and among the She Oaks.

"It's lovely," she agreed.

"If you want to discuss art, perhaps I should put some more clothes on," the artist said.

To Carmen's surprise, Anne replied, "Oh don't bother. It doesn't offend me." She glanced at Carmen and blushed.

To her own surprise, Carmen nodded. "Nor me." Then, to justify herself she added, "I knew that Jill was a bit of a prude, but I didn't realise that Jacob had such strong views."

"Even so," the artist replied, keeping himself covered. "You girls aren't as old as that blonde. I might be able to convince a magistrate that she had told me she was eighteen, but not you two."

Anne laughed, and Carmen said, "Letitia! Oh the lying little minx! She's only sixteen."

The artist laughed. "I'll just cover up a bit more," he said.

With that he strode across to the beached dinghy and put down the sketch to pick up a towel. Carmen could not resist a peek as he wrapped the towel around his waist. Anne also looked, then met Carmen's eye and blushed, giggling as she did. Feeling guilty Carmen checked where Jacob and Jill were. She saw that Jacob was now on top of the rocks at the end of the point. For a moment they looked at each other and she thought she detected a disapproving hostility in his look.

I think our relationship is over, she decided sadly. Then, on reflection, she shook her head and felt happier. *No, better to find out we are not suited now, before I had made any serious emotional commitment.*

The artist walked back to them, pulling on a shirt and buttoning it up as he did. He then stood beside them and explained his painting. Carmen asked how it was he could make it look so real and he showed her the tiny touches of white that gave the impression of sunlight reflecting on water.

"Do you have any other paintings?" Anne asked.

"Over in my beach hut," the artist replied, pointing across the small creek to where the sandy foot track Letitia had taken vanished into the She Oaks.

"Could we see some please?" Anne asked.

"By all means, as long as you don't mind my poor housework," the artist replied. He grinned, then spent a minute cleaning his brush and screwing the tops on tubes of oil paint.

They then walked across the tiny, ankle-deep trickle of a creek. As they went past the boat, Carmen gave it a knowledgeable appraisal and noted it was an aluminium dinghy about five metres long. It had lockers under the thwarts and was fitted with an outboard motor. A rope led from the bows up to a tree. There it was fastened by the simple expedient of passing the anchor rope around the tree and then hooking the anchor into the rope.

"Have you been on the island long?" she asked as they went up into the trees.

"Only a week. I've got another week yet and then I have to head back," the artist replied.

Twenty paces into the trees a second track branched off to the left and ran parallel to the beach for about 25 metres. The right-hand track went on inland towards the ridge. They came to a small, sandy clearing with a hut built in it. The hut was only a single room with one door and two windows. It was constructed of timber planks and sheets of corrugated iron. Out the front a tent fly had been strung between the trees to make a shady 'porch'. A blanket spread on the sand provided 'outdoor' furniture.

With a graceful gesture the artist suggested they sit. As she sat down, Carmen looked around, then said, "Oh, what a lovely view!"

Through a gap in the trees she could see down onto the beach and out over the sea. In the distance were more islands and a view of the coastal mountains.

The artist said, "I won't invite you in. It's a bachelor flat and not very tidy. Would you like some tea?"

They both said yes, and the artist went into the hut. Carmen looked in through the door and saw that the artist was right. There was a bunk with an untidy tangle of bedclothes, a couple of boxes and a suitcase overflowing with clothes, some tins of food, and a stack of paintings. The only illumination she could see was a hurricane lantern. The artist lit a small spirit stove and placed a kettle on it.

"Don't you get lonely?" she asked, as the artist returned with tin cups and spoons.

He shook his head. "Not at all. Most of the year I am surrounded by people. I either live in Sydney or in London, and I get a bit tired of the human race in the mass. This is bliss compared to those places."

He came back and poured out the tea, then offered them sugar and biscuits. "No milk, sorry," he explained. The artist took the sugar back inside then sat down as well.

Over a cup of hot, black tea they discussed painting and the artist's lifestyle. "I'm sorry about not wearing much," the artist apologised. "But when you grow up in England where the sun doesn't shine properly for much of the year, and where it rains every bloody week, you can get a bit of a thing about the sun."

"Do you paint people?" Anne asked.

"Do you mean portraits or nudes?" the artist replied.

"Both, I suppose," Anne answered, blushing as she did.

"I am trained to do both, but I prefer nudes. You would make an excellent model," the artist said.

Anne blushed bright pink, but Carmen could see she was actually pleased and took it as a compliment. As for herself, she was mildly peeved that the artist had not thought the same of her.

What has Anne got that I haven't? she wondered.

She had always considered Anne to be a bit of a 'Plain Jane', but now took a more critical look at her.

Anne made no reply to that but steered the conversation back to paintings. The artist stood up, then went into the hut. A minute later he brought out a large canvas and stood it against a tree.

Carmen suspected that the artist was quite aroused and wondered whether it wasn't time to leave. Then she shook her head.

No, there are two of us. He won't do anything, and if he tries it is our fault. He is probably turned on by having girls here. So she decided to stay, sensing that the artist was actually a nice man.

In all the artist brought out four works and stood them against trees. One that instantly appealed to Carmen was a picture of the wreck. It had been painted from the rocks where they had first seen it and it looked really good.

Andrew would love that as a present, she thought. Somewhat hesitantly, and fearing to be disappointed, she asked if it was for sale.

The artist nodded. "Yes, that is how I make my living."

"How much?" Carmen asked.

"Five hundred dollars," the artist replied. Then, seeing the disappointment on her face, added, "It took nearly four days to do."

Carmen nodded but could not reply. She did not have money like that. To change the subject, she asked about a painting that was done from inside the creek at Fishermans Bay, looking out to sea through the tunnel of trees.

"Have you seen the old ruin and cemetery?" she asked.

"Yes, but I haven't had a chance to paint there yet. I was going to but there were some very unfriendly people there," the artist said.

"Oh yes, that awful family with the dog and the bad-mannered kids," Anne said. "They have gone."

The artist shook his head. "No, not them. Some nasty looking characters off a yacht. One of them was missing an eye and a leg and looked like he was an extra from a remake of *Treasure Island.* He was Long John Silver to a tee."

"Oh I saw him in Cardwell," Carmen replied. "He is certainly a nasty looking piece of work."

"So when do you people leave?" the artist asked. "Not that I mean any offence by that. I just want to paint the scenes on your side of the island."

"We are here till Friday," Carmen replied.

The artist nodded. "So that will be next week's work then. That's alright. It will give me time to finish the one I am working on now," he replied.

After discussing the ruin and possible scenes on the other side of the island, the conversation moved on to the problem of painting the sea so that it looked real. That got them talking for half an hour about the problems of capturing on canvas the moods and colours of the ocean. Carmen was particularly interested to hear the painter say that he found it more difficult to paint the tropical sea with its bright colours than the North Atlantic in winter, with its sombre greys and dull greens.

The sound of the boy's voices ended the talk. Through a gap in the trees Carmen saw Andrew and Martin in the distance. They were heading back along the beach towards the campsite.

"We had better get going," she said, while thinking, *Andrew will not like it if he finds we have been talking to a strange man for an hour.*

As she got up, so did Anne and the artist. Then he stood and said, "Thanks for calling."

"Can we come again?" Anne asked.

"If you like. Just call out to warn me so I have time to dress respectably," he said.

Carmen blushed and then said goodbye. As she could hear Andrew and Martin getting closer, she hurried off. Anne followed. At the track junction Carmen turned left.

"Where are you going?" Anne asked.

"Up over the hill," Carmen replied. "The painter said this track goes over the ridge to the campsite. Besides, I don't want the boys to know we have been talking to a strange man for an hour."

Anne giggled and followed her. They were 50 metres inland by then and the track had begun to climb, winding up the side of the slope beside the tiny creek. It was easy walking and the track was clear and smooth. As they walked along, the two girls discussed men and what they liked and were like. Carmen realised that Anne was genuinely interested, and was assuming that because she had a brother, she knew all about such things. It embarrassed her to discuss the subject, but she responded to her friend's unspoken plea.

She needs to know, if only so that boys don't take advantage of her ignorance, she reasoned.

The whole subject of sex puzzled, interested and disgusted her. What really bothered her was that she knew her information was incomplete and what she had read about or seen on the internet she found both fascinating but also worrying, if not downright repellent. She understood that much of what was on the internet was inaccurate and that the whispered 'girl talk' of her friends was also of dubious value and wished that her parents were not so embarrassed by the subject. Not once had she been given a serious 'Mother-daughter' talk and she was now at the age where she felt she really needed that.

The track did a switch back to the right at the point where it crossed the small creek. This was in the jungle and there was a small pool dammed by the stones used to make the path. Then the track angled south up the side of the slope, to emerge on the open, rocky ridge top a few hundred paces further on. Here they were granted a wonderful view of half the horizon. Clearly visible below them was the wreck on its reef.

"There are Jacob and Mark," Anne said, pointing.

Carmen saw the tiny figures down on the rocks beside the sea. Then she saw Jill and her brother. Martin climbed into view as she watched. She did not call out or linger. In her mind it was important to get back to camp to talk to Letitia before the others returned.

So they crossed the ridge top and plunged into thick rain forest on the eastern slope. The track angled down fairly steeply but was still a definite bench cut, very clear and easy to follow. About 50 paces down the girls came to a fork in the track. One track went off to the left, southeast. Carmen paused for a moment, thought, then took the right-hand track.

"That other track goes down to the ruin I think," she said, remembering the track which went past the pump shed and small dam near the ruin.

Her guess was correct. Five minutes later they came down into almost flat jungle and reached the creek just across from their tents. By then Carmen was in a lather of self-doubt. She was heartily ashamed of herself and was thinking that maybe Jacob had been right: that they should be more modest. That got her worrying about what to say to Letitia when she found her.

She need not have bothered. Letitia wasn't at the camp. Nor was anyone else.

"Let's check the beach," she suggested.

After a quick drink, for she was thirsty again after the walk over the hill, she led the way out to the end of the jetty.

Letitia was on the beach. Carmen saw her sitting in the shade near the three pandanus palms near the cemetery. She was now wearing a white T-shirt and shorts and was staring out to sea.

"There she is. Let's go and talk to her," Anne said.

Carmen stood at the end of the jetty and bit her lip in indecision. "No, not yet," she replied.

Now that they had found her, she could not think of what to say. She stood there, looking out to sea to avoid staring at Letitia. That made her aware of Letitia's parents. They were still fishing out on the water and were at least a kilometre away. The two girls turned and walked back into the shade of the closest trees.

As they sat downs Anne said, "I can't compete with her."

She said this with such bitterness that Carmen glanced sharply at her. "What do you mean?"

"Letitia, with Andrew. He can't take his eyes off her and he hardly even notices me," Anne replied.

Carmen wanted to say something comforting, or to deny, but she could only sigh and agree.

"He is certainly infatuated with her. I really worry that he will get hurt."

For a while the two girls sat in gloomy silence. Most of Carmen's thoughts were centred on her own situation regarding Jacob but after a while she consciously thrust these aside and tried to think of a strategy to help Anne win Andrew's attention, if not her affection. But she had to admit that competing with Letitia's uninhibited attitudes and ample charms was not going to be easy.

Anne agreed with that observation. "Besides, I am not the sort of person to act like that," she said. "I don't want him to think I am cheap or easy."

"You are right," Carmen replied, feeling sad for Letitia as well. She glanced in her direction, then pointed along the beach. "Here come the boys now. I wonder what they found."

Chapter 17

DARE

As Andrew and Martin walked back along the beach at Careenage Bay, Andrew was in a ferment of lust and inner conflict. The sight of Letitia had set him on fire with urgent desire. His mind flooded with fiery memories of those few ecstatic moments back in January when she had joined him in the shower. The gentle smoothness of her skin, the softness, the sheer magical pleasure and burning desire! But gnawing at his lust was guilt. Self-doubt and self-loathing tormented him. He knew he was causing his sister worry, and he knew he was hurting Anne's feelings. There was also the moral issue.

Pure lust is anything but pure, he told himself. *It is immoral, and sinful.*

Jacob's Biblical injunction came back to trouble his conscience. Andrew was not very religious, rarely went to church, but he had imbibed enough good old Hellfire theology to feel stabs of doubt, and to worry.

Then other concerns crowded in: of despising himself for being weak enough to be tempted; and then despising himself for not being a 'real man'. That sent another spiral of worry swirling around his mind: *Am I good enough? Will I be able to do it if I ever get the chance? Will I turn out to be impotent?*

It was all a bit much and he tried to push the thoughts out of his mind. But they kept flooding back, with embarrassing effects on his body. Also he suspected that Martin had been deeply embarrassed by his sister's behaviour so made no mention of the incident.

From Bennet Point they had been able to see the lighthouse on Cape Saunders. Having observed the next beach, Stingray Bay, the two boys had turned back. After climbing back down the rocks to the beach, they had set off southward along it. As they walked, Andrew had kept straining his eyes for a sight of the artist but could see no sign of him.

The issue of nudity had also got him worried. He had rarely been seen naked by either his parents or his sister, at least not in the last few years, and he had never been naked in public. Thus he was amazed and anxious about his reaction this time. He had been annoyed and jealous. When the artist had told them that Letitia had just walked up to him and started talking to him, he had been astounded. Then the jealousy and hurt had followed.

Instinctively he had known the man wasn't lying. Letitia had approached the man. Andrew was sure of that. The thought of her standing there with the artist able to see everything, now got Andrew into an angry turmoil of resentment and jealousy. To his own disgust, he knew that he wanted to do such a thing with Letitia. Then the whole spiral of moral arguments began again.

Martin pointed to the left into the trees. "There's a hut there. That must be where that painter is living," he said.

Andrew glanced that way, saw no sign of the man and just grunted and kept on walking. He felt very mixed up and anxious and just wanted to get away from the place. As quickly as he could walk without betraying his fear by actually running, he led the way past the beached dinghy and across the shallow creek. He found it a relief to climb back among the rocks and around to Wreck Bay.

He had been hoping that the sight of the wreck might bring back pleasant daydreams, but this was not to be. As soon as they climbed around the small point, he saw Jacob, Mark, and Jill standing fishing on the rocks of Snapper Point. That brought back the sense of the incident with the artist and the harsh words by Jacob and Jill. In turn that led Andrew's thoughts into a fluster of doubt about how to handle the situation.

What will I say? he worried.

The solution came from doubt: he said nothing at all about it. Instead, he asked how the fishing was. Several silver and pink fish about 40 centimetres long lay on the rocks.

"Are they snapper?" he asked.

Jacob shook his head. "No, coral trout."

"They are good eating, aren't they?"

"Yes, if they don't have Sigratera," Jacob replied.

Andrew had heard of the sickness caused by poison in the flesh of some tropical fish, so they discussed the likelihood of this but then shrugged and philosophically decided the risk was low. All the while that they were talking, Andrew was wondering where Letitia was and his impatience to see her led him into saying he was going back to camp.

Martin came with him, the two boys following the walking track back around Snapper Point. As soon as they rounded the last rocks, Andrew saw Letitia sitting alone near the far end of the beach. Seeing her dressed induced instant regret, mixed with relief. Again there was the concern over what to say. This also came to nothing as Carmen and Anne appeared near the jetty and came to meet them.

Thus the awkward moment passed, and Letitia was left to join in the general conversation when she at last joined them. While they chatted about the lighthouse and fishing, Andrew saw the Schipholl's boat making its way in to the pier, so he and Martin walked there to meet them and to tie the boat up. The adults had caught a really fine red emperor and a couple of passable whiting so it was obvious what the next few meals would be. Andrew joined Martin when he offered to scale and fillet the fish.

"And don't throw the gut and remains into the sea," Mr Schipholl cautioned. "That might attract predators who might think we are their next meal."

Cleaning and filleting the fish kept them all busy for the next half hour. While they were doing that, Jacob, Jill ,and Mark joined them and their fish were also dealt with. The fish provided enough of a topic so that no mention was made of Letitia's incident with the painter. Andrew hoped that no-one would mention it, to save her from trouble or embarrassment and to his relief nobody did.

What Andrew had trouble doing was taking his eyes off Letitia. Every few seconds he found his thoughts, and then his eyes, wandering to her. In a determined attempt to stop this he devoted deliberate attention to Anne. That she appreciated this was at once obvious as she smiled and happily replied.

Satisfied he had a better plan to keep his mind from straying to evil thoughts of Letitia, Andrew walked back to camp with Anne. When he got there, he made a deliberate effort to avoid looking at Letitia. Anne responded by being friendly. That made Andrew feel guilty and anxious, and the few glances he gave Letitia were answered by anxious little smiles.

Tea was grilled fish. Andrew helped cook, savouring the aroma of the frying flesh. Not only did he enjoy the cooking, but it helped him to calm down. Much of the time Anne stood beside him and helped, the adults sitting back and insisting that, as they had done the catching, it was not their duty to cook.

By the time tea was eaten twilight had set in. It was still quite hot and humid and working near the fire added to this, but Andrew found he was now relaxed and content. However, he didn't stay that way for long. After the cleaning up was done, they all sat around the lantern and discussed the day's discoveries. This got Andrew both interested and anxious. His concern was that someone would mention the artist, so that Letitia's parents would find out what she had done. To his relief, no-one did, although they skated around the topic a couple of times and there were a few glances exchanged.

It was Mark who changed the subject, thereby sparking the dare. He said, "Who wants to go to the dunny?"

As the toilet was only about 30 metres away, Andrew thought this a strange comment. "The dunny is just over there," he said, pointing into the darkness.

Mark appeared to move uncomfortably on his seat. "I know," he agreed. Then he reluctantly added, "It's just that being so close to that cemetery makes it kind of scary going to it in the dark."

"Are you scared?" Martin challenged.

For a moment Mark did not reply. Then he nodded and confessed, "Yes."

Martin curled his lip in derision, but before he could say anything Jill said, "I think cemeteries at night are really spooky."

"Me too!" agreed Anne. "They are bad enough in the daytime."

"Oh piffle!" Martin scoffed.

"They are so!" retorted Carmen.

"Rot!" Martin answered.

Jacob now spoke up. "If you are so brave, you go out to the middle of it on your own then."

That put Martin on the spot. His face changed and Andrew could see he was trying to come up with some answer. Finally bravado won.

"Alright. What if we all go?"

"Okay," agreed Mark, "But let's go to the toilet first."

"Why? So you don't crap yourself when you see a ghost?" teased Martin.

There was laughter at that, but Andrew could see that the dare had taken hold on their minds. Letitia added to it by agreeing and saying, "We will all walk through the cemetery together, right across to Sandy Beach and back."

The teenagers all stood up and Carmen went to her tent and reappeared with a torch. Mrs Schipholl remained seated and said, "You children be careful. Don't do anything silly, and no running around in the dark. Make sure you have shoes on. And take your torches."

"Aren't you coming, Mum?" Martin asked.

"No, father and I will stay here, or we might go for a stroll out to the jetty," Mrs Schipholl answered.

"I want to listen to the radio," Mr Schipholl added. "I'd like to hear what the weather forecast is. I know it's the end of the cyclone season, but we would look a right pack of noddies to be caught here by one."

"Cyclone! The cyclone season ends in March," Martin replied scornfully.

"You still get the odd one in April," Mr Schipholl replied. "It's hot enough for one."

Andrew listened to this without much concern. Cyclones formed way out in the Coral Sea and usually took several days to form and make landfall on the Queensland coast, if they came that way at all. He knew there was an elaborate system of satellites and radar and weather stations to detect and track the huge storms, so he wasn't worried.

"We will get a couple of days warning," he commented.

The teenagers all trooped over to the toilets. Once away from the tents and the warm glow of the lantern, everything was very dark. The moon was not yet up, would not be up for nearly another hour. Andrew wondered if he should also get his torch but decided not to.

There is enough light to see, he thought.

Mark had his torch and when he turned it on inside the toilet the beam accentuated the shadows and made things even spookier. Martin did not help by waiting outside and jumping out to cry 'Boo!' when they came out.

"Don't be silly, Martin!" Mark snapped, betraying his anxiety by the quaver in his voice.

"Wait till you see a real ghost," Martin replied with a grin.

"Stop that nonsense," Carmen replied. "There are no such things as ghosts."

"Yes, there are," Jacob contradicted. "The Bible says so. Christians believe in the Holy Trinity: Father, Son and Holy Ghost."

"Holy Spirit," Anne corrected.

Jacob disagreed. "That is just modern jargon to try to make it sound better. The old versions called Him the Holy Ghost."

"I believe in ghosts," Jill added, sounding quite nervous.

"Don't forget there's supposed to be one who walks the island on the full moon," Martin said.

"Oh there is not!" Carmen said irritably.

"Yes, there is," Martin insisted. "I read it in those historical notes of yours. There was a murder at the tourist resort; a waitress was raped and strangled. The murderer then committed suicide."

Jill looked shocked. "Oh, stop talking like that!" she cried.

By then they had started walking along the track towards the cemetery. All the talk of ghosts now had Andrew feeling distinctly anxious. He did not want to admit to himself it was fear, and he tried to tell himself he didn't believe in ghosts but that did little to calm him. He now wished the subject had never come up but did not want to admit he was scared. So he walked along behind Jacob and Martin. Anne followed him and the others trailed along behind.

In the darkness the shadows among the bushes and trees beside the track looked dark and sinister. Andrew kept glancing at them anxiously, trying to consciously conjure up an exciting daydream to push the superstitious thoughts out of his mind. Even thoughts of Letitia did not help much. The group came out into the grassy clearing of the old cemetery just as the glow of the moon began showing above the hill ahead of them. The loom of growing moonlight seemed to cast an eerie glow over the place. In the dark the tombstones looked bigger and much spookier and Andrew, to his own dismay, shivered.

The sandy paths were easy to see, and the group had no trouble keeping to them. Every few paces Mark or Carmen shone their torch on a headstone to read it. Andrew rather wished they wouldn't as the torchlight spoilt his night vision. It also made the shadows darker and added to the creepy feel of the place.

Then something scuttled among the dead leaves and grass off to the left. "What's that?" Anne cried anxiously. She stepped over against Andrew and grabbed at his arm.

"Just a rat or a possum," Martin said with a derisive snort.

Then Jacob went, "Whooo! Hooooo!"

The hairs on the back of Andrew's neck prickled and he glanced anxiously around, even though his rational mind told him it was only Jacob playing the fool.

Carmen obviously wasn't amused. "Stop that Jacob!" she snapped.

Jacob did, but he chuckled. Andrew found he was holding Anne's hand and noted that she was trembling with nervousness. The group resumed walking, taking the track to the left which led past the end of the hill to the Secret Beach. The track was too narrow to walk side by side, so Andrew released Anne's hand, not sure if he was glad or sad.

Do I really want to have a romance with her? he wondered. She was nice enough but...

Coming out of the long grass and bushes at Pirate Cove was like stepping into another world. The rim of the moon was just peeking above the horizon, flooding a rippling silver path across the sea to them. The wind was cool and the waves just big enough to break with a flurry of foam. The beach was white under the stars and the shadows among the large boulders looked more exciting than menacing.

"Oh! Isn't this lovely!" exclaimed Letitia.

She pranced down the beach to the edge of the water. In the moonlight she looked radiantly attractive. Andrew had the distinct feeling that, but for the presence of Jacob and Jill, she would have peeled off her clothes there and then. But he had to agree. In the moonlight the little beach had a magical and romantic feel about it.

Perversely he reacted to his attraction and lust for Letitia by moving over next to Anne again. He did not take her hand, but he talked to her. Carmen joined them and seemed to nod approval.

Anne pointed out to sea. "What's that big black thing?" she asked.

Andrew looked. He could see the silhouette of several islands, looking like black cardboard cut-outs against the moonlight. Then a flicker of light caught his eye, and he saw what Anne meant. After puzzling for a moment he replied.

"It's a thunderstorm," he explained.

The storm was a long way off and, now that he looked more carefully, Andrew noted other banks of dark clouds along the horizon or against the stars.

"Oh I'd love to have a swim!" Letitia cried, still skipping and dancing around on the sand.

It was so hot and humid that Andrew had to agree that a swim would be lovely, but he had a deep-seated fear of swimming in the sea at the best of times, never mind at night.

Carmen vetoed the suggestion emphatically. "No way! Never swim in the sea at night. If you get into difficulties and slip under no-one will be able to find you, and remember that the sharks find you by electricity and smell as much as anything."

"Electricity?" Anne asked.

"They have little sensors along the sides of their body that pick up electrical discharges from living creatures," Carmen explained.

The thought of sharks instantly doused any further desires for swimming. Andrew shuddered and looked at the rippling waves, now showing back and silver as the moon edged further up.

You would never see a fin against that, he thought.

He well knew that sharks rarely swam with their fin sticking out of the water anyway. Any shark attack would be a totally unexpected surprise attack. His mind recoiled from even contemplating the savage ferocity of such an event.

"Let's go back to camp," Jill said.

"Through the cemetery or some other way?" Mark asked.

"The cemetery," Carmen replied. "It is by far the quickest and easiest way."

"Alone," Martin challenged.

Anne gasped. "Oh don't be silly!"

Jacob turned to Martin. "Bet you aren't game," he dared.

"Bet I am! I will if you are game," Martin replied.

"Who else?" Jacob asked.

That caused Andrew to feel distinctly put on the spot. His male pride was now on the line, and he found himself answering, "I will."

Carmen snorted, "Oh you boys are silly. I'm not having anything to do with this. I'm going back in a group. Who is coming with me?"

Jill, Anne, and Mark at once said they would. Martin then said, "You go first and wait at the toilet. You can then check that we do in fact do it on our own."

"Alright, but don't be long. I'm tired," Carmen replied.

"Five minutes before the first one," Martin replied, glancing at his watch to check the time.

The group set off back and as they disappeared along the track Jacob said, "Okay, what order?"

There was some discussion and it was during this that Andrew became aware that Letitia had stayed and was standing close to him.

Is she hoping to stay here to be alone with someone? he wondered. He met her eyes, saw them twinkle in the starlight, and that sent his heart rate soaring. *Surely it couldn't be me?* he thought, his hopes shooting up.

It was agreed that Martin would go first, then Letitia, then Jacob, and finally Andrew. He wasn't too happy about this, partly because he was scared and partly because he wanted to be with Letitia. However, there was nothing for it but to carry on. Martin set off chuckling along the path. They then counted out five minutes before Letitia followed, after glancing 'meaningfully' at Andrew.

Was she trying to send me a signal? he wondered.

That got him anxious. On top of being scared he found he was almost hyperventilating. By a mental effort he resolved to behave and to be nice to Anne.

Jacob checked his watch and set off, leaving Andrew alone on the beach. Now he did shiver. The place suddenly seemed much more threatening and lonely and he glanced anxiously around. For a couple of minutes he stood there, looking in all directions, deliberately imagining pirates coming ashore in a longboat. He watched distant lighting flicker in the thunderstorm, then tried to tell himself he wasn't scared.

Finally he set off, a minute or so early. To his annoyance, he found he was almost gulping air and was very nervous.

Don't be ridiculous, he told himself. *There are no such things as ghosts.*

Then he let out a gasp of horror as a white object rose from behind the first large tombstone.

"Got ya!" cried Letitia with a giggle.

"Holy shit!" Andrew gasped, jumping back, his heart leaping into his throat.

He had been expecting either Martin of Jacob would try to frighten him but not quite so soon, and not her.

"Shh! Get down," hissed Letitia, grabbing at his sleeve.

"Wha... why"" Andrew replied. Now his heart was hammering furiously and he was experiencing waves of hot and cold.

She moved over closer and whispered in Andrew's ear. "Because Jacob and Martin are hiding along there further. They want to scare me," she replied.

She was so close he could now smell her. Her scent caused his heart to hammer in a different way.

"What do you want me to do?" he asked.

"Come with me and we will sneak around them," Letitia said.

"Which way?" Andrew asked, puzzled and wondering what it was Letitia really wanted.

"Down to the front beach and along to the jetty," Letitia suggested.

Andrew nodded. He raised his head and studied the cemetery. The moonlight was now lighting it up, causing the rows of headstones to gleam whitely. It looked even more spooky and there was an un-nerving silence. Andrew looked around to select the best route. He noted that there was a faint foot trail leading southwards towards the beach. He knew it was that direction because the moon was on his left and the stars of the Southern Cross were visible ahead of him. After a careful study to try to detect any lurking 'ghosts', he started moving at a crouch in the direction of the dark line of banyan figs which edged the beach.

The trees were 50 metres away and looked black in the night. The shadows under them were inky. Andrew moved slowly from one row of headstones to the next, pausing to listen and to peek around each one before moving to the next. He found it hard to hear because his heart was hammering so hard. Now he was very anxious, worrying about what the others might be thinking. Letitia moved close behind him.

A few minutes of careful creeping got them to the line of trees. Andrew saw that they were just near the rocks and three pandanus palms. Here they paused, hidden in the deep shadows. Andrew stood against the trunk of a tree and scanned the now moonlit beach. There was nobody in sight, but he realised that they could not go that way.

The others will guess what we are doing and will wait under the trees to catch us, he reasoned.

As he stood there, he became very aware of Letitia. She stepped close and their arms touched. She leaned even closer and whispered, "Hold me, I'm scared."

Before Andrew could decide what to do, she had snuggled against him. It was both a shock and a delight. Andrew felt her press against his arms and chest. Stabs of mixed alarm and pleasure shot through him.

Carmen and Anne will work out I am with Letitia, he reasoned.

He was unable to decide if that was good or bad, but it made him feel guilty. It also made him feel scared. He sensed that Letitia was serious. Faced with the possibility of having reality thrust upon him, he quickly got cold feet.

She's a bit too full on for me, he thought.

"We had better get going," he said, his voice coming out as a shameful croak. "Or everyone will wonder where we are."

"Let them wonder," Letitia said, snuggling closer and putting her arms around him.

Now Andrew felt trapped. He knew he was becoming aroused but equally he felt so anxious and cornered that he just wanted to get away. Before he could say anything, she kissed him, pressing hard against him as she did. To Andrew, it was almost overwhelming. He had kissed Letitia before but this time she was panting hard. The fear that he might be about to do something he would later really regret began to grip him.

His senses received another shock when she gripped him tightly. The result was almost overwhelming in desire and sheer pleasure. Lust surged, to mingle with the mounting panic. It was now very obvious to him what she was in the mood for.

What should I do? he wondered.

He was gasping now, almost sobbing as the passion and emotion mounted. He knew his body was all but out of control of his mind, his hands starting to roam her body.

Someone was coming! Andrew saw the movement out in the moonlight in the graveyard.

"Someone heading this way," he whispered, his mouth so dry that it came out as a hoarse croak. "We must get out of here!"

Chapter 18

CAUGHT OUT

Anne turned to Carmen and said, "They are taking a long time. I wonder where they are?" They were waiting near the toilet.

Carmen had been thinking the same thing. She noted the anxiety in Anne's voice and that gelled with her own worries. It was the fact that Letitia was one of the last group that was causing her worry.

I hope Andrew isn't doing something silly, she thought.

At that moment, a boy screamed in fear out in the darkness. Then Jacob's angry voice sounded clearly.

"Bugger you, Martin! You scared the living daylights out of me!"

There was the sound of chuckling and then some shouting that Carmen did not catch. "Jacob is chasing Martin, I think," she said.

Anne nodded. In the light of the lantern Carmen saw her bite her lip. She looked quite down and anxious. Next to them Jill looked around.

"Where has Mark gone?" she queried.

Carmen and Anne both looked. Carmen was surprised. "He was here a minute ago."

"I'll bet he's joined the other boys in their silly game," Anne said.

Jill pursed her lips. "Letitia is still with them too," she said.

There were more shouts and then someone yelled, "Boo!" Another short scream and expletive were followed by more laughter, disrupted as the person doing it was obviously running.

"Silly boys! They are chasing each other around the cemetery," Anne said.

"I hope nobody hurts themselves," Carmen commented.

Mrs Schipholl looked up from her reading. "I thought I told them not to run."

Jill answered. "You did, but they are boys and their brains aren't that good."

There was more distant laughter and then silence settled, broken only by the swash of the waves on the beach and the gentle rustle of leaves. A faint breeze reached them.

"Oh thank heavens!" Carmen commented. "It was getting much too hot."

The girls stood listening, staring into the darkness. They had now been back at the camp for over twenty minutes. The faint grumble of distant thunder reached Carmen's ears as she strained to work out what was going on out in the darkness. With every passing minute she became more anxious.

Ten more minutes went by. There were no more noises from the cemetery. Then the swishing sound of someone walking on sand sounded from along the track leading to the jetty. The girls all turned to look. Into view walked Andrew.

"Andrew! Why did you come that way?" Carmen asked.

Andrew stopped when he reached them. "I was dodging around the others. I reckoned they would try to jump out and scare me, so I went around them along the beach," he replied.

"Have you seen Letitia?" Anne asked, stepping closer to Andrew.

Carmen saw a momentary look of distress cross Andrew's face and she instantly feared the worst. Then he hesitated before answering. Even as he opened his mouth Anne attacked.

"You have, haven't you?"

Again Andrew hesitated and his mouth opened and shut. Then he nodded. "Yes. I saw her back in the cemetery."

"What was she doing?" Anne asked, her voice very soft but full of hurt.

"She jumped out to frighten me," Andrew replied. To Carmen, he looked very uneasy and she was sure that he and Letitia had done something.

"Where is she now?" Jill asked.

Andrew gestured vaguely. "Back there somewhere. She was trying to hide among some bushes when I last saw her."

Anne looked unhappy but she said nothing. Carmen studied Andrew's face by the light of the lantern and was sure he and Letitia had been doing more than hiding. That got her worrying about what exactly they had been doing.

More thunder growled in the distance. "That storm is getting closer," Andrew said, obviously trying to change the subject.

There were more shouts out in the cemetery, but Carmen could not tell who it was making them. Then there were more footsteps from the direction of the jetty. Mark appeared.

"Where have you been?" Jill snapped.

Mark stopped and looked worried. "I just went to check if the boat is alright," he replied.

Jill stepped over beside him. "Did you see Letitia?"

"No," Mark answered immediately.

Jill quickly leaned forward before stepping quickly back. "You did so! You've been with her! I can smell her," she cried, hurt and anger sounding in her voice.

Mark looked stunned. He tried to speak but Jill spun on her heel and stalked off to her tent.

Oh dear! Carmen thought. *Mark has been sneaky, and he has now been caught out. Oh, what a silly boy!* Then she shook her head sadly. *What a fool! Why would any boy pass up a girl like Jill for a trollop like Letitia?* But in her heart she understood. Letitia was alluring. Letitia had the reputation of being easy. *Males!* she thought in angry exasperation.

Then Carmen became aware that Andrew was frowning and looking shocked. That opened another can of worms. She guessed that, if Letitia had also kissed Mark, he was feeling betrayed and cheated.

Poor Andrew. I hope he doesn't think he is in love with Letitia, she thought.

An uneasy silence settled on the group. Carmen saw that Mrs Schipholl was glancing at them with a worried frown on her face and that got her worrying about what she might have heard.

After all, Letitia is her daughter.

Carmen did not want a really embarrassing scene that would make things so unpleasant that the holiday would be spoilt. She wasn't exactly enjoying the holiday but equally she did not want it all to end in frosty resentment or harsh words.

That got her thinking about Jacob. She was well aware that her initial high hopes of love had turned to dust.

Jacob is not the man for me, she told herself.

That got her feeling sad and wistful. Part of her felt jealous of Letitia, fleeting fantasies of being kissed in the moonlight adding to this.

Oh well, plenty more fish in the sea, as Mum says, she thought.

It was Letitia who appeared next. She also walked in from the beach, reinforcing the suspicions that she and Mark may have met. When she saw them there, she smiled and said, "That was fun! I really scared Martin."

Anne made no reply. Mark looked uncomfortable and just nodded. Andrew grunted. Letitia looked from one to the other and frowned.

"What's wrong?" she asked.

Anne answered her. "Jill thinks you met Mark down on the beach."

"Oh I did not!" Letitia cried. "I was in the cemetery."

"You saw Andrew there," Anne said flatly.

Letitia opened her mouth, shut it, looked from Anne to Andrew, then scowled. "So what? I just gave him a fright. Anyway, it's none of your business. You don't own him," she said.

Carmen had been following all of this with close interest. To confirm or allay her suspicions, she moved to catch a whiff of Letitia's perfume. Then she sidled over beside a very uncomfortable looking Andrew, who was now eyeing an unhappy looking Mark. Very faintly she detected traces of Letitia's scent on him.

He has been with her, she thought.

There was a brittle silence. It was clear to Carmen that both boys were too shocked and unsure to know what to say. They just kept exchanging worried and faintly hostile glances. Anne stood looking unhappy. Both Mr and Mrs Schipholl sat and watched but did not join in. Carmen was sure both parents were embarrassed.

I would be, if I had a daughter like Letitia, she thought.

She eyed Letitia with fascinated askance, wondering if she really had been at least kissed by two boys within a few minutes of each other.

For the next few minutes the tension seemed to crackle like the electricity in the distant storm. The situation was changed by the return of Martin and Jacob, both of whom were puffing from running. They were happy and laughing and their comments on the game of hide and seek in the cemetery eased the tension and allowed a semblance of normality to return. Mrs Schipholl moved things along more by getting up and asking them if they wanted supper. She gave people jobs and asked Anne and Carmen to prepare Milo.

Another, louder, rumble of thunder caused Mr Schipholl to get up.

"I don't like the sound of that. You boys come with me and we will move the boat right up to the trees," he said.

"It's not a cyclone, is it?" Anne asked anxiously.

Mr Schipholl shook his head. "No, just a thunderstorm. It may not even hit the island. Thunderstorms are usually quite localised and only last a few hours. Cyclones are massive and last for days."

He and the boys vanished into the darkness. Letitia followed them, her retreating back earning an unfriendly glare from Anne. Carmen then stood watching Anne spooning sugar and Milo into cups, wondering what to do.

Should I try to speak to Jill? Or should I just let her get over it in her own way? she worried. The whole situation had her annoyed. *Blast Letitia! Why can't life be nicer, and less complicated?* she thought.

Finally, Carmen decided she would try to draw Jill out. She went to the tent and said, "Supper is ready if you want some Jill."

From inside came snuffles and then Jill muttered, "I don't want any, thanks."

"You alright?"

"No, just leave me alone please."

All that Carmen could then do was withdraw and rejoin the others at the table. When the group returned from securing the boat there was more tension, but the hot drinks and food helped ease this. It was after 9pm by then and Carmen felt quite tired. As soon as the washing up was done, she retreated to her tent. Letitia joined her, acting defiantly defensive. Rather than make an issue of it, Carmen just prepared her bed and got ready, then slipped into it. As usual, Letitia again stripped off her trousers and pulled on a big T-shirt before getting into her own bed.

That disturbed Carmen slightly, more because she found she had an urge to look than from any prudery. She resisted this and lay back, pretending to be asleep. Then she heard Anne and Jill muttering in the next tent. Most of the words were too muffled but their general tone was clear. The words were unhappy and there were sniffles and tears. Once Carmen thought she heard Jill say, 'cheap slut' and another time she thought it was 'two-timing tart'. She hoped Letitia could not hear but did think the comments justified.

Carmen lay in her sleeping bag worrying. She tried hard to think of a plan to retrieve the social situation before it became intolerable, but no sure design came to her. Instead, she found she was sweating. It had become so hot and still that she pushed her sleeping bag open and half off her. Then she got up and opened the front flap of the tent and brailed it up. Outside was now a bright dapple of moonlight and the shadows of the leaves.

She lay down on her side, facing away from Letitia and returned to trying to come up with a plan to make the holiday a success. After a time she drifted into a restless sleep.

KA-BAM!

Carmen sat up, her heart hammering in fright. Then lightning lit up the whole place and there was another massive crack of thunder.

"Only a storm," she told herself, reassured.

Beside her, Letitia had also sat up and was holding her arms across her bosom, her eyes wide. "Bloody hell!" she cried. "That gave me a fright. I was just having a nice dream too."

Carmen was about to make a sarcastic rejoinder about what type of dream when there was another flash of lightning, then more thunder. The time between the flash and the shattering bang was only moments and she guessed that the bolt had struck somewhere up on the ridge to the west. With that came a rush of fear. She tried to be rational and tell herself hardly anyone ever got hit by lightning and that being in a tent down among the trees on the low ground was safe, but even so the next flash caused her to jump and her heart to palpitate. Then another sound reached her ears and she tensed.

It was the sound of the wind roaring in the trees. Within seconds it had reached them and with it came rain: heavy, driving rain. Heavy drops began to stream in through the open tent flap. Letitia at once cried out and moved to try to close it. As she did, the wind gusted and rain blew in.

"I can't untie it," Letitia shrieked.

Carmen scrambled up, pushing against her as her own fingers groped at the knots. By the time she had the flap untied and rolled down both she and Letitia had been soaked on their heads and upper bodies. They both sat back on their bedding gasping and wiping drops from their faces. More lightening flared. Carmen shook her head and groped around for her towel.

Then another problem revealed itself. Water was flowing into the tent along the ground. Worse still, one of the corner pegs was suddenly wrenched out by the wind and began failing dangerously around. With difficulty, Carmen gripped the edge of the tent with one hand, using the other to protect her eyes. She managed to grab the loose peg, but the tent kept straining and flapping in the wind. Carmen was both amazed and frightened at how strong the wind was.

"This needs two people to fix," she yelled to Letitia.

"I'll get the hammer," Letitia called back.

Before Carmen realised what Letitia intended, she slid out of the tent. Another flash of lightning illuminated her as she ran across to her parent's tent. Carmen crouched, gripping the flogging tent tightly. She saw Letitia kneel and call inside. Mr Schipholl's head appeared and he pointed. As Letitia made her way to the woodpile, Mr Schipholl came crawling out of his tent. All he wore were a T-shirt and a pair of shorts.

Letitia went to a box under the table and began rooting through it. Mr Schipholl joined her and they both scampered across to where Carmen was. Mr Schipholl quickly grasped the tent corner and held it down, then looped a piece of rope around an exposed tree root and secured it to that. By then Letitia had found a small spade and she came and bent over near the tent and began digging.

"Storm drain," she yelled above the noise of wind and rain.

That was something Carmen knew about. She pointed and called back, "It has to be close, in under the edge of the tent. And shovel the sand into the tent. The drain will only channel some of the water away. What we really need is a dam to keep the flow out."

Letitia looked doubtful so Carmen repeated what she had said, adding, "The drain is also a borrow pit to get the soil for the dam. Quickly, water is flowing in."

At that, Letitia began carefully scooping sand to where Carmen could pile it up. She glanced around and saw that faces were peering from both of the boy's tents and also from the other girl's tent. In the next flash of lightning Carmen saw that Jill and Anne were both looking, Jill's face a mask of sour disapproval.

Mr Schipholl was now busy digging around the parent's tent and Carmen saw that Mark and Andrew had both come out into the rain and were digging.

She called to Letitia, "Letitia! The boys can see you."

Letitia glanced in the direction of the boy's tents but just shrugged. "They won't see much, and anyway, they won't mind."

Another flash of lightning clearly revealed Letitia's wet T-shirt clinging to her. "Letitia, they can see you. Come inside," she said.

"It'll be right."

"Jill and Anne can see you."

"Stuff Jill!" Letitia replied, or at least that's what Carmen thought she said as a huge clap of thunder drowned most of it.

"Please, don't make things worse," Carmen pleaded.

"What about the drain?"

"We have enough sand," Carmen replied.

"Okay, just a sec." Letitia replied.

She then stood up and walked quickly through the downpour across to where Mark was digging with his bare hands. He looked up in surprise as she spoke to him. Carmen saw Mark's eyes goggle as Letitia handed him the spade and for a moment Carmen thought she was going to stay and help him dig. Then Letitia turned and hurried back, Mark's eyes on her the whole way.

Oh I hope Jill isn't watching, Carmen thought. She looked across at the other girl's tent and saw that she was, and that she did not look happy. *Oh dear caught again!*

Letitia crawled into the tent, giggling and gasping. "It is wet!" she cried, adding, "And bloody cold."

"Letitia! Get better dressed please," Carmen snapped. She was now both offended and embarrassed.

Letitia made a face but then reached for her towel. While she dried her face and hair, Carmen concentrated on patting the low earth dam she had constructed into a firm wall. Outside the boys and Mr Schipholl were still busy.

Finally holding the towel over her front, Letitia leaned forward and asked, "Do you think it will flood?"

Carmen shook her head. "No. The storm is already passing."

"I meant the creek," Letitia replied.

Carmen now realised she could hear water rushing down the nearby creek. That was a something she hadn't considered. After a moment's thought she again shook her head.

"No, I don't think it will come that high."

"I'll have a look. Where's your torch?" Letitia replied.

"Letitia, for heaven's sake! Stop running around like that before you upset everyone. Please stay in the tent," Carmen cried.

To her relief, Letitia did. She pouted and looked as though she was going to argue but then sat back on her damp bedding.

"The boy's won't mind."

"Jacob does," Carmen answered, "And I don't want Andrew all aroused. It's not fair to tease them."

At the mention of Andrew's name, Letitia sniffed and glanced in the direction of his tent. She opened her mouth but then seemed to change her mind and closed it again. That got Carmen worrying.

Oh dear! I wonder what happened out there tonight?

Chapter 19

BUCCANEERS

As Andrew looked out of his tent, he was certainly aroused. Letitia had stood only a metre away and the lightning had revealed seemingly every curvaceous detail of her lovely shape, the wet cloth clinging to her. Then, as she had walked back to her tent and crawled in, another flicker had allowed him to see her clearly. It had all been a bit much, on top of the earlier events of the night. The rain and the cold had no effect on the surge of lust he experienced, and he was glad that Mark was busy outside.

Having finished their storm drain, Andrew moved back to his own side of the tent and sat on his damp bedding. He had been wearing a T-shirt and shorts, but the shirt was now soaked so he peeled it off. Mark crawled in beside him and groped around for his towel.

Mr Schipholl appeared at the front opening. "You boys come with me while I check the boat," he said.

Both boys crawled out and followed him along the path. Mr Schipholl had a torch, but it was not really needed as the lightning flashes were so frequent. Andrew was quickly soaked but did not mind. To his mind it was a real adventure and he at once began to embellish it with fantasy: the buccaneers had rescued the beautiful Mistress of the Plantation and were making their way back to their boat. The face and figure of the rescued girl were at first Letitia's, but those images seemed to blur and waver as Andrew thought regretfully about the earlier incident in the cemetery.

When Letitia had started kissing him at the cemetery, he had been surprised and then mesmerised. He had felt like a bird hypnotised by a snake. The feel of her had sent his lust soaring. Even so, he had felt somehow trapped, as though he was being pushed too quickly into something he feared he might regret. When they had been hiding from Jacob, she had insisted on continuing to kiss. It had all been a bit overwhelming.

To his whispered queries of what if somebody caught them, she had just laughed and said she didn't care what they thought.

"They'll just be jealous and want it too," she had replied.

167

That had both shocked and scared Andrew. He finally realised that Letitia was willing to let him do more, was in fact urging him to. At that, stage he had faltered. Part of him had urgently desired such a thing, but inside he felt sick, as though he was being used. He sensed that, if he did anything serious with Letitia, he would strongly regret it, even if there were none of the more dire consequences like disease or pregnancy.

But then his courage had been tested and he had all but faltered. How to say no? The old saying that 'Hell hath no fury like a woman scorned' burned and emasculated him.

She will despise me and think I am not a man, he had thought miserably.

He had hoped that Jacob would come back, to give him an excuse for stopping and getting away.

Finally he had croaked, "No," and had broken free from her grip.

Sobbing in emotional turmoil he had run off along the beach. For ten minutes he had walked back and forth, calming down but still in the grip of lust. Several times he had been tempted to go back to her but finally had forced himself to walk away. As he did, a person had come the other way and he had hidden under a bush. Now he knew that other person was Mark and that hurt too. Had Mark met Letitia? Had they done anything? Jill had certainly seemed to think so. It was all a bit much and helped Andrew to calm down.

Inside he was still torn, except that he had a deep conviction that he had done the right thing. By then they were at the jetty and the sheer splendour and fury of the scene brought his thoughts back to the present. For several moments the spectacle of the storm held Andrew's attention. Lit by the flashes of lightning the whole bay seemed to seethe like a boiling cauldron. Waves were churning in from several directions, crossing and colliding and swirling into a welter of foam and spray. Out of the shelter of the trees the wind was much stronger, driving the rain and chilling the skin. The tide was in and the spray was foaming onto the jetty. Waves were surging right up the beach to tug at the boat.

A quick check showed that the boat was in no danger. It was securely fastened to a tree and the waves were barely moving it. They dragged the boat a bit further up, then stood and looked at the sea again. On an impulse, Andrew walked over to the end of the jetty, then made his way slowly out along it, thrilled and enthralled. In his mind he was now the captain of a square-rigged sailing ship beset by a hurricane. The masts were all gone and the ship was being driven ashore by the storm.

We must get ready to try to get ashore, he thought.

But who with? A fleeting image of Letitia crossed his mind, but he quickly substituted it for one of Anne, or better still, 'Lady Anne', the daughter of a rich English nobleman. Andrew pictured her in 18th Century costume: rich gold and green brocade, gold jewellery, eyes adoringly pleading for him to save her.

He took a few more paces out along the jetty, getting drenched by rain and spray. The larger waves were washing up over the decking ankle deep, causing delicious little thrills of fear to shiver through Andrew. Salt tasted on his lips, and he cried out for the sheer joy and thrill of it. Then Mark joined him and spoiled the daydream.

"Pretty wild, isn't it?" Mark said.

"Hmmm," replied the disappointed buccaneer.

Mr Schipholl shouted above the storm. "Come on you kids, I'm getting cold, and it's not safe to be out on that jetty. It could give way."

Reluctantly, Andrew followed Mark back to the beach. Then he imagined that the survivors were staggering into the trees to find cover.

The sailors quickly made tents from torn sails, he thought as he crawled back into his own tent.

Mark then surprised him by saying, "Bloody hell I'm wet. I'm going to take off these wet clothes. Do you mind, Andrew?"

"No," Andrew replied, blushing as he did.

He actually thought it a good idea and quickly dried himself as well as he could with his already damp towel. By then Mark had stripped off and begun drying himself. Andrew was very careful not to look in his direction, being both embarrassed and ashamed of possibly being accused of being either a Peeping Tom or gay. Then he groped in his bag until he found another pair of shorts and changed. He did this inside his sleeping bag, even though it wet the inside, as he did not want to expose himself to Mark.

Having changed his shorts Andrew lay back in his sleeping bag and closed his eyes. To his relief, Mark also pulled on dry clothes before lying down. Andrew rolled the other way and tried to sleep, his attempts frustrated by occasional peals of thunder from the now passing storm, and by his own tortured thoughts about sex and relationships.

All his anxieties returned instantly when he woke up. It was daylight. As quickly as he could, Andrew pulled on his sandshoes and grabbed a shirt. He then crawled out and stood up. All the time he kept glancing towards Carmen's tent. To his mild regret, he noted that the tent flaps were down and tightly laced.

To hide his interest, and to avoid being accused of being a Peeping Tom, Andrew strode quickly away, pulling on his shirt as he did. While he walked, he found that his mouth had gone dry and his heart had started to hammer very fast. To his dismay, he was gripped by an intense urge to see Letitia. Shame and fear both gripped him, as did the lust. He knew it was lust because his body was now so aroused his whole being felt like an itch that needed scratching. So ashamed was he of his reactions that he almost ran to get away.

A minute later he was at the beach. To his dismay, he saw that Jacob was sitting out on the jetty. Not in the mood to talk to him at that moment Andrew stopped and busied himself with checking that the boat was still securely tied to the tree. He was surprised to find it was half full of water so crouched to begin bailing it out. That kept him busy until Jacob came walking back along the jetty a few minutes later.

Jacob's presence restored a sort of brittle normality. Andrew stood up and look around. He found it hard to imagine there had been so much climatic violence a few hours before. Now the sea was flat and only a gentle breeze ruffled its surface. The sky was clear blue and cloudless.

"Going to be another hot day," he commented, for something to say.

Jacob nodded and grunted. He didn't seem very happy. "I wonder what we will be doing today?" he said.

"Exploring?" Andrew ventured.

"Exploring! We've seen everything there is to see on this boring little island!" Jacob retorted.

Andrew had to bite back from saying, *If that's how you feel why did you come?* Instead, he said, "I heard Mr Schipholl say something about looking for pirate treasure."

"Pirate treasure! Strewth, you're a little kid!" Jacob sneered.

That really hurt and Andrew was left on the edge of tears, staring out to sea while Jacob strolled along the path towards the camp. The sound of laughter from the camp told him that others were awake. To his relief, he found Letitia awake and dressed (well, almost dressed as she wore a T-shirt and bikini bottom). She was busy smearing suncream onto her legs. Andrew's gaze travelled down those legs, then up again and he muttered with frustration and looked away. Luckily, Jacob was nowhere to be seen so Andrew relaxed.

Mrs Schipholl was preparing breakfast, and she told Andrew to wake all the others. That done, they were ordered to tidy their tents while they waited for breakfast to cook. In spite of his earlier humiliation, Andrew cheered up, helped by the smell of frying bacon. Ropes were tied between trees and damp sleeping bags and clothing were hung to dry in the sun.

Jacob strolled back from the direction of the toilet, but Andrew avoided looking at him. Instead, he helped keep the fire alight under the barbeque. The others all seated themselves at the table and began to eat cereal. For Andrew that was Weetbix with syrup on it. Fruit juice, then bacon and eggs on toast followed, making a really satisfying meal.

"Sorry about the bread being a bit stale," Mrs Schipholl said.

"It's fine, Mrs Schipholl. It toasts really well," Carmen replied.

Mrs Schipholl nodded and said, "It does. Never mind. We will get some fresh bread tomorrow."

Mark swallowed a mouthful and asked, "What are we doing today, Mrs Schipholl?"

"We are going to be buccaneers and are going on a treasure hunt," Mrs Schipholl replied.

At that, Andrew met Jacob's eyes, then blushed when Jacob's lip curled into a derisive sneer. However, Jacob said nothing and Mrs Schipholl went on to say that they were all to dress up as pirates for the morning. She indicated a large cardboard box which stood in the corner of her tent. It was only now that Andrew saw that Mr Schipholl was not present, but he did not like to ask where he was.

A few minutes later, Mr Schipholl came walking into camp from the direction of the beach, but he offered no explanation, just sat and commented on what a fine day it was. When breakfast was over, and the cooking utensils and plates cleaned up, Mrs Schipholl told them all to dress in long sleeves and long pants and to make sure they had good footwear on. Letitia pouted at that a bit, but her mother insisted so she went and pulled on a pair of jeans and a long-sleeved cotton shirt. As this was some sort of gauze and almost see-through, and with half the front buttons undone, it was only a token effort.

When all were dressed Mrs Schipholl opened the cardboard box and began handing out items of pirate costume. Jacob again curled his lip but, to Andrew's secret relief, did not make a scene and got dressed with everyone else. They were each given two large handkerchiefs, one to tie around the neck as a scarf and one to tie around their head. Cardboard 'bicorn' hats with white 'skull and crossbones' on them were handed to each. Then black cardboard eyepatches with elastic straps were added. Next, some large clip-on, gold coloured, plastic earrings were offered. Andrew declined but Mark accepted, as did all of the girls. The offer of a plywood cutlass and plastic flintlock pistol were more to Andrew's liking and he stuck these in his belt.

Martin and Mark both entered into the spirit of the thing and began singing, "Yo ho ho! Fifteen men on a dead man's chest," and making calls of, "Avast there ye lubbers!" and "Aye me hearties!" and other supposed pirate talk.

Then they began to poke each other with their cutlasses until told to stop it by Mrs Schipholl. "It's all fun and games till somebody loses an eye!" she reminded.

Anne then said, "Carmen, I don't think you should go on this. Remember what happened last time you went on a treasure hunt."

At that, Andrew saw Carmen go pale, but she managed a smile. "Don't be silly," she replied. There were a few moments silence and Andrew could tell that Carmen was shaken by the comment. To change the subject he said, "Where's my parrot? Has anyone seen Polly?"

"No, but I can see what he did on your shoulder," Martin quipped.

Andrew actually glanced to see if there was bird poop on his shirt and the others laughed. Mrs Schipholl scolded Martin. "That's enough talk like that, thank you. Now, who wants this plastic sword?"

By the time everyone was dressed up, the whole mood had lifted to one of excitement and happiness. Andrew began to daydream again, imagining himself ashore with Captain Flint's crew and with a desperate search and battle ahead. The hurtful comment by Jacob still rankled but he thrust it aside and cheerfully entered into the spirit of the game.

Then a more stressful twist was added to the game. Mr Schipholl explained that the treasure hunt was a race and that they would be in teams of two. These were selected by drawing names out of a hat. To Andrew's secret delight, he was teamed up with Jill, although he gave

Anne a look that was meant to convey that he really wanted to be with her. She ended up with Jacob, and he did feel sorry for her then. Martin and Carmen were the third team, which left Mark and Letitia as the last.

That drew a frown from Jill, but Andrew was secretly relieved. He now feared being alone with Letitia, partly because he was afraid he would give in to her and then probably regret it, and partly out of anxiety over her scorn or anger if he rejected her again.

Mr Schipholl then explained that they all needed pencil and paper and proceeded to hand each team two small notepads and two pencils.

"That is because the clues are all in some sort of code and you won't be able to crack them in your head," he explained. He then went on, "To make sure there is no cheating you have to show either Mum or I the full decoded message written out before you can move on the next place."

Anne smiled. "Just like the treasure hunt we did at cadets."

"It is," Mr Schipholl agreed. "That was what gave me the idea. But I think this will test you."

Satisfied they understood the rules Mr Schipholl next opened a notebook and read aloud, "First clue. Ready to write? Romeo, Oscar, Bravo, India, November."

As Mr Schipholl spoke, Andrew and the others at first gaped. Then Andrew saw Carmen's face light up and she began to write furiously. Suddenly it came to him.

Mr Schipholl is reading letters from the Phonetic Alphabet.

By then Mr Schipholl was saying, "Sierra." Andrew silently cursed himself but began to write, hoping to find out the letters he missed later.

"Oscar, November, Charlie, Romeo, Uniform, Sierra, Oscar, Echo, apostrophe, Sierra."

Andrew could see that the others were now starting to switch on but Letitia and Anne both looked plainly mystified and Jacob looked annoyed. The message kept coming, "Foxtrot, India, Romeo, Sierra, Tango, Papah, Romeo, India, Oscar, Romeo, India, Tango, Yankee, ends."

For a second of two Andrew waited, pencil poised. Then, as his mind grasped that they had the complete message he began scanning it and wondering how to get the missing letters at the beginning. Jill leaned over and studied the note, gently touching Andrew's arm as she did. Now Andrew began to get flustered. He was stimulated by her touch and also wanted to create a good impression of being clever.

Oh what does it mean? he wondered, his eyes flicking along the line of letters that he had printed.

Suddenly Jill pointed and said, "Does that say 'priority', that last bit?"

It did, but everyone else heard her and also looked at their notes. "Sssh!" Andrew hissed.

But by then he had identified the word 'first' and put a pencil circle around it. As he did, Mark cried, "First Priority."

Letitia shushed him, making the others laugh. By then Andrew had worked out the method. *It is just one long run of letters, and we need to break it into words,* he reasoned.

He tried several combinations before it struck him. He nudged Jill and used his pencil to underline another group of letters.

"Crusoe's," he whispered.

She nodded and Andrew felt a surge of relief. *The letters I missed must spell 'Robinson',* he decided, noting that he had 'son' as the first letters he had copied.

Taking Jill by the elbow, he moved away. "Robinson Crusoe's first priority," he said.

Jill nodded, leaning close to whisper. "Sshh! Not so loud. Loose lips sink ships."

Her closeness got Andrew even more stimulated as he was able to look into her eyes and scent her perfume.

"What was his first priority?" she asked.

That had Andrew stumped. He closed his eyes and tried to conjure up images of Robinson Crusoe dragging himself ashore on the island (he was sure it was after the shipwreck).

What would be my first priority if I was shipwrecked on a desert island? he wondered.

Thoughts like seeing if he was the only survivor, of helping his shipmates ashore, flitted through his mind. Then he thought of things like weapons in case of savages, or a rowboat.

"Food?" Jill queried.

"Fishing hooks, or maybe..." Andrew replied.

He stared at the jungle and felt hot and bothered. *What could it be?* he thought anxiously.

He was not alone. All the others were now in huddles discussing it.

Suddenly it came to him as he watched Martin lift a drink bottle to his mouth.

"Water," Andrew whispered. "Drinking water. Without that he would be dead very quickly."

"The creek" squeaked Jill.

To Andrew's annoyance and her embarrassment, everyone else heard her and all heads swung to look in the direction of the creek.

"Water!" Martin cried.

They started to move but Mr Schipholl's bellow stopped them. "Show me your written message first!"

They rushed into a jostling line to show Mr Schipholl. Mark and Letitia were at the front and they raced for the track down to the creek. Jill went to follow but Andrew grabbed her sleeve.

"It will be the mouth of the creek on the beach where he came ashore," he said. He turned towards the beach.

By then Jacob and Anne were following Letitia and Mark but Andrew saw that Carmen had reached the same conclusion as himself. She and Martin began running along the path towards the beach. Andrew and Jill followed. The four ran as fast as they could out to the beach, then turned right and ran along it towards the mouth of the creek. In his mind's eye, Andrew could picture Robinson Crusoe staggering along the beach towards that point.

He was right. Taped to a tree trunk at the mouth of the creek was a piece of paper with letters printed on it. As soon as he arrived, Andrew crouched and began to copy it down. Carmen scribbled furiously beside him. As they were finishing, shouts and splashing indicated the others were running down the creek. They arrived wet and panting and obviously annoyed with themselves.

Andrew and Jill moved away and sat in the shade to puzzle over the next message. It read:

ACR YEF TIH BEL RXE DAC NFY COP TIH KEL ROS LVV IRV TOZ RAS

For a minute or so he stared at it completely nonplussed. "I've seen things like this on a Command Post Exercise with the Army Cadets," he said. "They have Code sheets with these Trigrams, that's the three letter groups. Each Trigram has next to it its meaning, either a word or a sentence, things like 'enemy' or 'withdraw' and so on."

"So we need a code sheet," Jill replied. By then Mr Schipholl had caught up and she called to him. "Mr Schipholl, can we have a code sheet please?"

Mr Schipholl, now dressed as a pirate and wearing a long blue coat, shook his head. "Nay me hearties. Ye cannot. Ye have no need of such things."

Jill nodded, bit her lip and looked down to study the message. Andrew glanced anxiously around and noted that Carmen was already doing something to hers, writing quickly.

"Maybe we do something to the letters," he suggested. Dimly he remembered word puzzles and 'secret code' activities in primary school. For a moment he struggled to remember how they worked. Then he said, "Let's try rewriting it backwards."

A moment's work caused him to shake his head. SARZOT, it read.

That doesn't make sense, he reasoned.

To add to the pressure, Carmen and Martin stood up and moved over to Mr Schipholl. After showing him what they had written, they went running off westwards along the beach.

Oh no! Andrew groaned inwardly. *Jill will think I am a real dill! Oh, how does it work?*

Chapter 20

TREASURE HUNT

Carmen paused at the end of the beach to look back. She was feeling anxious lest the whole Treasure Hunt become an unpleasant experience.

If any group really falls behind it could hurt their feelings, she mused. Already there were signs of tension.

It had been she who had broken that last code. There had been a similar type of problem on the infamous 'Treasure Hunt' on which she had been kidnapped. When that had been jokingly mentioned she had experienced an amazingly strong emotional reaction which had taken some self-control to hide.

"Try crossing out every second letter," she had suggested to Martin.

They had both started with a different letter: Carmen with the first and Martin with the second. Within seconds Martin had nudged her and shown her ARE THERE.

"This is the method," he muttered.

Carmen had nodded and quickly started doing the second half of the message. Within a minute they had ARE THERE ANY OTHER SURVIVORS.

Martin frowned. "What does that mean?" he asked. "Survivors of what?"

"Robinson Crusoe," Carmen had replied, remembering the first clue.

Martin had looked along the beach and at the trees. "Can't see any," he muttered.

"Of the shipwreck," Carmen said, also puzzling.

Then it came to both of them simultaneously. They looked at each other and Martin breathed, "The wreck!"

After showing the message to Mr Schipholl, they set off running, leaving a worried looking group behind. The heat and the sand soon took their toll, slowing them to a jog, then to a fast walk. When, on reaching the end of the beach, they could see none of the others following they slowed to a walk.

The clue wasn't on the wreck. It was taped to a rock beside the foot track on the end of the point overlooking Wreck Bay. Carmen saw it from 25 metres away.

"That makes sense," she said. "We can see the whole beach near the wreck and there are no survivors on it."

By then they had reached the clue. A muttered "Bloody hell!" from Martin made her look at the message and she saw what he meant. It wasn't in words at all, it was a series of small, coloured flags.

She groaned. "Those are the International Signal Flags used at sea. Oh bummer! I wish I'd paid more attention in those lessons at cadets!"

There were 14 flags, all coloured and in neat rows. Carmen shook her head and sat to start puzzling them out. A couple she could tell. The pair settled to decode the message. Carmen thought hard and pointed.

"That one there is the 'Blue Peter' I think."

"What letter is that?" Martin asked.

He had only been a Navy Cadet for a few months and Carmen knew it was unlikely he had ever been taught the signal flags.

"P," Carmen replied.

"It isn't very blue," Martin suggested doubtfully.

"No, you are right," Carmen said. Now it came to her, a teaching point from Petty Officer Fox during a lesson. "It isn't 'P'. It is 'S'. Its colours are the reverse of the Blue Peter."

The letter 'S' was written down and Carmen studied the others. She noted that the same flag appeared three times and that two others appeared twice each.

"That red and white one is 'H', I think," she said.

This was added and then Martin asked, "What about that back-the-front French flag?"

That jogged Carmen's memory. "That is 'T'."

It was added but the message still looked woefully empty. "Four out of fourteen," Martin wailed.

As he did, the sound of running came to them and Jacob and Anne appeared. Jacob, being a leading seaman, just stood back and wrote the letters out as he looked at the flags. Within a minute he had shown the message to Mr Schipholl, who had puffed up in his wake. Mr Schipholl nodded, and Jacob and Anne trotted on towards the wreck.

As they went down onto the beach of Wreck Bay, Andrew and Jill arrived, followed soon after by Mark and Letitia. Carmen noted that the front of Letitia's shirt was now completely unbuttoned. That drew a pained frown from Jill, who then pointedly looked away and whispered to Andrew.

To Carmen's chagrin, Andrew also just stood back and muttered the letters down as he wrote them down. He obviously knew the flags well enough to do that.

Drat! she thought, peeved at the thought of being beaten by her little brother. Within a minute Andrew and Jill were on their way down to Wreck Beach.

Before Andrew left, Carmen had heard him mutter 'C' a bit too loud. She also saw that Jacob and Anne were now wading out towards the bow of the wreck.

"The word 'wreck' must be in the message," she whispered to Martin.

They looked at the clue. Carmen tried to work out the language structure to insert a 'C'. She tried to fit 'wreck' in at the beginning, but it did not make sense. Then she placed it at the end, making 'C' the second last letter. It seemed to fit.

Martin pointed and said, "So if that is 'C', then the letter before it must be 'E'. That is the same as that flag after the second 'H'. So if that is an 'E' then there might be the word 'the'.."

That made sense to Carmen, and she wrote 'E' in both those places. Then she wrote it in after the 'S' at the beginning.

"Now we are getting somewhere, I hope!" she said.

It was more than Mark or Letitia were managing. They were looking frustrated and hot and were obviously making wild guesses. By now Andrew and Jill had also reached the wreck, wading out of sight on the far side. Once more Carmen scanned the structure of the words.

"We have four out of six letters in the first word," she said, pointing to them. "If that last word is 'wreck', then the fourth last letter must be 'R', and that is the same flag as the fourth letter."

S- E- question- R- C- H THE WRECK, Carmen wrote.

"Search," Martin cried.

"Yes," Carmen agreed.

Then she shushed Martin, noting that Mark and Letitia had overheard this. That got them going again. Carmen scrambled to her feet and showed the message to Mr Schipholl.

He nodded, then said, "Get moving. I'll give this pair a few more minutes before I start feeding them clues."

Carmen and Martin ran down to the beach and along it, then waded out to where the other four were standing in knee-deep water beside the rusty bow of the wreck. A piece of paper was taped to a hull frame.

"Lucky the tide isn't in," Martin commented and then laughed.

"It's coming in," Andrew added. "It will be high tide at about ten, at two metres and something."

Carmen checked her watch and was surprised to see it was only 0830hrs. Then she focused on the clue and began writing it down. This one was also in Trigrams. It read:

EDD AEM DNT OLE TLL ASE

As soon as she had it copied down, Carmen indicated to Martin to go back to the beach. The pair waded ashore and sat down. The others also came ashore, seating themselves some way apart.

Carmen said, "Martin, you try backwards and I'll try the one we just did of random letters."

They set to work. As they wrote, Letitia and Mark came hurrying down from the headland, followed by a smiling Mr Schipholl. However, when Letitia saw where the note was, she pouted and said to Mark, "You go and write it down. I don't feel like getting my pants wet."

Mark obediently waded out. He wrote down the note and came ashore. He and Letitia sat on the sand nearby and began working on it, Letitia leaning on Mark and placing one hand on his leg.

Poor old Mark! Carmen thought. *I hope Jill doesn't get jealous and make a scene.*

Then she glanced around to see what Jill thought of the situation, and got another shock. Jill was pressed up against Andrew and did not even appear to have noticed.

Oh dear! I hope Jill isn't going to put poor old Andrew under stress again, Carmen thought, remembering the rivalry that had led to blows in January.

Carmen liked Jill, and thought she was a very nice person. She also thought she was extraordinarily pretty. Her black hair had a sheen to it that seemed to make her face glow and she had a very trim figure. At the moment this was set off nicely by her blue and white striped sailor jersey and the hip-hugging jeans she wore. All Carmen could do was shake her head and hope, and feel a bit sad and left out as it was obvious that Jacob had lost interest in her.

Suddenly Mark said, "Swap."

Everyone looked at him and he looked back, blushing with guilt at having spoken too loudly. A frantic scrabble of pencil work began as each group vied to try that method:- of swapping every two letters. As Carmen wrote, the message appeared rapidly before her eyes. It read:

DEAD MEN DO TELL TALES

That got them. Mark frowned and looked around. "Dead men? What dead men?"

Martin and Carmen both opened their mouths to speak and met each other's eyes. "The cemetery!" they whispered to each other.

They sprang up and showed their message to Mr Schipholl, then hurried back the way they had come.

What a sneaky trick! Carmen thought, *making us back-track.*

It became a race as the others quickly worked out the message and then set off after them. Carmen very quickly had to slow down to a puffing walk, bemoaning her unfitness. In the end this did not matter because Mr Schipholl had laid down that the pairs had to stay together for safety and no one pair had two fit people. Thus it was that the whole group came hurrying back along Picnic Beach in a lather of perspiration. They passed the jetty and turned up under the fig trees to the cemetery.

Carmen and Martin found the clue first, but only a few seconds before the others. It was taped to the headstone of Captain Simpson's grave and was easy to see from the inland side. It was in Trigrams and very short. It read:

UPJ MFU

It had them stumped. The pairs sat under the trees, sweaty and becoming increasingly frustrated as they tried the various ways of re-arranging the letters. Then 9:30 came and went and the sun climbed higher and became hotter. Because of the rain the previous night the humidity was very high and their clothes stuck to their sweaty skins. Carmen regretted not having her proper hat and considered ducking back to camp to get it. She noted that Mark had lost his cardboard bicorn.

She also noted that Letitia was using her open shirt to fan her front, all the while exposing half her breasts right in front of Mark. Carmen saw Mark's eyes flicking continually up to look at Letitia's cleavage and that made her give a sour smile.

Letitia is doing that deliberately, she thought.

It was clear that Jill was aware of what was going on and she looked grumpy.

It was Martin who finally cracked it. After twenty minutes he whispered, "What if the letters aren't the right ones?"

"What do you mean?" Carmen asked.

"What if other letters have been substituted?" Martin suggested. "I read somewhere that the Roman Emperor Hadrian used to encode his confidential messages by moving his letters one to the right or left."

"So that A becomes B and so on do you mean?" Carmen queried.

Martin nodded and they at once began to experiment. "You do one letter to the right and I'll do one to the left," Carmen said.

It was Martin who got it. The word TOI LET was the result. With gleeful glances at the others the pair stood up and showed Mr Schipholl, then set off at the run through the cemetery towards the toilet. When they got there, they found the clue taped to the back wall. It was just a long run of numbers.

0615121215232008050615152016180914$2019$

For a full minute Carmen stared at in baffled silence. Martin was also stumped.

"Bloody hell!" he cried. "How does this one work? Is it grid references or something?"

"Don't think so. Might be compass bearings as well," Carmen suggested.

They were joined by Anne and Jacob who stood panting and staring in similar bewilderment. Carmen took the opportunity to go to the toilet, then went to the camp to have a big drink. She met Anne there. Anne was laughing and red in the face.

"This is fun!" she said. "But Jacob is a bit of a bore."

That hurt a bit because Carmen had thought he was wonderful. *But that was before I got to know him,* she told herself sadly.

The two girls returned to the toilet to find Andrew and Jill also here. For the next five minutes they all wondered, often aloud, how to decode the mysterious numbers. Then Anne took Jacob aside and whispered to him and Carmen was peeved to see them start to write. Whatever it was obviously worked as their facial expressions told her. Within a minute Anne and Jacob had their message written out, but as Mr Schipholl had not arrived and Mrs Schipholl was nowhere to be seen they ran back into the cemetery.

A minute later they came running back out and started looking around. Mr Schipholl appeared, followed by a sulky looking Letitia and a worried looking Mark.

Then Martin distracted her by saying, "Alphabet place."

"What?"

"The numbers are the place each letter has in the Alphabet. Zero Six is F, and fifteen is O."

Carmen saw that he was busy writing the Alphabet down the side of a page. Next to each letter he then wrote a number, starting with 01. Then it was the work of moments to decode the message:

FOLLOW THE FOOTPRINTS

"What footprints?" Carmen queried, then cried "Oops! Loose lips sink ships!" and covered her mouth when she saw the others all glance at her and then follow her gaze.

Anne and Jacob had obviously found them as they had vanished in the direction of the camp and not come back. Carmen went in that direction as well, Martin following and all the others busy writing Alphabets and muttering. As they did, a drum began to beat away off in the jungle. They both stopped.

"What on earth is that?" Martin asked.

"A tom-tom from the sound of it," Carmen replied, mystified.

"I wonder who is playing it," Martin said.

"Don't know," Carmen answered, although she did have a strong suspicion.

"I suppose it is part of the Robinson Crusoe theme, you know, cannibals and head-hunters and so on," Martin suggested.

"Possibly, now keep looking for footprints," Carmen said.

The footprints started on the far side of the camp near the fireplace. They were little cardboard cut-outs placed on the ground, one every ten metres or so.

Martin laughed and said, "Look how long the paces are. I hope we don't run into a giant!"

Carmen laughed as well. She was really enjoying herself now and was glad to be back in the shade of the trees, rather than being out in the heat of the open. The 'footprints' led across the creek heading in the direction of the ridge. When they reached the creek they stopped by mutual consent and rinsed their faces and had a drink. Then they hurried on, wanting to catch up to Anne and Jacob. All the while the jungle drum kept thudding away off to their right somewhere.

The footprints turned off the track and led them along the top of the creek bank for 50 metres, then stopped abruptly at a piece of white paper taped to a tree. It read:

FIN DTH EDR UMX

This time they cracked it in seconds. Carmen just looked at it and the words seemed to leap out at her. "Find the drum," she said.

"What about the X?" Martin asked.

"Just a random letter to make up the Trigram," Carmen replied. "Come on."

"What about Mr Schipholl? We are supposed to show him the message," Martin replied.

"He isn't here. He is probably playing the drum," Carmen replied.

She set off through the jungle. Martin shrugged and followed. Luckily the jungle was fairly open and easy to walk through, with only a few vines and prickly bushes. There was even a faint trail which Carmen followed. As they headed off, Andrew and Jill came hurrying along and stopped to read the clue.

As Carmen and Martin walked northwards, the drumbeat got louder and louder. The trail was parallel to the creekbank so there was no real danger of getting lost, but it was still a bit of an adventure.

The drummer was, as Carmen suspected, Mrs Schipholl. She was seated on a log beside another foot trail and was wearing a grass skirt and floral lei. At first glance Carmen thought that Mrs Schipholl wasn't wearing a top but then noted a bikini top under the flowers. Her bosom wobbled in time to her thumping of the drum. Carmen found the sight both interesting and embarrassing. She could tell that Martin was highly embarrassed.

Poor Martin. He is ashamed that his mother behaves like this, she reasoned.

Mrs Schipholl grinned and pointed to a faint trail heading further upstream. "You must go that way and cross the creek by walking across the concrete dam. Do not fall in or the crocodiles will get you. Watch out for cannibals. For the next clue ask Squire Trelawney. Now hurry up. Jacob and Anne are beating you."

Carmen and Martin continued on. Carmen now saw that there was a deep pool ahead of them on her right.

"I know where we are," she said. "This is the pool behind that little dam near the concrete pump house."

Martin agreed. He was leading and soon pointed to where the low concrete wall dammed the creek. "That must be the way we go."

Without hesitation he climbed onto the narrow concrete dam and strode across. Carmen followed. As she walked out over the water, she could see the bottom, but she still felt uneasy. She had assumed that the talk of crocodiles was just part of the story to make it scary but now she wasn't so sure.

A croc could make his home in this pool, she thought.

It looked big enough and was deep and murky enough to hide one. For a few moments she hesitated, scanning the water, until her reason told her that no saltwater crocodile was going to crawl half a kilometre up a shallow freshwater creek. Even so she was careful, and thereby nearly lost her balance and fell in.

"You need to go faster to keep your balance," Martin called from the far bank as she teetered there, waving her arms to regain her balance.

On the other side they found a concrete path, almost hidden by a mush of rotting leaves. It led up through a tangle of bushes to the concrete pump house. There was no clue there, so they pushed on to the ruins of the house.

"The squire will be at the Big House," said Martin confidently.

He was. Mr Schipholl stood there in full 18th Century dress: tricorn, lace ruff, white shirt and plum-coloured coat, knee breeches and long white socks. For a moment Carmen could only admire him and think how much he looked the part.

Later, when they were alone, Carmen said to Martin, "You've got a great dad. I love the way he enters into the spirit of things."

"He can be a big kid at times," Martin replied, again plainly embarrassed.

Mr Schipholl pointed to a piece of paper taped to a corner post. It was more Trigrams and read:

STE RCE SYL IMA FRA EHN ETF OST NAV RES EHT

As there was no sign of Jacob and Anne, Carmen reasoned that it must be an easy one. She said, "You do random letters and I will try reversing it."

Reversing it was the method. Within two minutes they had: THE SERVANTS OFTEN HEAR FAMILY SECRETS.

"Servants Quarters!" Martin cried, pointing further along the mowed vehicle track.

On an impulse Carmen grinned at Mr Schipholl. "Many thanks squire," she said, knuckling her forehead with a mock salute.

Mr Schipholl laughed and called, "Take care ye buccaneers! There be savages in these woods."

As Carmen and Martin hurried off, she saw Andrew and Jill come puffing up the lawn from the creek. Both were red in the face and had obviously been running.

We had better hurry up, she thought, although she really did not mind who won. She was just enjoying the game.

The clue at the burned-out servant's quarters was also Trigrams. The method was alternate letters, and they had only just written it down when Andrew and Jill arrived. Both pairs cracked the code almost simultaneously and Andrew reached Mr Schipholl a few paces ahead of Martin. Mr Schipholl had walked after them to the wall of orange trees that separated the two lawns. He nodded at both messages and then went back to where Letitia and Mark could just be seen at the ruin.

The message was: ARE THERE CANNIBALS ON THE BEACH?

The four ran towards Sandy Beach through the overgrown coconut plantation and it was only when they were almost the sea that it occurred to Carmen that it might be the wrong beach.

It wasn't. There was a clue there and Jacob and Anne could be seen 200 metres away hurrying south along the open sand towards Oyster Head. By then it was 11:00 and only the fresh sea breeze made it bearable in the sun. The method was random letters and Andrew and Jill got it first. They went hurrying off and Carmen could only fume as she tried yet another method. By the time she and Martin had worked it out, Letitia and Mark had joined them.

It read: SECRET COVE.

There wasn't the slightest doubt about where that was, so she and Martin set off at the run to try to catch up. Unfitness soon brought this back to a steady walk but by then Carmen did not care. She was just enjoying the sun, sea and salt air, and the delightful scenery.

At Secret Cove they found Mrs Schipholl, now fully clad again. She was seated on a towel and was rubbing sun lotion all over her face and neck. Jacob kept glancing at her and frowning, making Carmen even gladder she had not actually fallen in love with him.

He is going to develop into a real wowser and prude, she thought.

The clue was in plain English. It read:

BROOK, FIREFLY, SCHOONER, GOULD.

That had stumped the others, and they were still puzzling over it when Letitia and Mark caught them up. Their arrival drew a frown from Jacob, sour disapproval from Jill, and a warning to put on some sun cream from Mrs Schipholl.

Andrew worked it out. Carmen heard him say to Jill, "Those are the names of islands around here."

Then she saw him stare out to sea. He frowned with annoyance and Carmen saw him moving to try to look for something. Then she heard him mutter irritably and glance up the ridge. He went over to Mrs Schipholl and whispered to her. She nodded, so Andrew and Jill set off up the hill.

Carmen instantly understood. She whispered to Martin, "I reckon we need to be somewhere you can see all four islands."

When this was said to Mrs Schipholl she smiled and nodded. Martin and Carmen set off at a run, leaving a grumpy looking Jacob and huffy looking Letitia behind. It was a hot, sweaty climb up the rough foot track, but the view was worth it. The lovely, island-studded tropical sea looked superb. For a few seconds Carmen just stood and rank in the view. Then she made her way over to where a piece of paper taped to a rock said:

AESEHTYBEERHT.

They were puzzling over this when the sound of aero engines made them look around. A red and white twin-engine aircraft came into view as a distant spec. It travelled past Gould Island, coming from the south and flew on almost directly over their heads. It vanished off to the northeast where the masts of a large freighter could just be seen poking up above the horizon.

"Coastwatch," Andrew observed, watching the aircraft for a few minutes before returning to the puzzle. Jacob and Anne joined them.

Martin worked it out. "Backwards," he said.

It was. It read:

THREE BY THE SEA.

"Three by the sea? What does that mean?" Andrew asked aloud.

Carmen saw it first. She moved to get a bit of shade from a large bush and that gave her a good view along the Fishermans Beach. Below her she saw the small patch of sand right at their end of the beach, where Mr and Mrs Schipholl had been sunbathing. Mr Schipholl was there, still in his Squire Trelawney costume, standing under one of the figs at the edge of the cemetery. Near him, close to the clump of rocks, were the three pandanus palms.

Carmen led a scramble down the rocky hillside to where Mr Schipholl waited. He grinned and called out, "Ahoy there shipmates!" as they came running, red-faced and sweating.

On the pandanus was a note and when she saw it Carmen's heart leapt.

Morse code! she thought happily. Now she was very glad she had mastered it, being part of her signallers course the previous year.

By the time the others had caught up she had decoded FIVE PACES WEST DIG and had paced it out. She and Martin knelt and began to dig with their hands in the soft sand at a point that looked like it had been recently disturbed. Almost at once they discovered a metal container.

As she went to pick this up, Andrew cried out, "Watch out, Sis! Remember what happened last time we dug up a treasure box in a beach."

At that, Carmen went cold with shock and jerked her head up, to scan the beach and bay.

Chapter 21

HARD WORDS

For a few moments Carmen felt her heart hammer and her breath catch in her throat. Then she forced a smile, even though she felt sick in the stomach. Her searching glance had shown her that there was nothing there. The bay was empty and the only people on the beach were her friends and Mr Schipholl. For a fleeting second, she saw a look of guilt cross Andrew's face.

Their eyes met and he said, "Sorry, Sis. I just remembered last time."

Carmen nodded. She understood. It was the sort of thing that stayed with you, long after the event. She dusted the sand off the metal box and saw that it was only a cheap cash box. It had a keyhole but was not locked. As she lifted the lid, all of the others bent closer to look.

Inside was a note. It said: YOUR TREASURE IS IN THE ESKI. PLEASE SHARE IT.

At that, Carmen smiled and stood up. She put the box under her arm and said, "Back to camp."

The group trooped back along the beach, past the outcrop of rocks and along to the end of the jetty, then into the camp. Mrs Schipholl was waiting for them there. She beamed and opened an eski. From inside she extracted chocolates in gold wrapping: Crunchie bars, and gold doubloons. There was also a large jug of cold orange and mango cordial.

"Thank you very much," she said to both parents. "That was great fun. You are making this into a really enjoyable holiday."

Both the Schipholls smiled and made light of her thanks. Andrew added his agreement and then smiled at Jill. That caused a twinge of concern to Carmen as she did not want any ill-will to spoil the pleasant atmosphere.

Lunch came next, bread with various spreads. While they were sitting around eating, Mark asked the question that had been drifting in Carmen's mind, "What do we do this afternoon?"

Mrs Schipholl answered, "We thought you should have an easy afternoon after all the running around this morning."

"Good idea," Martin agreed.

"I think I'll just lie in the shade and read a book," Andrew said.

"We can go fishing," Jacob suggested.

"If you like," Anne said to him.

She said this in a way that caused Carmen to speculate. *Surely Anne doesn't see anything in Jacob?*

Mrs Schipholl nodded. "We can do all of those things," she agreed.

"I want to go for a swim," Letitia said.

"Snorkelling," Mark suggested.

Mrs Schipholl now shook her head. "No swimming in the middle of the day. You are to keep out of the sun till after three o'clock, and Letitia dear, you put some more sun cream on."

That caused them all to glance at Letitia and Carmen again marvelled at how alike the mother and daughter were.

Will I grow up to be just like my mum? she wondered.

The upshot of all this was that they retired to their tents to change and to collect gear. This led to another of those embarrassing little incidents. To change into her bathers, Carmen closed the tent flaps and then sat and took off her joggers and then her jeans. Next, she tugged off her undies. As she did, Letitia suddenly pulled open the tent flap from outside. Carmen saw that Martin was just outside and the look on his face told her that he could see inside.

"Letitia! Please! I'm getting changed," Carmen cried. She blushed with shame at being seen with no pants on.

"Sorry," Letitia replied, bending down to crawl in.

She didn't sound sorry and that further upset Carmen. *Bloody cow!* she thought, *Showing off all the time!* Then she felt guilty for such unkind thoughts. *She can't help it,* she thought. *That's how she was made.*

There was a twinge of pity, tempered by irritation that Letitia didn't make a bigger effort to be modest instead of showing off. As quickly as she could, Carmen pulled on her bathers, turning her back as she did. Then she slipped on the long-sleeved shirt again.

The Schipholls had brought a box of snorkelling gear: face masks and snorkels but no flippers. The box was carried down to the beach and the group spread itself in the shade along the top of the sand. Towels and rugs were spread and pillows added. Then they all lay down. Carmen lay beside Anne, with Andrew on her other side. Jill lay next to Andrew and

Mark lay next after Jill. Letitia placed herself beside Mark at the end of the row. On Carmen's other side, beyond Anne, was Jacob. The parents took up places 20 metres along.

Almost at once there was a subtle rise in tension. Letitia began smearing sun cream on herself as she sat looking out to sea. Carmen could see all the boys glancing at what was happening. She almost opened her mouth to protest but Letitia finished and put the sun lotion down.

It was a relief when Letitia lay down, but this was on her back in a very revealing way. Carmen curled her lip in disgust and turned away. As she did, she saw Mark staring with fascination. He licked his lips and shook his head, then rolled over.

Poor boy! she thought. *He is being tormented by her.*

Carmen could only shake her head and look away as she found the sight quite unsettling. In doing so she caught Jacob looking. He noticed her glance and went stony-faced and looked away.

He is at least male enough to be interested too, Carmen surmised.

The group at last settled. Time went slowly by and Carmen relaxed and drifted into a restful doze. This was disturbed by Andrew.

He commented to no-one in particular, "Look at this lizard. I wonder how it got to the island?"

Carmen swivelled her head and located the reptile. It was quite a small creature, about 15 centimetres long, but brightly coloured green, a dragon of some sort. It was clinging to the trunk of the nearby tree, all the while tilting its head from side to side to study them.

Martin answered, "Probably dropped by a bird."

"Or washed out of a flooded river clinging to a log," suggested Anne.

"More likely came in a boat," Jacob commented.

"What boat?" Andrew queried.

"Noah's bloody Ark of course!" Mark cried.

That got Jacob angry. He sat up and snapped back, "Probably, but please don't swear about things in the Bible."

There was a moment's silence before Letitia who got the tension ratcheted up again. She rolled over and arched her back to undo the back strap of her bikini top. When this was undone, she lay face downwards, her breasts squashing out very noticeably.

"Mark," she called. "Will you please put some suncream on my back?"

That got everyone's attention. Carmen saw Mark cast a guilty glance towards Jill before nodding and getting to his knees beside Letitia. Jill looked hurt and her mouth trembled. Jacob gave a disapproving sniff. Martin looked embarrassed and Andrew tried to pretend he wasn't interested.

Mark began gingerly smearing the cream on Letitia's shoulders. Carmen could see that he looked flustered and embarrassed. Letitia added to the pressure.

As he reached her lower back, she half-lifted herself to look and said, "Don't miss anywhere. I don't want to get sunburnt."

At that, Mark blushed bright red, but he nodded and obeyed, his hands sliding right down to the edge of the material. Then he started on her sides. To Carmen, he appeared to be flushed and panting fast and his eyes had a sort of glassy look.

He is stressed all right, she thought. She began to cast around for a way to divert things. Andrew was watching and Carmen could see his pupils dilating with interest. *I must stop this,* she thought.

But again she was too late. Letitia arched her back. She twisted to look at Mark and said to Mark, "That's alright. Don't miss anywhere,"

That was too much. Jill exploded with jealous rage. "Oh stop it, Letitia! Don't be such a tease."

Letitia turned to glare at her. Mark instantly withdrew his hands and went even redder. Letitia then snapped back, "Don't call me names, you frigid bitch!"

"Why, you slack tart!" Jill screeched.

Letitia flamed into anger and went to sit up, exposing her front even more. What she called back was lost in Jacob's bellow.

"Cover up, you shameless creature!"

By then the Schipholls had both sat up. Before either parent could intervene, Letitia sprang to her feet, scooping up her top and towel and covering herself with them.

"I wish you hadn't come on this holiday!" she screamed at Jacob. "I don't know why you did anyway. I hate you!"

With that she stormed off towards the camp, ignoring her mother's anxious calls. Mrs Schipholl hurried after her. Carmen bit her lip with anxiety and wondered how to calm things. Mr Schipholl looked worried but as nothing more was said he lay back down again. The friends lay back in tense and embarrassed silence. After a few minutes Mrs Schipholl came back. She knelt and whispered to her husband and then lay down again.

Oh, what a shame! she thought. She hated fights and ill-will.

A few tense minutes ticked by. Andrew sat up and had a drink. Then Anne said something to Jill about the ants. It was such an obvious attempt to ease the atmosphere that it had the opposite effect. Very slowly the tension eased. Carmen decided it needed more positive action. She sat up and announced she was going snorkelling.

"Who else wants to come?" she queried.

"Not me," Mark said. "Something might bite me."

"Then you sit on the jetty and keep watch for sharks," Carmen said.

Mark nodded. "Good idea. I will do some fishing at the same time," he replied.

There was a general stir and the group thankfully set about other tasks. Jacob and Anne opted for fishing from the jetty while Andrew, Mark, and Jill said they would also come snorkelling. The goggles and facemasks were dug out and handed round and snorkels fitted and tested. Carmen had been snorkelling a few times so felt quite confident. She rinsed her facemask, spat in it, smeared the saliva around, swilled it clear and then pulled the facemask down. Then she waded carefully in. With a sigh of pleasure she slipped under water, the cool liquid swirling refreshingly around her heated skin. She also found it a great relief to escape from the tension of the social situation.

Because the sea was so calm the water was crystal clear. As always, Carmen was thrilled by the sensation of sinking into the cool water and of being able to see. She marvelled at just how far she could see and felt reassured that she might be able to spot any prowling shark before it got her. Andrew started swimming beside her and she could see that he was continually lifting his head to look anxiously in all directions. She knew he had a deep and irrational fear of sharks.

Very slowly she swam out into deeper water, keeping close to the jetty. The bottom was so sandy and clear that it held little of interest but there were schools of tiny fish flitting around the barnacle encrusted jetty pilings. There were also a few small purple and grey crabs. Several times Carmen surfaced and looked to check that Mark and the others actually were on the jetty. She was being careful not to swim into a fishing line.

Towards the end of the jetty she was startled by the sudden appearance of a number of long, thin garfish. These were silver and had yellow teeth. They moved with quite amazing speed, dashing into a school of tiny, banded fish. The tiny, banded fish scattered and swam around and around the piling in desperate attempts to escape. One of the tiny fish got separated and swam frantically away out into the open water. Carmen watched, both fascinated and appalled.

The water is so clear he will never be able to hide, she thought.

Nor could it. The tiny fish managed to avoid several ferocious lunges by the long, thin fish but then was gone, snapped up in the twinkling of an eye. Once again, she was reminded that nature was not necessarily very nice and certainly wasn't very forgiving. That thought got her eyeing the band of blue darkness that began 50 metres out in the deeper water.

I don't think I will go any further out, she decided.

Instead, she turned and swam parallel to the beach, heading towards the rocks on Oyster Point. She had an idea she might find things of interest there but, apart from a few fish and some oysters, there was nothing much. After swimming for about twenty minutes, the others following in her wake, she waded ashore near the three pandanus palms.

From there they swam in the shallows back to the jetty. After returning her snorkelling gear to the box Carmen returned to her towel in the shade. The others joined her, even Jacob and Mark.

As they walked back Carmen asked, "Not fishing then?"

"Nothing there," Mark answered.

"We might try out on Snapper Point again," Jacob suggested.

Carmen had been looking around and worrying about Letitia. She now pulled on her sandshoes and shirt. Andrew looked at her quizzically.

"Where are you going?" he asked.

"To see how Letitia is," Carmen replied.

That drew sniffs from Jill and Jacob, but Anne said she would come with her. Carmen walked with her past Mr and Mrs Schipholl, who both appeared to be asleep, then back to the camp. It was deserted. For a minute Carmen lingered, having a drink and enjoying the cool shade. Then she looked at the toilet and down in the creek near the camp. Letitia was not there. Concern became anxiety and she began to worry.

Anne looked anxiously around. "I wonder where she is?" she queried.

An awful suspicion had begun to form in Carmen's mind, but she did not like to voice it. *I'd like to check,* she thought, *but I don't want the others to know.*

But she could not think of an excuse to get away from Anne. Her dilemma was intensified by the arrival of Martin and Andrew.

"Where is she?" Martin asked.

"Don't know," Carmen replied. "Why don't you boys check the ruins and Sandy Beach. She might be at Secret Cove."

Andrew looked doubtful and Martin made a face but reluctantly agreed. They hurried off. Carmen then accepted the inevitable. She turned to Anne and said, "Come on. Let's check over the ridge."

Anne's mouth opened in shock, and she gasped, "At the artist's?"

"Yes."

Once it was said there was nothing else to do but start walking. By this time Carmen was genuinely anxious and she walked quickly, ignoring her pounding heart and the sweat that dripped off her. They crossed the creek and followed the walking track up the side of the hill through the jungle. The hill seemed to be higher and steeper than she remembered but they reached the crest of the ridge at last. Here they paused for a minute to get their breath back and to be refreshed by the breeze. Then they started down the other side.

As they went down the western side of the hill, Carmen found it even hotter. The breeze was cut off completely and the afternoon sun shone directly on them. By then it was nearly three hours since Letitia had run off and Carmen became increasingly fretful and irritated. Her annoyance was increased when she heard voices behind them and then the thud of running feet. It was Andrew and Martin.

"I thought I asked you two to check the ruin and Sandy Beach?" she snapped.

She really didn't want either Andrew or Martin hurt more by Letitia. Her stomach was now churning with a sense of unpleasant foreboding and she wanted the boys elsewhere.

"We did," Andrew replied, looking stubborn. "I went to the ruin and servant's quarters and Martin went to Secret Cove and Sandy Beach. Then we came up the other track past the little dam near the pump house."

"I think you should go back," Carmen said.

"And I think you should," Andrew replied firmly. "I don't want my sister being exposed to that pervert painter."

Anne cried out at that. "Oh, he's not a pervert! He's very nice."

"How do you know?" Andrew challenged.

Anne went very red and bit her lip. Carmen answered, "Because we talked to him."

At that, Andrew looked hurt and Carmen felt even more upset. He gave Anne an accusing sort of look, then went to keep walking. Carmen blocked him by continuing to walk herself.

Andrew called angrily, "Go back! I don't want you seeing a deviate."

"No!"

"Carmen!"

"No!"

"Please!"

"No!"

The futile argument continued to the base of the slope. The group hurried through the dry scrub on the flat, passing the turn-off to the artist's hut. A minute later they burst out of the bush at the bank of the tiny creek near the rocks. The sight that met their eyes brought them to a shocked standstill.

Oh no! Carmen thought.

Standing on the beach with his back to them was the artist, clad only in brief nylon bathers. Standing a few paces away, and facing them, was a totally nude Letitia. She was obviously posing for the artist. He was busy with brush strokes on a canvas, the outline of which was clearly Letitia.

She saw them at once. Her mouth opened but then she defiantly held her pose. Carmen stopped and tried to prevent Andrew and Mark seeing, but she was too late. She turned, in time to see a look of jealous anguish cross both their faces.

The artist looked over his shoulder and half-turned. Annoyance registered on his face. Carmen was both shocked and fascinated. For a minute all she could do was stand and gape, too surprised to think what to do.

The suspense was broken by a completely unexpected act. From out of the rocks across the tiny creek strode Jacob, followed by Mark and Jill.

Jacob began to shout, "Harlot! Slut! Pervert! Beware the wrath of God! You will be punished!"

Then Jacob splashed across the shallow creek, fishing rod raised to strike.

Chapter 22

ALL UPSET

Andrew stood and stared. He was stunned. The sheer beauty and sexuality of Letitia's nude form held his gaze. He was simultaneously amazed at her boldness and delighted by her beauty and he swallowed as his heart rate shot up. He was also highly embarrassed, mostly because the artist was standing there and could see everything.

Then shock began to transform as jealousy added to the embarrassment: jealousy that Letitia was letting this man, this strange man, stand and drink in her every intimate detail with his lustful eyes. Anger was stirred, to mix with desire and jealousy. As his rage mounted, Andrew gritted his teeth and moved to confront the man.

Before he could, Jacob appeared and went striding forward, splashing across the shallow creek while brandishing his fishing rod. His face was suffused a shade of purple. He began shouting angrily, "Disgusting creatures! Have you no shame! Harlot! Deviate! Pervert! Let her go! Get dressed woman! Cover yourself, you shameless hussy!"

The artist spun to confront Jacob. In doing so he turned side on to Andrew, who saw he was holding a brush and palette daubed with paint. Letitia looked shocked and frightened but made no attempt to cover herself. The threat of violence was so apparent that the artist dropped his palette and brush and raised his fists to defend himself. Andrew watched, appalled at the confrontation and the possibility of a serious fight.

Jacob strode over to the artist but stopped short by a few paces. He screamed at him, "You evil creature! How dare you expose these young girls to sin! How dare you seduce this girl! Cover yourself and repent of your sins!"

With that Jacob again raised the fishing rod. The artist's face mottled with anger and he snarled back, "Hit me with that and I'll knock your ignorant block off! Now back off you bigot and leave us alone!"

For a second it seemed that Jacob would completely lose control, but then he hesitated. Andrew saw the artist's jaw clench and sensed that he would not back out.

There will be a real fight alright! he thought, anxiety now taking over.

As well, his first angry reactions were now being replaced by dislike of Jacob, and of his cruel and savage accusations and harsh words.

Jacob gabbled and gestured, pointing both at the man and then at Letitia. Waving his arms he screamed, "You have no right! This is wickedness! This is the sinful desires of the flesh! Evil lust!"

At that, he slashed the fishing rod down. It whistled through the air, striking the artist hard on his left forearm, which he raised just in time to protect himself.

In a flash the artist grabbed the fishing rod with his left hand and stepped forward and punched hard with his right.

"Too right it is chum," he snarled.

The punch took Jacob full in the face. He reeled back, let go of the fishing rod and fell on his back. The artist took a couple of steps forward, casting the fishing rod aside as he did. Both Carmen and Jill cried out not to hit him, but the artist merely watched Jacob as he rolled on the sand. The artist lowered his fists. Andrew saw a livid weal appear on the man's forearm.

There was a moment's shocked silence, everyone frozen in place. Then Jacob gabbled again. He groaned and clutched at his jaw. He seemed amazed that he had been hit and kept shaking his head. His eyes rolled around and he was clearly stunned.

Jill now confronted the artist and screamed at him, "You bully! You filthy creep! Cover up in the presence of ladies!"

The artist half-raised his fists as anger at her words stirred him. Then he lowered them to his hips and glared angrily at her.

"Don't call me names girl! I haven't done anything."

Jill stabbed her finger towards Letitia, who still stood defiantly naked. "What about her?"

"I haven't touched her," snapped the artist angrily. "She came here of her own free will and asked me to paint her picture. I didn't ask her to take off her clothes."

"You are a liar!" Jill yelled. "You just want to have sex with her!"

At that, the artist's face broke into a grin. "Too bloody right! And if she wants it, I'll give it to her, and so will all these young buggers if they get the chance."

At that, Andrew burned and ground his teeth, knowing in his heart that the artist was right. A glance at the others showed guilty anger on all of their faces, except Martin's. He looked so miserable that Andrew thought he might burst into tears.

Jill was rendered incapable of coherent speech for a minute and then gabbled and snapped, "I don't want to see any of this! Cover up!"

"Then piss off!" retorted the artist. "I didn't invite you here, and you knew I live here and that I don't wear much. If it offends you, then you leave!"

Jill was nearly purple in the face by this. She shook her head and looked wildly around. Carmen now took command of the situation. She stepped forward and grabbed Jill.

"Calm down, Jill! The man's right. We have barged in uninvited and with no warning. We should leave. Help Jacob up."

Jacob was helped to his feet. He still looked stunned and kept shaking his head and touching his nose and right cheek. Mark hesitatingly moved forward to help, his eyes flicking continually from the artist to Letitia. Andrew stayed where he was, feeling somehow detached from it all. He did not approve of the artist, or of Letitia's behaviour, but he was disgusted by what he felt was an extreme over-reaction by Jacob and Jill. He was conscious that Anne had moved close beside him, and that she was watching everything closely.

The artist bent down and picked up Jacob's fishing rod and tossed it to Mark. "Here! Take this, and if he tries to hit me with it again, I'll thrash him to within an inch of his life. Now clear out and leave me alone!"

Carmen nodded. She said, "We are going. Come on, Letitia."

Letitia stood and shook her head. "No! I'm staying here."

"You can't," Carmen tried to reason.

Andrew could only stare, his jealousy now mingled with large helpings of lust. The sight of her nude body, and the fiery spirit of defiance was moving him to admiration.

"Yes, I can!" Letitia retorted. "I'm old enough. Anyway, I just want my picture painted."

She gestured to the canvas. Andrew had glanced at this several times. So far all the artist had done was a quick pencil or charcoal sketch and roughed out the shape of Letitia's body but it looked very attractive to him.

Jill now tried to reason with her. "But this... this... this is just improper."

At that, Letitia laughed, thrusting her hips forward as she did. "It is not! Life drawing has always been part of art. We even have life classes at school. And I like it, so leave me alone."

"Letitia!" Carmen gasped. She was obviously distressed and shocked.

"Oh give it a break!" Letitia snapped. "I've had enough of being criticised by bastards like Jacob who secretly want me. He's just a bloody hypocrite and bigot. Now go away!"

Jacob responded to that. His face mottled and he spluttered, then cried, "I'll tell your parents."

"Tell them! See if I care."

"I'll tell the police!" Jacob threatened.

Letitia just curled her lip in contempt and looked away, presenting such a profile of out-thrust breasts and curve of hip that the sheer beauty of it took Andrew's breath away. He knew he was staring.

Carmen gently pushed Jill and Jacob to get them moving back towards the rocks. Then she turned to Letitia again.

"Please Letitia!"

Letitia shook her head. "No! Go away!"

Carmen turned to Martin with a beseeching look. Martin called to Letitia, but she just turned her back. "Go away Martin!" she called, "Just because you are my brother doesn't mean you can tell me what to do."

"I'm just trying to look after you, to keep you safe!" Martin wailed, his voice cracking with anguish.

When Letitia refused to answer, he turned and, with a sob, ran off back up the track. Andrew half-turned to follow but Anne took his arm.

"Let him go," she said. "He's just ashamed of his sister, poor bugger!"

By then Carmen had urged Jill, Jacob and Mark back to the rocks. She now turned and called to Andrew. Anne answered for him, now gripping his arm.

"We will follow. You get going," she said.

Carmen did not look happy, but half her attention was now taken up with persuading Jacob to keep going as he was now recovering from the blow and showing signs of wanting to renew the battle. Andrew still stood and stared at Letitia and the artist. He was appalled at the thought of Letitia and the man being together and was desperately casting around for something to say to talk her out of such behaviour.

As Carmen and her group vanished among the rocks on Bennet Point, the artist turned to face them. Andrew had assumed that Anne had the same plan as he did and was quite amazed that she had stood her ground facing the man.

Now she surprised him even more by calmly saying to the artist, "Sorry. We should have warned you we were coming. I didn't realise that Jacob would fly off the handle like that."

The artist grunted in acceptance of the apology. Nor did Letitia help, as she again turned to face them, her face a mask of sulky defiance. The artist glanced briefly at Andrew, then turned back to Anne.

"Not your fault. He's got a problem that one. Don't marry anyone like him or your life will be a misery. All religion and no Christian charity or compassion."

Anne calmly stood there. "Yes," she agreed. Then she looked at Letitia and quietly said, "Please come back, Letitia."

"No," Letitia snapped.

She was very emotional and Andrew watched with dry-mouthed desire and thumping heart as her bosom heaved to her own rapid breathing. It was all too much.

He croaked to her, "Please Letitia!"

"No. Go away!"

"Please don't do anything," Andrew cried, now upset and shaking.

"You aren't my boyfriend, Andrew, so don't try to tell me what to do."

Anne took Andrew's arm and turned him around. She called over her shoulder, "Take care, Letitia. See you later, Mister Mason."

Andrew wanted to stay, to try to persuade Letitia but that last comment completely disarmed him.

Mr Mason! he thought, stunned by the implication. *How does she know his name?* Then he became suspicious of Anne's whole demeanour and behaviour. *Has she been seeing the painter secretly? Does she know him?* They were crushing thoughts and he just crumpled up inside.

Anne led him back along the track into the dry jungle. As he walked, Andrew was in absolute turmoil. All morning he had been enjoying himself, daydreaming about pirates and playing the treasure hunt. He had enjoyed lying on the beach watching Letitia and had relaxed reading *Treasure Island*. In his mind's eye he had pictured a stately 17th Century sailing ship gliding into the bay and he had wished he had a model ship to play with. And now this! It was all so adult, so grown up. He found it hard to cope.

Inside he felt like his stomach was a mass of maggots and worms. The thought of the artist doing things with Letitia made his flesh crawl and he wanted desperately to stop it happening. But thinking about it just filled him with self-loathing, knowing that it was exactly what he urgently desired to do himself. Suddenly the tears came, and he could not stop them. That made it worse as he was ashamed to cry in front of Anne.

They were near the small creek crossing by then and both stopped, and she shushed him and put her arms around him, holding him tight. "It's alright Andrew. Just have a good cry," she whispered. As she held him, she stroked his hair and patted his back.

"It... it... it's... Let... Letit... ia," he sobbed. "I j... just... d... sob... don't want her to get hurt or to d... d... do anything."

"Are you in love with her?" Anne asked.

"No," Andrew answered, now sure he didn't. "I just... just like her, and... sob."

Again Anne patted him and then said, "I think from what I've heard you are too late to stop her doing things. So don't let it upset you. You've done all you could. It is her life."

Sadly Andrew knew this to be true and he cried some more. After a while he calmed down a bit, ashamed of his outburst and of his own hypocritical attitude, his own lustful fantasies about Letitia. Then he became conscious of Anne's physical presence and that unsettled him as well.

He said, "I was annoyed at that disgusting man."

Anne just shrugged. "He's only a man. Seen one you've seen 'em all my mum says." Then she giggled and added, "Although there is a lot of variety."

That simultaneously shocked and interested Andrew, as they separated and resumed walking. To save awkward conversation he walked fast, pausing only for breath on the crest. On the downslope through the rain forest he almost ran. Near the bottom of the hill they met Mr and Mrs Schipholl coming the other way. Andrew paused, heart hammering and emotions once more in turmoil.

Do I tell or not? he wondered. Then he pointed back up the track and stammered, "Letitia."

"We know," Mr Schipholl said. "Carmen told us."

Feeling highly embarrassed, Andrew stepped off the track to let them past, then continued on, Anne close behind. A couple of minutes later they reached the creek. The pair paused here to wash their faces and to have a drink, before going up to the camp. Andrew was dreading that, but when they got there it wasn't as bad as he had imagined. Carmen and Jill were sitting talking and there was no sign of anyone else.

"Where are Jacob and Mark?" Andrew asked. He had trouble meeting his sister's eye.

"Out on the jetty fishing," Carmen replied.

"What about Martin?"

"Haven't seen him," Carmen replied.

"We had better look for him," Andrew said.

"No, let the poor bugger lick his wounds in private. He must be so embarrassed," Carmen said.

There were several minutes of silence. Andrew sat there wondering what would happen next. Finally he lifted his head and said, "It's all wrecked, the holiday I mean."

"Certainly a bit upset," Carmen agreed.

"What do you think will happen next? To Letitia I mean?" he asked.

At that, Carmen shrugged and shook her head. "I have no idea. If it was Mum and Dad, they would be appalled."

That was certainly a sobering thought and Andrew mentally chewed at it for a minute. Then he shook his head.

"Nah! Can't ever see you running around in the nuddy. It would never happen."

Carmen blushed and nodded.

Jill had been listening intently. "I wonder what will happen to Letitia?" she said.

Anne shrugged. "Nothing much, probably."

"Oh there must!" Jill replied. "If I behaved like that my oldies would have a fit and ground me for life!"

"Yeah, but your oldies aren't like her parents," Anne replied. "Letitia's are very broad minded. They are probably sitting down right now having a cosy chat with Mr Mason."

"With who?" Jill asked.

"Mr Mason, the artist."

Jill gave her an odd look and said, "How do you know his name?"

"We talked to him the other day," Anne replied.

That caused an awkward silence while Jill thought about that. It also got Andrew worrying again.

After a minute Jill looked up. "What will we do now?" she asked. "What will we say?"

That was the heart of their problem and they had no sensible answer. Finally Carmen said, "I think we must play it as it comes. Maybe we should act normal and pretend nothing unusual has happened."

"Oh how can we!" Jill cried.

"Easily," Anne replied. "We all practice deceit of one form or another all the time. That's normal human behaviour. It is just more of that."

That was a very uncomfortable thought for Andrew, and he worried at it. He put the idea that they might all be going home tomorrow and then dreaded the long night such a decision would bring.

Then Carmen stood up and said, "I will look for Martin. You others stay here and tidy the camp and get ready for tea. Even if the sky has fallen in, we still have to eat." With that she walked off towards the ruin.

They did as they were told. More time went by. The sun went behind the ridge and the evening shadows settled. Andrew began to be very anxious, hoping that Martin was alright. Then 5:30 came and went. Still nobody returned to camp. The food was ready by then and the fire laid waiting for a match. With nothing else to do the three sat and brooded over what might happen. Andrew felt sick at heart and deeply saddened.

Why is life so complicated, so disgusting? he wondered unhappily. He could never remember feeling so upset in all is life. *Except when Carmen got kidnapped by those smugglers,* he qualified. Then he heard voices in the jungle across the creek and tensed. *Here they come! Oh bum! What will we say? What's going to happen?*

It was the Schipholls. Mr Schipholl was leading and Letitia, now clad in her bikini, brought up the rear. As she came up out of the creek her eyes met Andrew's briefly, then she looked away. Her face looked flushed and sullen, but she put on a brave show of normality when she greeted the girls.

"Where are the other boys?" Mrs Schipholl asked.

"Fishing," Anne answered.

Mrs Schipholl looked at the food laid out and said, "Then one of you go and get them. It is teatime. It will be dark soon."

Andrew watched and marvelled. To his eyes both Mr and Mrs Schipholl appeared to be quite normal and relaxed.

Maybe Anne was right? Their daughter being with that artist hasn't bothered them much?

It certainly looked as though that was the way it was as Letitia was then spoken to quite casually by her mother. Jill offered to go and get the boys and that notched the social tension in Andrew back up again.

How will Jacob react to Letitia? he wondered. *And how will we explain to Mr and Mrs Schipholl where Martin is?*

Chapter 23

IN THE EYES

When Carmen had offered to go and look for Martin, she was feeling sick at heart. She had been deeply shocked and upset by the events of the afternoon and was feeling quite unsure about how to speak to Martin, even if she could find him. Her mind swirling with options, all seemingly difficult, she had walked along the track towards the ruins.

Walking through the overgrown coconut plantation on her own she found an eerie experience. By then the sun had moved so far down to the west that the place was in the shadow of Mt Gore. Carmen's thoughts were almost as gloomy as the thickets of rainforest over to her left.

How could Letitia do that? she wondered.

But the idea of standing naked in front of a man caused Carmen to blush and tingle with what she recognised as sexual arousal, and she then doubted herself. Then, try as she might, she could not push the picture out of her mind.

This is ridiculous! she told herself. *I'm not like that!*

But that was an uncomfortable thought and led to secret, niggling doubts that maybe she wasn't as strong and nice as she had always seen herself to be. That led to other thoughts, to wondering what sex might be like, and whether she would enjoy it. Up to that moment it had mostly seemed disgusting and unpleasant, something a married woman might put up with as part of her 'wifely duties' to have babies and to appease her husband's carnal lust (She had no doubt that male desire existed!).

Now, thinking about Letitia, she was simultaneously sickened and fascinated. Obviously, Letitia did not think sex was all that big a deal whereas Carmen had always thought it to be one of the great taboos until married (in spite of what she heard from other girls at school). Having told Mrs Schipholl about the artist had helped ease her conscience after not being able to talk Letitia into returning with the others.

It had been a stomach-churning experience to tell Mr Schipholl and Carmen was ashamed that she had not told the whole story (about the fight, or Letitia's comments about doing what she liked). It was all very distressing, and made worse by the fact that the whole situation obviously deeply embarrassed Martin.

What would Andrew think if I was a tart? she pondered.

That got her very anxious about Martin. What if he became so ashamed and depressed that he did 'something'? (Suicide she meant, but did not want to frame the word in her thoughts). That got her thinking about Martin's parents and their reaction. What must it be like to live in a house where you sometimes saw your mother and father butt-naked? That made Carmen smile. Never in her life had she seen either of her parents naked and she formed a wry smile.

Compared to the Schipholls, Mum and Dad are boring normality personified. But with that came another unsettling thought. *Are Mum and Dad any happier than the Schipholls?*

Over the last few days she had witnessed the Schipholls give each other frequent signs and touches of tender affection and they seemed very much in love.

By then she was at the ruin. Martin was not there. She looked down the other trail as far as the dam, then checked the concrete pumphouse. Still no sign of him. Next, she looked at the remains of the servants quarters. Still nothing. For a few minutes she stood there alone, gripped by emotional turmoil and a mounting sense of apprehension. In the hush of evening she heard the swash of surf.

"Sandy Beach. I'll look there," she muttered.

She did not feel like calling out. With her emotion catching in her throat she hurried down the side track to Sandy Beach. The beach was in shadow as well by then, the sunlight still lighting up the islands out to sea. Still no sign of him. Carmen stared both ways along the beach, screwing up her eyes against the fresh breeze and the fine sand and salt spray it was whipping up.

For half a minute she stood there, biting her lip and wondering where to go next. Back towards the camp seemed the most sensible option so she set off south along the beach. Five minutes later she came to the Secret Cove. It had a fair surf pounding in and did not seem to be nearly as pleasant as she remembered. By then the wind had begun to chill her.

Where to next?

She hesitated between going back to camp through the cemetery, or up over the hill on Oyster Point. The cemetery did not appeal so she set off up the hill. Twilight was setting in by then and she knew the others must be wondering where they were.

The Schipholls must be back by now, she thought.

That got her speculating about what had happened over at the artist's. In turn she began thinking about the incident and she blushed again.

She shook her head. *No. I could never let anyone look at me naked. Well, maybe, if the conditions were right.*

She tried to imagine how she would feel if a man saw her naked. The idea made her squirm and feel deeply anxious.

"No!" she said emphatically.

"What?"

It was Martin. He was sitting on a rock right on top of the hill. He was hunched up, gripping his knees with his arms and was staring out to sea.

Carmen walked over and sat beside him, relief flooding through her. "Nothing Martin," she replied. "I was just talking to myself."

Martin merely grunted and hunched lower. That left Carmen groping for the right thing to say. She decided the thing to do was confront the issue, so she said, "You must be feeling pretty rotten at the moment; really embarrassed and ashamed I mean."

For a moment Carmen feared she had done the wrong thing. She saw Martin stiffen and then he turned tear-filled eyes to her.

"You have no idea how I feel!" he cried in anguish.

"No," Carmen conceded, her heart going out to him in such obvious distress. "But I do care, and I want to help. So do the others."

"Not Jill, or Jacob," Martin said, his face a picture of utter misery.

"No, but Andrew is your friend, and so is Anne," Carmen replied. "They don't judge you."

"They do! Everybody does! How do you think it feels when your sister has a reputation around the school? Have you any idea how much it hurts when you walk over to your mates, who are all laughing at some joke, and they suddenly look sideways at you and go all red and shut up and you realise they were sniggering about your own sister!"

That burned and Carmen had no words to answer. Instead, she placed her hand on Martin's arm and shook her head sadly. She could see that Martin was struggling to hold back tears and wanted to spare his pride. She felt him go tense at her touch but gently patted and kept her hand there. Unable to stop herself, she sighed loudly and shook her head.

"I'm sorry, Martin, but don't be too harsh on Letitia. Maybe that is just the way she is? Maybe she has needs that... that..."

"It hurts!" he wailed. The tears had started to flow now but Carmen tactfully ignored him. "It really hurts to know everyone is calling your sister easy, and a moll and a slut and a trollop!"

Hearing Martin use those names scorched Carmen's compassion and she put her arm around his shoulders. For a few minutes she just held him while he sobbed. Then she wiped away a few tears from her own cheeks, and said, "Have you thought about why she acts that way?"

"Probably because... because... I don't know," Martin replied.

Because of your mum and dad, Carmen thought, finishing his sentence in her mind.

Instead, she said, "I think she does it because she is feeling very insecure and desperately wants to be loved and wanted."

Martin looked at her in scornful disbelief. "Wanted!" he cried.

Carmen ignored that. "Yes. Most girls get very anxious about whether they are good enough, about whether they are attractive enough to get a boyfriend. And they have a deep need to be accepted and loved, and to have friends."

"Those sort of friends?" Martin sneered in a sarcastic tone, but Carmen could tell her words had gone home.

"Any sort of friends. When you are really lonely you get desperate," she replied. "Letting boys do things is one way to get their attention."

"It's disgusting, and shameful!" Martin said.

"Yes, it is," Carmen agreed. "But perhaps she is very lonely and insecure." She paused for a moment, and when Martin made no answer, added, "I don't know why. Letitia is very good looking and is such a nice person. It would be different if she was a hard-hearted bitch."

Martin was still sniffling but had stopped the anguished sobbing. It was plain to Carmen that he was thinking hard. She now pressed her advantage.

"You need to tell her how you feel."

At that, Martin seemed to shrivel. Carmen continued, "I know, easier said than done. But she is your sister, and I can tell you love her. So help her and at least accept her for what she is. And try to keep her safe if you can. Now, it is getting late, and I am sure your mum and dad will be wondering where we are. It must be teatime. Let's go down."

For a moment Carmen thought Martin was going to refuse, but he nodded and stood up. As they did, Carmen took her hand away. She at once turned and started down the rough track towards Fishermans Beach. To her relief, Martin followed.

They descended the hill in silence, but at the bottom on the small strip of beach near the three pandanus palms he muttered, "Thanks."

To avoid making it more stressful, Carmen just graciously acknowledged his gratitude and kept on walking. Rather than detour through the gloom of the cemetery she kept on along the beach to the jetty. A minute later she and Martin arrived back in camp. All the others were there and were seated in a circle at one of the tables and around a lantern next to it.

She had been dreading the return, but Mrs Schipholl merely cried, "Oh there you are! Good. Just in time. Here, sit down and have some grilled fish. Mark caught it."

The fish provided a topic to carry them over the first few embarrassing minutes. To Carmen's relief, neither Jacob nor Jill made any comments and she caught looks of relief and sympathy on the faces of Andrew and Anne. She also noted that Andrew and Anne were sitting side by side and that got her wondering. From a couple of looks, she guessed that Mrs Schipholl was also wondering. But that was something for Martin to address, so she tried to relax and 'suss out' the social situation.

That things were tense was plain, but most of them were trying to hide it. Letitia was now fully dressed and conducting a cheery chatter that revealed she was in a brittle state. Jacob sat looking surly and said little. Mark was looking anxious, most of the time looking at Letitia. Jill was quiet and stony-faced. Only Anne and Andrew seemed relatively normal, and they were as much taken up with talking to each other as with anyone else.

To Carmen's eyes Mrs and Mr Schipholl were looking a bit anxious, but she decided they were worried about the whole camping trip. That got her wondering what they might have said to the artist, and to Letitia. Letitia's actions gave very little clue, but Mr Schipholl appeared to be quite calm.

As the minutes ticked by, conditions slowly eased. The fish was excellent and was followed by tinned fruit and cream. This was washed down by tea or coffee, prepared by Anne using the gas stove. As soon as the meal was over, Andrew at once began washing up, having heated the water in a pot on the barbeque plate. Anne and Martin moved to help him. The others were told by Mrs Schipholl to tidy up and then get ready for a campfire sing-along.

That produced a few cries of protest and a sneer from Mark, but they were all over-ruled and told to get on with it. Mr Schipholl, who still wore part of his Squire Trelawney costume, stood up and said, "No mutiny, me hearties. Aye, and ye can all dress up in yer buccaneer's outfits again."

"Oh, do we have to?" Mark asked.

"Yes, me hearty. The dress of the day is 'Pirate Rig'," Mr Schipholl replied.

Andrew stood up and grinned, then knuckled his forehead. "Aye, aye Squire!"

Carmen saw Letitia pout and it crossed her mind that the dressing up might be a way of getting Letitia covered up, without making any fuss about it. She personally had no problem with the idea of costume and went happily off to her tent to change. A silent Letitia joined her a few minutes later. As she crawled into the tent their eyes met and Letitia gave a wry smile.

More a grimace than a grin, Carmen thought, noting the little lines of stress around Letitia's eyes.

To her relief, Letitia made no fuss and pulled on a red and white striped T-shirt and jeans. Carmen dressed in a similar way, rolling up the bottoms of her trousers and tying a handkerchief around her head.

Twenty minutes later they were all at the beach between the jetty and the mouth of the creek, dropping their pieces of firewood and spreading rugs or sleeping bags on the sand. Once again, Carmen noted that Andrew and Anne were sitting side by side.

And quite close too. Good!

Mr Schipholl appointed himself chief firelighter and Mark helped him. Soon a cheerful little fire was blazing on the sand. Mr Schipholl then stood as Master of Ceremonies and invited them to join in. From the pocket of his blue 'captain's coat' he produced a harmonica and began to play. Carmen was quite astonished at how good he was. Usually she disliked harmonica music intensely, but this seemed just right for the time and place. It was a lilting tune that got her feet tapping and she saw the faces of the others changing as they tried to not laugh or sneer.

"That be a tune called 'Portsmouth'," explained Mr Schipholl. "A sailor's hornpipe. Great dancers the old sailors were, so me hearties, let's be havin' ye all on yer feet and we'll try it."

That took some persuading, but Carmen, Anne, and Mrs Schipholl stood up straight away. Andrew and Martin followed and that shamed the rest into getting up. Then Mr Schipholl demonstrated the steps and began to play. Carmen tried, making a deliberate attempt to ignore her self-consciousness.

Dance like nobody is watching, she told herself

She actually enjoyed it and was flushed and happy when she sat down. She suspected some of the others also enjoyed it more than they let on. The eyes gave it away. They also betrayed who was looking at who. After they had seated themselves, she noted with pleasure that Andrew and Anne kept exchanging glances, but with disquiet that Mark was making eyes at Letitia. She was pretending not to be interested but the by-play was drawing pained glances from Jill. Jacob's eyes also kept flicking to Letitia, but Carmen could not read their meaning. Martin's eyes looked sad, even though he had a smile on his face.

Mr Schipholl next coaxed them to sing sea shanties: He had taken the trouble to photocopy the words and handed them each a song sheet. Having no excuse about not knowing the words they all sang, the volume increasing as they started to relax and enjoy themselves. They sang: 'What shall we do with the drunken sailor', 'Hey, hey and up she rises, early in the morning', 'Yo ho ho, and a bottle of rum' and 'Anchor's aweigh!' Then Mr Schipholl gave a solo rendition of 'Shenandoah', singing in a fine, rich baritone that quite pleased and surprised Carmen. Mrs Schipholl then stood and sang 'The Skye Boat Song'. That was so well done that she drew spontaneous applause from Carmen and Anne.

More dancing followed, then Mr Schipholl recited 'The boy stood on the burning deck'. After that he got them all on their feet in pairs spaced around the fire.

"You are to pretend that you are sailors working the capstan to wind up the anchor," he explained.

Then he got them doing 'Stamp and Go!' and singing 'Bound for Botany Bay' and 'To South Australia'. They all chanted and stamped around on the sand and even Jacob smiled so Carmen thought the whole idea of a campfire an excellent one.

Anne then surprised her by standing and singing 'The Belle of Belfast City'. It wasn't a sea song but was sung with such clear, true notes that they all clapped. As Anne sat down, Andrew made a point of telling her how well she had done. To Carmen's delight, she saw them move so close together on the rug that they were touching.

The campfire lasted nearly two hours and changed the whole atmosphere of the group. The gloom lifted and there was laughter, jokes and cheering. Only a couple of sour notes intruded: Mark saying that the only sea song he knew was 'The Good Ship Venus' (Carmen had only ever heard one or two verses but knew it was very, very crude); and the obvious forced smiles of Martin and Letitia. Even Jacob seemed to lighten up and enter into the spirit of the thing.

At 9 o'clock Mrs Schipholl led them all back to camp for supper: hot chocolate and cream biscuits. By the time supper was over, Carmen felt quite tired.

It's been a long day, she mused, her mind roving back over the treasure hunt and then the dramas of the afternoon. That got her thinking about the artist and Letitia, and she blushed as she knew she was pruriently interested and was ashamed of herself.

Bed was ordered by Mr Schipholl, who had come in from making sure the fire was completely out. "And no hanky panky tonight!" he added.

As he said this he glanced at Letitia, who gave a faint curl to her top lip. Carmen also noted her eyes then flick to Mark, whose (she thought) glinted.

Did Mark just give Letitia a nod? she wondered.

There was no doubt that Andrew and Anne were exchanging glances and that got Carmen both pleased and anxious.

Oh I hope they are making up, but I also hope they aren't planning anything foolish later.

With that thought on her mind she crawled into her tent and changed for bed, slipping off her jeans but leaving on her T-shirt. Letitia came in a few minutes later and avoided her eyes, adding to Carmen's suspicion.

I'd better keep an eye on her tonight, she decided.

"Good night, Letitia. Sleep well."

"Yes, good night. I will," Letitia replied.

She lay down and stretched out. Carmen was self-consciously aware of Letitia so lay on her side facing away from her. Outside, the camp settled down. The moon was now well up and still very full. It cast a dapple pattern from the leaves on the tent and Carmen lay staring at these for a while. From time to time she would glance at Letitia to check she was there. She found it a relief when Letitia pulled a rug over herself as the night air cooled. After a time she drifted into a restless sleep.

What woke me? she wondered.

She lay still and listened but all she could hear were the usual night sounds and the gentle swash of waves on the beach. No strange sound indicated anything unusual. For a time she lay there wondering if she had heard one of the others moving about, but despite straining her ears she could not detect anything to indicate that. She closed her eyes and tried to go back to sleep.

But sleep would not come. Carmen lay there listening to the small night noises of insects and birds in the surrounding forest; of one of the boys snoring lightly (Mark or Andrew?); all the while thinking deeply.

I will go for a walk, she thought. As quietly as she could, she got up and slid on her jeans. Letitia appeared to be asleep.

Very carefully she left the tent and crept across the clearing. Taking the track to the beach she walked slowly along it, her mind and body relaxing as she left the camp behind. She found walking along the track an odd experience. The moonlight lit up the sand so that it seemed to glow, making the patches of dappled shadow under the trees seem to be even darker. When the gentle sighing of the wind in the leaves, and the murmuring swash of the waves on the beach were added, it was very romantic.

She reached the edge of the beach and stopped, breathing deeply and gazing with delight at the ripple of silver and black as the sea danced in the moonlight.

Oh, I wish I had a man who loved me, she thought, brushing a fleeting image of Jacob from her mind and hugging herself.

Suddenly she tensed. From behind came the sound of giggling and the scuff of footsteps on sand. Glancing behind her Carmen saw movement.

I'll bet it is Letitia and Mark, she thought.

On an impulse she stepped into the darkness under the nearest tree. Her idea was to step out and thwart their plan before they actually did anything. Then she saw the moving figures clearly in a patch of moonlight and was appalled.

Oh no! It is not Letitia and Mark. It is Mr and Mrs Schipholl!

In the bright light Carmen could plainly see both of them. To her relief, Mr Schipholl wore a pair of loose shorts and Mrs Schipholl had on a large T-shirt. But their arrival threw her in a fluster. As the two passed within arm's reach, she found she was so anxious about embarrassing them (and herself) that she stayed hidden.

I will creep back to camp as soon as they are gone, she thought.

But to her dismay, they did not go away. Mr and Mrs Schipholl stopped only ten paces from her, near the end of the jetty. The moonlight was so bright that Carmen could see every detail and she could only stare in embarrassed interest.

Mr Schipholl hugged his wife to him and they kissed very tenderly. As the kiss went on and on, the couple stroked each other, and Carmen's embarrassment and anxiety grew.

I hope they aren't going to do anything serious, she thought.

By then Carmen was in a near panic. She was so ashamed that she just wished the sand would open up and hide her. She thought of making a noise to warn them but her throat seemed to have thickened up and dried out. All she could do was bite her lip and gasp little breaths.

I must sneak away, she told herself.

But the moment she tried to move she trod on a dry stick which snapped loudly. She froze but neither adult seemed to hear. Mr Schipholl and Mrs Schipholl continued to hug and kiss for a few more minutes. By this time Carmen was desperately anxious that her presence not be discovered so she slowly edged around behind the trunk of the tree.

Mrs Schipholl sighed with pleasure and then Mr Schipholl kissed her again and said, "You are wonderful. I love you."

That really got Carmen going. Now what she was seeing just seemed wonderful and natural.

Oh I hope I find a man who can love me like that! she thought.

To her enormous relief, Mr and Mrs Schipholl released each other from their embrace and went strolling hand in hand out along the jetty. Carmen was so emotional that she stood and trembled, her heart only slowly easing its urgent hammering. To her surprise she discovered that, far from feeling disgusted at the exhibition of passion, she felt she had witnessed something very special.

I wish it was me kissing the man I love, she thought, thinking the setting of the moonlight shining across the ripples of the ocean and with the pleasant tropical breeze rustling the palm leaves very romantic.

As soon as the Schipholls were out near the far end of the jetty, Carmen risked being seen and crept back through the moon dappled shadows to her tent. Back at the camp all was quiet. Very carefully she slid into her tent, noting Letitia's sleeping form.

Good, Carmen thought. *She hasn't snuck out and got up to any mischief.*

After rearranging her bedding and slipping off her joggers and jeans, Carmen lay back. For at least half an hour she lay there with her mind and body in an aroused state, reliving what she had just seen and wondering what it might be like for her when the time came. Then, as the excitement ebbed, she slowly drifted into a relaxed sleep.

Some time later something woke her. For a minute or two she just lay still, wondering what and noting the bright moonlight. Then she glanced sideways and her anxiety shot up. Letitia's bed was empty.

She was gone!

Chapter 24

IN THE MOONLIGHT

Andrew was having a wonderful dream. He had managed to get Letitia alone and they had started a fairly torrid 'pashing' session, but being a dream, nothing ever going quite right. Then she had said 'yes' and things had started to go wrong. Andrew found himself torn, and then the dream faded.

His eyes blinked open. He lay there, staring at the dapple of leaf shadows on the roof of the tent, wet with perspiration and feeling very frustrated. He was extremely aroused and glanced quickly at Mark to check whether he had noticed. To his relief, Mark was sound asleep. Then Andrew remembered.

Anne! I am supposed to meet her at 1 o'clock! he thought. Panic surged. *What time is it?* A check of his watch in the beam of moonlight coming in through the door showed him it was after 1:30am. *Oh no! Half an hour late! I wonder if she has waited?*

Feeling wretched he crawled to the entrance. Then he reached for a shirt, grabbing his dark blue work shirt as the first one that come to hand.

I had better wear a shirt or she might get the wrong idea, he reasoned.

Of course he was hoping for a kiss and a cuddle (Why else would she agree to meet him on the beach after midnight?) but he did not want her to draw the wrong conclusions about his motives. He was now clear in his own mind that he wanted to learn about girls but was also determined make sure neither they, nor he, were placed at any serious risk or harmed.

When Anne had agreed to meet him, he had been elated. She had insisted that it be well after all the others were asleep so that there was no possibility of them being found out.

"I don't want a lot of behind-the-hand snickering," she had explained.

"And now I've slept in and am late," Andrew muttered as he crawled out of the tent.

For a minute he stood, quietly listening, while he buttoned up the shirt. He began walking quietly across the campsite. Then another awful idea came to him.

218

What if she has given up and gone back to her tent?

He paused and stared in the darkness at the tent she shared with Jill. But the flaps were closed and he could not tell who was in it.

In an attempt to find out, he padded quietly over and stood listening. He could hear breathing inside but could not tell if it was one person or two. He did not dare try to open the tent, picturing the embarrassment and accusations if he was caught trying to sneak into one of the girl's tents in the middle of the night.

Jill will bung on a real turn, he thought.

Still unsure, he seemed to have no other option but to hurry to the rendezvous agreed on, in the hope that she was still there. He set off along the pathway towards the beach, rehearsing his lame excuse and silently wishing the moonlight was not so bright.

Once at the beach, Andrew turned left and hurried along it for a hundred paces, his bare feet sinking into the cool, damp sand. The scene was just made for love: the silver dapple of dancing waves, the gentle murmuring of the swash and the rustle of palm fronds, the moonlight. But most of it was lost on Andrew in his current state of anxiety. He reached the small outcrop of rocks and stopped. There on his left was the clump of three pandanus palms, the agreed meeting place.

But no sign of Anne.

Andrew moved up to the pool of shadows cast by the large banyan fig growing at the top of the beach, but she was not there either. He went on a few paces into the grass and weeds until he could see the tombstones of the old cemetery, glowing pale and ghostly in the moonlight. She was definitely not there. When Anne had suggested the three pandanus palms as a meeting place Andrew had been astonished.

I wonder how serious she is about this? he thought. He really wanted a bit of a kiss and a cuddle but really did not want it to go too far. Then he shook his head. *Nah! She's not like that. The best I will get tonight will be a kiss and a bit of a hug,* he thought. But that would be fine he decided. But what to do? *Should I go back to camp and see if she is in her tent?* And if she was, could he wake her up without also waking Jill? *And what will her reaction be after being stood up?* he thought gloomily.

Then his hopes soared: someone was coming along the beach.

Andrew moved down towards the outcrop of rocks to get a better look, and froze in alarm. It was not one person but two.

Oh no! Who are they? he wondered.

Not wanting to have to explain to any of the others what he was doing on the beach at that hour, Andrew stepped behind the rocks. When the people continued towards him, he became anxious and looked around for a place to hide. The nearest was a small hollow between the rocks. This was just in the circle of shadow cast by the fig tree. His rapidly racing mind calculated that he had no chance of reaching any other cover without being seen or heard. Feeling both foolish and embarrassed, he crouched down in the cleft.

Even as he did his eyes registered that the people were fully dressed. There was something decidedly odd about them and he tried to identify who it was. They were carrying things and were talking softly. Then Andrew gaped and shook his head.

They are wearing their pirate costume, he noted.

That got him wondering if the others were playing a game of buccaneers and why he hadn't been told. He noted the tricorn hat on the person on the right, and the striped sailor's jersey on the person on the left. Then he gaped again. A third person had appeared back near the jetty and was hurrying along behind the others.

They are looking for me, Andrew decided.

Thinking it must be a game of hide-and-seek or something, he crouched even lower. Then he gaped again. By now the closest two were clearly visible in the moonlight, and he did not know them!

Both strangers appeared to be men. The one with the tricorn hat had a huge black beard and wore a dark flowing coat of 17th Century cut, complete with rows of brass buttons. He had knee breeches and old-fashioned sea boots with the tops turned down. He also had a sword and a pistol. The blade of the sword shimmered briefly in the moonlight, causing Andrew a first shiver of apprehension. Then he noted the pistol and he was gripped by real concern. It was a modern automatic.

It isn't Mr Schipholl or Jacob dressed up, he thought. *These are strangers!*

The other man wore loose, baggy white trousers, rolled up to the knees, and a long-sleeved, striped sailor's jersey. He also had a black eye patch and a handkerchief tied around his head. A large gold earring dangled from his right earlobe. The sailor had a cutlass thrust through his belt and was carrying a shovel.

For a moment Andrew wondered if he was dreaming. Then the men spoke and he knew he wasn't and fear flooded in.

These men are up to no good, he told himself. *They are real pirates.*

The two pirates stopped on the beach and looked at the three pandanus palms. Then the one with the black beard put down a metal box and said, in a very English accent, "This be the ones, I reckon."

"Ain't no others I can see," agreed his companion, also with an English accent.

"I'll pace it out. You keep watch," Captain Blackbeard instructed. He moved right up to the pandanus palms, then let out a sharp cry. "Ouch! Bloody thing's got thorns on it!"

"Heh! Heh! Do ye good, ye lubber," chortled the other pirate.

But any humour in the situation was lost on Andrew when he saw him unsling what could only be a sub-machinegun.

Who are these men? he wondered. *And what are they doing playing pirates in the middle of the night?*

Captain Blackbeard faced towards Andrew and paced out five paces, counting them loud enough for Andrew to hear.

Then he said, "Here. Start digging, Smee."

Smee? Andrew wondered. *Wasn't he a pirate in Peter Pan? Am I dreaming this?*

But he knew he wasn't. Ants had found him and started to bite, and they hurt. From fear of these strangers with guns Andrew could only bite his lip and endure the pain. He tried to crouch even lower in the cleft.

As Smee began to dig, the third person arrived. It was another man dressed as a pirate, except that he also carried a wicked looking sub-machine gun.

Very modern pirates, Andrew thought. *And up to no good.*

He began to sweat with fear, worried about what they might do to him if they found him.

As the third pirate arrived, Captain Blackbeard asked, "Well Bosun, anyone there?"

"Aye Cap'n. There be five tents up under the trees, but all's quiet," Bosun replied.

"Silver was right then," Captain Blackbeard said. "Good, you go back and keep watch in case any of 'em wakes up."

"What do I do if they do?" Bosun asked.

"Tell 'em to piss orf. And if they won't, bash 'em," Captain Blackbeard replied.

"Aye, aye Cap'n," Bosun replied. He turned to go back towards the jetty.

As he did, Captain Blackbeard called after him, "Keep watching. When I signal with my torch, bring the boat along here. That'll save us walking all that way back."

Bosun grunted acknowledgment and hurried off. Andrew quickly lost sight of him as he dared not raise his head to see over the rocks. All he could do was crouch there, in rapidly increasing discomfort, while Smee shovelled sand a few metres away.

Captain Blackbeard watched for a minute, then looked past Andrew. With a grunt he strode up the beach and into the shadows of the fig. Andrew hardly dared to breathe but did slowly turn his head. He heard leaves crackle underfoot and some dry twigs snap.

Then Captain Blackbeard came back and said, "Only a bone orchard."

"A what?" Smee asked, resting for a moment.

"A bone orchard, a graveyard," Captain Blackbeard replied.

"Dead centre of town, eh?" Smee joked. Then he bent to his digging.

Captain Blackbeard chuckled and fingered his pistol while looking down at Smee. "Aye, dead men tell no tales."

When Andrew heard that his hair stood on end with dread. *Is he going to shoot Smee, to leave a ghost to guard his treasure?* he wondered.

He had no doubt the hole was being dug for the metal box that lay on the sand. Captain Blackbeard stood so close to him he could see every detail: the lace ruffles at the end of his shirt cuffs, the sash around his waist, the folded neckcloth and stock. The word 'swashbuckling' flitted across Andrew's mind. So did pain. Having to crouch and stay still for so long was resulting in cramps. All he could do was grit his teeth and try to carefully flex the muscles.

Smee grunted and stopped digging. "That do?"

Captain Blackbeard looked and nodded. "Aye. Enough. Here, take the box."

The two men hoisted the box into the waist deep hole. Once again, Andrew feared Captain Blackbeard would shoot while Smee was bending over settling the box in the bottom. But nothing happened and he climbed out and began shovelling the sand back in. As he did, Captain Blackbeard took a small torch out of the side pocket of his coat and flicked it on, aiming it towards the jetty. That got Andrew really anxious.

If he shines it this way he must spot me, he reasoned.

Within a couple of minutes the hole was filled in and Smee set to work smoothing the sand. As he did, Captain Blackbeard walked down to the edge of the water. Andrew heard a low muttering noise which he decided was a motor. Into view slid a black boat of some sort with one man in it. The boat nosed in close to the beach and the man in it jumped out and held the bow.

Andrew now saw that the boat was of the 'Rigid Raider' type. *Yes, very modern pirates,* he told himself.

Captain Blackbeard waded out and clambered aboard, then turned and called, "Come on, Smee. We want to be well away by sun-up."

"Aye, aye. Just smoothin' this sand so no nosy parkers notice it," Smee replied.

He was now so close that Andrew could have almost touched him, and he feared he might hear him breathing, or even smell him. But Smee was puffing too much himself, and sweating heavily. He brushed the sand off his hands on his trousers, picked up the shovel and shotgun and trotted down to the boat.

As soon as he was aboard the boat, Bosun pushed it off, clambered aboard, then made his way aft to the controls. The motor sound increased to a deep, purring noise and white water boiled at the stern. The boat slid backwards, then spun on the spot. A moment later it was accelerating out of the bay.

Andrew began to move even before it had gone from sight as his muscles were now so cramped that he was hard put not to cry out in agony. With a gasp of relief he straightened up and walked down the sand to watch. By then the boat was just a tiny black blur, the foam from the propeller being more visible than the craft itself. Within a minute it had vanished, heading east around Oyster Point.

I wonder where they are going? Andrew thought, as he massaged his thigh and calf muscles.

For another couple of minutes he stood, staring out to sea. All the while his mind was racing. Who were the pirates? Where had they come from- a ship? Why were they dressed that way? Why did they bury the box, and, above all, what was in the box that they buried in the sand?

Curiosity now got the better of Andrew. *I could dig it up and find out,* he decided.

So he walked back to the spot where the box was buried and began scooping sand out with his hands. As he did, he kept glancing out to sea, just in case the pirates came back.

Suddenly, all his hair seemed to stand on end with fright and his heart leapt into his mouth. The sound of whispering voices had reached his ears. The sounds came from just the other side of the rocks. Andrew sprang to his feet, heart hammering. In the moonlight he saw two people walking towards him. One person was wearing what looked like a large white T-shirt but Andrew could not make out what the other had on.

The two stopped and came together and Andrew saw that they were kissing and hugging. He had been about to call out but the cry died on his lips. Now he closed his mouth and strained his eyes to see. The sound of a giggle came from the pair.

Letitia! Andrew thought, his body going tense with instant jealousy and hurt. *But who is that kissing her?*

The pair continued walking towards Andrew. By then they were only 20 paces away and again Andrew cast urgently around for an escape. Once again, he realised he had left it too late, so he stepped back to the cleft in the rocks and began lowering himself into the shadows. But this time he remembered his cramped legs and positioned himself so he could straighten them.

Letitia asked, "Why are we coming all the way along here?"

A man answered: the artist. He replied, "Because if anyone comes looking for you they are more likely to go the other way, now give me another kiss."

Andrew was stunned. Letitia and the artist! He was so horrified he almost stood up and cried out. To his added dismay, the pair stopped right where the box was buried, only about five metres from Andrew. Feeling rapidly growing hurt he watched while they kissed. When the artist slid his hands over Letitia's buttocks and in under her white T-shirt Andrew burned with jealousy. He saw that the artist only wore a pair of shorts and the flame turned to white heat.

The knife of envy was twisted even more by the way Letitia kissed the man. What really got at Andrew was the shame of knowing that he was a hypocrite, that he would love to have Letitia kiss him like that.

Now maggots of jealousy swirled amid the growing arousal he was experiencing.

I should let them know I am here, he thought.

But he didn't. He was frozen in place by shame and embarrassment. He was even denied the idea of trying to rescue Letitia as it was blatantly obvious that the pair had met by arrangement, and that she was a very willing participant.

Oh I hope they aren't going to! he thought.

His emotions were now a seething mixture of anger, jealousy and lust. He felt sick to the bottom of his stomach, as much by his own mounting desire as by anything. He gritted his teeth and clenched his fists, trying desperately to decide what to do. The temptation to jump out and stop them kept rising to the top of his mind but he was held back by feeling sure that if he did, Letitia would not only be mortified, but would never speak to him again.

Then it got worse, much worse!

Letitia stepped back and peeled off her T-shirt. She wore nothing underneath and the artist drew her hard against him and they resumed kissing.

Andrew crouched in both mental and physical agony and bit his lip. He began to silently cry, misery and jealous rage warring with his desire. But still he could not bring himself to stop them. He yearned to cry out not to do it, to stop, but his lips remained closed. For that he despised himself as a weakling, while rationalising that his intervention would be fiercely resented, possibly violently.

Suddenly the pair stopped kissing. The artist pointed along towards the jetty.

"A light, coming this way," he said. "I wonder who that is?"

"Oh shit!" Letitia cried. "Two torches. I'll bet they are looking for me."

"This way, quick!" the artist whispered.

Still holding Letitia's hand he ran up the beach past Andrew. A moment later the pair had vanished into the old cemetery, only the crackle of dead leaves and dry grass marking their exit.

I'd better get out of here too, Andrew decided.

If the searchers had torches, they were sure to see him. He painfully raised himself so that he could see over the rocks. To his dismay, he saw two people with electric torches walking towards him. They were only about 50 paces away and were shining their torch beams in under all the trees at the top of the beach.

Andrew moved out at a crouch, keeping low behind the rocks, his eyes flicking in all directions while he tried to decide which way to run. There seemed only one practical alternative, into the old cemetery.

But I might run into Letitia and the artist, he thought.

In spite of that it seemed the best option. The other was to run along the beach and scramble up the side of the rocky hill on Oyster Point.

Having made his choice, Andrew set off at a scampering, crouching run. That was a mistake because he crunched the dead leaves and twigs and the people with torches heard him.

A torch beam flashed across and he heard Carmen's voice call out, "Who's that? Letitia, is that you?"

By then Andrew was behind the fig tree and into the dry grass. The last thing he felt like doing at that moment was explaining to his sister what he had just seen. Normally he would have been scared stiff at the idea of walking through the cemetery on his own at night but now fear gave him speed. It was almost his undoing as his ankle struck an iron railing which was hidden in the long grass. He went sprawling, striking his face very hard on the next tombstone. For a moment he lay there stunned, clutching his face. Then he heard voices behind him and saw the torch beams flickering through the trees. He scrambled to his feet and continued on, limping and with tears of pain running down his face.

Two minutes later he reached the toilet. Here he paused to get his breath back and to listen. He did not want to go running into a camp of fully awake people. That would mean some awkward explanations. However, all seemed quite so he walked forward into the shadows under the big trees. There was no-one there and the tents all appeared to be closed up, so he padded over to his own. A careful check showed that Mark was still asleep. With a sigh of relief Andrew crawled in.

After closing the tent flap, he lay down on his bed. A fit of trembling and emotion then gripped him.

Chapter 25

THE MORNING AFTER

Before leaving her tent, Carmen pulled on her jeans and joggers. She then picked up her torch and crawled out. As she stood up, she heard movement nearby. Flicking on the torch she was surprised to find Anne standing fully dressed and fixed in the beam. Anne let out a gasp of fright and stood open-mouthed. To Carmen, she looked more than surprised.

She looks guilty, she thought.

"Who's that?" Anne cried.

"Carmen," Carmen replied. "Have you seen Letitia?"

"No, should I have?" Anne replied. She then moved to crawl back into her tent, then paused. "I just went to the toilet," she added.

The attempt at an excuse convinced her that Anne really was feeling guilty. But of what? However, that was secondary to finding Letitia.

She said, "I think she has gone to meet one of the boys."

"Oh! Which one?" Anne asked, her voice higher pitched than normal.

She is worried! Carmen thought.

But the question put her on the spot, and she shuffled boys' names in her mind as fast as a deck of cards. Mark was the obvious one, but Andrew's also flitted across. She quickly answered, "Mark."

"We could check and see if he is in his tent," Anne suggested.

Carmen did not really want to do that. She said, "What if they aren't decent?"

"Then we close our eyes," Anne said.

She walked across to the tent shared by Andrew and Mark and lifted the flap. Having no reason not to look Carmen went over and shone her torch inside. To her dismay, she saw that Mark was sound asleep but that Andrew's bed was empty.

Oh no! she thought. *I hope he isn't with Letitia.* Glancing sideways she saw a pained look cross Anne's face. *Uh oh! Anne isn't happy,* she thought. That made her angry. *That stupid little brother! Here is Anne wanting to be with him and he has to go running off after that... that...* With an effort she stopped herself from thinking awful names.

"Where do you think they are?" Anne asked, her voice trembling.

"The beach of course," Carmen replied.

She did not really want to go and look but equally she had a sick feeling of apprehension about the whole situation.

"Should we wake up Mr and Mrs Schipholl and tell them?" Anne asked.

"Not yet. Let's go and look first," Carmen replied.

She was now dreading the search, fearing she would catch Andrew and Letitia in a compromising situation.

"I'll get my torch and come with you," Anne said. Now she sounded positively miserable.

So the two girls had made their way to the beach. Once there, Carmen shone her torch on the sand, noting (but not mentioning) the many scuff marks at the sign and at the end of the jetty. What was plain was that there were no fresh footprints going right, which was what she had secretly feared. Rather, there were many going left.

So they went that way and heard, then glimpsed the figures scuttling off into the old cemetery. Carmen had been almost sure one of them was Andrew and was reluctant to follow. However, Anne turned left just before the outcrop of rocks and hurried up to the line of trees at the edge of the cemetery. From there she shone her torch out across the overgrown cemetery. Reluctantly, Carmen joined her.

"They've gone," Anne said, her voice full of hurt.

"I don't feel like chasing anyone through that cemetery in the dark," Carmen said with conviction.

"Nor do I," Anne agreed.

For lack of another plan, the two girls walked back along the beach and then to the camp. The first thing Anne did was check if Andrew was back in his tent. He was, lying on his bedding fully clothed. He was lying on his side with his back towards them. For a moment Carmen feared that Anne would speak to him, to question him. Instead, she sadly shook her head and turned away.

Carmen then went back to her own tent and looked in. Letitia was there, very naked and pretending to be asleep, the fact that she was not being betrayed by her rapid breathing. As well she was sweating and had sand stuck to her bare skin in places. Carmen realised that the beam of her torch was lighting up Letitia's bum and the backs of her legs.

Anne can see everything, she thought, aware of Anne's presence behind her. She clicked off the torch and crawled into the tent. Then she was unsure what to do next. *Do I confront her?* she wondered, picturing the ugly scene and probable lies. That decided her. *Even if I do, what good will it do?* she asked herself.

Instead, she called back out to Anne a 'goodnight' and sadly lay down. There was no real proof, but she had the ugly suspicion that Andrew and Letitia had been together on the beach.

And she didn't have a stitch on! she told herself.

Sleep was a long time in coming and when it did it was fitful, restless and full of bad dreams. The end result was a tired and unhappy girl in the morning. It was Letitia scrabbling among her clothes that woke her.

Carmen rolled over and opened bleary eyes to see Letitia tugging on a tight T-shirt. A pair of shorts followed and then Letitia crawled out and headed for the toilet. Carmen sat up and found her joggers, then followed. Inside the toilet she spoke to Letitia.

"Where did you go last night?"

"Nowhere," Letitia answered defensively.

At the lie, Carmen bristled. "Oh you did so! Anne and I went looking for you. You were down on the beach with Andrew, weren't you?"

"No."

At that moment, Anne came in. She had obviously overheard the exchange because she snapped, "Oh you were so! We saw you!"

"I only went to the toilet," Letitia retorted, her face turning red.

"You were with Andrew," Anne accused.

"I was not!"

"You're a lying bitch!" Anne cried.

"Don't call me names, you silly little thing!" Letitia yelled back.

Carmen was angry but she now became concerned that there might be a fight. She tried to calm the two, but they began swearing and calling each other horrible names. Mrs Schipholl, tousle-haired and wrapping a dressing gown around her, suddenly came in.

"What on earth is going on? Stop that yelling you girls!"

There was a moment's embarrassed silence. Then Anne began to sob and pushed past Mrs Schipholl and fled. Mrs Schipholl looked from Carmen to Letitia. Letitia shrugged so Mrs Schipholl looked at Carmen.

"Well? What was that all about?"

"Anne... we... accused Letitia of sneaking out to meet Andrew last night," Carmen replied, now strongly regretting having caused the confrontation.

"I did not! I haven't seen him since yesterday. Anyway, if I was going to the beach, I wouldn't be going to meet him. He's just a little boy!" Letitia snapped angrily.

Mrs Schipholl at once flared with anger. "That's enough talk like that, thank you! Now both of you get changed. We will all go for a swim, and we will have no more of this nonsense!"

Letitia gave Carmen a scowl and pushed past. "Fine by me! But I am not playing with these kids today."

Carmen followed them out of the toilet, only to be appalled by finding everyone else standing outside. They had obviously heard at least part of the argument. Her eyes at once went to Andrew and she gasped.

"Andrew! What happened to your face?"

Andrew gaped and put his hand to his face. As he flushed red, Carmen thought a look of guilt crossed his eyes. That made her even more anxious but to begin with she was concerned by the huge bruise that ran across his left cheek, over the bridge of his nose and onto his right forehead. The bruise was a dark, bluey-black and ran in a straight line. It had already gone yellowish around the edges and had also given him a black eye.

"It's alright," he stammered, clearly very embarrassed but unsure what the others could see. "I just tripped and hit my face on the dunny door last night."

The excuse sounded lame to Carmen. She touched the bruising and shook her head. "You should have told us. Is anything broken? Feel your nose."

Mr and Mrs Schipholl pushed forward through the others. Mr Schipholl looked and gently pressed Andrew's cheekbone and nose, causing him to wince.

"Maybe you should come with us when we go ashore," he said. "We can have that checked by a doctor."

"I'm alright," Andrew insisted, but he was obviously shocked when Mrs Schipholl held up a mirror to show him just how big the bruise was.

Mr Schipholl then said, "Come on, a quick dip to wake us all up, then breakfast. We want to get going quickly. I would like to be back here by midday."

Carmen remembered that the adults were going to Cardwell to do some shopping. That got her anxious. She wasn't sure that it was a good idea both adults going at once.

She said, "What if one of us gets hurt while you are away?"

"I will leave the mobile phone," Mr Schipholl replied. "We are only going for a few hours. As I said, we will try to be back by lunchtime."

The group dispersed to get changed. Carmen made a point of waiting till Letitia had re-emerged from the tent in her bikini. She had no desire to see Letitia nude, or to be seen in the same state by her. As quickly as she could, she changed into her bathers, slipped on an unbuttoned long sleeve shirt and sandshoes and crawled back out. The boys were all down at the water by then, swimming with Mr Schipholl. They had carried the boat down to the water and it now bobbed on the tiny waves at the end of its painter.

Letitia wiggled her way down the beach and into the water, but none of the boys made any moved to splash or duck her. They just followed her every move with their eyes, while pretending not to. That caused Carmen to give a sour smile.

She is not as popular today, she thought.

She quickly entered the water herself, gasping at how cold it felt. Anne and Jill joined them, then Mrs Schipholl.

I wish Mrs Schipholl would wear more, Carmen thought, eyeing with disapproval the bikini she wore. Then she shook her head and swam out a few strokes. *It is going to be a lovely day,* she decided, *but I'm not looking forward to it.*

Thinking about how they could repair the social rifts so as to get through the remainder of the camping trip without further unpleasantness occupied her mind for the next few minutes.

Oh well, only two days to go, she told herself.

Mr Schipholl only allowed them ten minutes then shooed them out of the water. They hurried back to camp in a mostly silent straggle. There they dispersed to tidy the camp and have breakfast. Carmen stayed dressed in her bathers and with the shirt slipped back on but left unbuttoned. The others all remained in their bathers or shorts, except Martin and Jill, who both pulled on shirts and shorts. Seeing Letitia still in her tiny bikini caused Carmen to silently fume but she held her tongue and tried not to look at her.

Breakfast was an almost silent meal. Letitia sat with her parents and Martin at one table and the others sat around the second table. During the meal Carmen could not help noticing the eye by-play. Andrew kept glancing at Letitia, while Anne kept giving Andrew hurt looks. Letitia avoided looking at anyone, instead staring off into the jungle.

To end an embarrassing silence, Mark asked, "What are we doing today?"

Mr Schipholl answered that. "You are making sandcastles. While we are away you are to stay in this area. No exploring or running around the island. Each person is to make their own sandcastle, and we will judge which is best when we get back."

"Does it have to be a sandcastle?" Jacob asked.

"Yes, a sandcastle. No mermaids (this with a look at Letitia) or dragons or anything else. I want to see towers and walls and a moat and crenelated battlements," Mr Schipholl insisted.

"Can we use sticks and things?" Martin asked, liking the idea.

"Yes. Now, any particular shopping requests? Okay, here is the phone. I will leave it on our bed. Come on dear, we had better get moving. It is nearly eight already and I want to be in town by nine."

With that Mr Schipholl walked to the parent's tent and placed the mobile phone on the bed. He and Mrs Schipholl then slipped on shirts, trousers and sandshoes, picked up bags and started walking.

As they did, Mr Schipholl called, "Now no trouble, kids. Play safe and be nice to each other."

Be nice to each other! Carmen thought sadly. *I wish we could.*

She watched as Martin, Jacob, Mark and Jill followed the parents towards the beach. She remained in the camp, pretending to tidy up. What she was actually trying to do was keep a surreptitious eye on Andrew and Letitia. Anne also seemed to be lingering. To make it less obvious, Carmen went into her tent and busied herself with rolling up her bedding and packing her clothes more neatly.

It was while she was doing this she saw Andrew walk off towards the toilet. As Letitia was still sitting at a table, apparently sulking, Carmen crawled out and moved to watch from behind the aerial roots of the fig. It was when Andrew looked back, apparently to check if anyone was watching, that Carmen became really suspicious.

He is up to something, she decided.

Andrew obviously had not noticed her, and both Anne and Letitia had their backs to him. He turned and hurried past the toilet and into the old cemetery. Carmen frowned.

Now that is suspicious. What on earth is he going in there for? she wondered.

She grabbed a straw hat and hurried after him. As she did, Anne caught her eye. Carmen did not want Anne to follow but could not think of any reason to fob her off.

"Where are you going?" Anne asked, hurrying to join her. She was still dressed in her bikini and sandshoes.

Carmen bit her lip, then shrugged. She realised she would have to hurt Anne's feelings.

"I am wondering where Andrew is sneaking off to," she replied, gesturing in the direction in which he had vanished. She then glanced back but Letitia was still sitting at the table, looking the other way.

"Can I come with you?" Anne asked.

"It... I... I don't know if it is a good idea," Carmen replied.

Anne turned eyes that were watering with tears to meet hers. "I was going to meet Andrew last night!" she blurted out.

Then she sobbed a bit, and Carmen grabbed her sleeve and started her walking, not wanting Letitia to hear. As they passed the toilet, Anne added, "I went to the beach to meet him, at the three pandanus palms, but he didn't arrive. That was just after midnight. I waited nearly an hour, but he didn't come. I felt really hurt. I came back to camp and saw that he was still asleep, but I didn't have the courage to wake him... in case Mark heard. So I lay down and must have gone to sleep. Then I woke up and checked his tent and saw he was gone. I was just about to go out to the beach when I met you."

"Probably just as well you did if he was with Letitia," Carmen answered.

Anne nodded and Carmen noted the tears trickling down her cheeks. *Poor kid,* she thought. It made her both sad and angry to think that Andrew could have done such a thing. *Surely, he didn't arrange to meet two girls in one night?*

The girls were in the old cemetery by then and out of sight of the camp. For a moment they stopped, and Carmen puzzled over where Andrew had gone. Then she glimpsed movement among the trees right over in the far corner near the beach. She glimpsed the dark blue shirt Andrew had put on.

She pointed. "There he is. He is going to the three pandanus palms."

"Why?" asked Anne.

Carmen had a shrewd idea, but she did not reply. She thought it though. *He is going to find something he lost last night.*

But Anne kept walking and Carmen felt she had no option but to go with her. By then the sun was up and there was almost no breeze in the old cemetery. The air was stifling and between that and the tense state of her body Carmen began to perspire freely. With every step she regretted following Andrew. Her anxiety rose so that she was biting her lip and her heart hammered rapidly.

The two girls arrived at the line of fig trees along the top of the beach. They were just to the left of the outcrop of rocks and Carmen saw the three pandanus palms quite clearly. She moved forward, trying not to stand on dead leaves, her eyes flicking to and fro, looking for Andrew.

Then she saw him. He was down on his hands and knees and in his right hand he was holding a white piece of clothing. At that moment, he saw them and he gave a guilty start, his mouth sagging open and his face crumpling with distress.

"That's Letitia's T-shirt!" Anne wailed.

Chapter 26

AWKWARD EXPLANATIONS

When Andrew heard footsteps crunching on dead leaves and looked up and saw who it was, he was aghast. The feeling seemed to run out of his face, at the same time as the T-shirt in his hand felt like it was scorching his skin.

Oh no! he thought in horror. *How will I explain this? They will never believe me now!*

Ever since he had woken up he had been in a state of emotional turmoil- anger, jealousy, misery... and curiosity. He had meant to creep back down to the beach once everyone had gone to sleep, but had drifted off to sleep himself. When he had been woken by Mark, he was shocked to find it was daylight. Then had followed the excruciating personal aguish of watching Letitia, and of hearing the girls yelling accusations and insults at each other.

The impossibility of intervening and telling the truth had so gripped him he had felt almost paralysed. What was almost as hurtful was seeing Letitia apparently acting as though nothing unusual had happened the night before. It shocked Andrew deeply to find that what was so terribly important to him was apparently of little consequence to her. It was all very saddening and upsetting.

Then he had remembered the pirates. *How do I explain them?* he wondered.

That had led to him wondering if it all hadn't just been a bad dream. Curiosity then gripped him. For over an hour he struggled to act relaxed and normal, while all the time he was on the razor's edge of nervous excitement.

It had seemed he would never get a chance to sneak away. Only after the Schipholls had set off did he decide no-one would notice his absence. After a quick check that nobody was looking, he had slipped off behind the toilet and into the old cemetery. On arrival at the three pandanus palms, he had been appalled to see Letitia's T-shirt lying on the scuffed-up sand. For a minute or so he dithered, trying to decide whether to hide it or to somehow sneak it back to camp and place it there where she could find it.

Finally he had decided to hide it. *If I take it back Letitia will wonder how it got there and then she will suspect I saw what she did,* he reasoned. So he had knelt down to bury it, only to have Anne and Carmen arrive.

He gaped at them, scorching waves of shame sweeping through him. He knew he was blushing, and blushed some more. He knew he was looking guilty and could not help himself.

"It... it... it's not what you think," he blurted out.

The look of hurt in Anne's eyes made it harder, twisting his conscience so that he felt nauseous. It was plainly obvious that neither Carmen nor Anne believed him. Andrew just shook his head and bit his lip. Through his mind swirled the images of Letitia and the artist kissing there, right where he crouched. That hurt, it really did.

"We didn't do anything," he cried, tears welling into his eyes.

Carmen walked down the beach and looked at the T-shirt. "So whose is that?" she asked.

"Letitia's. I just found it here," Andrew mumbled miserably, still burning with shame.

"So why did you come sneaking down here?" Anne snapped, her hurt turning to anger.

Andrew stood up and looked around, seeking for the right answer. All he saw was more trouble. Walking along the beach towards him from the jetty were Jacob, Martin, Mark and Jill. Heading out to sea, and already a distant, tiny shape, were the Schipholls in the boat.

Anne pointed accusingly at the T-shirt. "So if that is Letitia's, how did it come to be here?"

"She obviously took it off," Andrew replied.

By now he was so upset he could hardly speak his mind filled with images of Letitia and the artist.

"Did you see her do that?" Carmen asked.

Andrew could only nod. He just wished he could run away and hide. By then Jacob, Martin, Mark, and Jill had joined them.

"What's going on?" Jacob asked.

Anne answered. "Andrew found Letitia's T-shirt and said she took it off here last night."

That caused new waves of embarrassment. Andrew swallowed. He shook his head and bit his lip, then broke into a sweat. Having Martin there added enormously to the pressure.

I don't want to hurt him any more, he thought.

Jill pursed her lips and said, "Were you with her?"

Andrew shook his head.

Jill did not let up. "Was she with someone?"

At that, Andrew looked up and briefly met her eye, then looked away, nodding.

"Who?" Jill demanded to know.

Andrew was now blinking back tears but just shook his head.

"What was she doing here?" Jill asked, her voice harsh and spiteful.

Andrew made no answer. Instead, Mark snorted, "We can guess!"

At that, Andrew met Martin's eye and saw the pain. It made him even more miserable. He just shook his head and wished they had never come to the island for the holiday.

Jill then twisted the emotional knife some more. "So, if it wasn't you, who was she with?"

That got them all glancing at each other. Andrew saw Mark blush and that hurt too. *I've got to end this,* he thought.

"I'm not going to say," he replied. "I came down here last night to meet Anne, but she wasn't here."

Anne met his eyes and he saw she was crying. Jill sniffed and looked around. "Where is the moll anyway?"

Martin reacted to that. "Don't talk about my sister like that, please," he said, his voice filled with distress.

The thought that the group was going to disintegrate into squabbling factions got Andrew talking. He cried loudly, "Don't start name calling please! This..." he waved the T-shirt, "wasn't why I came here now. I came back to see what it was that the pirates buried."

Jacob's face curled into a sneer. "Pirates! Have you been drinking jungle juice or something?" he said in a voice laden with sarcasm.

"No!" Andrew snapped back. "There were pirates here last night, three of them."

Jacob gave a mocking laugh. "Oh sure! Captain Kidd, Captain Hook, and Henry Morgan!"

"No, Blackbeard," Andrew retorted. He was stung by the ridicule and at not being believed. He pointed. "I was waiting just here for Anne when

I saw them walking along the beach from the jetty. One had a sword and carried a metal box. He was Blackbeard. The other was called Smee and..."

"Smee!" Jacob rudely interrupted. "Are you sure you haven't been sniffing petrol or paint or something? This is fantasy."

"It is not!" Andrew shouted. "They came right to the three pandanus palms. Blackbeard, he had a big black beard and wore a three-cornered hat, paced out five paces from the tree to here, then told Smee to dig a hole."

Jacob jeered and Mark and Jill both looked sceptical, but Andrew saw that Carmen was looking anxious and puzzled. He turned to her. "I'm not making it up, Sis! They buried a metal box right here. Then a third man called Bosun came along in a boat and picked them up and they went back out to sea."

While he had been talking he had been pointing, first at the three pandanus palms then at the footprints leading from it, then at where he stood and finally at the edge of the water. As he did, his hopes went up and down. All around the three pandanus palms were numerous footprints, mostly from their own treasure hunt. To his disappointment, these were well above the tide level where the sand was dry and did not retain the shape of any feet or footwear. Where he stood was all stirred up. But down on the edge of the water where it was still damp was a very obvious mark showing where the keel of a boat had slid down into the sea. Better still some really clear boot prints showed in the damp sand.

Andrew saw Carmen bite her lip as she looked at them. She then walked down the beach to stare at the marks in the sand.

"These are fresh," she said. "High tide was at about 1am, I think."

Martin nodded. "Yes, and only a low one, about two metres."

It was low tide as they spoke so the water hadn't washed out the prints. "See! I'm not making it up," Andrew insisted. He then added more details, of how the men had been dressed and of the guns they carried.

"But why the fancy dress?" Anne asked.

"Probably just a disguise," Martin suggested.

"Where did they go?" Mark asked, looking out to sea.

Andrew pointed to Oyster Point. "Around that. They were in a boat like a Rigid Raider, and it had a really big outboard motor on it. And that was really quiet."

"To some ship then," Martin suggested, staring out to sea.

Andrew looked but the only vessel in sight was a sail yacht about a mile off.

"But why?" Mark asked. "Why bury a treasure?"

"Search me," Andrew answered, happier now the others were starting to believe his story.

Jacob still wasn't convinced though. "Where did they bury this box?"

"Somewhere around here," Andrew replied, pointing down.

"And where were you during all this?" Jill asked, still not convinced.

Andrew pointed to the cleft in the rocks. "Just there."

"How come they didn't see you?" Mark asked.

"I was in the shadow of the fig tree, and I lay low," Andrew answered. "I was scared, I can tell you."

"So why didn't you tell us last night?" Carmen asked.

"Because... because... because you came along and I didn't want you to see me, so I ran away," Andrew replied, again blushing and feeling upset.

"Were you here while Letitia was here with someone else?" Mark asked.

Andrew could only nod at that, shame choking him up.

"What were they doing?" Mark went on.

Andrew blushed and shook his head but then mumbled, "Kissing." Shame almost choked him.

Mark's eyes widened. "Oooh! So you could see everything?"

Again Andrew could not answer... would not.

Jill pursed her lips and snapped, "That's disgusting! Who was she with? Was it you?"

"No," Andrew croaked. "Look, never mind her. Let's dig up the treasure."

"Good idea," Martin agreed. "How many paces from the trees?"

"Five... I think," Andrew replied.

He badly wanted to divert the conversation back away from Letitia. It was just too painful to think about, and he writhed inside, knowing he was a hypocrite.

Martin obviously had the same aim as he determinedly paced out the distance and then dropped to his knees.

"Come on, let's dig it up and see what it is," he said.

That got them moving. They all knelt and began scooping sand away with their hands. Andrew sighed with relief and began to dig. After a few minutes they had all scooped out hollows about thirty centimetres deep.

"How far down?" Martin asked.

"About a metre I think," Andrew estimated.

"We should get a shovel," Jacob suggested.

"You can. There's one at camp," Martin replied.

Jacob dusted his hands and set off back through the old cemetery. The others kept scooping sand away but soon stopped. It was actually quite painful after a while. Andrew was the last to give up, ignoring the scraping, abrasive pain as long as he could in his eagerness to be proved right. To Andrew, it all became a very intense experience. He was so torn up by jealousy and shame that he felt miserable and confused. As he dug, he noted how the fine, dry sand in the surface layer stuck to his sweaty skin, especially on the forearms and legs. The damp sand deeper down also stuck but was much coarser in grain and had a noticeable salt tang. There were tiny fragments of coral and broken shell which scraped and scratched at the skin and Andrew noted how red his hands had become. However, he was in such emotional distress that the physical pain was almost a release.

The others sat on the sand next to the rocks and discussed who the pirates might be.

"Smugglers?" Carmen suggested.

Andrew saw she looked quite anxious. "Could be," he replied. "Ah! Here's Jacob."

Jacob had returned with a small spade used for making sandcastles. "It's all I could find," he said. "And Letitia's not at the camp."

"I'll bet I know where she is," Jill said, eyes narrowing, lips pursing.

"We should go and look for her," Carmen said.

"No!" Martin cried. "Please... Don't. Mum and Dad know, so please, just let her be."

Andrew's heart went out to his friend. Martin looked so upset that the word 'harrowing' crossed Andrew's mind.

Poor bugger! I'm glad my sister doesn't behave like... with... He said, "Never mind her. Dig up the treasure."

Carmen looked worried but nodded. "Alright. But as soon as we have, I am going to look for her."

Jacob curled his lip at that but set to work digging. It seemed at first they were not going to find anything, and Andrew became anxious lest he be made to look a fool and a liar. He suggested digging a bit closer to the rocks. Jacob gave him an 'I-told-you-so' look but did so.

Suddenly the spade struck metal and all were instantly excited. Jacob quickly shovelled away more sand and then reached down. Andrew watched him brush sand off the top of a grey metal box. The box was about the size of a large shoe box, only wider. Jacob then took hold of the handle on top and pulled. As he lifted it up and the sand fell away, Andrew experienced the most peculiar sensation of *déjà vu* He looked up and met Carmen's eyes.

She was wide-eyed. "It... it looks exactly like the box we dug up at Simpson Point!" she cried.

She reached out and took it from Jacob. As she did, all the others stood up and crowded around. Carmen brushed more sand off and turned the box to reveal a keyhole.

Andrew saw that it was a brand-new container. "That's what it will be, the smugglers have made a drop."

"And that means those horrible crooks will be coming to collect it!" Carmen cried, fear flooding her face. As she said that she looked anxiously around. Then her mouth dropped open and she tried to speak.

Andrew looked, and gaped as well. Tied up at the jetty was the yacht he had seen earlier, and striding towards them along the beach were four pirates!

"P... Pirates!" he gasped.

It wasn't the same crooks as the last time, but one look was enough to send a chill of fear flooding through him. All four were grim-looking, tough-looking men, and all carried a gun of some sort. The leader was dressed in what looked like a blue and white striped jersey, blue long trousers and a black tricorn hat. He was a tall man and carried a pistol. The next one looked vaguely familiar to Andrew, and he then recognised the man with the earrings and pony tail who had been flirting with Letitia in Cardwell. He wore blue jeans and a red and white striped T-shirt, topped by a handkerchief tied around his head. In his hands was a rifle of some sort. The next 'pirate' wore blue shorts and a white T-shirt. He carried a shovel and a pistol. The fourth man wore blue trousers and blue T-shirt and had a red cloth tied around his neck. He had a shotgun.

It was obvious that the pirates had seen what was going on and that they had been spotted. Their leader suddenly yelled out, "Oi! You bloody kids! Drop that box, or else!"

At that moment, the pirates were about a hundred paces away. Carmen cried "Oh no!" and there were gasps and comments from the others.

Martin asked, "Are these the pirates that kidnapped you Carmen?"

"No. I've never seen them before," Carmen replied.

"Oh, let's get out of here!" Anne cried.

At that, Carmen dropped the box and turned to run. Andrew saw her drop the box and hesitated, thinking to take it with him. But he was not quick enough. Martin bent down and snatched it up.

"These are drugs, are they?" he asked.

Andrew nodded. "I'm not sure, but the last lot were," he said.

Carmen had run up under the tree. She looked back in horror and cried, "Oh leave it! Drop it!"

The pirates now all began yelling. Anne and Carmen both started running. Mark began pulling at Jill's arm, but she seemed to be transfixed. Jacob stood there shaking his head. Andrew looked at the angry men, who were now running along the beach towards them, and he fled. Martin followed, still holding the box.

Seeing them running the pirate leader screamed angrily and there was a loud bang. Andrew nearly wet himself with fear as he realised the man had fired a shot. He bent into a crouch, jinked wildly and raced up into the old cemetery. Mark and Jill followed. Martin dashed past, going to the right and still clutching the box.

The pirate leader shouted, "Stop or we will shoot! Stop, you bloody kids! Drop that box!"

There was another vicious crack and Andrew whimpered with fear. He knew that the sound was a bullet going past. It did not stop him however. He was now so scared that all he wanted to do was get away. Carmen and Anne were running ahead of him, crouching low and trying to keep the few tombstones and long grass between them and the pirates. Mark and Jill came running up past the fig tree, Jill audibly whimpering. Martin angled off to the right.

Carmen began running to the left. Andrew called to her, "Don't go that way!"

"The phone," Carmen gasped back.

That made sense. Andrew began to master his rising panic and thought, *Which way now?* The camp seemed a good starting point, even though it meant running left across the front of the pirates. He was now gripped by a sense of unreality. *This can't be true!* his ordinary mind cried, but he knew instinctively that it was.

There was another shot. This time the bullet struck a headstone and ricocheted with a spine-chilling screech. Andrew flinched.

"Those men mean to kill us," he cried.

"Then give them the box," Anne called.

To Andrew, she looked terrified. He looked around but could not see Martin. That got him really worried but he did not stop running. He fully agreed with the idea of letting the pirates have the box. Luckily, he now knew his way around the old cemetery very well and was able to dodge the worst thickets of spiky bush or long grass and avoided tripping on the old grave markers hidden in the grass. This meant several sharp zig-zags around graves.

As he ran, Andrew kept glancing back, noting that Mark and Jill were still following but were twenty or thirty paces behind. Jill was hobbling and limping and Andrew decided that was because she was barefoot and was stepping on the prickles that abounded in the old cemetery. There was no sign of Jacob.

The friends reached the line of cottonwood trees along the west side of the old cemetery without the men shooting anyone. As he dashed along the track through the thicket Andrew glanced back and glimpsed the man with earrings appear a hundred paces back. Even as he shouted at them to stop, he was lost to sight.

"Keep running," Andrew gasped. "We must scatter and hide."

"We must call the police," Carmen said.

By then they were at the toilet. They dashed past it, crossing the main track as they headed towards the camp. As they did, Andrew glanced left towards the jetty and was shocked to see two of the pirates running along it towards them. They were the one in the white shirt and blue shorts and the one all in blue. As soon as they saw the teenagers, the pirates began yelling.

By then Carmen had reached the Schipholl's tent. She dived inside and picked up the mobile phone. Andrew glanced behind and was appalled to see the pirates. They were near the toilet, and were fleetingly visible through the foliage. To his further dismay, Andrew saw that Mark and Jill had stopped and were raising their hands.

"Keep running!" he cried at Anne.

A frantic urge to escape spurred him on. It also occurred to him that Carmen would not have time to use the mobile phone before the pirates arrived.

"Car! Bring the phone, run!" he called. With that he continued running.

By then Anne was at the bank of the creek. She looked back at him, her face a frightened query. *She is wondering which way,* Andrew deduced. He was now thinking the same thing, but the options appeared to be limited.

He nodded and called, "Go on along the track, run!"

Anne dashed down into the creek, Andrew close on her heels. It only took them seconds to splash across. As they scrambled up the other bank, Andrew glanced back.

Where is Carmen? he wondered. Then he glimpsed her behind the Schipholl's tent. She was on her hands and knees and was scrabbling amongst the dead leaves. *What is she doing? She will be caught*, he thought anxiously.

For a moment he slowed and wondered whether to go back for her. But then he saw a pirate running into the camp site. Carmen obviously saw the man as well because she slid over the bank out of sight.

If I don't run, I will be caught too, Andrew rationalised, although it went right against the grain to leave his sister behind.

The thought that Anne might also get caught if he didn't help her helped him to make the choice. With that he ran on along the track. Within seconds he was hidden from the camp by the jungle. Behind him he could hear shouting and barked orders but could not distinguish clearly what was being said.

Anne kept running but was plainly making hard work of it. She glanced back from time to time and he urged her on. Then they reached the hill section of the track and within 50 paces Anne slowed to a gasping plod. Andrew wasn't much better, his heart hammering while he sucked in great gulps of air.

Oh, I am unfit! he berated himself. *We will be caught!*

With that thought, and all the nameless fears it conjured up, he kept going, urging and helping Anne along. They plodded up the track, sweat pouring out of them. All the while Andrew kept straining his ears to listen for sounds of pursuit. He was also anxious about what was happening to the others. After only a few minutes of pushing themselves, Andrew and Anne reached the crest of the ridge and the track junction. That presented a dilemma.

Anne stopped and pointed to the other track. "We could go down that to the ruins," she suggested.

"We could," agreed Andrew.

He had been thinking about that. That had the advantage of giving several routes by which he could sneak back to try to find out what was going on. But a moment's thought caused him to shake his head. He was prepared to do that but did not want Anne with him.

I must get her to safety, he told himself.

The other option was to go on down the other side to the artist's. The instant he thought of him Andrew knew he must go that way.

Letitia might be there. I must warn her, he told himself. Then he remembered that the artist had a boat. That settled it.

Andrew pointed left and said, "Down to the artist's. We must warn him and Letitia."

Anne nodded and set off down the path. As Andrew resumed walking, he heard voices down in the jungle behind him. Quite clearly he heard a man say, "Hurry up, you slug! They'll get away."

"We are being followed," Andrew called to Anne. "Run!"

They both did, pounding down the track as fast as they could. Now knowledge of the track helped. They were able to anticipate the twists and turns and the stones and tree roots which might have caused them to stumble or trip. Even so they found it hard going. Both were winded and only fear kept them moving as fast as their legs could be forced to move.

During that run down to the beach Andrew was in emotional turmoil. *I will probably see Letitia naked again,* he thought, *and maybe the artist.*

For a horrible few seconds the thought came to him that he and Anne might find the pair kissing, or worse, and he groaned and wondered if he could somehow change the plan. But no obvious alternative other than turning off to hide in the jungle came to mind. That plan he had to reject as it meant not warning Letitia. Realising he would have to endure whatever was ahead of him wrung several sobs of anguish from him, but he steeled himself and kept going. All he could do was gasp a warning to Anne.

"They might not have any clothes on."

Anne just shrugged and kept on running, her long legs now a distinct advantage. Within a minute the pair had reached the bottom of the hill and Andrew gasped and sobbed again, knowing the moment of truth was just ahead.

He mentally braced himself for another awkward explanation.

Chapter 27

CARMEN CALLS

Carmen was both furiously angry with herself and gripped by fear. The moment she had seen the pirates she had almost fainted with fright. Then she fled, terror spurring her legs. She ran desperately through the old cemetery, her frantically racing mind seeking the best way to escape. To her own surprise, part of her brain was still acting rationally as she remembered the mobile phone.

I must call the police, she thought.

With that idea in mind she dived into the Schipholl's tent. To her enormous relief, the phone was on the groundsheet. She snatched it up and scrambled out the back of the tent, spurred on by Andrew's urgent cry to run.

Her haste was her undoing. A strap from Mr Schipholl's carry bag caught her right foot and she tripped. As she fell hard on the leaf mould the phone went skittering out of her hand. She also struck her face on a small tree and for a moment was stunned and disoriented.

The phone! Where's the phone? she thought.

She scrabbled frantically among the dead leaves till a fearful glance over her shoulder revealed a pirate only metres away. The man was on the other side of the nearest fig tree and had not seen her yet. As he moved so that the tent hid her from view, Carmen crawled forward and slid down over the bank of the creek.

As she did, she saw the phone. It was lower down, resting against a tree root. She reached for it but, to her dismay, a cascade of sticks and leaves that her movements had dislodged, slid down and covered it. For a second, she hoped the tiny avalanche would not dislodge the phone but, even as her left hand reached for it, she saw it slide from its precarious perch. To her horror, the phone dropped down the steep bank and into the creek.

So appalled was she by this that she quite forgot the pirates and slithered quickly down as well, jumping the last metre. She landed in the knee-deep water with a splash, bent down and snatched up the phone. As she lifted it dripping from the water, she muttered a few words of which her mother would not have approved. Then she tut-tutted.

"Oh, I hope it still works!" she said.

As she did, shouts penetrated her consciousness and she remembered the pirates. There were voices, strange male voices, yelling angrily just up on top of the bank. With her heart catching in her throat Carmen cast a fearful look upwards. To her relief, there was no-one in sight. Then the voices became clearer.

One shouted, "And keep your hands up!"

Another yelled, "Gary, get after those other kids, the ones that went along that track there."

A third called, "Come on, Silver!"

Silver? Carmen thought, her frightened mind racing. *Does he mean 'Long John Silver'? Am I dreaming this? Or do these pirates all use nicknames?*

She pressed herself in among the tree roots on the creek bank and looked upstream. A man went racing down the bank and splashed across. She recognised him as the man with the ponytail and earrings who had flirted with Letitia in Cardwell. He was followed by a second man, the one with the three-cornered hat and carrying a pistol. Carmen had a fleeting impression of blonde hair and rugged good looks.

The second man splashed across the creek as well and followed 'Earrings' up into the jungle on the other side. Within a few seconds they were gone.

Andrew and Anne went that way, Carmen thought, hoping they would get away but deeply anxious.

There were still voices above her in the camp, but she decided she had to risk looking to be able to size up the situation. With pirates that close she did not dare try to turn on the mobile phone, knowing it would emit its tell-tale beeping sound when she did. After a careful look she waded slowly downstream ten paces and then crawled up a tiny gully. That brought her to a big tree with buttress roots which provided good cover. Using that, and the leaves of a plant growing on top of the bank to hide her, she raised her head and looked.

Standing 20 paces away were two groups of people. One group comprised Jacob, Mark, and Jill. They had their hands up and looked scared. Jacob had blood running down his face, presumably from a blow to the nose. The other group were two pirates: the one all in blue and the one in white T-shirt and blue shorts.

The one in the white T-shirt said, "Tie 'em up, Sammy. No nonsense, you kids, or you are dead! Remember, dead men tell no tales."

The one all in blue, Sammy, put his hand behind his back and slid the pistol he carried into the waistband of his shorts, then moved forward. As Carmen watched he drew a knife. Using that he cut off some of the rope holding the tarpaulin up. Then he told Jacob to turn around and to put his hands behind his back. Quickly and with seamanlike efficiency Sammy then bound Jacob's wrists together. Jacob was then seated to one side and Sammy began the same process on Mark.

Can I rescue them? Carmen wondered as she lay there, her heart hammering.

The two pirates were each about 20 paces away and the one in the white T-shirt held a shotgun. That decided Carmen. She had heard that shotguns caused horrific wounds and she felt sure that the pirate would use it if attacked. Seeing no way to creep up on the men she could only lie and watch.

When all three prisoners were bound and seated the two men began questioning them, wanting to know how many in the group. Mark got stubborn and Sammy walked over and kicked him hard in the face, then hauled him up by his hair, at the same time holding the knife to his throat.

"Don't be a smart-arse, you little idiot! Answer our questions or I will cut the dame a bit."

At that, Carmen felt a chill of horror and dread clutch at her heart. *Oh my God! I must do something.*

Jill was obviously terrified as she cried out, "We will tell you! We've got nothing to hide. We haven't done anything wrong!"

Sammy shook his head. "Yes, yer have, Sweetie, ye've taken our treasure box. Now, how many of yer are there?" he asked.

Carmen bit her lip and trembled with frustration. *Oh what can I do?* Then she realised she still held the mobile phone. *But they will hear it if I try to use it here,* she reasoned.

She also thought she might need to get up higher to get a clear signal from the mainland. That got her thinking about where to go. The only way that appeared possible, with the least chance of being seen, was down the creek.

I will go down the creek till I reach the beach, then keep inside the jungle and make my way up onto the ridge above Snapper Point, she decided.

Having decided that she edged herself slowly back down the creek bank. As she did, she heard Jill explaining that the Schipholls would not be back till lunch time or later.

She doesn't have to volunteer information like that! Carmen thought crossly. It went against her normal feelings to leave her friends in such a situation but she could not see any practical alternative. *It will take the police a few hours to react, so the sooner I call them the better,* she told herself.

Once she was down in the creek Carmen set off, wading slowly downstream. All the while she kept looking back to check that she was not visible to the pirates. It was a relief to round the next bend in the stream and be hidden. After that she increased speed but was still careful not to make a splash. As she waded along, Carmen worried about whether Andrew and Anne had escaped.

That got her thinking about where they might have run to. *Over the hill to the artist's,* she decided. *Andrew will want to make sure Letitia is safe.* That also gave her a spurt of hope. The artist, for all his eccentricity, was an adult. But she shook her head. *But he won't be able to cope with two pirates with guns.*

A fleeting image of the artist and a probably naked Letitia (Carmen was sure she would be) being confronted first by Andrew and Anne, and then by two angry and armed pirates, gave a momentary spurt of malicious pleasure. Then she felt guilty and anxious about what might then happen.

The artist does have a boat, she remembered. *Perhaps they will all escape in that?*

But she knew they would have to be very quick. Carmen now had doubts about whether Andrew would be able to convince the artist in time? It seemed very doubtful and increased her sense of urgency and dread. The need to use the mobile phone became even more imperative. She thought that the artist would almost certainly have a mobile phone, but she did not know what reception might be like from that area.

By then she was at the last bend and could see the sea through a tunnel of jungle. It was a beautiful picture of shimmering blue, white sand and lush green, but the sight was quite lost on her at that moment. Very slowly she crept forward till she could see both ways along the beach, being careful to remain inside the edge of the jungle while she did. There was no-one in sight.

The only sign of the pirates was their yacht, an ordinary sort of 12- or 15-metre sailing yacht, white hull, single mast. It was moored on her side of the jetty, out near its far end. A dinghy was streamed astern on a painter. The yacht was about a hundred metres away and appeared to be deserted. Satisfied that nobody would hear Carmen turned her attention to the mobile phone. After studying it for a moment she pressed the power button. Nothing happened so she pressed it again.

Oh no! The water got into it, she thought, her anxiety shooting right up.

Guilt at her own clumsiness, and then frustration and anger, all welled up to upset her. She tried again but no sound indicated electronic life, and no picture of any sort appeared on the display.

Oh no! What will I do? Oh you clumsy girl! she told herself.

For a few minutes she just crouched there, so upset and defeated that tears prickled. She began to feel both angry and desperate.

If anything happens to the others it will be my fault, she reasoned miserably. It was an awful feeling. Even so her mind kept actively searching for a means of getting help. *If only we had some flares, or a radio,* she told herself.

Then she made a wry face. The mobile phone was a radio, a tiny, hand-held one to be sure, but a radio.

Radio! The yacht must have a radio, Carmen thought. From the back of her mind came a comment by one of the Navy Cadet Petty Officer Instructors that, by law, all craft over a certain size had to have a radio. *That yacht is sure to have one,* she thought.

Now that was food for thought! Carmen was now starting her Third Year in cadets, and was an Able Seaman Signaller. She had been trained in Morse code, semaphore, signal flags, and the use of marine radios. So she was sure that she would be able to use one, if only she could find it. The real question was: were there any pirates on the yacht?

Now that the idea had come to her, she was gripped by it. She stared at the yacht, cursing the sweat that threatened to trickle into her eyes. She thought that a boat of that sort usually had bunks for four people, but she wasn't sure. But she had never been that interested and had only ever visited a couple of similar craft.

There was certainly no-one on deck. *Surely, they would all have come rushing ashore to try to catch us,* she reasoned.

That got her trying to picture what the pirates would have done as they sailed into the bay and saw the group of children digging at their treasure site.

Four men chased us? she reasoned. That raised bowel-watering doubts and the awful thought that she really had no honourable option. *If I don't try to save my friends, I will despise myself for the rest of my life,* she mused miserably. *However short my life is,* she added, giving a bitter laugh that was half sob.

She bit her lip and knew she had to try. But fear held her there for a couple more minutes. In an attempt to get herself to move, she puzzled over the best way to reach the yacht unseen.

Should I adopt the bold course and just walk along the beach and out along the jetty, or should I swim out and try to stay underwater as much as possible?

Intellectually she knew that the bold course was often the best. But the thought of walking along that jetty while exposed to the guns of the pirates terrified her. Then she pictured swimming and at once made up her mind. In her imagination she viewed the moment of surfacing after each breath.

My eyes will be all blurry from the water and it will take me vital seconds to clear them. If there is a pirate on the yacht, I won't even see him, not until it is too late.

But how to make herself move? She was really scared and knew it. Finally it was shame at her own cowardice that motivated her. With a sob she stood up and began walking to her left, keeping just in among the trees. As she moved along her eyes flicked too around, searching for the slightest hint of danger. Her heart began to hammer so loudly it sounded like the swashing of surf in her ears. She found she was gulping air and had to consciously slow her breathing. Perspiration seemed to trickle from every pore.

Two minutes later she was at the end of the jetty. For perhaps another minute she crouched behind the tree where she had watched the Schipholls the previous night. Now fear almost did paralyse her. She looked back along the track towards the camp and strained her ears for any sound of the pirates.

What is happening back there? she wondered.

Now the jetty seemed to stretch out for an immense distance, not the mere 50 paces it was. After another careful scrutiny Carmen at last pushed herself to move. With beating heart and shaking legs she stepped out into the open and strode across the sand to the end of the jetty. Then she hurried out along it, casting continual fearful glances over her shoulder.

If I am seen now, I will dive in and swim for it, she decided.

Thirty seconds later she stood on the jetty beside the yacht. The vessel rode easily at her moorings, the deck just below the level of the jetty. Once again, Carmen paused. There was certainly no-one on the yacht's deck, but what about below?

No. If there was anyone they would be up on deck watching the action, she reasoned.

Then it occurred to her that the longer she stood on the jetty the more likely she was to be spotted. Gritting her teeth with determination she stepped aboard, then crouched beside the small cabin. She was now so anxious and frightened that she felt sick and for a moment was afraid she might faint. Annoyed with herself she shook her head and told herself to get on with it.

Moving slowly and quietly she crept along and peeked in through a small round porthole. Inside was what she expected, a cabin with a galley and table and so on. A small door in the forward bulkhead led into the forward half of the vessel. Now that she was moving Carmen found it easier to continue. Seeing no-one, and not getting any obvious response to the movement of the vessel under her weight (she was surprised at how much movement it had, even on the gentle ripples that passed for waves), she moved aft.

This brought her to a small half-cabin and the cockpit. She peeked around the corner and then nodded with satisfaction. It was as she expected: the wheel, navigation equipment, and a door leading below into the cabin she had looked into. After a quick check back along the jetty she stepped around into the cockpit.

The door was open and just below she saw what she sought- the radio. It was on a bench at the bottom of the small companionway. But to use it meant going down inside and that was much more of a challenge than stepping aboard! She had to grit her teeth and tell herself she was a weakling and a coward before she could force her limbs to move.

A few seconds later she stood in front of the radio. After a few nervous glances around the cabin she focused on the set itself. The need to think technical thoughts quickly calmed her.

Yes! I can use this! she told herself, her spirits rising.

The set was not switched on, but it took her only seconds to find the 'on' switch. She then studied the tuning dials and other switches.

Hesitantly she picked up the microphone and went to press the transmit switch. Then she stopped and silently swore.

Oh bugger! I don't know the name of the yacht, she thought irritably.

She had forgotten to look over the transom to find out. She cast a quick glance around to see if she could find any clues, but none was immediately obvious. What she did see was a radio schedule with frequencies. A few seconds of sliding her fingertip down the list told Carmen that she could transmit on the frequency the set was already on and should gain contact with the coastal shipping radio station.

"Never mind all that!" she muttered. She pressed the transmit button firmly and saw the needle in the dial swing over and the set hummed in the way she expected it to. "Good, it is transmitting," she said. Then she lifted the microphone to her mouth and said, "Mayday! Mayday! Mayday! This is Endeavour Island. Endeavour Island calling. Anyone who can help, over."

Carmen released the switch and waited. The set crackled and hummed for a second. She was just about to call again when the sound of a man's voice crackled from the speaker.

"This is VKC calling unidentified station, say again, over."

"VKC, this is Carmen Collins. I am holidaying on Endeavour Island and we have an emergency, over."

"This is VKC. I got that. Is it Carmen? Over."

"Yes VKC. Carmen Collins. I am a fifteen-year-old girl. I am on Endeavour Island with seven other kids, and we are being chased by smugglers with guns, over."

"This is VKC. Which Endeavour Island? Over," the man answered. He sounded calm but slightly sceptical.

"The one off Cardwell. Oh please call the police! This is an emergency.

There are four men and they have guns and they have already caught Jacob, Jill and Mark," Carmen answered.

She was sweating now and feeling very anxious. *What if the man doesn't believe me?* she wondered.

The man obviously didn't as he asked again who she was. This time Carmen gave her full name and her home address in Cairns, plus her parent's telephone number.

The man then asked, "And who are these men?"

"Smugglers, I think. Last night three men dressed as pirates came ashore and buried a box in the beach. We dug it up this morning but then this yacht arrived with four men on it and they are chasing us. Oh please hurry," she answered. Then she remembered she was supposed to say 'over' to indicate she had finished speaking so she pressed the switch and said, "Over, Oh! Oh help!"

There was a man on the yacht!

The door at the forward end of the cabin had just opened and a man was looking through. Carmen instantly recognised him—the villainous looking man with one eye and a peg leg she had seen on the jetty at Cardwell.

Chapter 28

RAW

Peg Leg glared at Carmen with evident astonishment in his one eye. Carmen saw anger or hate flare in it and then he swore and came charging through the door. At that, Carmen fled. All that saved her was the table in the way and the fact that the man was slowed by his crutch and peg leg. Even so he was terrifyingly quick. Even as she bolted up the companionway he grabbed the tail of her shirt. Feeling him haul at it sent a wave of sheer panic through Carmen. She grabbed the brass handrails and heaved herself upwards.

Fear helped her think fast. As the man hauled at her shirt, Carmen half-turned and let it slide off one shoulder. As her right arm came free, she twisted the sleeve off. Peg Leg grabbed at her ankles with his other hand, but she was so scared that she screamed, kicked and jumped. The shirt tore and she squirmed the other way and let that sleeve slip off her left arm as well. Carmen broke free but then found that the man was clutching at her ankles. She stamped his hand and struggled and broke free again, only to trip on the coaming and go sprawling into the cockpit.

With quite unbelievable speed, Peg Leg hopped up the companionway and struck at her with his crutch. She was really scared now because there was a wicked-looking sheath knife on the man's belt, and he looked really cruel.

As Carmen rose to her feet, Peg Leg stomped into the cockpit behind her and his right hand hooked into the back of her swimsuit. Carmen cried out in fear and squirmed frantically, trying to break free and at the same time reach the railing. In the process she felt the right shoulder strap of her swimsuit stretch and slip off her shoulder.

Peg Leg swore and snarled, "Hah! Got ya, ya little mermaid!"

Terror swamped Carmen. In desperation she half turned and tried to rip free. To her dismay, Peg Leg kept a firm grip of her swimsuit strap. Only the slipperiness of her suncream prevented him from getting a hold on her wrist. The Lycra swimsuit stretched even more. Carmen's attempts to break free became frantic. She jumped and squirmed, stretching the material more. She was dimly aware of darker fears of what her fate might be if caught.

Carmen slid her elbow back through the stretched strap and shrugged her arm free. The man swore and tried to grab at her again. Seeing his evil looking eye flick over her sent Carmen into ever more desperate attempts to get away. Peg Leg hopped quickly forward, his clawing fingers reaching for her arms. Fearful that he would get hold of her, Carmen jumped backwards to get away. As she did, she felt another stab of terror because the man's right hand still gripped the strap of her swimsuit.

She shrugged and squirmed frantically. She had managed to haul herself to the portside, her swimsuit stretching all the while. In her mind all she wanted to do was get into the water to escape so she tried to jump but Peg Leg's grip spoiled her leap. The low railings caught her behind the left knee.

Unable to stop herself, she fell sidewards over the railing. As she did, her swimsuit peeled off her like the skin off an over-ripe banana. A moment later, she found herself hanging upside down over the side, and before she could react in any way she slipped right out of her bathers and headfirst into the water.

As she went under, a swirl of emotions engulfed Carmen. Dominant was relief at her escape. Closely mixed with that was the terrifying knowledge that it was only a temporary reprieve. Now she had to get right away from the man. There was also scorching shame at being naked, tempered by the absurd physical pleasure of the cool water on her bare skin.

With her mind racing with desperate speed, Carmen opened her eyes. She peered through the blur of seawater and bubbles and tried to orient herself. At the same time she tried to come up with a plan to escape. The immediate problem was physical: she had not been ready to dive underwater and was both short of breath and had water up her nose and in her throat. She began to gag and cough. There was no other possible option but to surface to clear her breathing passages and to get a good lungful of air.

It took her an effort of willpower, but sheer necessity helped. Turning over she struck out for the surface, her eyes squinting and hurting. As she broke surface, she strained to clear her vision at the same time as she coughed and gasped for air.

And there, only centimetres from her head, was a grasping hand!

Peg Leg was leaning right over the railings, his ugly face contorted by anger, his mouth working as he swore vile obscenities. Carmen almost choked as water went down her throat, but she managed to cough enough to clear her windpipe. At the same time, she used her arms to backwater. This enabled her to squirm out of reach of those clawing fingers. Then she sucked in a deep breath and slid under.

Now her mind was working more clearly. *Which way should I swim?* she wondered; *and on the surface, or under water?*

Under water she decided, thinking of guns. But the direction was a problem. She badly wanted to reach the shore, to hide in the jungle. For an instant she considered swimming in under the jetty, but a moment's thought discarded that plan.

Peg Leg can hobble in along the jetty and catch me at the beach, she reasoned. So she decided to swim under the yacht and under the jetty and make for Oyster Point. *That might confuse him for a few minutes,* she decided.

It had the added advantage that he would have trouble running along the sand with his peg leg, and probably even more difficulty clambering over the rocks.

So she turned and side-stroked down. The hull of the yacht was close beside her and easy to see. So was the sandy bottom. But it seemed to require swimming much deeper than she had expected. The keel went down for what seemed like an amazing depth. Before she reached it, Carmen began to think she had made a serious error.

Will I be able to hold my breath long enough? she wondered.

But then she was there. She saw that the bottom of the yacht was thickly encrusted with weed and barnacles, so she made an extra effort to push herself well clear, not wishing to lacerate her soft skin. With a mental sigh of relief she swam under the hull, twisting her head upwards to look as she did. The pilings of the jetty stood out as solid black bars and were easy to avoid. She swam into the shadows under the jetty with strong strokes, very aware that her breath was fast running out.

Black dots began to dance before her already blurry vision and she felt a sharp throbbing in her head. She knew she had to come up.

I hope Peg Leg hasn't grabbed a gun, she thought. But fear or no fear she had to breathe, so up she went.

By the time her head broke surface, Carmen was in such emotional turmoil that she was almost in a state of shock. Fear, shame, and physical distress all swirled in a body that felt like it was squirming and quivering with intense sensitivity. Before she surfaced, Carmen had retained the presence of mind to turn to face her enemy. As she blinked the water from her eyes, she also gasped a fresh breath.

Then she gasped again. Her eyes frantically flicked from point to point. *Where is Peg Leg?* she wondered.

He was not on the jetty above her, where she had expected him to be. Nor could she see him on the yacht. She at once sucked in another big breath and went under. As she went down, she twisted to face away from the dark shadows of the jetty. She began swimming directly away from it, hoping that she was heading for Oyster Point.

This time her swimming was more controlled and she did not go as deep. Before she had to surface for another breath, she covered a good 25 metres she estimated. Once again, she cast a fearful glance behind her. This time she saw Peg Leg. He was standing on the jetty and appeared to be shaking a fist at her. He was shouting something but the words did not register, just the sense: anger and obscenity.

Carmen resumed swimming, but now remained on the surface. She used an economical side stroke so was able to look back as well as breathe. What she saw got her heart rate shooting up again with fear. Peg Leg jumped back onto the yacht and then lowered himself over the stern into the aluminium dinghy moored there. Within seconds he had cast loose the painter and then heaved himself aft to start doing things to the outboard motor at the stern.

He was so obviously going to pursue in the boat that Carmen cried aloud in terror. For a few seconds she changed her plan and turned to swim for the beach, only to choke up in fear. A second pirate had appeared, the one with the three-cornered hat. He was hurrying along the beach parallel to her. With a sob of desperation, she resumed swimming towards Oyster Point.

Now the rocks looked much further away, and she began to seriously doubt if she could reach them before Three-Cornered Hat had also run to the same spot. In a frantic effort to swim faster she changed to an overarm stroke, but not for long. It was too hard to do and tired her too much. Also it made it harder to see where she was going and to breathe in the choppy salt water. She changed to breast stroking, her head swivelling from side to side to keep watch on the two men.

The sound of the outboard motor starting up sent a shudder of pure terror through her, tinged with deep despair. By then she was at least a hundred metres from the jetty, but still had just as far again to swim to the rocks at the end of the point. The pirate on the beach was now passing the three pandanus palms and her mind calculated that he would obviously reach the rocks before she did. She was out in deep water now and other fears edged in: of sharks, of drowning, of jelly fish stings, and of a hundred nameless dreads.

The dinghy came accelerating out around the end of the jetty, its hull slapping against the small waves with a series of very audible smacks. Watching it approach caused Carmen to tread water, her heart sinking with feelings of despair and defeat. She could just see Peg Leg's head above the raised prow of the dinghy, and he looked very menacing and angry. Her eyes searched for signs of a weapon of some sort, but she saw none. Then she got stubborn.

How is he going to catch me? she wondered. She did not think he would jump in. *Most likely he will try to run me down,* she decided.

The thought of that racing propeller mincing her soft flesh made her cringe, but the fear also gave her strength.

Having decided to resist, Carmen now floated and waited. Peg Leg saw her and steered to come close alongside. As he did, he throttled back. When the dinghy was only a metre or so from Carmen, he throttled back and then reversed the thrust to bring it to a bobbing standstill.

He glared at her and snarled, "Get aboard!"

Carmen shook her head. Her heart was now hammering with intense anxiety and she half expected him to pull out a gun. When she refused to obey, Peg Leg's face contorted with rage and he again shouted angrily at her. By this time she was in such a heightened state of emotion that she was hypersensitive. She was acutely aware of her nakedness. She had a strong desire to cover herself and was intensely ashamed of him being able to see her. Yet she needed to use her arms to swim, so she kept treading water.

When she refused a third order to climb aboard, Peg Leg leaned forward and picked up a gaff hook. As the pole with its sharp, curved hook was lifted into view Carmen nearly lost control of her bodily functions.

The thing was designed to jag large fish to drag them aboard boats and she knew it would rip and tear her flesh if it caught her.

Even as he swung it over towards her, she sucked in a deep breath and ducked under. Driven by sheer terror, Carmen used her arms to thrust herself deep, expecting at any moment to feel the sharp hook snagging at her skin or body. When it did not, she kept swimming down. Glancing back up through the blur of bubbles and rippling sunlight on the water, she saw the blurred silhouette of the boat and then the threshing disturbance where Peg Leg was reaching down to try to get her.

But what to do next? The dilemma was exacerbated by the need to come up for air. Carmen decided to move away from the boat and come up for a quick breath, then dive again. She struck out sideways but was appalled to hear the motor rev and then see the black shape of the boat turn in the direction she was swimming. At once she reversed direction and swam in under the boat. By then she was badly in need of air and she had no other option but to come up.

She decided to come up behind the boat so swam that way. As she did, she eyed the shiny propeller with deep concern. It had stopped for the moment, but she had no doubt it could instantly whirr into deadly life, and that if it hit her it could inflict fatal injuries. With that in mind she took two extra strokes and came up about two metres behind the boat.

As she broke surface, she saw Peg Leg twist around to glare angrily at her. He swung the gaff hook towards her and shouted, "Give up, yer silly bitch and ye won't get hurt."

Carmen again shook her head. She wanted to say that she didn't trust him not to harm her, but a wave slopped into her open mouth and left her coughing and spluttering. As she floundered there trying to get her breath, she saw him drop the gaff and reach over to the throttle. She knew at once what he was going to do as his wrist twisted the controls.

He's going to reverse over me! she thought. In desperation she slipped under and struck out sideways.

The motor roared. The propeller became a whirr of bubbles which slid quickly towards her. Carmen could only see it as a blur in the water, but it was enough. She gave a convulsive jerk and tried desperately to thrust herself away from it. She felt a tingling knick on her right ankle even as she noted the dark shape of the boat slide over the top of her.

Missed! she thought as she watched the shape slide on. Then it stopped and she was again confronted with the dilemma of where to come up. *Beside the boat, but out of reach,* she reasoned, thinking she could get inside the turning circle.

She was partly right but had not taken into account the fact that, by turning the outboard motor's direction of thrust, Peg Leg could make the stern skid around towards her. She just had time to suck in air, note the movement and then slip under again. This time the propeller passed so close that she felt the turbulence on her face and felt her hair being sucked in a swirl towards it. Somehow she twisted away and the boat slid close over her.

She came up panting and feeling exhausted. *This can't last!* she thought, fear and despair mingling in her emotions.

"Give up yer stubborn bitch!" Peg Leg shouted.

He slewed the boat back towards her but had too much forward momentum. Carmen stayed on the surface and gulped air, her mind racing in an attempt to come up with a plan. Then she dived deep again as the boat came churning back towards her.

She was able to easily avoid it this time, but she knew she was weakening. Then a peculiar murky streak in the water caught her eye. She glanced and saw that it seemed to come from her leg. Only then did it dawn on her. The dark film swirling away from her ankle was blood!

I've been hit by the prop, she thought. Then real terror gripped her. *Blood! The smell will attract the sharks!*

She looked hastily in all directions and noted with dismay that she was now in water so deep she could hardly see the bottom. Worse still there was that dark gloomy limit to visibility hedging her in from about twenty metres away.

A shark will just appear out of that and attack without warning, she thought.

Chapter 29

RED RAW

By this time Carmen was so tired and so scared that she knew she was on the edge of hysteria. The boat now seemed the safer option. She saw that it was stopped right above her again and she could even see Peg Leg's head silhouetted against the sky as he leaned over to watch her. She realised that the water was so clear that he could watch her movements most of the time.

The need for air again forced her upwards. As she rose, the glimmer of a desperate plan formed and she resolved to try it. Just before she reached the surface, she changed direction and swam in under the boat, apparently aiming to surface on the side away from Peg Leg. Almost at once she swung her legs around and changed direction, kicking up to the surface. As she broke surface, she put up her hands and grasped the gunwale and heaved herself up.

As she blinked, the water clear of her eyes Carmen saw that her little trick had worked. Peg Leg had moved to the other side and was leaning over to look down. Knowing that it was now all or nothing, Carmen heaved herself up, putting all her weight on the side of the boat. She put her head down and rolled into the boat onto her back, her legs flailing as she did. Peg Leg began to turn and straighten up, and then lost his balance. To steady himself, he put his left hand down to the side, at the same time swinging the gaff hook. The pole whacked against Carmen's legs as she landed in the bottom of the boat, but she was desperate now and kicked out with all her strength.

Her feet struck at Peg Leg and he reeled back. Caught by surprise, he cried out and then dropped the pole in an attempt to clutch at her. The boat rocked wildly and he stumbled. He was now completely off balance, and the side of the boat caught him behind the knees and he went over backwards. Carmen saw his arms wave wildly in an attempt to regain his balance or to grab at something. Next, his foot and steel leg appeared, silhouetted against the sky. Then he fell out of sight.

For a few seconds Carmen could not believe what had happened.

Then she struggled to get up, ready to fight off any attack. But he was gone.

He's fallen overboard! she thought in disbelief.

The bottom of the boat was full of junk: ropes, poles, fishing lines, a toolbox, fish scales. It all hurt her bare back and buttocks, but she ignored this and scrambled to a crouching position, ready to fight.

Peg Leg's head surfaced in the midst of a swirl of bubbles and froth. As it did, Carmen clenched her fists. Then she looked around for a weapon. The gaff hook was there against her leg, so she snatched it up. In fear of her life she jabbed the blunt end of it into Peg Leg's face. He let out a gurgle and went under again.

But what to do next? Carmen looked around and knew she could not win in a fight with Peg Leg.

He will be too strong. I must get out of here, she reasoned.

But how? She considered swimming, but only after damaging the boat's motor. But Three-cornered Hat was still on the beach and had stopped to watch.

Take the boat then, she decided.

But that wasn't as easy as it sounded. Carmen had often been in power boats but had never been taught how to operate the motor. All she knew was from her casual observations. And there was the problem of Peg Leg. He had come up again and was coughing water and mouthing murderous threats.

As Peg Leg started swimming towards the boat, Carmen acted. She again thrust at him with the blunt end of the gaff hook. This time he was ready for that and instantly grabbed at it. Carmen had been expecting that so now she leaned on it and pushed with all her might. The boat slid away from Peg Leg, and she almost lost her balance and tumbled over the side. Just in time she gave a last heave and then let the gaff hook go, letting Peg Leg have it.

The shove had worked in pushing the stern of the boat another couple of metres away from Peg Leg. Now Carmen sprang to the motor. She knew she had only a few seconds and her eyes had trouble focusing. Suddenly she seemed to be all a-fluster and she dithered, her hands waving and fingers wriggling in indecision. Then her eyes noted what she was seeking, the small lever that engaged the power to the propeller. She reached forward and clicked it towards her. At once the motor noise changed as the propeller began to rotate. The engine noise dropped so quickly that Carmen feared the motor might stall. She bit her lip as she grasped the throttle, the cylindrical moving part of the handle. She gave this an exploratory twist and to her relief the engine at once picked up revolutions.

A glance over the side showed Peg Leg splashing towards her using an awkward overarm stroke. He had pushed the gaff hook aside and was now only a metre or so from the boat. In desperation Carmen twisted the throttle further and pulled the steering across to angle the stern of the boat away from him. The motor roared and smoke and water both sprayed out of the back. The boat began to move but to Carmen it seemed much too slowly. She saw Peg Leg's head close to the side and then watched in horror as his hand reached up.

She clenched her fist to hit at his hand. Peg Leg reached up but by then the boat was not only moving but slewing around and she saw the hand miss by centimetres. Suddenly Peg Leg was slipping astern and away. For a ghastly moment Carmen feared that he might be hit by the propeller, but he flung both arms back and heaved himself away. There was a slight bump but he appeared to be safe. As the boat picked up speed Carmen saw him start treading water, his mouth working and his fist being shaken at her.

She sighed with relief, then sat down, instantly regretting that as the thwart was covered with sand and fish scales which felt awful on her bare bottom. Taking a better grip on the throttle and steering, she eased the motor and looked around.

If I keep well clear of Peg Leg there is no way he can get back aboard, Carmen reasoned.

She allowed the boat to go around in a wide circle while she considered what to do next. One of the things worrying her was whether Peg Leg could swim. She had no desire to cause his death by drowning. That concern was quickly put to rest as she saw him treading water and shaking his fist. Then he began swimming towards the rocks of Oyster Point. Carmen saw that the point was now only about 75 metres away and was much closer than the beach. She also noted that Three-cornered Hat had stopped near the rocks at the end of the beach. He now began walking back towards the jetty. That put Carmen in a quandary. She really wanted to go back ashore to try to help the others but now she was unsure. She allowed the boat to go around in a second circle while she considered what to do.

I could sail around Oyster Point and land on Sandy Beach before Three-cornered Hat arrived, she thought. *Or I could go the other way, around to the artist's.* She considered both options but then shook her head. *I should really go and get help.*

That she decided was the sensible (if cowardly) thing to do. She was quite unsure if the radio operator she had spoken to had understood or believed her story. After a third circle she nodded to herself and said, "That is what I must do. I will go to Cardwell and get the police."

She looked around and was able to easily note the course she must take as all of the islands were clearly visible. For a few seconds she thought about going back to the yacht and trying to use the radio again and she even headed that way but that got Three-cornered Hat running back along the beach and caused her to shake her head.

I wouldn't have time, she decided. *He will arrive before I can get aboard and use the radio properly.*

After another look to check that Peg Leg was swimming and not drowning, Carmen turned the boat and pointed the bows out of the bay and towards the distant shape of Hinchinbrook Island.

Looking down at her nakedness she made a wry face. *Oh heavens, I will look a sight walking along the main street of Cardwell like this!*

She looked at the litter of fishing junk in the bottom, searching for a cloth or something to cover herself but there was nothing.

"I am going to get cooked red raw by the sun!" she muttered, hunching over to try to cover herself.

Then she saw the blood. It was still trickling from her lower calf and had formed quite a pool in the bottom of the boat. The sight gave her a shock and made her feel both nauseous and anxious.

I might bleed to death!

But a closer inspection showed her that the cut was only a couple of centimetres long and did not seem to be very deep. Once again, she searched the bottom of the boat for something to cover or bind it with but found nothing. The best she could do was lift her leg up and grip the leg.

Satisfied that the bleeding was not too serious she turned to look back. What she saw caused her to suck in her breath in dismay. A white sail was climbing up the jib stay of the yacht.

They are going to chase me! she thought.

She bit her lip and turned to study the sea and islands. That calmed her. Already she could see that the yacht was a long way behind- probably a couple of kilometres. The islands ahead were already looking larger and with details of vegetation showing. The only vessel in sight was the tiny speck of a small boat away off to the starboard bow but it appeared to be heading inshore as well.

Too far away for me to signal to, she decided.

Then she saw the yacht swing around and begin sailing westwards across the bay. A mainsail began to climb the mast, but slowly. That puzzled her but the distance was too great for her to see any details.

Maybe the pirates are leaving? she wondered.

Once she was sure that the yacht was definitely not following her, she began to relax. She again focused on her bleeding ankle, noting with relief that the flow seemed to be definitely easing. She also fussed over her rapidly burning bare skin. The tanned skin of legs and arms was clearly marked, and it left the white of her body even more obvious. Looking at her body got her all anxious about what to do when she reached civilization.

There might be people on the beach, and I will run up and quickly grab a towel, she decided.

Then, as she pictured this, she giggled nervously. "I'm as bad as Letitia!" she told herself.

Feeling better she settled to her navigation. She was thankful that the sea was calm and that there were no obvious problems. After looking astern several times she felt even better. The yacht had vanished from sight behind the small island and was obviously not chasing her. Also the bleeding seemed to have stopped. Carmen sighed with relief and turned to watch where she was going.

"Oh good! Only half an hour or so and I will be safe," she told herself.

Even as she did the motor gave a blip. Her heart leapt with concern and she turned to glance at the motor. As she did, it blipped again. She bit her lip and worried, but it seemed to pick up and run smoothly. Then, just as she was relaxing again, it began to splutter and cough. To her dismay, it suddenly stopped. There were a few more short splutters and then it died altogether. The boat came to a rocking standstill and Carmen could only sit in silent dismay.

She looked around and saw that she appeared to be a long way from any island or land. Worse still, there wasn't another boat or ship visible anywhere. She had the sea to herself and was now drifting slowly on the breeze. Her initial panic died away when she noted that the direction of drift was northwest, towards the mainland.

I will get washed ashore eventually, she reasoned.

But she also calculated that it would be many hours before that happened. That got her very anxious. Not only was she now feeling very thirsty and becoming painfully sunburnt, but it meant she would not be able to get help for the others.

She looked the motor over and soon discovered the problem: out of fuel. That upset her too because it meant that there was nothing she could do to fix the problem. All she could do was hunch in the seat feeling defeated and miserable. She bit her lip and wept a few salty tears, then tried to cover herself against the now scorching sun.

Sunburn and dehydration became her primary concern as the time began to drag by. The sun was so hot that it felt as though it was actually causing flames on her back and shoulders. She sweated for a while and then stopped sweating and that worried her even more. She knew it meant she was drying out and would soon be getting heat exhaustion. To compensate, she used a bailing tin to scoop up seawater. This was poured over her head and back and brought some relief, but it did not stop her becoming very thirsty.

As she sat there in the boiling sun, her misery and physical distress both mounted. She was deeply upset at not being able to help her brother and her friends and not knowing became an almost unendurable tension. Time dragged by and she began to feel dizzy. Her eyes felt sore, the result of dry salt and glare. A headache developed and she kept trying to lick dry lips that were starting to crack. Only by pouring seawater over herself could she gain any relief.

Then, as she stared around the horizon with growing desperation, her eyes noted the flecks of white. She rubbed her eyes and squinted against the glare. Yes! The white was spray from a moving boat. The boat was white. It appeared to be heading straight towards her and her spirits lifted immediately.

"Saved!" she croaked.

She saw that the vessel was a large motor launch: a cabin cruiser with a steering position on the upper deck. At first she thought it was similar to one of the game fishing launches that were common along the coast but as it got closer she saw that it was even larger and that it actually had a sizeable foredeck over a row of portholes. The focsle gave way to a covered half deck at the stern, more cabins being visible there. A wheelhouse structure was set atop this.

Then Carmen saw that the launch was not actually heading for her at all and she began to panic. To attract attention she stood up and began waving. That got her all anxious again as there did not appear to be anyone visible on the launch. She began to fear that she would not be noticed as it headed on its way. She saw that too would pass several hundred metres off so she waved even more frantically and began to scream.

Only then did she remember that all boats were supposed to have compulsory safety gear, including flares, an EPIRB, and a small radio. She stopped waving and began searching. Now she was almost frantic as the launch was passing abeam and she could not find any sign of even a lifejacket, never mind the other items. A flare was what she wanted but the boat had no lockers and there was no container.

"Oh please! Here I am. Please see me!" she cried, standing up to wave again.

To her despair, the launch went surging on its way, its sleek bow slicing into the small waves and throwing up a fine spray. To add to her frustration she now saw shapes that could only be people. They were lying of the foredeck.

"Oh see me please!" she sobbed, jumping up and down so much she almost overset the boat.

Suddenly, a person on the front of the launch sat up and she saw an arm point. A second head popped up beside the first and then one appeared up on the upper steering position. To Carmen's intense relief, the launch began slowing and turning. As it became obvious that it was now heading directly towards her, she sank down and burst into shivering sobs.

Then she remembered her nakedness and waves of shame and anxiety began to sweep over her. She curled up to try to hide herself. As the launch drew closer, she decided that the people on it were not liable to be bothered by her undressed state as she saw that both of the people on the foredeck were women and they both appeared to be wearing very brief swimsuits. By rubbing her eyes and blinking Carmen saw that one woman had black hair and wore only a red one-piece bathing costume. The other woman was a busty blonde and she appeared to have only a brief bikini.

That got Carmen all embarrassed and she braced herself for a difficult experience. By then the launch was slowing and steering to stop close alongside. Carmen looked up and saw a man appear on the side outside the cabin doors. The head showing in the upper steering position was also a male. Carmen hunched herself into an even tighter ball and braced herself for being ashamed.

The launch came to a standstill with a grumble of powerful diesels and Carmen made herself look up at the people. She saw grinning faces and shame scorched through her. This was almost instantly replaced by a wave of cold shock.

The dark-haired woman in the red bathers was Lana the smuggler! Beside her stood the blonde. Carmen blinked and gaped, unable to credit what her eyes told her. She gasped and looked at the man leaning over the rail at the upper steering position. Then her stomach turned over with fear. It was Mr Barrett, the smuggler. Even as Carmen's mind recoiled in disbelief and fear she saw that the man giving her the evil grin from the main deck aft was Ponytail Dan.

Chapter 30

ANDREW ACTS

Letitia was naked and the artist wore only a grubby pair of grey shorts and a white cloth hat. At the first glimpse, Andrew felt the hurt. Jealousy and distress warred in his chest. It made him feel so upset that his skin seemed to itch and his stomach heaved. Letitia was standing thigh deep in the edge of the water, posing for the artist. He was working at his easel ten paces away to her left.

As Anne and Andrew came racing along the track the artist looked in their direction, his face a mixture of annoyance and alarm.

"You bloody kids aren't going to cause more grief, are you?" he challenged.

Andrew came to a gasping stop beside Anne. Next to them, floating on the rising tide in the small creek, was the boat. He shook his head and pointed to the boat, a plan forming instantly in his head.

"No. Quick, into the boat and get going!"

Astonishment showed on the artist's face. "What? What on earth? Why?"

"There are men with guns; drug smugglers. They are chasing us. Oh quick! Don't argue. Get the girls to safety," Andrew pleaded.

That had become part of his plan: send both Anne and Letitia away in the boat to keep them safe.

To Andrew's relief, the artist accepted his story. "The same one's that kidnapped Carmen?" he asked.

"Yes," Andrew lied. "I think so," he added, to salve his conscience.

As he spoke, his eyes were drinking in Letitia's nude form. She made no attempt to cover herself and stood holding her pose. To Andrew, she appeared as a vision of wonder and delight.

"What makes you think that these men are dangerous?" the artist challenged.

"They fired shots at us," Andrew replied. He cast a fearful look over his shoulder, half-expecting to see the pirates at any moment. "Oh hurry! Don't argue please! Just get in the boat and go!"

As the artist still hesitated, Andrew acted. He ran to where the boat's anchor rope was looped around a tree trunk and quickly untied it. With the anchor in his right hand he ran back down to the boat, ignoring the artist's protests.

"Get in! Don't waste time arguing," Andrew snapped angrily, fearing for both Anne and Letitia.

Andrew's tone of voice and his determined actions seemed to convince the artist as he put down his palette and brush and began moving towards his camp. Andrew shook his head and pointed to the boat.

"Where are you going? Get in and get the girls to safety," he cried.

"Clothes," the artist replied, gesturing towards where Letitia's lay on the sand.

Andrew was now so agitated that he just seized the man's arm and pushed him around. "No time! Get in! Get going!" he ordered.

The artist looked doubtful, but Anne ran past him and scooped up Letitia's bikini and towel. "Letitia, get in the boat," she cried, tossing the clothes into it as she did.

The artist quickly splashed in to help as Andrew tossed the anchor and rope into the boat, and he and Anne began pushing it down the creek.

Andrew flamed with shame and worry about Anne seeing Letitia, but in his urgency he thrust such thoughts aside. To the artist he snapped, "Get in and start the motor. I will turn the boat around."

The artist obeyed, clambering into the boat. He began working on the motor while Andrew threw his weight on the side of the bow to spin the boat around. He was in waist deep water by then but saw that there was a shallow bar at the mouth of the small creek. Pushing with all his strength he shoved the boat towards it.

"Anne! Letitia! Get aboard, quickly!" he ordered.

Impatiently he gestured to Anne, and she splashed into the water and he held out a hand to help her aboard. She scrambled in and sat down near the bow.

Andrew then held out his hand to Letitia, who had finally started to move. As she waded over to him, he did not know where to look. He flamed with embarrassment as his eyes flicked from one part of her body to another. She looked puzzled rather than anxious and took her time, much to his annoyance.

"For God's sake, get in!" Andrew snapped.

He held her hand to steady her as she climbed in. Seeing her in intimate detail from so close got him so flustered he could hardly think straight. Despite that, the urgency of the situation drove him and as soon as Letitia was aboard he threw his weight on the boat and completed pushing it around. He pushed so hard that Letitia lost her balance and fell on her bum, crying out in protest as she did.

Andrew shook his head and splashed to the stern. Once there he started pushing hard. He slipped a few times on the sandy bottom and found himself in knee deep water and then, after a few rapid strides, in waist deep and then chest deep water.

"We are over the bar," the artist called. "Get in and I will start up."

Andrew shook his head and shoved with all his might, sending the boat surging out into the low waves. "No. You get the girls to safety. Go to Cardwell and get the police. I am going back to help Carmen and the others. I will decoy the pirates away. Get going."

Having said that, Andrew turned and began splashing ashore. He heard Anne cry out, calling for him to get into the boat but he ignored her. The artist, seeing he was determined, at once pulled the toggle to start the engine. To Andrew's intense relief, it started at once and a puff of blue smoke billowed out, followed by white smoke and a spurt of cooling water. By then Andrew had splashed ashore, his head swinging rapidly from side to side as he tried to watch the boat and look back along the track at the same time.

The surge of sound as the boat's motor was accelerated was a great relief to Andrew. He glanced back and saw white foam cream at its bows as it began to move. Froth swirled at the stern and it began to punch into the small waves with audible smacks. But now Andrew had focused on the easel and painting. The painting was a good one and already was a recognisable Letitia. For a few seconds Andrew gazed at in a sort of awe. The shape of Letitia's nude form appeared to him to be excellent, and it was obviously expert work.

I'd like to own this painting, he thought as he grabbed both easel and canvas.

Some irrational desire not to let the men see Letitia's picture made him pick them up and run with them. Holding both tightly, if awkwardly, he splashed across the shallow creek towards the rocks at the end of the point. By the time he reached them he was relieved to see that the boat was already 40 or 50 metres out from the beach and picking up speed.

Andrew ran in among the boulders, following the tracks they had made over the last few days. For a moment he paused to thrust the painting and easel out of sight behind a large rock that was well above high tide level. Then he ran on. Seconds later he was scrambling up over the rocks. As he climbed up onto a rocky outcrop the boat came back into view. He saw that it was now 75 metres out.

At that moment, movement behind Andrew attracted his attention. It was the pirate wearing the three-cornered hat. He came running out of the scrub. One glance told Andrew that he was seen. It was enough. He fled, and Three-cornered Hat charged after him, splashing across the small creek with a skittering of spray, to vanish from sight among the rocks. Andrew scrambled over the boulders as fast as he could go, at great risk of slipping or losing his balance. He knew that a fall would be disaster, and several times slowed down rather than take a foolish risk.

Because he had been that way half a dozen times, Andrew was confident that he could outrun the pirate on the rocks. What he was worrying about was whether the pirate had a gun and whether he would use it, and also if he had seen the boat. Frequent glances behind at last revealed the pirate's head bobbing up and down among the boulders. It also showed Andrew that the boat was now at least a hundred metres offshore and heading directly away from the island.

They should be safe now, Andrew reasoned, noting the inshore islands and line of distant mountains.

He had not seen a rifle in Three-cornered Hat's hand and did not think a pistol could accurately fire that far. As he clambered up over another boulder, Andrew saw Three-cornered Hat on top of another rock about 50 paces back. The pirate had paused to study the boat but, beyond shielding his eyes with one hand and looking puzzled, he took no other action. Then he turned and looked at Andrew. Their eyes met momentarily and the pirate yelled at him to stop. Andrew ignored the man and scrambled down the boulder and hurried on along the rocky shore.

By the time Andrew reached the beach at Wreck Bay, the boat was hundreds of metres out to sea and starting to turn to port towards Schooner Rock and Cardwell. Satisfied that the girls were safe, Andrew began to worry about what to do next. As he ran along the sand past the wreck, he considered just running into the jungle to hide. Other options were to sneak back to the campsite to try to locate Carmen, or to find out what had happened to the others.

Another problem was sheer physical fitness, or lack of it. Andrew was now gasping for breath and starting to develop a stitch. Sweat was pouring out of him and he knew he was tiring. However, a glance behind showed him that his pursuer was no fitter and had not gained any distance on him, indeed had lost ground.

I'll decide what to do once I am over the ridge at Snapper Point, Andrew thought.

He reached the end of the beach and went trotting up the foot track, all the while panting and wiping perspiration from his eyes. Three-cornered Hat, visibly slowing and puffing, came trotting along the beach behind him, a good 75 metres back.

Andrew slowed to a panting fast walk as he made his way up the slope. Now he was starting to regret not wearing a shirt or hat as the sun felt blisteringly hot on his bare skin. By the time he reached the crest of the low ridge he was gasping for air and his heart was hammering furiously but he was cheered by seeing that Three-cornered Hat looked to be going even slower and had fallen further behind.

As Andrew crested the rise, he slowed and cautiously scanned the beach and bay. He half expected to meet another of the pirates coming the other way but saw that the path and beach in front of him were deserted. The pirate's yacht was still moored at the jetty but there was no sign of movement on it either. Then a fleck of white moved on the deck of the yacht. Andrew paused to look and saw a person go down into the stern companionway.

"There is someone on the yacht," he muttered.

He decided he had better take to the scrub rather than risk being seen. Having enemies both in front and behind did not seem like a good idea. With that in mind, he bounded down the last of the rocks and onto the main beach, then turned left and hurried into the thicket of prickly bushes which grew at the back of the beach.

Almost at once he regretted that decision. Not only were the bushes prickly but they grew so close together that he could not push through between them. He could only proceed by crawling. This was very unpleasant, the branches scratching his bare back and dead leaves sticking to his sweaty skin. For a moment he contemplated backing out but then realised he was committed. He had wasted too much time and knew that Three-cornered Hat must now be over the crest and hurrying down to the beach.

Then Andrew made another unpleasant discovery: He had miscalculated the lie of the land. Only 25 paces in was the steep lower slope of the hillside. He had been hoping to find flat jungle but now saw he had to either try to force his way up a steep, rocky slope thickly matted with vines and bushes, or work his way along to the right. One glance up at the thicket on the steep slope decided him. He began crawling and pushing his way along near the base of the hill.

As he did, he kept peering over his right shoulder for any sign of Three-cornered Hat. *If he has a gun and sees me he will just be able to shoot me,* Andrew reasoned.

The fear made him sweat all the more and tended to freeze him up. It was just as well because the belt of bushes and scrub was not complete, and he could get frequent glimpses through to the beach.

It was just as he reached a more open area where several gaps allowed a good view out to the sea that Andrew glimpsed movement. He immediately froze behind a bush and tried to quieten his ragged, gasping breathing. Into view only ten paces away came a very red-faced and angry Three-cornered Hat. The pirate was sweating profusely and held a pistol in his hand.

"Little bastard! Where's he gone?" Three-cornered Hat muttered. His eyes swept around the scrub, then along the beach.

Andrew felt a spasm of real terror. *Oh no! He will see my tracks and follow me,* he thought, panic mounting. He tensed, ready to flee.

At that moment, a girl's scream sounded. Andrew flinched and crouched lower. Three-cornered Hat heard it as well. He jerked around and stared towards the yacht. Andrew could not see the yacht clearly but as another female scream reached his ears, he recognised who was making it and his whole body went cold with shock.

Carmen! And she is in real trouble, he told himself.

That was incredibly distressing. Andrew's instinctive reaction was to rush to his sister's aid, no matter what, but the sight of the perspiring pirate and the automatic pistol in his hand caused him to remain crouched under cover, his whole being filled with despair and anguish.

Three-cornered Hat remained staring towards the yacht. Suddenly, he shook his head and muttered, "What the bloody hell is going on?"

He moved a few paces further out onto the beach and kept grumbling angrily. Next, he took off his hat and wiped sweat from his forehead before settling the hat firmly again. Then he stood with his back to Andrew while staring towards the yacht.

It was too much for Andrew. He just had to know. Moving very carefully he edged across behind another bush and risked a look. What he saw made him bite his lip in frustrated impotence. Carmen was struggling in the cockpit of the yacht with another pirate. The man had hold of her and she was hitting at him and trying to get away. Andrew stared in horror as she suddenly fell backwards over the side, her green bathers peeling off and being left in the grip of the man.

As Carmen vanished into the water, Andrew felt a surge of relief. *She's broken free,* he told himself. *But how can she possibly get away?*

With heart in mouth he watched her surface, then evade the pirate's grasping hand and dive again. When Carmen did not resurface, Andrew's anxiety shot up. Only when he saw the pirate on the yacht peer over the stern, and then over the side nearest the jetty, did Andrew's hope return.

She's swum under the yacht, he decided.

He could not see her but watched with growing hope as the pirate scrambled up onto the jetty. Then Andrew understood. The pirate had an artificial leg and used a crutch. When he heard Peg Leg shouting angrily to come back or else Andrew broke into a grin.

She's got away! he thought happily.

Then his smile faded and a frown returned as he watched Peg Leg clamber back onto the yacht, then down into the dinghy moored astern. It was obvious the pirate was going to pursue her in the motorboat.

Three-cornered Hat had also been watching this with growing agitation. Andrew heard him curse, then mutter, "What the hell is that old fool doing? Bloody hell!" With that he cast an angry glance back at the scrub where Andrew was hiding, then set off running along the beach towards the jetty.

Andrew saw him go but for a few moments could not believe his luck. Then he heard the motor of the dinghy splutter to life and concern for Carmen became his dominant emotion.

I've got to help Car, he told himself. But how?

Chapter 31

THE DEVIL AND THE DEEP BLUE SEA

Andrew crouched behind the bushes, quivering with tension and anxiety. Driven by a compulsive urge to help Carmen he crept forward to try to get a better look. To his amazement, he saw that Three-cornered Hat was still running along the beach and had almost reached the end of the jetty. For a moment Andrew contemplated running after him, but caution stopped him. Instead, he began moving as quickly as he dared through the bushes and then from tree to tree just inside the edge of the jungle.

As he moved, Andrew got glimpses through the pilings of the jetty of what was going on. What he saw appalled him. He watched in horror as the dinghy surged forward towards Carmen's head. Andrew was aghast.

"He is trying to kill her!" he cried in anguish. Frustration at his own inability to help caused him to grind his teeth, then hurry on.

To his enormous relief, Andrew saw Carmen duck just in time. When her head came up behind the boat and the pirate swore and tried to gaff her, but failed, Andrew almost cheered aloud.

Good girl! Keep it up Car! he thought.

But watching had Andrew's heart right up in his dry throat and he felt sick with apprehension. It seemed that the unequal struggle could result only in Carmen being badly hurt or killed. The thought of her being minced by the boat's propeller was so disturbing that Andrew tried to thrust it out of his mind.

He came to the mouth of the creek and splashed across, then hurried through the line of trees behind the picnic area. He was still being cautious because he knew there were at least three other pirates somewhere, and blundering into them and getting caught would not help Carmen in any way. Every few steps he risked a look along the beach and noted with satisfaction that Three-cornered Hat had run on past the jetty and was now near the three pandanus palms where they had found the treasure. The pirate was obviously heading for the rocks on Oyster Point to cut off Carmen's escape.

Andrew reached the last tree beside the track leading into the camp site and paused. A glance left along the track showed no sign of any pirates. And then, just as he looked the other way, he did cheer. Even as he watched he saw Carmen heave herself into the dinghy and then kick Peg Leg over the side of the wildly rocking boat.

"Oh, well done! Keep it up!" he called. Then he watched with bated breath her struggle to keep Peg Leg from getting back aboard. "Start the engine! Get away from there!" Andrew muttered.

To his intense relief, she did. As the dinghy moved clear and began to circle, he heaved a huge sigh of relief. She was safe- at least for the moment.

From under cover Andrew watched Carmen circle in the dinghy. She was obviously trying to work out what to do next.

She could pick me up, Andrew decided. *Then we could go around to the other side of the island and land, then try to help the others.*

With that thought in mind Andrew leaned out and looked along the beach. To his consternation Three-cornered Hat was running back in his direction.

He can't have seen me, Andrew thought. *So why is he running this way?*

He noted that Peg Leg was now swimming towards Oyster Point while Carmen was pointing the dinghy out of the bay. Then his gaze travelled out along the jetty and stopped at the yacht.

Maybe Three-cornered Hat is going to chase her in the yacht? he wondered.

Andrew had no idea how fast the yacht could go. He assumed it had an engine as well as sails and reasoned that it would make better progress in the waves than a small boat.

The yacht. I've got to stop the pirates using it, he decided.

How he wasn't quite sure but no sooner had the idea formed than he acted on it. He broke cover and began running out along the jetty.

That he was seen was immediately apparent from the shout directed at him by Three-cornered Hat. As he ran, Andrew glanced left and saw that Three-cornered Hat was still running, had passed the three pandanus palms and the clump of rocks and was now sprinting along the sand towards him.

Oh help! I'll have to be bloody quick! he told himself.

Ideas crowded Andrew's racing mind: disable the engine and swim for it; set fire to the yacht and dive overboard; try to set sail and get clear. Whatever he did he knew must be done very quickly as Three-cornered Hat was covering the distance fast; and he had a gun!

By the time Andrew had reached the yacht he had made a decision: cast the yacht off and then try to do something.

I must get her clear before Three-cornered Hat arrives, he reasoned.

With that in mind, he stopped at the first mooring pile and bent down to grasp the ropes looped over it. There were two: a spring and a mooring line. Andrew heaved on the spring to loosen it, then hauled it up over the top of the post. With a strong heave he threw the end aboard the yacht. The bight of the rope was too heavy and the rope slid down into the water, but he ignored that and tugged at the mooring line. It scraped up the post but came free. In the process Andrew collected several very painful splinters under his fingernails but he was so excited and frightened that he barely noticed.

A fearful glance showed him that Three-cornered Hat had reached the end of the jetty. The pirate looked furiously angry and was waving the pistol in the air threateningly. Andrew gasped in desperation and ran on along the jetty to the aft mooring pile. Now he was frantic and just reefed the spring upwards. To his dismay, it jammed and his mind told him that the breeze had pushed the now free bow of the yacht out, pulling the spring tight. He had no option other than to grasp the line and heave with all his strength to pull the bow back towards the jetty.

He managed this and cast the loop off the top of the piling, but knew he had lost. The thunder of running feet on the jetty warned him and he looked sideways even as he began to struggle with the aft mooring line.

Oh no! Only one rope to go and I don't have time! his frantic thoughts told him.

Three-cornered Hat was now almost at the bow of the yacht, and he had the pistol raised. Even as Andrew tried to pull the yacht back to take the strain off the mooring line, Three-cornered Hat shouted, "Drop it kid, or you are dead!"

Andrew gave a convulsive heave to try to get the loop free. Then he saw the look of fury in Three-cornered Hat's eyes and the gun come up. Driven by sheer survival instinct Andrew dropped flat.

Bang!

Andrew heard the bullet crack past close overhead. He had no doubt that the pirate had tried to kill him. Terror and rising panic now took over. Leaving the last rope attached, he rolled sideways and sprang up.

Bang!

That shot also missed, but it was obvious to Andrew that Three-cornered Hat was trying to shoot him. His initial thought had been to dive into the water but then he considered having to come up for air and being shot in the head as he did. Instead, he swerved and jumped the other way, onto the yacht.

Bang!

This time Andrew heard the bullet strike the boat near him. He did not see where but did not care. It had missed. There in front of him was the open companionway leading below and he jumped quickly down it. Even as he did, he thought he had made a mistake.

Now I will be trapped below decks! his mind told him

His head then struck the deckhead and almost stunned him. He landed on the deck with a crash, which bruised his left arm and knee. For a second he lay there dazed, but the motion of the boat told him that Three-cornered Hat had jumped aboard.

Get up! Run! his panicking mind screamed.

Andrew dragged himself to his feet, banging his ribs painfully on the table as he did. His eyes flicked round the cabin searching frantically for either a weapon or a way of escape. He noted the radio and a chart table and stove but no knife or other such object visible. Footsteps above him and the flicker of shadow past a port hole got him moving. The sight of a sandshoe stepping over the coaming and onto the top tread of the companionway was enough. He fled.

But there was only one way to run, around the table to the door at the forward end of the cabin. Andrew ignored banging his hips against the table in his frantic rush. He reached the door and twisted the handle even as the pirate's legs came down the steps. As the gun came into sight, Andrew reefed the door open and scrambled through it, pulling it shut behind him.

To his dismay, he found himself in a cabin lined on both sides with bunks, but with no obvious escape other than through yet another door in the forward bulkhead. Reason told him this should lead to the sail locker and storage area.

There should be a hatchway there, he thought, remembering seeing sails being handed up through such a hatch when out sailing one weekend. *But will I have time to get through and open that door?*

Before he could even move, the door he had just closed was kicked violently open and Three-cornered Hat appeared. Andrew blanched and terror coursed red through his veins. Even as the gun swung round towards him, he acted. Close to his hand was a fire extinguisher. Yellow, his brain noted. In a flash he grasped the top of it, wrenched it free from its hook, and swung it up in a desperate attempt to save himself.

Pistol and fire extinguisher met.

Bang!

The bullet missed, thudding into a locker. Andrew lashed out in desperation, hitting out with the fire extinguisher again. Three-cornered Hat tried to grab at it but failed. The extinguisher took him hard across the nose and he reeled back, striking his back and head on the doorframe. The pirate swore and put his left hand up to his face, at the same time as he went to aim the pistol again. Again Andrew lashed out. The extinguisher cracked down hard on the pirate's wrist. To Andrew's astonishment, the pistol went flying out of the pirate's hand and landed on the deck.

For a couple of stunned seconds both stared down at it. Then Three-cornered Hat, still holding his nose and cheek, darted forward, bending down to retrieve it. Andrew changed his grip on the extinguisher, meaning to hit the pirate on the head with it. To his surprise, it began to hiss and squirt white liquid. He was so caught off guard by this that he almost dropped the extinguisher. Then he saw that the spray of liquid was hitting the pirate about the head, causing him to jerk back.

Instantly, Andrew changed his plan. He gripped the extinguisher and aimed the spray into the pirate's face. The pungent odour told Andrew's nose what his mind had already partially known from the colour: it was a chemical extinguisher for electrical fires. That the chemical was having a disabling effect on the pirate was at once obvious. The man reeled backwards, crashing into the bulkhead and bunks, while he tried to shield his face and eyes. He began to retch and cough and his eyes rapidly blinked and watered.

Andrew tried to keep directing the stream of liquid onto the pirate's face, but the man was now jerking and moving so convulsively that most of it missed. Then the hissing slowed and the jet turned to a dribble.

Oh no! It's run out! Andrew thought.

The pirate was still on his feet, although plainly in distress and likely to collapse. As the spray slowed, Three-cornered Hat gripped the edge of a bunk to steady himself, then wiped his face with his sleeve and glared at Andrew. Wracking coughs caused him to gasp and retch, but Andrew could see that he was only temporarily incapacitated. He could also see that the man was now murderously enraged, his eyes blazing and spittle dribbling from his rapidly working mouth.

Oh help! I've really made him mad now! Andrew thought.

He backed away a couple of steps, fear of the probable consequences almost paralysing him. In an attempt to knock the man out, he cast the fire extinguisher at him with both hands. The pirate saw it coming and managed to raise his left arm just in time. The extinguisher struck him a hard blow on the forearm, then fell to the deck. That left Andrew even more afraid and he stepped back another pace.

As he did, his foot kicked the pistol. Andrew knew at once what it was and acted without conscious thought. He bent and scooped the gun up, jumping further back in case the pirate tried to pounce. Then he stepped back two more paces till the bulkhead behind him prevented further retreat. With fumbling fingers, Andrew turned the pistol around and held it ready for use in his right hand, his finger on the trigger.

"Keep back or I'll shoot!" he croaked.

For a couple of seconds Three-cornered Hat stood glaring at him, his whole body heaving as he gasped for air. He wiped his streaming, red-rimmed eyes and ground his teeth. At some point his three-cornered hat had fallen off and Andrew noted that he had long, curly blonde hair.

Then Three-cornered Hat snarled and reached behind him. To Andrew's dismay, his hand reappeared holding a wicked looking knife. The pirate sneered and said, "You are going to pay for that you little bastard, now give me that gun."

"No! Drop the knife!"

"No way. You drop the gun, or I'll cut your guts out!" he said, and moved into a crouch and took a step forward.

Andrew swallowed and felt sick with apprehension. "Stop! Stay there! Drop the knife or I will shoot!"

At that, a wicked sneer crossed Three-cornered Hat's face, and he replied, "You wouldn't be game."

"Yes, I would," Andrew cried, aware that he was taking huge, gasping breaths and that the pistol was shaking in his grip.

Three-cornered Hat took a very deliberate step forward. Andrew cried out in desperation, "Stay there and drop the knife or I will shoot!"

To his shame, his voice cracked as he cried this and it caused a mirthless smile to cross the pirate's face. Andrew was in anguish by now, desperately afraid he might have to pull the trigger and fearful that he would not be able to. As the pirate took another step forward, he took an involuntary step backwards.

Behind Andrew the bulkhead door suddenly swung open. In an instant he took his decision. He felt for the doorframe and then ducked backwards through the doorway. As he did, Three-cornered Hat dashed forward. Even faced by that attack Andrew could not bring himself to shoot. He tried to swing the door shut and failed. The pirate smashed it open and lashed out with his knife. Andrew jumped back just in time.

It was the sail locker and storeroom. A loosely bundled sail was next to Andrew on a bench. He grabbed it and dragged it in front of him as Three-cornered Hat lunged again. The sail was just enough to block the attack. The sail entangled the knife point and caused the pirate to stumble. By now Andrew was sure that the pirate wanted to kill him, and fear drove him into flight. Close behind him was a short companionway and an open hatch. He turned and scuttled frantically up this, expecting to be grabbed and slashed at every step.

Gasping with fright, Andrew stumbled out onto the foredeck. Because of the way the ladder faced, Andrew found himself in the bows facing forward. He had been going to jump onto the jetty but now saw to his dismay that, by his earlier efforts, he had defeated himself. The bow had swung away from the jetty so that the yacht was moored only by a single stern line. Next, he looked at the water and wondered how well the pirate could swim. But the thought of fighting off a big, strong man armed with a knife underwater was more than Andrew could face. He turned and fled along the deck, clambering up onto the cabin roof next to the mast.

Through the hatchway appeared Three-cornered Hat's head. The pirate was facing away from him and paused to look around. Seeing Andrew he glared and held up his knife. Andrew looked frantically around for a way of escape and saw only the options of fighting or swimming.

Trapped! he thought. *Between the Devil and the deep blue sea!*

Chapter 32

ALL AT SEA

Andrew knew in his heart he could not shoot the pirate. That knowledge engendered such a feeling of helpless desperation that he was driven to act. In an attempt to bluff, he used his left hand to pull back the slide on the automatic pistol to check it was cocked. In his mind was the desperate expedient of trying to shoot the man in the leg. As he did, he sprang sideways, away from that knife.

Three-cornered Hat glared at him, slashing forward as he did. The knife blade flashed in the sunlight and Andrew jumped back again, his finger tightening on the trigger but failing to make the gun go off. A feeling of despair surged through him as he thought he had made a fatal mistake.

Safety catch? he thought.

A malicious grin spread across Three-cornered Hat's face, and he sprang forward across the open hatchway, knife point leading. Andrew had no time to glance at the pistol to find the safety catch. All he could do was make a desperate jump sideways, narrowly avoiding the stabbing blade. In a frantic attempt to save himself he swung his arm back, preparatory to hurling the pistol at the man.

In attempt to slash at Andrew before he could throw the gun, the man twisted and took a step sideways. But he miscalculated and his foot went down into the open hatchway. Before Andrew's astonished gaze the pirate suddenly fell, striking his forehead on the coaming around the hatchway. There was a very audible bump and then the man crumpled and tumbled down the companionway to sprawl on the deck below.

Andrew saw him go and watched the knife drop onto the deck with a sort of disbelief. He shuddered with relief and reaction. The pirate was lying unconscious at the bottom of the ladder. Andrew stood and stared down the hatchway, his heart hammering and his chest heaving. He tensed, ready to resume the fight, but then noted that the pirate was not moving. Fear changed to a sort of sickly dread.

Oh no! I hope I haven't killed him, Andrew thought.

Very cautiously he lowered himself down the hatchway. A step at a time he made his way down, ready to jump back or to lash out. As he went down, his eyes kept scanning the pirate for any sign of movement. By the time Andrew reached the bottom, the pirate had not moved at all and did not even appear to be breathing.

Feeling utterly wretched as well as intensely nervous, Andrew stepped off the ladder and moved around behind the pirate, then bent to check whether he was alive. As he did, Andrew quivered with tension, expecting it to be a trick and for the pirate to suddenly open his eyes and try to grab him. However, nothing happened and the other fear, that he had killed the man, became dominant. Steeling himself to touch his enemy, Andrew reached down and placed two fingers on the man's throat.

Andrew could not feel a pulse and his heart turned over with sickening apprehension. Then he noted a slight movement in the pirate's chest.

He's breathing. Oh thank heavens! Andrew thought.

Even as Andrew checked, the pirate gave a snuffle and moved slightly. Andrew sprang back in fright, banging his shoulder and head against the ladder. But the pirate remained still, obviously unconscious.

He is really hurt, he thought.

Then another horrible thought galvanised Andrew: what was the other pirate, Peg Leg, doing? Andrew had last seen Peg Leg swimming for the rocks but by now he could well be ashore and heading for the yacht.

And there are at least three other pirates. Where are they?

For a few seconds he dithered over what to do about Three-cornered Hat. Then he shook his head and turned to the companionway.

"I will just check whether any of the pirates are coming, then tie him up," he muttered.

Quickly but cautiously he went up the ladder and peeked out of the hatchway. To his relief, there was no sign of anyone else on the yacht. Nor was there anyone on the jetty. Andrew raised himself higher and looked around. Very carefully he scanned the beach but saw no sign of anyone. Then he turned and looked seaward, hoping to see Carmen. It took him a few seconds searching before he detected flecks of white that indicated the bow wave of a boat. It was a long way off in the direction of Hinchinbrook Island.

"That must be her," he told himself. He estimated she was now at least a nautical mile away. "Well, she is quite safe now," he assured himself.

That gave him the problem of what to do next. *I should try to find the others and help them,* he decided. But what to do with the yacht? *Treasure Island,* he thought. The idea seemed to form in his head.

"I will do what Jack Hawkins did and steal the *Hispaniola.* Then I will hide her and go ashore to negotiate with the pirates: my friends in exchange for their ship."

As soon as he thought of it, Andrew decided to carry out that plan. He climbed quickly up on deck and hurried aft. Arriving at the stern he again scanned the jetty and beach but still found them deserted. That worried him and he paused to look at Oyster Point.

Where on earth is Peg Leg? he wondered. There was no sign of movement on the rocks or on the hillside above them. *Perhaps he drowned?* Andrew thought.

Then he shrugged and thrust that unpleasant thought aside. He placed the pistol on the steering console, then bent to untie the stern mooring line, wanting to get the yacht away from the jetty so no other pirate could get aboard. However, he found he had the same problem that had baulked him before: the line was too tight to undo. The breeze had pushed the yacht away from the jetty and she was held by the stern line, which was bar taut.

There was nothing for it but to grab the line and heave. It took all of Andrew's strength to move the weight of the yacht but with a gasping, sweating effort he managed it. He was able to haul her back close to the jetty, allowing the mooring line to go slack. Then he almost muffed it. He tried to flick the loop of the line off the mooring pile but it caught and he had to pull the yacht in again and lean over to lift it clear.

As he did, the thought came to Andrew that the yacht was not the *Hispaniola.* "I wonder what her name is?" he said.

As soon as the mooring line was free, he leaned over and looked at the flat counter. He was able to read the name and then chuckled. "The *Jolly Roger.* That's good!"

He also noted with interest that the port of registry was Nassau. *In the Bahamas. Very appropriate for pirates,* he decided. It also fitted the accent of the pirates. All the ones he had heard had all spoken with distinct English accents.

The motion of the yacht then recalled Andrew to present reality. He saw with concern that she was drifting quite rapidly away from the jetty.

One glance confirmed the worst. *Oh bloody hell! What an idiot I am,* he berated himself. The yacht was now drifting diagonally across the bay and would plainly run aground near the mouth of the small creek if he did not act very fast. *I should have got a sail ready before I cast off,* he thought as he hurried forward.

But which sail? Part of Andrew's being burned with embarrassment at his poor seamanship. The remainder struggled to come up with the correct answer.

A jib, he decided.

Having caused himself the crisis he moved to the foredeck almost in a fluster. His gaze swept quickly over the ropes and fittings and noted that he wanted. There was a jib. It was bent on and crumpled into an untidy furl at the foot of the forestay. A halyard ran up from its hoist and the sheet was lying loose across the deck. Obviously the pirates had not wasted time doing a harbour stow after they berthed.

Andrew hurried to the mast, located the halyard, and quickly cast it off the cleat. Then he began to hoist, working with short, rapid heaves. To his relief, the sail at once began to slide up the stay. The wind caught it immediately and pushed the bow around to face almost directly towards the beach. That got Andrew even more anxious and he stopped heaving and made fast, even though the sail was only about halfway up the stay. He pounced on the sheet and quickly made it fast to a cleat on the base of the mast. It was not the correct place to secure it, he knew, but he was now starting to panic lest the yacht run aground.

A dozen rapid strides had him at the cockpit. He jumped in and gripped the wheel. An exploratory pull showed that it was free to turn, and he quickly spun it and then waited to see what would happen. He was aware that too much rudder could counteract his plan and he was very aware that he did not have the 'feel' of the boat. Sweat trickled down his forehead and he knew he was breathing too fast and flustering but all of his concentration was now on the trees on the rapidly approaching beach.

"Turn! Turn!" he cried, trying to will the yacht to change direction.

As the beach came closer by the second, he bit his lip and began to mutter. Then, ever so slowly it seemed, the trees began to slide sideways past the forestay. For a few more seconds he dithered over whether to increase the helm or not. In the end he held her as she was and prayed that she would not run aground.

It seemed to him that the yacht must touch ground, as the water was so clear he could plainly see the bottom. He even noted a stingray suddenly scoot off in a flurry of sand as the shadow of the yacht slid over it.

Oh no! I have mucked it up! he thought unhappily.

But then the bow came round even more, swinging in a gentle curve so that the rocks at the end of the beach appeared ahead, then the bulk of Snapper Point. For what seemed an age but was actually only a few seconds, the yacht slid along parallel to the beach and only about ten metres from it, before smoothly turning to point towards the end of the point.

Andrew gasped with relief and then started to get anxious again. As the yacht swung around, the wind came across the port bow and the poorly set jib flapped and shook. Andrew bit his lip and began to ease the steering back.

"If I am not careful, I will end up with her luffing up and stalling," he told himself.

That would mean the yacht would then drift backwards and he knew there was not enough room to let her head fall off to gather speed for another attempt. The knowledge that there was both an anchor and an engine were no help. Andrew knew he did not have time to try to use either. All he could do was hold the steering steady and hope.

To his immense relief, the bow stopped swinging up into the wind and settled on a course pointing out past the end of Snapper Point. The feeling of relief was short-lived as memory of the rocks and reef off the end of Snapper Point reminded Andrew that he might run the yacht aground there. He bit his lip and tentatively added a touch of port helm. This angled the bow well clear and he then centred the steering. A look around satisfied him he was still well within the angle at which his sail would function.

"I had better set that sail properly," he thought.

That got his eyes roving over the controls and they quickly located what they sought: the lock for the steering. He set this and went scrambling forward. Another glance showed him he was sailing parallel to the rocks on Snapper Point but had only about 25 metres of sea room.

One mistake and we are aground, he told himself. Then he blushed again at his own mistakes. *The mooring lines are still trailing in the water. If one of them snags on the bottom I could end up on the reef!*

That got him moving. He dashed to the bow and pulled up the lines, ignoring the water that dribbled and splashed on him, only conscious that it felt cold. Having dealt with the bow lines he raced aft and did the same at the stern. Then he stopped, chest heaving, to consider what to do next.

After a rapid study of the rigging and fittings, he cast another look to check that the yacht was in fact steering clear of the rocks. Satisfied she was, he cast off both sheet and halyard and began to pull the jib up. Now that he had thought his actions through it all went smoothly. In a few seconds he had the sail right up and secured and before the yacht had lost both way and steerage he had refastened the sheet.

Only as he stepped past the hatchway in the foredeck did Andrew remember the pirate. He gulped with anxiety and bent over to look down. To his mingled relief and concern, Three-cornered Hat was still lying crumpled on the deck below, apparently still unconscious.

"I must tie him up as soon as I have the yacht safe," Andrew muttered.

He also had the nagging worry that he might have badly injured the man. The image of one of his First Aid instructors appeared in his mind and he remembered being told that internal bleeding from head injuries could have fatal results. That thought caused Andrew to feel really sick.

But the yacht needed his attention so he hurried aft, his head swivelling continually to judge distances and angles. He also scanned the now rapidly receding beach and noted with relief that there was still no sign of any pirates. Satisfied that the yacht was going to steer well clear of Snapper Point and its reef, Andrew now began to worry about Schooner Rock which was sliding into sight ahead and looming closer ever minute.

On this course I will hit it, he reasoned.

But which way to steer to avoid it: to windward? Or to starboard and through Falcon Passage? It all seemed to be happening so fast!

Andrew had read about that being how things were like at sea. He even had limited experience of the phenomena from sailing Sabots and Corsairs, but a full-sized yacht was another kettle of fish altogether!

"Mainsail," he said. "That will give more speed and manoeuvrability."

Having decided that he stood at the wheel and studied the rigging. A minute later he was hard at work. Having satisfied himself that the mainsheet was secure but slightly loose he cast off the lashings of the mainsail and then hurried to the 'coffee grinder' winch that hoisted it.

After unlocking the ratchet he began winding rapidly. The mainsail slid smoothly up the mast. In doing so it caught the wind immediately and caused the yacht to both heel and veer slightly to port.

As the bow started to turn towards the wind, Andrew stopped work and hurried to the wheel. He adjusted the steering and then rushed back to the sail, very conscious of the fact that the yacht was sailing rapidly towards Schooner Rock. By the time he had the mainsail up and secured, he could plainly see the bird's nests and birds perched on the steep slopes of the rock.

There was no longer any choice about which side of the rock to go. The only safe option was to turn downwind and go through Falcon Passage. Andrew licked his lips and worried about a possible gybe, then spun the wheel to bring the yacht around. For a few anxious moments he thought she was not going to respond and he stared at the approaching rock in horror. Then the bow fell off the wind and she seemed to spin. In fact he had applied far too much starboard rudder, and she kept on spinning until her bow pointed at the shallow reefs and rusty wreck of the *City of Perth.*

That got Andrew madly spinning the wheel the other way, and all in a fluster. To his added dismay, the boom suddenly slammed over. Luckily, he had kept the mainsheets taut and the gybe was not a violent one. It did throw the steering again but a few seconds of wrestling with the wheel had the bow coming back around again. Andrew watched in dismay as the reef and wreck slid closer and closer. The brown-coloured shallow water seemed to reach out to the bow. Then, just as he was bracing himself for the shock of running aground, the bow slipped sideways and the wreck slid across his vision to starboard. The yacht steadied on a course which seemed to skim the very edge of the coral reef.

Sweating with effort and anxiety, Andrew eased the steering and then fretted as she gybed again. But it worked. The bow came further around and the yacht headed away from the reef and into the open channel. By his time Schooner Rock was well astern and Andrew was able to steady his nerves and thoughts, having open water ahead for several miles.

"Heavens, I'm not a very good sailor!" Andrew told himself ruefully.

Now, where do I go next? That got his mind working on details of his hastily conceived plan of emulating Jack Hawkins. *I need to anchor the yacht safely somewhere,* he thought. *But where?*

291

It only took him a minute or two to reason out the answer. *I can only bring her to in sheltered water. If I try to go around to the windward side of the island, I might muck it up and put her ashore.*

That meant Sandy Beach was not a safe option, so Andrew decided to make a virtue of necessity and bring the yacht round into Careenage Bay.

I will anchor near the artist's hut and go ashore there, he decided.

There were flaws in the plan he knew, the main one being the possibility that one or more pirates might be in that area. But it seemed the only practical plan. The idea of sailing off and leaving his friends without trying to help them did not appeal.

So Andrew eased the steering and turned the yacht slowly to starboard. This caused another gybe, but he was ready for it and did not lose control. By then the wreck was astern and the rocks at the nearer end of Careenage Bay were abeam. The beach was about 200 metres away and Andrew hoped that was enough distance to turn and anchor without running aground. He did not know how deep the bay was but reasoned that, if it was called Careenage Bay, then it must have sufficient depth for vessels to get in close at high tide.

Now, how do I anchor this thing? he worried.

In his mind he tried sort out all the things he would have to do and the correct sequence in which to do them. Unhappily he shook his head.

Strewth! I'm all at sea this time.

Chapter 33

JACK HAWKINS

Andrew moved to the bow and studied the anchor arrangements. The anchor itself was not large and was held in place on the foredeck by a steel frame and wing nut. The chain was locked in place by a similar arrangement. There was only a small hand winch to work it. Satisfied he understood how it worked, Andrew unscrewed both wing nuts and then heaved several metres of chain up out of the chain locker by hand, coiling it on deck.

He then hurried aft as the yacht was losing speed. On the way he glanced down into the hatchway and saw that Three-cornered Hat still lay in the same position. That made Andrew feel bad.

The fall must have given him more than just concussion, he thought.

For a second he hesitated, thinking to go down and check and to tie the pirate up. But as he went to do this, the yacht was caught by a change of wind so he hurried aft to correct the steering.

By then he judged it was time to bring the yacht around. All of the beach at Careenage Bay was visible and there was no sign of any pirates. With as much care as he could manage, Andrew turned the wheel and brought the yacht around to starboard in a wide curve. This caused a gybe, which he was ready for, then brought the wind from the port quarter to the starboard bow. As the yacht came around, Andrew saw that he had miscalculated. To bring her to anchor near the artist's hut would mean turning almost directly into the wind, and he guessed she would lose way and luff long before he was close to the shore. Having a considerable fear of sharks, jelly fish and other marine horrors, he had no desire to swim further than he had to.

Instead, he brought her round until the sails began to flap and then let the bow drop away until they drew again. This aimed the yacht at a point about a hundred metres further along the beach but that, he thought, would be fine. He began peering into the water, trying to judge the depth. The yacht lost way and began creeping in. As the yacht sailed slowly in towards the beach, it went into the lee of the ridge leading up from

Snapper Point to Mt Gore and the wind died to just a light breeze. That brought the yacht virtually to a standstill.

Andrew bit his lip and again berated himself. *I should have thought of that and turned sooner,* he scolded.

By now the yacht was within a hundred metres of the beach but that looked a very long way to swim in the tropical ocean, so he held his course and tried to coax her further in. The yacht continued to creep towards the shore, a faint gurgle under her bows being almost the only noise.

It was in this relative quiet that Andrew heard the voices, and it gave him quite a shock as it was coming from the cabin below him. Then he gasped with relief.

Radio! he thought foolishly. *Why didn't I think of that?* But he could not leave his task so stayed at the helm.

Finally, the yacht came to a standstill about 50 metres out and the sails hung loose and flapped. Andrew held the steering a bit longer, hoping to gain a few more metres but then he saw that the yacht had lost steerage way and was beginning to drift astern. Rather than go back out to sea and try again, he opted to anchor. Dashing forward he released the brake on the winch and tossed the anchor over. The chain ran out with a very satisfying clatter. It went out so fast that Andrew began to fear that he had made another mistake.

I wonder if the other end of the chain is secured in the hull? he mused.

Feeling foolish for not checking he applied the brake to the winch. Once the chain had stopped running out, he pushed the pawl into the ratchet ready to winch in if needed. Then he had to wait to see if the anchor would hold. For a minute or so it seemed that it would not, but then the chain went taut and the yacht came to a gently rocking standstill. Satisfied that it was holding, Andrew hurried to the sails and let them down. He knew there was a proper length of chain needed for particular depths of water but had no idea what that was. All he could do was shrug, not knowing either the depth of water, or the length of chain run out.

Next, he made his way to the cabin and looked at the radio. It was turned on and working. Some fishing trawler was talking to a station called VKC. Andrew studied the set and decided he could use it. The handset microphone was dangling on the end of its lead, bumping gently against the locker door below the set. He picked this up and looked at it, noting the press to talk switch. He then waited till there was a break in the transmissions and called.

"VKC, this is Endeavour Island calling, over."

There was a crackle and then a voice said, "Roger that *Malita,* your ETA thirteen hundred tomorrow. Berth Six is booked. Over."

Andrew stared at the set in puzzlement. As he drew breath to try again, the ship again called VKC and requested fuel be available. VKC acknowledged this. In the pause Andrew tried again.

"VKC this is Endeavour Island, emergency... er Mayday... Over."

A voice called, "Roger VKC, this is M.V. *Malita,* Out."

Puzzled and irritated Andrew waited a few seconds, but the two stations had stopped talking. All he could hear was a soft hum from the radio. He tried again.

"Anyone, this is Endeavour Island, Mayday, emergency. Over."

He released the switch and listened intently. There was no response. He tried again. Still no answer. Then he made another attempt. A faint signal answered him and he strained to listen, then huffed in annoyance. It was some fishing trawler calling VKC.

"This set must be damaged or something?" he muttered.

After two more attempts he gave it up. The fishing boat and VKC were having a conversation and obviously neither could hear him.

The set must not be transmitting, he decided. He shrugged and thought about what to do next. *Go ashore,* he thought. *And take this.*

'This' was a high-powered, bolt action, sporting rifle which was in a rack right next to the radio. Andrew reached forward and lifted it out, then looked it over. It was a lovely gun with shiny, blued metal and a gleaming, polished stock. He pulled the bolt back and noted that the magazine had bullets in it.

Good. This will help equalise things, he told himself.

He had been worrying about trying to use the pistol if he had to. Andrew's speciality in the Navy Cadets was to be a Quartermaster Gunner and he had already done enough basic training to be safe when handling weapons and to be sure he could use the rifle. However, in his heart he doubted if he could ever pull the trigger to shoot a human being. There was also the nagging worry that he would be a rotten shot with a handgun, never having fired one, so the rifle was much better. A check showed five rounds in the magazine.

I'd better get going, he thought. *Carmen or Anne will contact the police.*

He made his way up on deck and slung the rifle. That made him aware of just how sunburnt his shoulders had become and he wished he had a shirt or hat. However, he did not feel like wearing any of the pirates' clothes, so he made his way to the rail.

Now he had another test of courage. While he was a good swimmer, he had a mortal dread of sharks and such things. He now scanned the ocean for any sign. The water was clear and he could see the bottom, but the shimmering effect of the waves was no help as that caused the illusion of shadows flitting across the seabed. He knew he would probably not even see the shark that attacked him, not until he was gripped by its jaws, by the rending, tearing teeth, by...

"Stop scaring yourself and get it over with," Andrew told himself.

He realised he was hyperventilating and trembling. Gritting his teeth with determination he climbed over the low railing and lowered himself into the water. The sea was surprisingly cold and he shivered for a few seconds. Then he had to force himself to push away from the apparent security of the hull.

It took him an effort of willpower not to swim fast. Using a slow breaststroke he headed for the beach. His head kept swivelling, scanning the rippling wavetops for any sign of a fin.

It seemed a long way to the beach, but it only took him a minute to swim the distance. To his immense relief, his feet touched the sandy bottom and he stood up and dashed ashore. For a moment he stood on the beach, gasping with relief.

Safe! Oh golly gosh no! There might be pirates.

With that thought he unslung the rifle and checked it was cocked. He did not think that the water would have affected the ammunition but knew he could only hope.

Commandos and Clearance Divers swim with weapons all the time, he reasoned. *Now don't stand out here like a dork on the beach where everyone for miles around can see you,* he told himself.

Rifle at the ready he trotted up the beach to the scrub. His first surprise was how hot the sand was. The second was how thick the scrub was. The third was the green ants. Every second bush he pushed past seemed to be infested with the little, nipping monsters.

After a few minutes of this, Andrew gave it up and pushed back to the fringe of the scrub. He then made his way along the top of the beach, keeping inside the cover as much as possible. Within two minutes he found himself staring in towards a small clearing with a hut in it.

"The artist's hut," he muttered.

He had been expecting this, so he turned left and carefully crept towards it. As he did, he wondered how Anne was getting on in a boat with Letitia.

She will certainly have seen it all by now, he decided. Then he blushed and was ashamed of himself for thinking about things like that.

The hut was deserted. It only took a moment to glance inside. The place had no possible hiding places, being just a room with a bed, small table and spirit stove. A stack of canvasses and a couple of boxes completed the furnishings, along with a scatter of clothes and bedding.

A track led off towards the south, so Andrew took this. A minute later he was on the foot track that led back over the ridge. Rifle at the ready he turned left and headed that way. He was feeling very anxious now, fearful that he might bump into one of the pirates and have to use the rifle. What bothered him the most was the fear that he might shoot someone. There was also the doubt that he would be able to pull the trigger and that he might then be killed by one of the pirates.

At the base of the hill he paused and contemplated leaving the rifle. Then he shrugged. There was no guarantee that being unarmed would save him from being shot.

Besides, I might need it to save the others, he reasoned.

Gritting his teeth with determination he resumed his walk. It took him only five minutes to reach the crest of the ridge. There he paused to think and to get his breath back. Behind him he could see the yacht floating on the bay and that made him feel easier. He had been worrying that the anchor might drag and the yacht drift off out to sea. As nothing could be done about it now, he continued on, only to stop at the junction of the two tracks.

Which way to go? Right and down to the campsite, or left and down to the ruin?

Andrew was inclined to take the right-hand track but while he stood there thinking about it he heard a voice calling. At once he moved off the track and took cover behind a tree.

Who the Devil is that? he wondered, his heart rate shooting up with anxiety.

For a few seconds he considered creeping off into the jungle to hide but then decided to wait and to start sorting things out. As he waited, he strained to listen and was amazed to hear Mark calling out Martin's name at the top of his voice.

What on earth is he doing that for? Andrew wondered. *That will attract the pirates.* Which got him wondering whether the pirates had gone. Then he shook his head. *They can't leave. They haven't got a boat; and when they find it is missing, they are going to get really annoyed!*

Andrew crouched there, rifle at the ready, while the sound of Mark's voice came closer. He was coming up the track from the camp. A minute later he came into view at the bend in the track. Andrew strained his eyes to see if he was alone but could not see anyone following him.

As Mark drew breath to shout again, Andrew called softly, "Mark! Here I am."

Mark flinched in fright and gave a gasp, then stared in Andrew's direction. "Martin? Is that you?" he called.

"No, Andrew," Andrew replied, stepping out from behind the tree.

Mark gave a great sigh of relief, then said, "Have you seen Martin?"

Andrew shook his head. "No. Are you alone?" he asked.

Mark nodded, then stood trembling and looking utterly wretched. "Yes," he croaked.

"Where are the pirates?" Andrew asked.

Mark pointed back down the track. "There are three of them back at the camp and they... they've got... got Jill. They say they are going to do horrible things to her if we don't give them the treasure."

Andrew was shocked, embarrassed, and then deeply angry. He pressed his lips together grimly, then said, "Why are you here?"

"They let me and Jacob go. They said find the treasure within one hour or they would start ... start... enjoying themselves. And they said if we didn't come back, they would mutilate her afterwards and then kill her," Mark explained, his voice cracking and breaking into sobs.

"Then we had better find Martin quickly," Andrew replied.

Now he was glad he had the rifle and he placed it on safe and hefted it to a more comfortable position.

Mark pointed to it. "Where did you get that?" he asked.

Andrew was about to answer but then decided not to tell Mark the whole story. He replied, "Off a pirate. I knocked him out."

As he said this, Andrew realised that he had not tied Three-cornered Hat up. He silently berated himself. *You bloody idiot!* he thought. He pictured the pirate waking up and finding himself on the yacht.

For a moment Andrew considered running back down to the yacht to make sure the pirate was secured. Then he shrugged. That would waste half an hour and Jill was in danger. He pointed to the left-hand track.

"We will go that way."

"Do you know where Martin is?" Mark asked hopefully.

"No, but I've got a good idea," Andrew replied. "Follow me."

He set off down the left-hand track at a fast walk. Now that he knew Jill was in danger, Andrew felt his fear evaporate, to be replaced by grim determination. Instead, he was deeply angry and the rifle seemed to be a necessary instrument of justice. He kept it ready as he strode quickly along. Now he felt sure he could use it.

It only took five minutes to reach the bottom of the hill and another two to reach the point on the track where Mrs Schipholl had sat playing the drum. Andrew paused to study the ground, searching for any sign that Martin had been there. However, he could not see anything among the sticks and dead leaves so could only hurry on along the track, a deeply anxious Mark close on his heels.

They came to the creek crossing just below the small dam and paused. Satisfied that no-one was on the other bank, Andrew crossed and hurried up the track to the edge of the clearing around the ruin. Here he stopped under cover and carefully looked around. Seeing no-one, he scouted along the edge of the clearing to the left until he came to the track leading down to the concrete pump house. This he approached with extreme caution.

The rusty iron door was shut. Andrew crouched behind a nearby tree and studied it, then looked carefully in all directions. Mark joined him. Both boys were sweating, and Mark looked a sickly, pale colour.

"Do you think he is in there?" he asked.

Andrew shook his head. "He would be silly to get trapped in a place like that, but I reckon he is somewhere around here."

"You cover me, and I will open the door," Mark said.

Andrew nodded and Mark crept over to come in from the side. After a gulp of air he reached across and pushed the door. It squeaked open and Mark jumped back out of the way. Andrew had the rifle sighted on the opening but nothing happened. Mark moved back and looked in, then shook his head. Andrew nodded and pointed on down the overgrown track.

"That way," he said.

Mark nodded and set off down the track. As he did, he called softly, "Martin! Martin! Where are you?"

"Here!"

Andrew and Mark both jumped with fright. From among the bushes above the track appeared Martin. To Andrew's relief, he was still clutching the treasure box.

"What's going on?" Martin asked. "Where are the pirates? Where are the others?"

Andrew and Mark quickly gave their accounts of what they thought was happening. Mark became very distressed when he described how Jill was being threatened by the pirates. He reached out for the box.

"Give me that! I am going to save her."

Martin went to hand the box to him, but Andrew stepped forward and shook his head. "No Mark. That won't work."

"Yes, it will! They said if we give them the treasure they will let her go."

"Do you believe that?" Andrew asked, his face grim.

Mark looked wildly back at him, then his shoulders slumped and his face crumpled. "No, but we have to try! What else can we do?"

"You are right, we have to try," Andrew agreed. Then he held up the rifle. "They don't know we have this. We can negotiate with a bit of strength."

Mark looked hopeful and Martin nodded agreement. "How?" Mark asked.

Andrew had been thinking fast. He bit his lip, then licked them before deciding. "You must go back and tell them we will hand over the treasure. They are to be in the middle of the clearing at the camp. Insist that they free Jill, and Jacob, if he's there. Tell them that all three pirates must be present. When they let our people go, Martin will walk out from this side of the creek with the box and he will place it down on the other bank when all three of you are safely past him. Is that alright Martin?"

Martin nodded. Andrew went on, "That way you will all be in the bed of the creek if any shooting starts and will have some cover. If the crooks start shooting, I will cover you and you are to go down the creek to the beach, then around the coast to the artist's hut. I will hold them off for twenty minutes, then meet you there."

"Do I tell them you have a gun?" Mark asked.

"No. We will keep that as a surprise," Andrew answered.

And the fact that we have stolen their yacht, he thought with satisfaction- till he remembered that he had not tied up Three-cornered Hat. With a mental shrug he thrust that anxiety from his mind. *Doesn't matter,* he told himself. *We don't need the yacht. Now that we have a gun we can hide in the jungle till Carmen or Anne bring the police, or the Schipholls return.* Thinking of them got him worried. *Oh I hope the parents don't return till this is over. They could get hurt.*

Martin now said, "What if the pirates try to double cross us?"

"They probably will," Andrew replied. "Now let's stop talking. We are wasting time. We will go down that track we followed during the treasure hunt and sneak towards the camp from across the creek. Let's go."

Andrew turned and started walking. To his relief, neither Mark nor Martin made any argument but followed him. He led the way back to the clearing, then went right and recrossed the creek. Reaching the faint trail they had followed during the Treasure Hunt he turned left and began walking along it. As he did, his mind raced with options and possible problems. On top of all the worries was the deep fear that he might have to shoot.

I will if I have to, he resolved.

Saving Jill was terribly important to him. He squared his shoulders and hurried on towards the camp.

Chapter 34

JILL

A ndrew held up his hand to signal halt to the two boys behind him. About a hundred paces ahead he could just glimpse the camp and movement. For the last few minutes he had been able to hear voices. Now he crouched behind a tree and carefully studied the ground. From where he was there was not much to see, the jungle was too thick.

"We will have to get closer," he whispered. "Martin, you stay well back and when we reach the track cover our rear."

Moving cautiously from tree to tree the three boys carefully approached the camp. They were just back from the bank of the creek and with each few steps Andrew could see the tents more clearly. He gripped the rifle and steadied his breathing. Now he was acting with a cold determination. His earlier doubts were swept aside. To save Jill, he was sure he could use the rifle.

Five minutes careful creeping had the three boys crouched behind bushes and trees beside the track at the point where it crossed the creek. Now visible was the centre of the camp. What he could see sent a chill of cold anger through Andrew and made him even more determined. Tied by her waist to the thick aerial roots of the fig was Jill. Her head hung and she looked so helpless and stressed that it was all Andrew could do not to just attack.

Despite his resolve, Andrew found it very hard to control his impulses. The view he had of Jill was in profile and her face was partly obscured by her hair and by the way her head hung. But to his eyes she was a vision of loveliness and for a few seconds he admired her.

We must save her, no matter what, he resolved.

Jacob was also there, seated against the same tree and very unhappy, presumably having returned without finding Martin. Blood trickled from his nose, which suggested that the pirates had struck him.

Also present were three of the pirates: 'Earrings', one in a white shirt, and the one all dressed in blue and carrying the shotgun. They were busy arguing and barely glanced at the surrounding forest.

Angry and shocked hissing from Martin and Mark caused Andrew to look back and raise a warning finger to his lips. He saw that Martin looked absolutely horrified and that Mark was weeping with shame and distress.

Beckoning them closer he whispered, "We need to do this quickly. I don't know how much of your hour is left but probably not much. And we don't want to give the bastards any time to think up any tricks. Mark, you walk across now and give them the message. Do it from the top of the creek bank. Next to that big tree, got it?"

Mark nodded. Andrew pointed to his right. "I am going over there to get a better view and so I can shoot without you being in my line of fire. Martin, you watch back up the track. There's another pirate somewhere, a mean mongrel with a peg leg."

As soon as Martin nodded, Andrew pushed Mark. Mark gave Andrew an anguished and scared look, but then moistened his lips and moved forward. As he did, Andrew slipped across the track and began crawling from tree to tree, seeking the best fire position he could. It was hot and steamy and sweat poured out of every pore, but Andrew ignored it. He also ignored the scratches and bumps from the bushes and vines. His whole being was focused on the task in hand.

He was still not in the best position when one of the pirates said loudly, "Well, times up! That little turd hasn't come back. Let's start having some fun. I reckon if we get her to scream loud enough he will soon find the one with our stuff."

Andrew cursed and struggled into a fire position. It wasn't the best, but he could see well enough into the camp to watch the look of sheer terror on Jill's face. Earrings moved towards her, his face one huge evil leer.

Mark's voice sounded loudly, causing all the people in the camp to look in his direction. "Don't touch her!" Mark shouted. "Leave Jill alone!"

Earrings paused when his hand was just touching Jill's shirt. He drew it back. In doing so he probably saved his life because Andrew was deeply angry and so determined to save her that he had sighted the rifle and even taken the first pressure on the trigger. To his relief, Earrings stepped back and turned to sneer towards Mark.

"Well, well, if it isn't the boyfriend. Well kid, where's the loot?"

"Here," Mark cried, gesturing behind him.

"Hand it over, or we go to work on your girlfriend," Earrings replied.

"Let her go first!" Mark shrieked.

Andrew did not look towards him but could tell from the tone that Mark was feeling desperate.

"Pig's bum!" Earrings retorted. "You hand over our stuff first."

To Andrew's annoyance, the one in blue hoisted his shotgun up to his hip and the one with the white shirt took out a pistol.

Mark, tell them the deal! he thought irritably.

Mark did. He described the arrangement. The pirates listened and then the one in the white shirt said, "No way kid. You can't bargain with us. Just get the stuff and give it to us."

"No!" Mark cried.

"Okay Stevo, strip her. See if that helps him decide," the pirate said.

Anger almost overwhelmed Andrew's self-control. He yelled loudly, overriding Mark's pleas. "You do that you mongrel and I will drop you!"

At that, the pirates all looked in his direction, their guns coming up. It was obvious to Andrew that they were surprised, and he also felt sure they could not see him.

The one in the white shirt jeered and said, "Oh yeah kid, what with?"

"I've got a rifle," Andrew answered, still keeping low but holding his aim on Stevo.

For a few moments he was tempted to start shooting, wondering if that wasn't what he should have done right from the beginning, in case the pirates tried to hold hostages.

White Shirt sneered and called back, "Bull! Now give us the box before the girl gets hurt." With that he pointed his pistol at Jill.

Exactly the situation Andrew had feared had now developed. He licked his lips and steadied his breathing and aim, determined not to miss. Then he called back, "You will die, mister. You might hit her, but you are a dead man. Now start talking sense."

White Shirt looked uneasy but then called back. "I don't believe you."

"I have a rifle, and I can use it," Andrew replied. He was getting anxious and flustered now as things weren't going to plan but he was still absolutely determined. "I am going to fire at the bottle on the table," he yelled. "Just to prove I have a rifle, so don't shoot anyone by accident."

As he sighted on the bottle on the picnic table Andrew knew he was taking a terrible risk, and also that he was giving away his position. However, he did not see any other alternative. He shrugged, then settled to get a good aim.

Orange and Mango cordial, he noted as he steadied the sights.

Crack!

The plastic bottle full of yellow cordial suddenly exploded in a shower of liquid. All of the pirates flinched and swore but none fired. Andrew swung the barrel back to point at White Shirt and at the same time worked the bolt to reload.

"Do you believe me now?" he yelled.

"Yeah kid, but we still got these two as hostages," White Shirt replied, his pistol swinging back to aim at Jill.

Jill now looked in Andrew's direction, her face a mask of hope and horror.

"Stop being stupid!" Andrew snapped. "You want the box, not a murder charge. We will give you the box and you let our friends go."

"He's right, Sammy," said Stevo.

"Shut up, Stevo!" Sammy snarled. Then he ground his teeth angrily before calling out, "Yeah alright. You bring us the gear and then we will let your friends go."

"No way," Andrew replied. "Untie them now and we will put the box up on your bank of the creek. Then one of you can walk forward with them to get the box."

There was a tense wait for a few seconds before Sammy nodded. "Yeah, righto" he said, but he did not sound happy.

"Untie them," Andrew snapped.

To his intense relief, Sammy nodded and spoke to Earrings who moved forward, drew a knife and cut Jill loose. She flopped to the ground and lay there sobbing while Earrings turned to Jacob. One slash of an obviously razor-sharp knife cut Jacob free. To Andrew's concern, Stevo began edging sideways, the shotgun still pointed in his direction.

He is trying to get some cover, he decided.

Then he shrugged and glanced to his left. Mark was just visible ten metres away. He was looking very agitated and his hands were twitching.

He wants to help Jill, Andrew reasoned. To forestall this he called out, "Mark, you move back. Martin! Come forward and wait in the creek bed till I tell you."

Mark turned a haggard, distressed face towards him. That only strengthened Andrew's resolve. "Mark, move back. We don't want any more potential hostages," he called.

For a moment he thought Mark was not going to obey, but then he reluctantly turned and made his way back across the creek. In his place Martin came scuttling forward, to remain crouching below the top of the far bank.

Over in the camp, Jacob had now climbed to his feet. Jill was then helped up by Earrings. She hung her head in distress and was sobbing.

"Come on Jill," Andrew called. "Start walking. Jacob, help her!"

Sammy swore and pointed his pistol at Jacob. "Wait a minute, buster! Where are the goods?"

Andrew called to Martin. Martin climbed up the bank and stood on top, the metal box held in front of him. When he saw it, Sammy nodded and said, "Go with them Gary and get the box, and check it hasn't been opened before you let these kids go."

"We haven't opened it," Martin called. "We haven't got a key."

"You'd better not have!" Sammy warned. "Okay, get going."

'Earrings' Gary walked forward holding Jill in front of him, his knife at her back. Jacob, instead of helping Jill, hurried on ahead. Andrew shifted his aim to Stevo, who had now sidled right over almost behind the Schipholl's tent. Martin held the box out and handed it to Earrings. The pirate looked hard at the lock and then shook the box. Then he grunted and nodded. Martin took Jill's arm and helped her down the bank. Jacob scurried on ahead of them and ran up the other bank and along the track. Earrings turned and walked calmly back towards Sammy.

As soon as Martin had helped Jill up the other bank, Mark rushed out to help her. Andrew kept his rifle aimed but called loudly, "Okay Martin, Mark, get her out of here." Then he called to the pirates. "You pirates clear out. And don't try to follow us or I will shoot you!"

To Andrew's annoyance, Sammy ignored him. Instead, he took the box from Earrings and placed it on the picnic table. Then he produced a key and unlocked the box. After lifting the lid he reached inside and lifted out a plastic packet of white powder.

Definitely drugs, Andrew decided.

It was what he had suspected. Sammy nodded and placed the packet back, then relocked the box. He then picked it up and turned to walk away. The others followed, Stevo edging backwards from cover to cover.

As soon as he was sure that the pirates were not going to shoot or immediately attack, Andrew slipped on the safety catch and stood up.

Now, we had better get out of here fast, he thought. *Once they find their boat is gone, they will come hunting.*

Andrew set off at the run along the track. He caught up with the others within a minute, near the base of the hill.

Martin turned and called, "What's happening?"

"Keep moving, fast!" Andrew replied, glancing over his shoulder.

They did, a sobbing Jill being helped along by Mark. She was shaking so much she had trouble walking. She kept stumbling on sharp sticks or stones and then hobbling and limping. Andrew found her slow progress very frustrating and quietly fumed but said nothing. The group walked as quickly as it could up the hillside track. Jacob was so far in front that they only glimpsed him occasionally. Martin commented and curled his lip at this, and Mark grumbled but privately Andrew thought that was a good thing.

If there is trouble ahead Jacob will run into it first and that should give us a bit of warning, he thought.

The military word 'scout' crossed his mind and that confirmed his thoughts. He was also ashamed to realise that he did not care what happened to Jacob and that he disliked him intensely. But the thought that he was actually so selfish and ruthless that he was willing to sacrifice another person was too uncomfortable for Andrew's conscience and he tried to thrust such a disquieting idea from his mind.

Despite Andrew's urging, it was seven minutes before they arrived puffing at the track junction near the top of the hill. Jacob had waited there and asked, "Which way? Where are we going?"

"Down to Careenage Bay, to the artist's hut," Andrew replied.

Jacob wrinkled his nose in distaste. "Why? What can he do?"

"Nothing. He's already left in his boat with Letitia and Anne," Andrew replied as he urged them to resume walking. "I sent him to get help an hour ago." Then he reconsidered. "More than an hour and a half ago."

That got Andrew calculating. *They should be at Cardwell, or nearly there. So the police should be on their way in another hour, I hope!*

He did not say this however but instead said, "The pirate's yacht is anchored down there. We will use that."

"What if there are pirates on it?" Mark asked.

That gave Andrew a jolt. *Three-cornered Hat! I hope he hasn't woken up and taken the yacht!*

He shrugged and replied, "There is, one who got knocked out when I took it, now hurry!"

"You took their yacht?" Martin asked incredulously.

Andrew nodded and blushed. He did not want to boast. "Yes, after a bit of a fight. Then I sailed it around here," he replied.

"You stole their yacht and sailed it single-handed?" Jill gasped, her eyes wide with admiration.

Ordinarily Andrew would have been overwhelmed by this but now he just nodded and urged them to hurry. He was now consumed by anxiety and it was not until, on cresting the ridge, he saw the yacht still floating quietly at anchor down in the bay ahead of them that he breathed easier.

Whew! Thank heavens! he thought.

But there was still that concern the pirate might wake up, so he urged them to greater speed. As they went over the crest, Andrew glanced back at Fishermans Bay. He saw that a large, white luxury motor yacht was heading towards the island.

I hope the people on that aren't going to land for a picnic, he thought, assuming they were holidaymakers. *We might have to warn them or the pirates will steal their boat.*

His estimate was that the luxury yacht was still about three nautical miles or so away and that it would not arrive for at least another ten minutes. He did not mention the launch but just urged the others to greater speed.

They ran down the track and reached the bottom within five minutes. By then they were all sweating and panting for breath, but Andrew would not let them stop.

"Keep running! We need to get aboard as quickly as we can," he cried.

He saw that Jill was now really gasping and near to collapse but urged Mark and Martin to help her along. He remained as rearguard, rifle at the ready. Jacob ran on ahead and Andrew was content to let him.

Out on the beach Jacob increased his lead. As the group hurried along on the hot sand, Andrew looked at the yacht and frowned. It appeared to be much closer in than he remembered. Then he bit his lip with anxiety.

Oh bloody hell! The tide is going out! I hope she hasn't grounded.

That was a sickening thought which got him running so that he now passed the three. By then Jacob had arrived opposite the yacht and had begun wading out. Andrew made sure that the rifle was on safe and slung it as he ran. He had been going to cover Jacob while he swam out but now decided to take the risk as there was no sign of Three-cornered Hat.

I hope he isn't waiting in ambush, Andrew thought as he ran into the shallow water.

Then he remembered that he had left both the pistol and the knife on board and felt even more anxious.

Chapter 35

THE WHITE CABIN CRUISER

Andrew was soon in chest deep water and had to start swimming. By then the yacht was only about 25 metres away and Jacob had already reached it. He reached up and Andrew tensed with anxiety as Jacob heaved himself aboard. Jacob made his way to the cockpit and bent to look down into the cabin. He then vanished below.

Anxiety sped Andrew's arms. He swam side stroke so that he could see and breathe properly. His strong, urgent strokes quickly covered the distance. As he arrived alongside the yacht, Andrew saw Jacob appear from the forward hatch.

"He's down here, unconscious," Jacob called down.

"Good!" Andrew spluttered back.

But he actually felt far from good. He was relieved that Three-cornered Hat had not been waiting, but he was also deeply concerned that the man was seriously injured. He swam towards the point where the yacht had the lowest freeboard, just forward of the cockpit. Jacob moved aft to lean over and help him aboard.

"Never mind me!" Andrew gasped back. "Start getting the anchor up."

Jacob nodded and made his way forward again. Andrew reached up and grasped the lower rail, then heaved himself up till he could get his foot on the deck edge. As he did, the rifle slid around and hit against his leg. Ignoring this he climbed aboard, then turned to study the situation. By then the other three were also wading in and he called to urge them to go faster.

"Hurry! We must get going!"

"Why? The pirates won't catch us now," Martin called back, turning to look back along the beach for signs of pursuit.

"There's a white luxury yacht, a cabin cruiser, heading for the island," Andrew called back. "The pirates might steal it if we don't warn the people first."

"So what?" Mark replied. "I don't care if the pirates get away."

"I was thinking of the people on the cabin cruiser," Andrew retorted. "I don't want any innocent people hurt."

Mark had the good grace to blush, then hid his confusion by starting to swim. Jill and Martin swam beside him, all using a breaststroke. By the time Andrew had hauled them dripping on board, Jacob had pulled up the anchor. As Andrew watched him securing the anchor in its bracket, he could only thank Navy Cadets for the training that made it easy. As a leading seaman, Jacob knew exactly what to do.

Jacob now moved to the jib and began sorting out the hastily secured lines. Andrew moved to the cockpit and said, "Martin, take the wheel. Mark, go below and check that pirate. Jill, get ready to hoist the mainsail. Okay Jacob, hoist away!"

They all moved to obey and only later did it dawn on Andrew that Jacob, as the senior rank in the Navy Cadets, should have taken charge. Andrew had given Jill a hard job to do, but quite deliberately. He wanted her mind busy and not dwelling on what might have happened. He himself stood behind Martin and looked around. He unslung the rifle and leaned it against the side of the cockpit, noting as he did that the pistol was still on the control console.

What he was worried about now was the feel of the yacht. As soon as he had climbed aboard, he had felt bumping and knew it was the keel hitting the sandy bottom as the yacht rocked in the tiny waves.

We are almost stranded, he thought anxiously. *Will she drift clear into deeper water?* he wondered.

He began taking bearings by eye, using the standing rigging and trees on the beach as marks to gauge movement. To his relief, the bows of the yacht began to come around. As the jib flapped its way up the forestay, the rate of swing increased. But so did the bumping! Andrew shrugged and called for Jacob to sheet the jib home, then ordered Jill to start hoisting the mainsail. She wasn't sure what to do so he had to explain each step to her. Jacob quickly made the jib sheet secure and then hurried to join her.

Under the influence of the jib the bows pivoted rapidly. Andrew felt a peculiar shuddering sensation and knew that the yacht was turning with its keel grinding on the bottom. He even imagined he could hear the sand scraping on the fibreglass hull. Despite that, the yacht came around easily and then resumed bumping. Andrew had to turn to face astern, the beach now behind them.

After a minute the bumping stopped and he was sure and began to relax. "We are afloat," he said. Then he pointed to port. "Steer to pass to starboard of Schooner Rock Martin," he instructed.

He had already thought about the course to steer and had decided that, with the wind coming from the direction it was, that it would be difficult and risky to beat up against it close inshore.

Tacking through Falcon Pass is not a safe option, Andrew reasoned.

With the mainsail set, the yacht rapidly picked up speed and Andrew almost cried with relief as they sped out into deeper water. Then Mark returned and his anxieties returned.

"That pirate is in a bad way," Mark said. "He's a funny colour and his breathing sounds horrible."

Andrew felt a swill of apprehension. "I'll come and look. Martin, hold that course. Jacob, come with us. Jill, act as lookout," he instructed.

He then followed Mark down into the cabin and made his way forward. As he did, Jacob came down the companionway behind him. He called to them as they reached the door to the next cabin.

"What about this radio?"

"I tried it," Andrew replied, "But you can have a go."

Jacob turned to the radio. Andrew followed Mark on through to the sail stowage. Three-cornered Hat lay in exactly the same position that Andrew had left him in. As Mark had said, he looked a funny colour, with a sort of sickly, pasty greenish tinge to his skin but with blue lips. His breath was coming in short, irregular snorts and snuffles.

Oh my God! Andrew thought in dismay. *I hope he isn't going to die!*

During First Aid lessons they had been warned about brain damage and bleeding inside the skull and Andrew now began to fear that might be the case. He began to pray, even as he bent to check the pulse. That was an unpleasant experience as the man's skin was clammy and cold. The pulse however seemed to be strong. That cheered Andrew somewhat. He stood and studied the man, biting his lip as he did.

"I think we should move him to a better position," he said. "On his side so he doesn't drown in vomit or something."

"Stable side position, or recovery position," Mark added, using the jargon from their First Aid lessons.

"Yes, you hold his head and neck while I move his body," Andrew instructed.

He hated touching the man, but they got him laid out on the deck and Mark collected a pillow from one of the bunks and gently slid it under the pirate's head. Andrew gingerly felt the top of the man's skull but that caused the man to writhe and moan so he stopped.

"What will we do?" Mark asked.

Andrew shrugged. "Get him to a doctor, I suppose," he said.

He was about to add, 'and tie him up,' when Jill called down to them through the hatchway, "Andrew, I can see that white motor cruiser."

"Keep an eye on him Mark," Andrew said.

As Mark nodded, Andrew turned and clambered up the ladder to join Jill on the foredeck. He was just in time to see the white cabin cruiser vanish inshore beyond Snapper Point.

"Damn! Too late!" he muttered.

His mind was now working quickly. He studied the angles and distances and then said, "We will have to try to cut through Falcon Pass after all. Martin, stand by to come about on the port tack. Bring her round slowly till you are going to pass close to port of Schooner Rock."

"Aye, aye sir!" Martin replied. He at once began to turn the wheel.

Andrew called down the hatchway, "Mark, come and help me with the mainsail. Jill, you keep the jib over to starboard. Hold it there if it starts to flap."

With that he hurried aft. He knew they were taking a risk and might have to try to go about again but decided it had to be done. Mark came hurrying up to join him and they eased the mainsheet and then hauled it taut as the yacht steadied on her new course. Andrew kept judging angles and distances and saw that Schooner Rock was already looking both large and menacing. It seemed to be all jagged outcrops, and the water was swirling around its base in a way that made Andrew's heart turn over with apprehension.

I didn't take tide and current into account, he berated himself.

But it was too late now. They were settled on the new course. Andrew bit his lip and watched the sails. These flapped a few times and Jill had to hold the jib sheet and lean out with it, but the yacht kept moving.

"We are as close to the wind as we can go," Andrew muttered.

Fearing he had miscalculated made him sick with anxiety. If the wind shifted, or the current swung them even a few degrees the yacht would end up head to wind.

Then she might fall off to starboard and put us on the rocks, he thought unhappily. *Or to port so we go ashore on the reef in Wreck Bay!*

For a few tense minutes Martin held his course, adjusting the steering with small movements. Schooner Rock drew closer and closer until it was sliding by only about 25 metres to starboard. Seeing the sharp rocks so close caused Andrew to swallow with concern but he was also secretly pleased.

We are going to make it, he told himself.

They did, but only just. A swirl of current caused the bow to shift and there was a slight bump and scraping noise which caused Andrew's heart to leap into his throat and turn over. Then they were past and slicing into the larger waves beyond.

"Whew! That was close!" he muttered. Then he turned his attention to port, where Fishermans Bay was now opening out.

The bump brought Jacob on deck with a rush. He stared in horror at the huge mass of Schooner Rock, which seemed to tower over them. Then he shook his head and said, "No luck with that radio. It is receiving but won't transmit."

"Thanks," Andrew replied. "Now get ready to help Mark with the mainsail when we come about."

He then looked to port, judging the moment to turn. About half a kilometre away, a bit over two cables Andrew estimated in the old-fashioned nautical style, was the jetty. The white cabin cruiser had now berthed alongside, on the far side and port side to, and a blonde woman in a bikini was on the jetty placing moorings. All Andrew could do was mutter in frustration. It was the sight of three men walking out of the jungle and onto the end of the jetty which caused his heart to stand still with dismay.

The pirates! We are going to be too late! he thought.

He shouted orders and they brought the yacht about onto the starboard tack but, by the time they had completed the manoeuvre, Andrew saw that the three pirates had almost reached the white cabin cruiser. The blonde woman had vanished back aboard.

Oh no! What can we do? Andrew thought.

He began casting about for a plan that did not involve too much risk for the yacht and its people. As he did, a sudden flurry of movement forward caught his attention. He was astonished to see Jill scampering aft, uttering cries of fright. Then his mouth sagged open with dismay as he saw a head emerged from the forward hatch. The pirate's!

"Bloody hell! We should have tied him up!" Andrew muttered.

Three-cornered Hat looked around, his eyes blinking in the sunlight. A puzzled frown crossed his face and he shook his head and blinked again, then looked directly at Andrew. Their eyes met and Andrew felt a chill of almost paralysing fear. For a second Andrew felt like running, thinking that it was all just going to start again. Then he remembered that he had others to help him.

And I've got the guns.

In two steps he was at the control console and had snatched up the pistol. He held it up for Three-cornered Hat to see.

"Don't try any funny business. Come out on deck and sit down."

To Andrew's surprise, the pirate nodded. He climbed up on deck and staggered aft, to clutch at the starboard shroud as the yacht rolled. For a moment Andrew feared the pirate was going to fall overboard, but then he slumped down to sit on the cabin roof. By then Mark had snatched up the rifle and was pointing that as well. Jill crowded in behind them.

"We will tie him up. Jacob, cut some rope," Andrew said.

As he did, Three-cornered Hat looked up and then shielded his eyes to study the white cabin cruiser, now only a couple of hundred metres away. Andrew saw the colour drain out of the man's face and was astonished to see him spring to his feet.

Scared that the pirate was about to attack, Andrew aimed the pistol and cried, "Sit down!"

Three-cornered Hat ignored the command, instead pointing towards the white cabin cruiser. He shook his head in apparent dismay and then cried, "That motor launch, d'ye ken who owns it?"

Andrew shook his head, mystified by the man's apparent fear, which was adding fuel to his own growing anxiety. "No, why?"

"Barrett!" Three-cornered Hat cried. "Are ye one of his lot?"

"Barrett?" echoed Andrew. He had heard the name but could not place where, or why it might matter. "No. We were just going to warn the people on that boat that those pirates might try to steal it, seeing we have taken theirs... yours."

"It's Barrett alright," Three-cornered Hat cried, gazing shoreward.

He straightened up and drew breath to shout. Even as he did, a crackle of sharp stuttering sounds rolled over the water and whatever he was going to say remained unsaid as he gaped in horror.

Andrew also stared in disbelief. He had heard that sound before, but only once in reality, though many times on TV or at the movies: machine guns firing.

Unable to credit what he was watching, he saw the three people on the jetty suddenly crumple up and fall, or be flung backwards to lie still on the planks. The shooting was coming from the white motor cruiser. Andrew clearly saw a large man wearing sunglasses, a white Panama hat, and a bright Hawaiian shirt lean over the side of the upper steering position and fire a sub machine gun down at the three bodies on the jetty.

This can't be real! his mind thought. But his eyes then focused on the man and his memory clicked. *Barrett! The smuggler who kidnapped Carmen at Simpsons Point!*

And it was! Andrew now recognised the man, also noting Ponytail Dan and a black-haired female in a red bathing costume; all three holding sub machine guns. At that moment, Barrett turned his head and looked straight at the yacht. Andrew felt a paralysing chill of fear and could only stare back, the sickening reality of it all now starting to sink in.

"Barrett! The smuggler!" he gasped. "And he's just murdered those three pirates."

"Aye!" snarled Three-cornered Hat, "And now he will kill us too."

"We must get out of here!" Martin cried.

Chapter 36

ABOUT!

A ndrew stared at the white cabin cruiser, aghast at what he was seeing and hearing. For a few more moment's he hesitated, then he cried, "Martin, bring her about!"

Martin began to spin the wheel. Only then did Andrew realise he had made a possibly fatal mistake. He saw the bow start to swing to starboard.

He's turning upwind to tack. I meant downwind to wear. I didn't give a clear order!

He almost choked in panic. "The other way! The other way!"

Martin heard him and hesitated, then began to reverse his steering. At that, Three-cornered Hat shouted, "No! Too late! Keep her coming around."

Andrew knew instantly that he had made a second mistake by countermanding the first order. A wash of bitter regret swept through him, but also steadied him.

"Hard a starboard!" he called.

Martin glanced at him distractedly, then began winding the wheel to starboard again. Andrew bit his lip and tried to judge the yacht's movements. He was well aware that he did not have the experience and did not know the vessel's sailing qualities so could now only watch and hope. He saw the bow start to swing back to starboard but felt sure it was swinging too slow.

I have mucked it up! he thought bitterly. *We will miss stays,*

The knowledge that they could end up just facing into the wind and going nowhere till the bow fell off one way or the other appalled Andrew. He shook his head and bit his lip.

"Jill, ease the jib!" he shouted. "Jacob, tighten the main sheet and get ready to go about. Mark, keep this pirate covered."

The bow came round very slowly, and Andrew groaned in despair as the way fell off the yacht. Then, just as he was sure they had failed, the bow passed through the eye of the wind and the jib suddenly flapped across. To his immense relief, he saw the sail billow and then drew on the port tack. Jill hurried along the port side, keeping well clear of the pirate, to adjust the jib sheet. Jacob set to work trimming the mainsail.

Andrew waited till he felt that the wind was on the beam before saying to Martin, "Hold her at that, Martin. We want a beam reach for speed."

As the yacht steadied on her new course, Andrew looked astern. He was surprised to see the blonde woman in the skimpy bikini but now carrying a gun leap down from the white cabin cruiser onto the jetty. She bent over one of the bodies and then picked something up and climbed back aboard the vessel.

Three-cornered Hat saw it too as he said bitterly, "That bitch has just picked up the box."

"The one with the drugs in it?" Andrew queried.

"Aye."

"Who is she? Who are they?" Andrew asked.

"A rival gang," Three-cornered Hat replied. "There are four of them: two men: Barrett and Ponytail Dan; a pair of gaybos; and those two lesbians: Blondie and Lana."

"How... how did they know to come here?" Andrew asked.

"I don't know," Three-cornered Hat replied grimly, "but I suspect treachery."

"Treachery? By who?"

"I don't know," Three-cornered Hat replied.

As they spoke, Andrew saw Lana and Ponytail Dan step off the motor launch and lift the mooring ropes free of the jetty pilings.

"Here they come," he said. "Do you think they will try to kill us?"

"For sure. My gang are their enemies, and you kids are inconvenient witnesses," Three-cornered Hat replied.

Andrew felt sick but kept watching. "What gang is that? Who are you?"

"Flint's Crew. I'm John Silver."

"John Silver? Is that just a nickname?" Andrew asked.

Silver shook his head and laughed. "No. It's my real name. When you have a name like that you play pirates too much as a kid, then you grow up to want to be one," he said. Silver stood up and began making his way aft. He held out his hand. "Now, if you want any chance of staying alive, give me the rifle."

"No!" Andrew cried with rising panic. "Stay where you are."

"Don't be stupid, kid!" Silver cried. "This is deadly serious."

"I don't trust you," Andrew replied, his voice almost cracking with nervousness.

"You won't survive without me," Silver said. "So give me the rifle."

"What about afterwards?" Andrew countered. "How can we be sure you won't just kill us yourself?"

Silver gave a wry smile. "You can't be sure, but think about it kid, if I'd been a killer I would have shot you when I was chasing you. I had a dozen chances. If we survive I will give you back the gun, on the promise you then land me ashore and let me go."

"You did try," Andrew replied, remembering those seconds of terror.

"I was angry then," Silver explained.

Andrew was terribly torn. Even as they argued he saw the white cabin cruiser swing away from the jetty. Then a froth of foam spewed out behind it, a white bow wave began to climb at the bow, and the vessel swung around in pursuit.

"It will catch us for sure," he said bitterly, watching the bow wave of the white cabin cruiser climb even higher.

Silver looked at it and nodded. "It will. It will do twice our speed. Our only chance is to hold them off till we get inshore."

That idea really bothered Andrew. He saw that their current course was south. *We are running at right angles to the way we need to go,* he thought.

He then pointed down. "This thing has an engine. Can you get it going?"

Silver nodded. "Aye. I'll do that and we'll be able to go a bit faster. And I suggest you come round onto a broad reach and run towards Cardwell, which is that way." He pointed.

That annoyed and embarrassed Andrew, but he nodded. "Bring her about Martin, steer southwest. Jacob, watch the mainsheet."

Still filled with doubt Andrew lowered the pistol, seeing no real alternative.

"Don't shoot him Mark," he said, well aware that the faces of the others were registering shock and disapproval. Silver walked aft. He gave Mark a wry grin and said, "I hope that thing is on safe," then vanished down the aft companionway with practised ease.

A minute later there was the rumble of a diesel engine starting up.

The yacht began to tremble and Andrew saw the turbulence of propeller vortices swirl out astern. The speed of the yacht at once increased noticeably, the bows punching into the waves and throwing up small showers of spray.

But a glance astern showed it was all just wasted effort. The white cabin cruiser had already halved the distance, was only a few hundred metres astern, and was rapidly overhauling them. Andrew was appalled at the obvious speed of their pursuer and felt a sour wash of defeat engulf him.

Silver came back up the companionway, rubbing his hands on some cotton waste. He tossed this aside and reached out to Mark for the rifle. Mark made no protest but reluctantly let him take it. Silver quickly examined the weapon and then looked up.

"Ah well, it will have to do. Now, who are you lot then, and what were you doing on the island?"

Andrew introduced them and quickly explained the holiday trip. Even now, however, he did not mention that Anne and Letitia had got away.

At least they are safe, he thought, eyeing the fast approaching, white cabin cruiser. Four black dots of heads showed above its upper steering position. The launch was overhauling them with what looked like implacable purpose and Andrew felt sick with apprehension, still not quite able to accept the reality of it all.

Silver pointed below. "Set her on automatic steering and you kids get below. Lie down and keep under cover."

"Shouldn't we try to do some manoeuvring?" Andrew queried, not wanting to give in and disliking intensely the idea of going below.

Silver shook his head. "Pointless. They will be able to run rings around us. Now get down and out of sight. I will try to equalise things a bit as they get closer. Go on!"

They did as they were told. Andrew waited till Martin had set the steering, using the controls Silver showed him, then went down last. Silver then lay down on the floor of the cockpit and steadied the rifle over the aft coaming. Jacob, Jill, and Mark did as they were told and lay down but Martin stayed upright, peering through the port porthole and Andrew remained on the steps, pistol gripped determinedly in his sweaty hand.

Silver slid lower and turned to look at Andrew. "How many bullets in this thing?" he queried.

"Four. I fired one," Andrew replied.

"See if you can find some more," Silver ordered. He then raised his head to peek over the coaming.

Andrew did not want to go. Instead, he crouched and looked into the cabin, then called to Martin, "Hey Martin, see if you can find some more bullets."

"Where?" Martin asked, glancing around the cabin.

"Look in the drawers and cupboards," Andrew answered, gesturing to where he had found the rifle in its rack.

Martin looked once more through the porthole. "They are getting close," he said, then climbed down and began to search.

Andrew edged up and risked a peek. All he glimpsed was the mast and upper steering position of the white cabin cruiser but that confirmed Martin's statement. The white cabin cruiser was now only about 50 metres away on the port quarter. To his own disgust, he found he was starting to tremble and sweat as terror took hold.

Andrew saw Silver lift himself and aim, the rifle barrel just above the deck level. He went very tense.

Crack!

"Got one!" Silver cried.

"Which one?" Andrew asked, simultaneously thrilled and sickened.

"Ponytail Dan," Silver replied. By then he had re-cocked the rifle and again raised it.

A sudden hammering sound filled the air. For a moment it puzzled Andrew, but then he saw holes appearing in the deck and splinters of wood flying. It was the enemy firing back! Absolutely frozen with fright, he gaped as bullets whacked through the side panelling near his face. Then he flinched and ducked, only to discover that bullets were also ripping through the cabin roof and sides and thudding into the furniture and panelling on the far side.

Suddenly the firing stopped and Silver fired again. Andrew saw his mouth working and guessed he had missed. The response was immediate and terrifying. Hundreds of bullets struck the stern of the yacht in the proverbial hail. Andrew guessed that every smuggler had a sub-machine gun. All he could do was crouch and whimper. There were vicious thuds against the panelling he was leaning on and right before his eyes the nose of one bullet splintered through and stuck fast.

That made him go cold with shock, but his mind told him that if the smugglers were using rifles or a proper machine gun then the bullets would have punched right through and he would be dead. Silver fired again, provoking another storm of return fire. At that moment, Martin touched Andrew, making him jump with fright. He turned to look. Martin was holding an open box of bullets. One glance at the short, round nosed bullets was enough for Andrew.

He shook his head. "Wrong sort. Those are pistol bullets."

Martin's eyes were wide with fear, but he nodded and turned to resume his search. More shots whacked through the cabin, shattering the port side portholes. Jill was screaming and Andrew saw that Mark was lying on top of her, shielding her with his own body. Jacob was huddled in a shivering ball in the far corner. Through the broken porthole Andrew glimpsed the bow of the white cabin cruiser. It was obviously edging closer.

He turned to warn Silver, thinking that, if the cabin cruiser got close enough, then the smugglers up in the upper steering position would have the drop on him. He saw Silver raise his head, then swear, before bringing the rifle up.

As he raised the rifle, he swore again. "Cop this, you bastards!"

Silver fired at the same instant as one of the smugglers. Andrew saw holes appear in the coaming, blood appear on the back of Silver's left calf, and splinters fly. To his horror, he saw Silver twitch violently backwards, dropping the rifle as he did. His hands flew to his face and he fell in a writhing heap, screaming with pain. Andrew went cold with shock and a feeling of absolute desperation welled up.

As soon as the storm of bullets ceased, Andrew lunged forward and grabbed Silver's shirt. A terrified glance sideways showed him the upper works of the cabin cruiser closing in. He did not hesitate but hauled. Normally he could not have done it but now he dragged Silver across the deck, over the ten-centimetre-high coaming and into the companionway in one mighty heave. Silver had both hands to the left side of his face and was still screaming and kicking but Andrew ignored that. He kept pulling until Silver fell on top of him. Both slid to the bottom of the companionway in a tumble of arms and legs.

"Help me up! Help me up!" Andrew yelled, frantic to get up in case the smugglers jumped aboard.

Hands pulled at him and Silver was dragged clear into the cabin. Andrew scrambled to his feet, oblivious to the bumps and bruises. He glanced down and snapped, "Do some First Aid, quick!"

Then he hurried up the companionway again. What was on the top of his mind was the rifle. *Without that we are dead!* he reasoned.

For a second he crouched, chest heaving, while he checked that the pistol was ready to fire. After taking a big gulp of air, he sprang up and out. As he did, he cursed being a right hander trying to shoot to the right. As he came out of the companionway he swung the gun up, steadied it on the row of heads leaning over the now very close upper steering position, and fired. There he paused, his eyes flicking frantically around for the rifle. To his dismay, and disbelief it was nowhere to be seen on the deck and he realised it must have slid over the side.

Oh no! he thought. But even as he did, he ducked.

He was just in time. Bullets began to hammer a savage tattoo on the roof and sides of the companionway and on the deck of the cockpit. Andrew bounded back down the steps, stumbling and crashing into Martin and Jill, who were both crouched there.

Martin steadied him, snarling, "The mongrels aren't short of ammo!"

"No," Andrew gasped, struggling to regain his feet. "We've lost the rifle," he added. Then he felt a sharp bump and knew that the cabin cruiser had come alongside. "They will board us!" he cried, raising the pistol to aim it up the companionway.

There were shots, lots of them, but nobody appeared against the rectangle of sky. A loud bang forward made them all jump with fear. Andrew glanced at the portholes and saw that the cabin cruiser appeared to be moving away again. He stepped over Silver and around Mark, who was holding his legs, then knelt on the settee to peek out through the shattered glass of a port hole.

He was right, the cabin cruiser had pulled away. Andrew glimpsed a face at a window on the main deck and aimed at it. Furiously angry and desperate to survive, he did not hesitate but pulled the trigger. He saw the window 'star' as the bullet hit it and the face vanished, but he did not know if he had hit the person or not. Then he ducked, as the anticipated response was immediate and deadly. Dozens of bullets smacked into the cabin roof and sides. A couple smashed right through and cracked across the cabin to bury themselves into the table or far side.

Once again, Jill screamed but she was also busy and kept working. Andrew knew that, if the smugglers had been using heavier weapons than sub-machine guns firing pistol bullets, they would all have been hit. Worry about whether the hull had been holed added to his concerns. Unable to tell, he turned and stared down and was amazed to see Martin and Jill both still working on Silver's head. Then, when his eyes focused on Silver's injuries, he drew in a sharp, horrified breath. A jagged splinter of wood about ten centimetres long was protruding from Silver's left eye!

Andrew felt nauseous and had to swallow. He was also amazed to see that Jill was busy fashioning a ring bandage. She kept at it, even though her hands were trembling violently. Martin held Silver's head still and Mark was busy bandaging a bullet wound in the pirate's left calf. Only Jacob remained out of it, huddling in the corner.

But it was Jacob that caught Andrew's attention. For no obvious reason, Jacob suddenly drew back into a kneeling position. His eyes riveted on the door to the bunk cabin.

"Smoke!" Jacob gasped.

"Open the door!" Andrew shouted. He could not easily step over the group on the deck, nor did he want to leave the companionway unguarded.

Jacob scrambled trembling to his feet and did so. As he swung the door open, a huge billow of brown smoke swirled into the cabin. He cried out in fear and slammed the door shut again. It had been enough for Andrew. He had seen right through to the sail locker and had been aghast at what he saw. Flames were roaring through the doorway of the sail locker into the next cabin and already the bedding on the bunks was alight. His mind instantly told him there was absolutely no hope of them putting out such a fire.

Jacob screamed, his voice rising in panic till it cracked. "We are on fire!"

Andrew ground his teeth and looked desperately around. He knew now what the loud bang had been.

The smugglers have fired a flare down the fore hatch, he thought.

Then he gritted his teeth as the appalling truth sank in. "They are going to burn us out," he said.

"Or shoot us in the water if we jump overboard," Martin added.

Jill raised terrified eyes to meet Andrew's. "Oh what will we do?" she wailed.

Andrew found he was gripped by an icy calm. "Put life jackets on to begin with," he said. "Then we will go down fighting!"

He swapped the pistol to his left hand, wiped sweat from the palm of his right, then swapped the pistol back. Face set with grim determination he turned to face the companionway. His mind began to roam over desperate options of trying to steer the yacht so as to board the cabin cruiser, and of using flares as weapons.

Chapter 37

BURNING

As the white cabin cruiser had slowed alongside the boat, Carmen had looked up at the grinning faces of the smugglers and a burning wave of shame swept through her. When she realised who they were she was aghast. It was obvious that they had also recognised her.

Ponytail Dan leered down at her and then quipped, "G'day sweetie! I didn't recognise yer without yer clothes!"

Black-haired Lana, leaned over the coaming of the upper steering position. "Who is it?" she called.

"Young Carmen, the Navy Cadet we took as a hostage a few weeks ago," Ponytail Dan replied.

"Why, so it is!" Lana called. "My, my! What a small world!"

Carmen hunched in fear, staring up them and wondering what would happen next. Somehow, she did not think that the smuggler's arrival was a coincidence.

This was confirmed when Barrett nodded and said, "Yeah, Sammy said there were a bunch of kids causing trouble on the island. Now we know who."

To Carmen's embarrassed astonishment, Blondie, clad only in a brief yellow bikini, appeared at the lower rail and looked up at Barrett. She held a sub-machine gun in her hands, the sight of which made Carmen go cold with fear.

"What will we do with her, Mr Barrett?" Blondie called up.

"Bring her aboard," Barrett replied. "She might be able to tell us some more."

"She can provide us with a bit of entertainment too," Lana grinned.

That set Carmen's heart racing and she broke into a feverish sweat of anxiety. *Little bit of entertainment! What does she mean by that?* she wondered. She looked desperately around, seeking for some means of escape. None was obvious.

Blondie pointed the gun at her and said, "Get aboard lovey, and no tricks."

Carmen looked up at the grinning face of Ponytail Dan, who had opened up a gap in the bulwarks and was now leaning out. This was obviously where the gangway was fitted as Carmen could see it lashed to the railings astern of the opening. Ponytail Dan put down his hand and indicated she should take hold of it.

Carmen hesitated and shook her head, causing Blondie to laugh and say, "Don't worry about Danny Boy. He doesn't like girls. You are quite safe, with him."

Seeing no option other than jumping into the sea, Carmen stood up and held up her left hand, still trying to cover her nakedness with her right. As she could not cover herself properly, she burned with shame. As soon as she had taken Ponytail Dan's hand and jumped up to the deck, she tried to use both hands for modesty.

To her surprise, Ponytail Dan picked up a towel from a nearby seat and held it out. "Here, put this around you. You don't want this pair leering at ya," he said.

Thankfully, Carmen wrapped the towel around herself, worrying that it might be too short but enormously relieved to be covered. Ponytail Dan took hold of her left arm and marched her to the covered area at the stern, to be met by both Lana and Barrett. To Carmen's added discomfiture, Lana ran her gaze slowly up and down. Carmen felt so embarrassed that she wished she could faint, or vanish through the deck.

She began to mentally brace herself, feeling sure that this time she would not survive the captivity. Mr Barrett also looked her up and down, causing a wave of heat to sweep through her already overheated body.

Lana also eyed her, but with an entirely different look in her face, one that caused Carmen to go cold with dread.

Lana then smiled. "She's a pretty little thing. What will we do with her?" she asked, adding, "Can we have her?"

Mr Barrett snorted and nodded. "Do what you like with her, but let's see if she can tell us anything. Well girlie, have you anything to say?"

Carmen pressed her lips together and shook her head, determined to die silent.

Blondie laughed, then said, "That's the spirit! Never mind, we will soon get her to talk."

Ponytail Dan shook his head. "You are a sad pair of bitches," he said.

"Each to their own," Lana retorted.

Carmen did not fully understand this by-play, but sensed it was bad news for her. At that moment, a mobile phone began to ring. Mr Barrett reached down to his pocket and lifted the phone up to his ear.

"Yes, Barrett here."

He listened for a minute or so, then said, "Righto. We are on our way Sammy. Meet you at the jetty." He then looked at his gang and said, "That was Sammy. He says they have the goods, but some kids have taken their yacht and he needs a lift. So we will have a little change of plan. Take this kid away and tie her up, then come up top so we can discuss our next move."

Blondie and Lana each took one of Carmen's arms and hustled her through a doorway next to the steps leading up to the top deck. As she was pushed through a saloon-dining cabin, Carmen felt a spurt of satisfaction.

Taken their yacht! Good! She felt sure that Andrew would have had a hand in that.

Beneath her feet powerful diesels began to rumble and she felt the cabin cruiser get under way again. She was shoved along a passageway that had cabins on both sides and which led to a ladder which she guessed led up to the upper steering position. Carmen was taken into a luxuriously furnished sleeping cabin on the port side of the corridor and pushed up onto a bunk.

"Face upward," Lana ordered.

Very reluctantly Carmen rolled over. This was obviously not fast enough as Lana gave her a sharp slap on her left buttock.

"Don't make it hard for yourself, Carmen Baby. Don't give us any trouble and we just might decide to let you go. Now just lie back and relax."

Carmen was now so scared and embarrassed that she was hyperventilating and feeling light-headed. For the next few minutes she lay there, using her hands to make sure the towel covered her while Lana went out to get rope. Lana returned and tossed a length of white rope to Blondie.

She then said, "Tie her legs, Baby. I will do the hands." To Carmen she said, "Now don't struggle. Make this easy for yourself or you will regret it."

As both women had placed their sub-machine guns on a sideboard, Carmen wondered if she could possibly escape. As they took hold of her limbs the idea of suddenly fighting them off went through her mind, but she quickly discarded that. The women looked too strong and ready for that. Blondie quickly looped a clove hitch around Carmen's right ankle, while Lana tied a silken pyjama cord around her right wrist.

Carmen was already scared and embarrassed, but emotions turned to scorching shame when Blondie grabbed her legs and pulled them together. Lying there while she was tied up was the most degrading thing Carmen had ever had done to her. But all she could do was lie and endure.

Lana tied the silken cord around Carmen's left wrist as well and then bound both together. Then, for lack of anywhere else to secure it, she tied both ends of the rope to a brass curtain rail above the row of windows on Carmen's right. Carmen closed her eyes and felt sick with guilt and fear.

Blondie tied the end of the other rope to a hinged steel bar that supported the fold-out bunk. That done both women stood back and looked down at her. In spite of herself, Carmen could not help looking back at them. Only then did the truth finally dawn on her. She began to shiver, fear of the unknown welling up to cause her panic. She was disgusted, appalled and ashamed.

A male voice saved her. It was Ponytail Dan. He had come to the cabin doorway and was standing there watching, a sardonic smile twisting his lips.

"Give the poor kid a break and come up top. Mr Barrett wants to brief you on what we are gunna do."

Blondie grinned at her. "We will be back, dearie. Just you lie there and enjoy it!" Then both women picked up their guns and followed Ponytail Dan out of the cabin, leaving a shocked and sobbing girl behind.

It took Carmen a few minutes to calm down and to get her mind working again. She was so ashamed and disgusted that she knew she was not thinking clearly. She lay back, sweating and panting, forcing her trembling limbs to relax.

Oh my God! I must get away from here, she told herself.

She was sure that when the two women returned they might do outrageous and disgusting things to her. Revolting possibilities she had only heard about flitted through from the darker corners of her mind. As panic mounted again, she began to twist and tug at the ropes. It was no good. They were stronger than her and had apparently been tied by people who knew what they were doing.

"Calm down! Relax, so you can think straight!" she told herself.

It took an effort, but she forced herself to lie still and steady her breathing and trembling limbs. Then she listened and studied the ropes. The engine note changed, and Carmen heard Mr Barrett's voice call, "Port side to!" and she decided they must be approaching the jetty. She was about to start struggling to escape when Lana appeared in the doorway again. She looked at Carmen and then blew her a kiss.

"Won't be long, Sweetie. Just a bit of business to attend to first," Lana said.

Ponytail Dan's face appeared at the doorway. "Hurry up and come and help me get the mooring lines ready," he said to Lana.

"Just checking she hadn't gotten free," Lana replied.

She and Ponytail Dan vanished from view. Carmen heard the engines slow even more and then felt a bump.

We are alongside the jetty, she thought. There were calls and the engines slowed to a faint ticking-over tremble. A feeling of desperation swept through her. *This is the best chance I will get to escape,* she thought. *I will jump into the sea.*

From the top deck she heard Mr Barrett say, "Here they come! Get under cover and get ready."

This is the only chance I'm going to get, Carmen decided.

She began pushing and pulling with her legs, trying to break the hinged metal bar holding the end of the bunk. She knew she could not break the ropes, and the bar seemed like the weakest part of the arrangement. With every muscle she could tighten she strained. But it was no good. The bar bent slightly but did not break. Carmen lay back, gasping and sweating, defeated but not yet ready to give up.

For a moment she relaxed to get her breath and made herself ease her tense muscles. Suddenly, from outside, she heard Mr Barrett's voice cry, "Now!"

There were cries of alarm from out on the jetty, drowned out by the shattering stutter of sub-machine guns firing.

Carmen twitched with fright. "Oh my God! They are shooting!" she cried.

The thought that the smugglers were gunning down Andrew and her friends sent a wave of sickening dread through her.

They will kill me for sure now, she told herself. *I must get away!*

In desperation she strained and pushed, placing all her effort against the bar at her feet. Gritting her teeth and praying for extra strength she tried again, sweat pouring from her. Suddenly everything came lose. For a second she lay there, wondering what had happened. She realised that the rope at her top end was lying loose all over her face and chest. She looked up and saw that the brass curtain rail it had been fastened to had given way. First it had bent and then one end had pulled from its socket. The rope now lay loose.

As realisation that she had a chance sank in Carmen heard a man's voice shriek, "No Mr Barrett, don't!"

Barrett called back, from above. "Sorry Sammy, but if you will betray one lot of friends, I can't trust you." Then a sub-machine gun rattled.

Fear helped Carmen. She jerked upright and was able to see out of the window. What she saw so appalled her that she sat there, stunned, for several seconds. Three men, pirates, lay on the timber decking of the jetty. Blood was trickling from a dozen wounds in each, flowing down through the cracks between the planks. Carmen had never seen dead men before, but she could tell that these men certainly were. The shock was tinged with relief as she realised that none of the dead people were her brother or friends.

From just above her, Barrett called, "Get the box, Blondie."

Blondie, gun in hand, passed in front of the window, causing Carmen to shrink back in terror. Through the now dangling curtains she watched as Blondie jumped down onto the jetty and picked up the box. As Blondie stepped back aboard, the fear that she would notice the curtains hanging at an odd angle caused Carmen to gulp with anxiety. But Blondie did not pass the window.

Then Carmen heard Ponytail Dan call out, "Hey, Mr Barrett! Look! There's their yacht."

At that, a thrill of hope ran through Carmen, to be swept out by a chill of fear as Mr Barrett snarled, "Bloody Hell! They saw us then. Blondie, cast off! Dan! Lana! Get those lines aboard, we must catch them!"

"What we gunna do, Mr Barrett?" Ponytail Dan cried near the stern.

"Make sure there are no inconvenient witnesses," Mr Barrett replied. "We will send them to Davey Jones's Locker. Dead men tell no tales!"

On hearing that a chill of absolute dread gripped Carmen. *They are going to kill Andrew and the others,* she thought.

Then she realised that she was also 'an inconvenient witness'. "They will kill me too, for sure!" she whispered.

With a shock she realised she had wasted valuable seconds. She at once bent forward and began working on the knots holding her feet.

As she did, she broke into a feverish sweat, expecting at any moment one of the gang to come into the cabin. Outside, she heard shouted orders to let go, followed by cries of, 'All clear forrard!' and 'All clear aft!' A person hurried by along the deck outside, causing Carmen to flinch in fear. She felt the engines begin to tremble and increase in power, then felt the launch lean over as it got under way and started turning.

With trembling hands she worked desperately to untie the knots. But they proved harder than she expected. Her feet she got undone fairly easily, there being enough slack for her to work the first clove hitch loose enough to slip the coils off her left ankle. After that it was easy to get her legs free. She then sat and struggled to free her hands, a much harder job because she could not use her fingers. Instead, she used her toes and projecting knobs like cupboard handles.

While she did this the launch accelerated and swung round, then raced under full power in pursuit of the yacht. Several times Carmen looked through the windows but all she could see was a sparkling blue sea. Minutes crept by and her anxiety increased.

I must get discovered soon! she thought.

That kept her working, and she knew that being a Navy Cadet helped because she was familiar with knots and ropes and could work out which bit was binding on which, and how to twist the strands to work them loose.

At last, and to her intense relief, she got her hands free. Just as she did, there was a loud snapping sound, followed almost at once by the hammer of sub-machine guns.

Oh no! she thought. *They have caught up with the yacht and are shooting everyone!*

Her heart lurched with sick dread and she dashed to the door and looked out. The shooting was coming from the starboard side, so she scuttled across into an open cabin on that side. As she did, the shooting started again, punctuated by much swearing and shouting.

She glanced out the window and saw with dismay that the yacht was close alongside. The deck, deckhouse and sides of the hull were pockmarked with bullet holes. She also saw a man's head and arms vanish down the companionway of the yacht, apparently dragged down by someone else. She could not see anyone on the deck of the yacht and presumed everyone was sheltering below. The launch closed right in and she felt it bump as the two craft touched.

Oh what can I do? Carmen asked herself in anguish. Part of her mind said, *Jump into the sea! Get away from here and hope they don't notice.* But another part cried out for her to try to help her brother. *I need a weapon. Oh, what can I use?*

She looked around the cabin in desperation. A loud bang outside and another savage burst of shooting caused her to look through the window again. To her dismay, she saw smoke starting to billow from the forehatch of the yacht. The launch began hauling clear, turning to port and slowing and the yacht was already ten metres away. Suddenly the window in front of her shattered and she flinched back. In stunned disbelief, she saw the concentric circles of 'starring' and the round hole left by a bullet.

Someone on the yacht shot at me! she thought in shocked amazement.

Her cheek started to sting so she put her hand up to rub it. Her fingers came away with blood on them. She stared at in horror, then gasped and began to shake. She knew she was on the edge of a hysterical breakdown. It was the sight of flames flaring up outside, and the savage cries of her enemies that got her thinking again.

One glance was enough: the jib of the yacht had gone up in a sheet of flame and the mainsail was now catching as well. Licking tongues of flame were leaping from the yacht's forehatch. The engines of the launch slowed, and Carmen saw that it was matching the slow speed of the yacht, now about 25 metres off to the starboard beam. Mocking laughter and jeering cries from the smugglers, who all sounded to be on the deck above, told Carmen their plan.

They have set fire to the yacht and will shoot anyone who jumps into the sea.

The sheer cold-blooded heartlessness of the plan chilled her, but also filled her with icy anger.

I must save them somehow, she resolved.

Chapter 38

CARMEN

Once again, Carmen looked around the cabin for a possible weapon. None was apparent but she did see a man's white shirt tossed on the back of a chair. She snatched this up and pulled it on, feeling an immediate sense of relief. As quickly as she could she buttoned it up. A glance down satisfied her that it was long enough. Being fully covered made her feel more able to face whatever was to come.

After taking a deep breath, Carmen made her way to the door of the cabin and aft along the passageway. She peeked carefully into the saloon, saw that it was empty and tip-toed across it to the stern door. Here she recoiled in shock. Lying on his back on the after deck with his arms outflung, and very obviously dead, was Ponytail Dan. A great wash of blood, starting at his shattered skull, was spread across the deck. Carmen stared at the blood in fascinated horror, appalled at how much there was, and at how it flowed in little trickles and rivulets according to the roll and pitch of the boat. Nausea welled up and she trembled. Fear gripped her so that she was unable to move for a minute or so.

Then she steadied herself. There was what she wanted, a weapon! Ponytail Dan's sub-machine gun lay on the deck. In two steps she reached it and scooped it up. For a few seconds she stared at it, trying to work out how it worked. She had never been trained to use anything other than the service Steyr rifle, but she had seen plenty of TV shows and movies. Quickly she identified the trigger, cocking handle and safety catch. She also noted the magazine release catch but that was no use as she only had the one magazine. She did not know how many bullets were left in it so all she could do was shrug and hope.

But what do I do now? she wondered. Again she contemplated just jumping over the side in an attempt to save herself. Shame at her own cowardice soon dealt with that idea. *I have to fight,* she resolved. That meant probably using the gun and she shied away from that. Then she steeled herself. *I must save Andrew and the others.*

A glance at the now blazing yacht told her she had only seconds to act. With a huge gulp to steady herself, she turned and made her way up the steps leading to the upper deck, the sub machine gun held ready in front of her. Her whole being seemed to narrow down to just a tunnel vision of the sub-machine gun, her hands, feet and the treads of the stairs. Terrified, but grimly determined, she forced herself to keep walking up.

As her head rose above the level of the top deck, her eyes took in the situation. Mr Barrett was at the controls but was steering with one hand while leaning over to look at the yacht. There was a sub-machine gun near his right hand, the weapon lying on a shelf above the controls. Both Lana and Blondie were leaning over the starboard bulwarks, their sub-machine guns resting on the rail.

Desperation, determination and anger all propelled Carmen up the steps. Once on the deck and only a few metres from the trio she raised the gun to her shoulder and sighted carefully. Mr Barrett, she thought, was the most dangerous, so she aimed at his gun. For another second she hesitated, appalled at the possible massacre she might provoke. Then she squeezed the trigger and let go at once.

There was sharp crack and the gun kicked. She saw the sub-machine gun leap and hit the windscreen and the drop back onto the bench. After another gulp for air, Carmen yelled, "Drop the guns! Put up your hands!"

Through a mist of sweat, fear and fury she saw their faces swivel to look in her direction. She noted Mr Barrett's mouth working but was not conscious of any words or sound. Then her brain registered what she feared: Mr Barrett was jumping aside and reaching across for his gun. Carmen squeezed the trigger. The sub-machine gun began to jump and smoke. She had fired the service rifle, the F88 Steyr, at the rifle range as a Navy Cadet, so had some idea of what was going to happen but was astonished at how wildly the gun bucked in her hands. She found the barrel vibrating upwards and began to panic. Part of her mind noted the used cartridge cases flicking out and another part was aware of the smell but mostly it was focused on trying to make those bullets go where she wanted them.

At least some of them did, but they found no target. Carmen saw Mr Barrett suddenly fall, then realised she had not shot him: he had accidentally stepped into the companionway leading to the lower steering position. He went down very fast, surprise clear on his face. Then his head struck the controls hard and he crumpled onto the deck and lay still

Unsure whether she had actually shot Mr Barrett or not, and appalled at what she had done, Carmen swung the gun to point at the two women. She was grimly determined to save Andrew and the others. To her vast relief, she saw that both still had their guns pointing out over the side. When they saw her aim her gun at them again both looked horrified.

"Drop your guns!" Carmen screamed. "Drop them, or I will shoot!"

She meant it and they clearly sensed this as they at once dropped the weapons to the deck and spread their arms out. As the guns fell heavily to the timber deck, they clattered on the dozens of used cartridges that littered it. Carmen gestured with the gun.

"Get over to the other side. Get away from the guns! Keep your hands up!"

To her relief, the women both began to do as she said. Lana licked her lips and cried, "Don't shoot! Be careful with that thing, dearie."

That 'dearie' almost got her killed. A surge of outraged anger made Carmen grit her teeth and tighten her finger on the trigger. Just in time she regained control.

Lana obviously saw this as she started to mutter, "Sorry! Sorry!"

"Shut up!" Carmen snapped in fury. Then another idea came to her. She aimed the gun at Blondie. "Stop the boat," she ordered.

A very scared Blondie at once nodded, turned to the controls and pushed two silver levers right up. The motors immediately died to a gentle vibration. Carmen felt the launch slow and risked a look around. She saw that the yacht was now about 30 metres away and slightly astern. It was a raging inferno, flames shooting ten or more metres into the air.

Blondie was still standing close to where Mr Barrett lay and his gun was near her hand. Carmen again gestured with her gun.

"Drag him away from there. Get him over to the other side," she ordered. As Blondie bent to grab Mr Barrett, Carmen looked at Lana. "You too! Help her."

Lana nodded and bent to help. The two women dragged Mr Barrett over to the port side, leaving a trail of blood on the deck. The sight of that made Carmen feel awful but then she noted his eyes were open and rolling around and she heard him groan.

Thank God! He's not dead! she thought.

Having succeeded left Carmen a bit stunned. *I needed a plan on what to do afterwards,* she told herself. Again she looked around, noted that the yacht was now almost totally enveloped in smoke and flames and felt even sicker. *They will get burnt to death if they don't get out!* she worried.

Then the horrible thought that maybe they had all been shot and could not get out, were possibly already dead, came to her.

I have to look, have to go back and help, she decided. But how to do that with the three smugglers. *The moment I drop my guard for a second they will jump me,* she reasoned.

The thought of Andrew burning to death steeled her heart. She pointed to the stern of the launch. "Drag Mr Barrett back there," she snarled.

The two women did as they were told. Carmen stayed well clear, edging over along the starboard side until she was standing amid the used cartridge cases next to the controls. She noted that the launch had now stopped and was turning into the wind, while the yacht still motored slowly on. A huge plume of black smoke was now rolling up from it.

"Put a lifejacket on him and throw him over the side," Carmen snapped. Lana opened her mouth to protest but Carmen just snarled, "And be quick about it!"

She could see now that Mr Barrett had not been hit by a bullet but was bleeding from his nose and lips. Blood was dripping and trickling off him and running across the deck in thin streams.

Blondie lifted a nearby seat and took out a lifejacket, doing it slowly so that Carmen did not think it was a weapon she was reaching for. She and Lana then quickly rolled Mr Barrett into the lifejacket. They then hesitated but Carmen was adamant.

"Throw him overboard!" she grated, shocked at her own ruthlessness, but did not care. Andrew had to be saved!

Lana and Blondie hoisted Mr Barrett up between him. Because of his weight and size they obviously found this difficult but they managed it at last. He was then rolled over the rail, to fall awkwardly out of sight. Carmen saw the splash and felt good.

Then she smiled. "Now you two jump over too," she said.

Lana blanched and looked over at the sea. "But... but... but there might be sharks. The blood!" she cried. "It will attract the sharks!"

Into Carmen's mind came the image of the three dead bodies on the jetty, then scorching memories of her own humiliation and outrage. Her self-control snapped, almost.

"Get over the side!" she screamed.

Then she lowered the gun and pulled the trigger, aiming at the women's feet. Only as the bullets began ploughing into the deck, or ricocheting, did she realise what a dangerous thing she had actually done. But it worked. Both women screamed and began dancing, then jerked themselves over the rail and fell. As the women vanished from sight, she took her finger off the trigger.

Another glance showed her that the blazing yacht was now about 50 metres away and she gasped with relief as she saw people scuttling out of the aft companionway and jumping into the sea. As soon as she saw that, she moved to the controls and pulled the throttles down.

I don't want those bitches climbing aboard again, she thought.

The launch surged forward and the three smugglers came into view, being swirled around by the propeller wash. Satisfied they could not climb aboard again, Carmen eased the throttles and put the gun down. Then she took the wheel and began slowly turning the launch to bring it around to the other side of the yacht.

As Carmen slowed the launch down near the first of the swimmers, a helicopter flew low overhead. She barely glanced at it until it began to circle, then hover. She shielded her eyes from the sun and looked up. It was a rescue helicopter from the Emergency Services.

Good! she thought. *My radio message must have been acted on.*

Then she saw Andrew in the water nearby. She shouted and waved and he recognised her and waved and grinned back. At that, a huge welling up of relief made her go weak. All she could do was grin and wave back, even when he was alongside and trying to get aboard. Only then did she realise that her help was needed. She stopped the launch and ran down to the main deck. At the gangway opening she reached down to take his hand. As he clambered aboard, she tried to embrace him but he held her off.

"We have to help the others," he said.

The others were Jacob, Jill, Mark, and Martin, all helping an injured Silver, his eye still bleeding and with the ghastly looking jagged end of the splinter protruding from the bandage they had wrapped around his head.

"Helicopter for him," Carmen decided, noting that the helicopter was starting to hover over the three smugglers.

In the lower steering position, just in a doorway near her, was a radio and she hurried in there and began calling. Luckily, she was able to raise VKC at once and they gave her the frequency of the helicopter. With trembling fingers she reset the radio and was just in time to contact them, even as a rescue medic was being lowered by winch. At first the helicopter pilot did not want to accept what she said, so she explained the situation and he changed his mind. The helicopter only hoisted Mr Barrett up, leaving the two women. It then moved over to hover above the yacht.

The medic came down and secured Silver, who was quickly hoisted up. The helicopter then turned and flew away, leaving the two women in the water. At that, Carmen did feel guilty and began to organise their rescue and detention. In the event she did not have to, as a Volunteer Coastguard Launch arrived with the local police aboard. The two women were fished out and taken into custody. Police transferred to the launch and stared in amazement at the guns, empty bullet cases and the very dead body of Ponytail Dan. Carmen then realised that the ordeal was all really just beginning, rather than ending!

For them it was back to Cardwell, another boat being sent to investigate the bodies on the jetty at Endeavour Island. Yet another was tasked to find her dinghy, then to stand by the now sinking yacht, to salvage flotsam so that it wasn't a hazard to shipping.

In Cardwell, Carmen found the Schipholls, Anne, Letitia, and Mr Mason. It was Anne who told them the tale of what happened at that end.

"When we got here the tide was going out so we could not reach the beach without trying to cross all that black mud," Anne said, "So Mr Mason took his boat into the jetty. There were a dozen people out on it: tourists and fishermen. Nobody took any notice of us, so we just hurried to the nearest shop and phoned the police.

"I'm glad you did," Carmen said. "The police arrived just in time."

"Oh they already knew," Anne replied. "They had been told by some radio message and were already getting organised."

"Oh good!" Carmen said. "That was me. I used the radio in the yacht."

Anne nodded. "There isn't much more to tell. Letitia saw her parents and went out to get them. They were preparing to return to the island. Of course, they were appalled at what had happened. By then a police car had arrived but there was nothing more they could do but wait. We saw the smoke and that got us worried," she added.

Andrew shook his head. "Not as worried as it got us!" he cried, his face and voice full of emotion.

They all laughed at that, and Carmen looked from Anne to Andrew and wondered if their romance was going to blossom or not.

It did not get much opportunity from then on because there were police interviews and then anxious parents arrived. By midnight Anne was back in Townsville and by midday the next day Andrew and Carmen were back in Cairns.

Oh poor Andrew! Carmen mused. *I do hope he finds his true love!*

POSTSCRIPT

For her part, Carmen was very careful, when telling her version of the story, that she made no mention of the fact that she had lost her bathers, and been captured stark naked. She noted that Andrew made no mention of it either and hoped that he had not actually seen her. The fear that the smugglers, or Peg Leg, might mention some embarrassing details at their trial was one of the things she was most anxious about.

I just hope nothing like that ever happens to me again! she told herself.

The white powder was a drug shipment: cocaine from Colombia. Mr Barrett, Lana and Blondie were all arrested and charged with murder. Their trial was an ordeal Carmen was not looking forward to. Silver was also charged with killing Ponytail Dan, but he escaped from hospital and managed to elude the police. Peg Leg, alias Ben Gunn, was found stuck on the rocks of Oyster Point. Apparently, the boat's propeller had cut his metal leg and when he had been making his way across the rocks it had snapped, jamming between two rocks. He was charged with attempted murder but claimed that he had been taken prisoner by the pirates, who had then stolen his yacht. His version was that, far from trying to run Carmen over with the boat, he had been trying to rescue her. He was released on bail and vanished.

As for 'Blackbeard', 'Smee' and the other midnight pirates, nothing more was heard of them.

Author's Note

This novel is a work of fiction. The names, characters and incidents portrayed in it are the work of the author's imagination. Any resemblance to actual persons, living or dead or events is entirely coincidental. The locations, except for Endeavour Island, are real and are described as during the author's most recent trip to the region. Endeavour Island is completely fictional but readers may easily find similar islands along the east coast of Far North Queensland.

Many of the places of interest in the story are fictional but are based on real places in North Queensland, as are the historical anecdotes used to give the story flavour and authenticity. Wonderful scenery, old cemeteries, shipwrecks and abandoned plantations or tourist resorts are very much part of the region's features. Visit and enjoy.

Enjoy more C.R. Cummings stories